THE REBEL

LIMITED EDITION

SOPHIE LARK

For all my beautiful Love Larks who have given me so much energy and inspiration for this series, and some great ideas that I steal while you're theorizing in our Facebook group ;)

Also thank you to all the ladies who make such gorgeous collages, edits, videos, Tiktoks, and playlists. Your art feeds me. There is no greater compliment than when you base your projects off my characters.

Xoxoxo

—Sophie

THE REBEL OFFICIAL SOUNDTRACK

Spotify → geni.us/rebel-spotify

Apple Music → geni.us/rebel-apple

1. Vintage - Blu DeTiger
2. Astronaut In The Ocean - Masked Wolf
3. POPSTAR - DJ Khaled, Drake
4. Money - The Flying Lizards
5. Asturias - Marc Lezwijn
6. Calm Down - G-Eazy
7. feel something - Bea Miller
8. Everyday - A$AP Rocky
9. Paint It Black - Vanessa Carlton
10. feel good inc. - renforshort
11. Plastic Hearts - Miley Cyrus
12. Drugs - UPSAHL
13. Just A Lil Bit - 50 Cent
14. Señorita - Shawn Mendes & Camila Cabello
15. Often - The Weeknd
16. Choke - Royal & the Serpent
17. Unchained Melody - The Righteous Brothers
18. Can't Help Falling In Love - Kina Grannis
19. Still Don't Know My Name - Labrinth

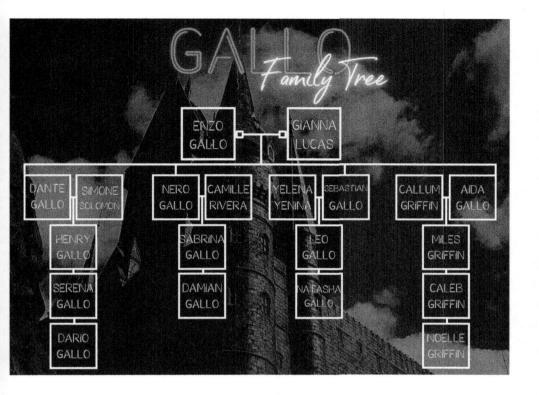

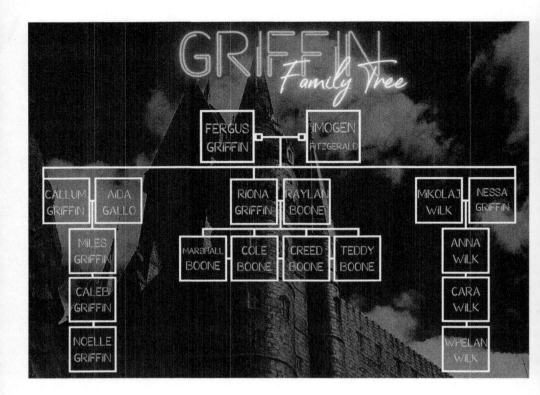

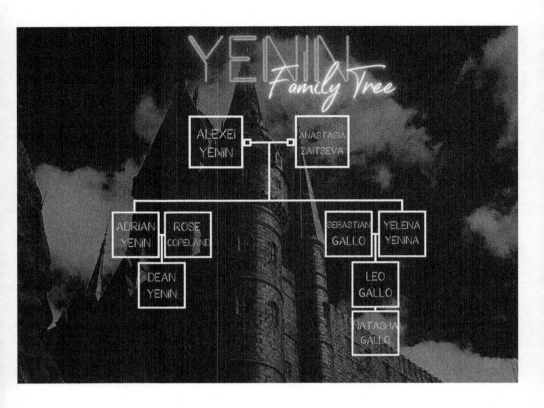

1

ZOE

It's my engagement party tonight.

I've never been less excited to celebrate something.

My stepmother Daniela sends her team of specialists to ensure that I'm in peak form, so Rocco and his family can be sure they're getting their money's worth.

They come into my bedroom at three o'clock in the afternoon and spend the next four hours scrubbing, exfoliating, waxing, moisturizing, painting, and primping every square inch of my body.

The fighting starts immediately when I demand to know why they're waxing my bikini line.

"It's an engagement party," I tell Daniela. "Not the wedding night. I don't expect anyone to be checking under my skirt."

I glare at my stepmother, who is already partway through her own exhausting preparations for the night ahead. She has a mud mask on her face and her hair up in rollers the size of soup cans. Far from looking ridiculous, it only makes her appear all the more imperious as the curlers encircle her head like a crown, and the mask obscures the few hints of emotion Daniela ever betrays. I can't tell if Daniela actually lacks all human feeling or if she's just very good at hiding it.

Daniela is only ten years older than me.

I was nine when my mother died, nine-and-a-half when my father remarried.

He used my mother up like an old sponge, putting her through fourteen pregnancies, ten miscarriages, two still-births, and the shameful arrival of me and my sister Catalina, none of which produced a male heir.

That last stillbirth was the death of her. She hemorrhaged on the gurney. The darkest part of me suspects that my father held back the doctor, allowing the life to drain out of my mother as punishment for the fact that even that final breath-less baby was a girl.

My father went into a rage.

There was no comfort for Catalina and me, no time to mourn our mother. Instead he ordered flower girl dresses.

He was already making arrangements to marry Daniela, the youngest daughter of rival Galician clan chief. Her sisters had produced two sons each for their husbands, proof in my father's eyes that Daniela would likewise be fertile and useful.

Daniela fell pregnant on the honeymoon, but an anatomy scan showed that the fetus was female yet again. My father forced her to abort it.

I only know this because I heard him shouting at her for hours, berating her into doing it. She was sick for several weeks after, pale and unable to walk from room to room without hunching over.

I don't know how many more times she was coerced into repeating that process.

Eventually, my father stopped trusting in fate and turned to science.

They saw fertility specialists. Daniela went through several rounds of IVF, harvesting her eggs for the sole purpose of selecting the gender ahead of time.

None of these attempts were successful. Daniela bore no babies at all.

I'd feel bad for her. But the sympathy wouldn't be returned.

Daniela hates me. She hates my sister, too.

Her loyalty is all to my father, no matter how he abuses her. She's his constant spy, acting as jailor to Catalina and me and helping carry out all my father's most insidious plans for us.

Like this engagement.

It was Daniela who brokered the deal with Rocco Prince and his family. She told Rocco's mother that I was intelligent, studious, obedient, submissive. And of course, beautiful.

When I was only twelve years old, she sent the Princes photographs of me laying by the pool in my swimsuit.

The Princes' first visit soon followed. Rocco was thirteen—just a year older than me—but I could already tell there was something very wrong with him.

He came out to the garden where I was sitting on a bench under the orange trees, reading *The Witch of Blackbird Pond*. I stood up when I saw him approach, smoothing down the white muslin skirt of the summer dress Daniela had selected for me.

Back then, I was innocent enough that I still had fantasies of a better life. I had seen movies like *Sleeping Beauty* and *The Swan Princess* where the prince and princess were betrothed by their parents, but their love was genuine.

So when I heard that Rocco was coming to see me, I imagined he might be handsome and sweet, and maybe we would write letters to each other like pen pals.

When he approached me in the garden, I was pleased to see that he was tall and dark-haired, slim and pale with the look of an artist.

"Hello," I said. "I'm Zoe."

He gave me an appraising look, not answering at first. Then he said, "Why are you reading?"

I thought it a strange question. Not, "What *are you reading?*" but "Why *are you reading?*"

"Are you trying to impress me?" he said.

I shook my head, confused and wrong-footed.

"I always read on Saturdays," I said. "When there's no school."

I didn't tell him there was nothing else to do at my house— Cat and I weren't permitted to watch TV or play video games.

He picked my novel up off the bench, examined the cover, and contemptuously tossed it down again, losing my place. I was annoyed but tried not to show it. After all, he was my guest, and I was already aware that our futures were meant to entwine.

"You're pretty," he said, dispassionately, looking me over again. "Too tall, though."

If that meant he wouldn't want to marry me, I was already starting to think that might be a good thing.

"You live in Hamburg?" I asked, trying to hide my growing dislike.

"Yes," Rocco said, with a toss of his dark hair that might have been pride or disdain—I couldn't yet tell. "Have you ever been there?"

"No," I said.

"I didn't think so."

I noticed little black flecks in the blue of his eyes, like someone had spattered his irises with ink.

"What's that noise?" Rocco demanded.

A parrot was screeching in the orange tree, swooping low over our heads, and then returning to its branch.

"It's annoyed because it has a nest full of babies up there," I said. "It wants us to leave."

Rocco reached inside his jacket and took out a pellet gun. It was small, only the size of a pistol. I assumed it was a toy gun, and I thought it was childish of him to carry it around.

He pointed it up at the small green parrot, following its flight path in his sights. I thought he was play-acting, trying to impress me. Then he squeezed the trigger. I heard a sharp puff of air. The parrot went silent, cut off mid-cry, dropping like a stone into the flowerbed.

I cried out and ran over to it.

I picked the parrot up out of the earth, seeing the small dark hole in its breast.

"Why did you do that?" I shrieked.

I was thinking of its babies up in the nest. Now that the parrot wasn't squawking anymore, I could hear their faint cheeps.

Rocco stood next to me, looking down at the moss-colored bird. It looked pathetic in my hands, its wings folded and dusty.

"The chicks will wait and wait," he said. "Then eventually they'll starve."

His voice was flat and expressionless.

I looked in his face. I saw no guilt or pity there. Just blankness.

Except for the tiny upward curl of his lips.

Those little black specks on his irises reminded me of mold. Like there was something rancid in him, rotting him away from the inside.

"You're horrid," I said, dropping the bird and wiping my palms atavistically on the sides of my dress.

Then Rocco did smile, showing even white teeth.

"We're just getting to know one another," he said.

Rocco has not improved on further acquaintance. Every time I see him, I loathe him more.

Tonight I'll be expected to dance with him, to hang on his arm, to gaze at him as if we're in love. It's all a performance for the guests.

He doesn't love me any more than I do him.

The only thing he likes about me is how much I despise him. That he enjoys very much.

That's the man for whom Daniela demands that I wax my pussy.

I stare at her with deep distrust, wondering what she knows that I don't. Why does she think it's important that I be perfectly smooth from the chin down? What does she expect to happen?

"I'm not doing it," I tell her. "He's not touching me tonight."

Daniela tilts her head to the side, eyes narrowed.

She's quite beautiful, I'd never deny that. She has the austere look of a saint in a painting. Like a saint, she worships a cruel and vengeful god: my father.

"You'd better learn to please him," she says quietly. "It will be so much harder on you if you fight. The things a man can do to his wife when she's trapped with him, all alone in a big house like this, with only his soldiers around. . ."

She blinks slowly in a way that has always reminded me of a reptile.

"You should learn how to flatter him. How to assist him. How to serve him with your body . . ."

"I'd rather die," I tell her flatly.

She laughs softly.

"Oh, you'll *wish* you were dead . . ." she says.

She nods to her team of estheticians. With something approaching force, they push me down on the chaise, pry my legs apart, and spread hot wax over the entirety of my pussy, all the way up to my anus. Then they rip the wax off in strips, until I'm bald as an egg absolutely everywhere.

Daniela watches the whole thing, then examines the final result. She checks my bare pussy for any sign of deformity that might derail her plans. Then she nods her approval.

"When I was presented to your father, I was stripped naked in front of a dozen of his soldiers. They evaluated me like a horse at auction," she says. "Be grateful it's only Rocco you have to impress."

She leaves me with the aestheticians so she can complete her own beautifying.

Daniela has already selected the clothing and jewelry I'll be wearing.

The aestheticians carry out her orders, zipping me into a suffocating gown that hoists up my breasts and cinches my waist to a fraction of its usual size. The gown is long, gold, and sparkling, with the sort of sleeves that are not sleeves at all, but only fabric draped below the shoulders. My hair is piled up on my head with a gold band as a tiara.

It's all undeniably beautiful, in impeccable taste.

I'm a glittering golden gift.

A black shroud would be more fitting. I feel like I'm going to my own funeral.

I'm like those maidens the Incas used to sacrifice to the gods: the Virgins of the Sun. All year they were fed delicacies—maize and llama meat. They were bathed and beautified with feathered headdresses and exotic shell necklaces. And then they were carried to the mountaintop tombs, to be sealed inside as an offering to a god that craved their death.

Catalina comes into my room, likewise dressed for the night ahead.

Cat perfectly suits her name. She's small and lithe, and she moves as silently as a little black cat. She has a pretty heart-shaped face, large, dark eyes, and a dusting of freckles across her nose. She's dressed in a pale lavender gown.

Even though we're only a year apart, she looks much younger.

She's always been timid.

I can see how nervous she is for the party, for everyone staring at us. Lucky for her most of the attention will be pointed in my direction. And she doesn't have to worry about being roped into some hateful marriage contract, at least not yet. That was part of my agreement with my father: Cat doesn't have to get married until she graduates college, and neither do I.

My father and stepmother are allowing me to attend Kingmakers for all four years, as long as I agree to marry Rocco directly after graduation.

It was a last, desperate ploy on my part to delay the inevitable.

They only agreed because Rocco is also at Kingmakers, as are plenty of his cousins and mine, always around to spy on me, to make sure I'm not drinking or dating or breaching any of the rules of the betrothal.

Kingmakers is no normal school.

It's a private college for the children of mafia families from around the globe, located on Visine Dvorca, a tiny island in the Adriatic Sea.

You couldn't imagine a more lonely or isolated place.

And yet, I almost enjoyed my Freshman year.

It was my first time living away from my father. The relief I felt, alone in my tiny dorm room, was like nothing I'd ever experienced. When I attended my classes I was free to study and learn, and even make friends without constant judgment, constant criticism.

Kingmakers is a castle fortress, a city unto itself. So vast and sprawling that I could easily avoid Rocco most of the time. Since he's a year older than me, we don't share classes together.

The relief I felt was painful. Because I knew it couldn't last.

Tasting freedom might only hurt me more in the end.

I felt guilty leaving Cat here alone. I know it was a hard year for her. I can see it as she sits down on the edge of my bed. She has a flinching reaction to noise that has worsened since I was gone.

But she should experience the same freedom soon enough—she's been accepted to Pintamonas and will be leaving in the fall, the same as me.

Cat is a talented artist. She loves drawing, painting, and graphic design. She'll flourish at school.

The further away from our world she goes, the better off she'll be. Maybe she'll escape it entirely, someway, somehow.

"You look stunning," Cat says to me, wide-eyed and impressed.

Cat is so innocent. I've always tried to protect her from the uglier things in our lives. Like how much I loathe Rocco.

She knows I'm not thrilled about being pushed into the marriage. But I've never told her how much he terrifies me. It would devastate her. There's nothing she can do to help me.

"The Princes will be so impressed by you," Cat says sincerely.

"You look lovely, too," I tell her.

"I made this for you," Cat says.

Gently, she lays a bracelet in my open palm. It's delicate and intricate, a net of tiny golden beads strung on woven wires. I can't imagine the hours of painstaking work to braid those fragile strands.

It makes me want to cry.

Knowing you're loved, truly loved, by at least one person makes all the difference in the world.

I put my arm around my sister and hug her hard, closing my burning eyes.

"Thank you Cat," I murmur.

"I'll help you put it on," she says.

She circles it round my wrist, closing the tiny clasp. It fits perfectly.

Daniela will be furious if she sees that I've augmented her meticulously curated look, but I don't give a fuck. I can't express to Cat how much it means to me to wear something I actually like, one good omen within this awful night.

"We'd better go down," I say to Cat.

Even though Cat and I are early, our father and stepmother are already waiting in the airy foyer. It shows how anxious they are to close this deal with the Prince family.

Daniela is wearing a sleek gown of deep bronze, her hair in an elegant bun. My father has on a black velvet jacket with a matching bronze pocket square. He's a man of substantial height and breadth, though Daniela is still always careful to select heels that will put her at least an inch or two below him. He has a mane of grizzled gray hair that makes him look like an elderly lion, and a broad, aristocratic nose. His mouth is the only weak feature about him—his lips thin and flesh-less, always pulling down at the corners.

They turn to examine Cat and me as we come down the stairs. I slip my left wrist into the folds of my skirt, so Daniela won't notice the bracelet.

Daniela frowns, displeased with something in our appearance. Maybe it's Cat's flyaway curls that can never be tamed, despite the best efforts of the professionals. Maybe she doesn't think my waist looks small enough. It's always something, and usually nothing we could actually fix.

My father nods his approval, so Daniela keeps silent.

"Be sure to curtsy to Rocco when you see him," my father says.

I crush down the rebellious part of me that cringes at that instruction. I hate this formal parade of false affection. I hate that I'm expected to bow and simper all night long in front of all these hateful strangers.

I follow my father out of the house to the waiting limo.

We live in a traditional-style villa in Sitges, on the south coast of Barcelona. My father bought this place because of the unusually large plot of land and the clear view to the ocean. The grounds include a spa and sauna, a Turkish bath, several ponds stocked with exotic fish, a large outdoor dining area, and an orchard. Surrounded on all sides, of course, by hedges and stone walls.

He likes to think of himself as a gentleman, though we're descended from fishmongers.

The Galician clans were all fishermen to begin with.

Then the Bay of Biscay ran barren, and they turned to tobacco smuggling instead. Smuggling was far more lucrative than fishing had ever been. The fleets multiplied and the fishermen grew rich with empty nets, and cargo holds stuffed with tobacco, hashish, and cocaine.

The Galicians made contacts in Colombia and Morocco. Spain became the entry point for the vast majority of the high-quality cocaine smuggled into Europe.

They built distribution routes to Portugal, France, and Britain, made alliances with the Albanians and the Turkish mafia to bring in heroin, too. They bought politicians and won the love of the people by sponsoring festivals, schools, and football teams. Juventud Cambados became the highest-paid football players in the nation, despite being located in a tiny town, all thanks to narco money.

But what had been a local operation between the tight-knit Galician clans became an international enterprise. The clans began to feud. Long-seated resentments flared up all over again, this time with exponential force behind them.

Threats turned into kidnapping. Kidnapping into torture and murder. A cycle of bloody reprisals split the clans apart.

This is where my father finds himself now: caught between the powerful Alonso clan who have allied themselves with the Brits, and the Torres family who owns the People's Party and the Galician Premier.

My father needs a partner, or he'll be swallowed up by one of the other clans. Or worse, crushed under their boot. He's clinging on to his empire by his fingernails.

That's where the Prince family comes in.

The Princes own the most powerful distribution network in Germany. With our product and their network, we'll all become wealthy beyond measure.

For the small price of my marriage to Rocco Prince.

I'm sure his parents know they're raising a psychopath.

He bounced around boarding schools across Europe to hush up the rumors of his cruelty, his depravity, his senseless violence . . .

I doubt there's a mafia family in Germany who would give him one of their daughters.

But a desperate Spaniard . . . yes, my father will gladly hand me over. As long as he gets the protection he needs.

As we seat ourselves in the backseat of the limo, my father pops a bottle of chilled champagne. He fills four flutes, his hand steady even with the unpredictable motion of the moving car as we head into the city.

"To securing our fortune," he says, raising his glass.

Daniela watches as I drink mine down.

They used to ply the Inca virgins with alcohol and coca to keep them docile. To help them accept their gruesome fate.

"Have another glass, why don't you," Daniela says to me. "For your nerves."

We drive down to Port Vell, to the Royal Shipyards. The old medieval dockyards have been renovated into grand venues for weddings and galas. The vast spaces that once held the bones of barquentines now host the elite of Spanish society in their tuxedos and gowns, their genteel laughter echoing high up in the rafters.

It's almost midnight. In Barcelona we don't even eat dinner until ten o'clock at night. This party won't reach its peak until the early hours of the morning. I'm already exhausted just thinking about it.

My father takes my arm in a steel grip and steers me relentlessly toward the center of the room where I can see Dieter, Gisela, and Rocco Prince holding court amongst their many admirers.

The Princes look just as regal as their name. Dieter could be a Kaiser with his immaculately trimmed black mustache and his military-style tuxedo. Gisela is fair-haired and pale, significantly younger than her husband. Rocco stands between them, black hair combed straight back from his brow, face lean and pale and cleanly-shaven, cheeks so hollow that a dark shadow runs from his ear down to his jaw.

My father shoves me forward so I'm forced to sink into a low curtsy in front of Rocco. I can feel his eyes looking down the front of this ridiculous gown. He makes me hold that position a moment too long, before putting his cool, slim fingers under my chin and tilting up my face.

"Hello, my love," he says in his soft, sensual voice.

His fingers feel as smooth and cold as a snake's tail. I want to cringe away from his touch.

Instead, he lifts me to my feet, allowing his fingertips to trail over my collarbone and the tops of my breasts as he releases me.

I give a small bow to his mother and father. Dieter Prince takes my hand and lifts it to his lips in a brief, dry kiss. I much prefer his indifference to his son's deliberate torment.

Gisela Prince briefly meets my eye then looks away. I've barely spoken to Rocco's mother, but if she knows anything about her son, she must feel some measure of guilt over the fate in store for me. I would assume there's a reason the Princes never had any other children. They might have worried that Rocco would strangle a baby in its sleep.

"Shall we dance?" Rocco says.

He doesn't wait for my response. He takes my hand and pulls me onto the dance floor, which is already filled with whirling couples. The light, lilting Spanish guitar contrasts the tense repulsion I feel whenever Rocco touches me.

The musicians are playing a gentle Arrolo, but as soon as Rocco has me on the floor, he snaps his fingers, ordering them to switch to tango instead.

Asturias — Marc Lezwijn
Spotify → geni.us/rebel-spotify
Apple Music → geni.us/rebel-apple

"I don't know how to tango," I tell him, trying to pull away.

He yanks me against his body, hand cradling the back of my neck, fingers digging into the vulnerable flesh at the side of my throat.

"Don't lie to me," he hisses in my ear.

The dual *bandoneons* play their introductory riff, their fingers flying over the strings. Rocco shoves his thigh between mine, dipping me back across his other leg until it feels like my spine will snap. Then he whips me upright again, our bodies pressed together from breast to hip, his face only inches from mine. He forces me to look in his eyes. He forces me to see how much he enjoys this.

He strides forward, shoving me backward in four long steps. Rocco is slim but horribly strong—there's nothing on his frame but muscle and sinew. Struggling against him is pointless, especially when every eye in the room is turned toward us and I can't cause a scene.

Raising his arm over my head, he spins me like a top, then bends me back again, exposing my breasts to the crowd even more than they already were.

This is the real purpose of us dancing together—so Rocco can display his control over me. There's no passion in his tango, no sensuality. His movements are rapid and technically precise, but without any feeling. Latin dancing is all about desire. The music is raw, insistent, all heat.

There's no warmth in Rocco.

I don't think he even feels lust.

He's flaunting my body because he knows it embarrasses me. All his pleasure comes from my discomfort, my desire to defy him juxtaposed with my complete inability to do so.

I feel like a marionette on strings. I actually like dancing—the few times I've been able to enjoy it without anybody watching. Rocco is poisoning this, as he poisons everything. My face is flaming, acid in my throat. The song seems interminable. The crowd around us is a blur of color and dark, staring eyes.

Finally the music stops and the guests applaud politely. This party is such a fucking charade. No one here cares about Rocco or me, or our upcoming wedding. Everyone present is fully focused on the deals they plan to make tonight, the connections and the agreements.

Rocco hasn't released me.

"That's enough dancing," I tell him. "I need a drink."

"Of course, my love," Rocco says.

He delights in pretending to be the doting fiancé. Using these terms of endearment, pretending that he has my interests at heart. When really everything he does is in pursuit of his own amusement.

That's why he forces me to take his arm as we head toward the bar. He wants me close, and he wants me touching him at all times.

"Just water, please," I say to the bartender. I already had enough to drink in the limo. I don't want to be inebriated around Rocco.

"Two scotch," Rocco cuts across me.

The bartender obeys him, not me. He pours the expensive liquor over single spheres of ice, then passes us the drinks.

"Bottoms up," Rocco says, his blue eyes boring into mine.

I swallow the drink. The sooner I get through these niceties— dancing with him, drinking with him, speaking to him—the sooner we can part ways again.

"Let's take a walk along the marina," Rocco says.

"I . . . I don't think we should leave the party," I protest.

I don't want to be alone with him.

"Nonsense," Rocco says quietly. "It's expected that the happy couple will want to slip away."

I set my glass down on the bar, the ice sphere spinning like a lonely planet.

"Alright," I say. "I won't be able to go far in these heels."

"You can lean on me," Rocco replies with a thin smile.

There should be plenty of people on the marina at this time of night. The docks are lined with restaurants, nightclubs, and shops. Still, I know he isn't taking me out there for no reason. He always has a reason.

I glance around for Cat as we're leaving, hoping to make eye contact with her so she'll know where I've gone. She's dancing with one of my father's associates, a lecherous old fuck with a spotty bald head, who's holding her much too close to him and whispering god knows what in her ear. Cat's smile looks pasted on her face.

She doesn't see me.

Rocco notices where I'm looking, and he smiles in a way that I don't like one bit.

He tucks my hand into the crook of his elbow once more and begins to parade me down the marina.

"You're very close to your sister, aren't you?" he says.

"No more than normal," I say.

The lie is instinctive and automatic. Rocco will use any leverage he can find to fuck with me. I don't want him to know that the one thing in the world I truly care about is Cat.

But he already knows. He doesn't ask a question without already knowing the answer. And he can always tell when I'm lying.

"Did she make that bracelet for you?" he asks, touching it with one long, slim forefinger.

I snatch back my wrist, irrationally outraged. I don't want him tainting the bracelet.

"No," I lie again.

It's my only protection against him—to refuse to answer him truthfully, even in the smallest details. I try to build a wall around myself, shutting him off from anything genuine. It's the only way to keep myself safe.

I hate lying. I'm an honest person. Deceit never tastes right in my mouth, no matter the reason for it. The way I'm forced to sneak and conceal, by Rocco and by my father and step-mother, sickens my soul.

Rocco likes making me lie.

This is what he wants: to break me down. To twist me and change me.

We're passing a seafood restaurant, the open patio full of diners enjoying their wine and poached fish.

Swifter than I can blink, Rocco grabs my arm and jerks me into the narrow alleyway between two restaurants. He shoves me up against the wall, the reek of empty mussel shells and fishbones filling my nostrils.

He seizes my jaw in his hand, pinching hard on both cheeks. The pressure of my flesh against my molars is intensely painful. He forces me to open my mouth.

"You weren't very friendly to me last year at school," he hisses, his nose inches from mine. "I almost felt like you were avoiding me, Zoe."

My bare back is shoved up against the filthy alley wall. My jaw is aching, and I feel absurdly vulnerable with my lips forced apart. I expect him to try to kiss me.

Instead, he spits in my mouth.

The cold saliva hits my tongue. I lash out instinctively, wrenching my face free and hitting him away from me while I wretch and gag. The unwanted scotch comes heaving up and I vomit on the cement, splashing my bare toes in their golden sandals.

My flailing arm knocks Rocco across the face. He scowls at me, either from the blow or from my extreme reaction to his spit on my tongue.

At least he doesn't want to touch me anymore now that I've puked.

"I expect your attitude to improve come September," Rocco says coldly. "If not, there will be consequences."

He strides away from me, leaving me alone in the alley.

My legs are shaking so hard that I can barely make it back to the party.

As soon as I enter the room, Daniela appears at my side hissing, "Fix your makeup, you look like a whore."

I stumble off toward the bathrooms. Sure enough, my eyes are watering from vomiting and my mascara is smeared as if I were giving an enthusiastic blowjob in that alley.

Daniela had no problem with that—it's what she expected me to be doing. It's the lack of care in my appearance that she can't abide.

Rocco's spit in my mouth was almost as bad as the alternative.

I wash my mouth out at the sink, rinsing over and over until I've recovered the ability to swallow without heaving.

I don't like this new demand from Rocco, but I don't see how he can enforce it. I agreed to marry him after graduation. I never said we'd be best friends at school.

He leaves me alone the rest of the night, and I think that's all he has in store for me. I think I got off relatively easy.

THE NEXT MORNING my father and stepmother breakfast with Dieter and Gisela Prince, to see them off before they head back to Hamburg, and no doubt to discuss details of their new collaboration.

I'm not invited. My spirits begin to rise, knowing that I won't see Rocco again until I board the ship to Kingmakers.

When we meet again, I'll have friends around me—Anna Wilk and Chay Wagner, for instance, who shared the same dorm with me Freshman year. They're formidable women, both proper Heirs who will actually inherit their families' businesses instead of being given the title in name only and then immediately married off.

Anna will run the Polish mafia in Chicago—she'll have a dozen *Braterstwo* under her command. Chay is the Heir of the Berlin chapter of the Night Wolves, a Russian motorcycle gang. With those two girls beside me, I'm not afraid to face even Rocco and his friends.

That is, until my father calls Cat and me down to his study.

I hate entering my father's office. This is a place I'm never invited unless I'm in trouble. Cold sweat breaks out on my skin just stepping foot over the threshold.

Cat is even more frightened. Her teeth are rigidly clenched to keep them from chattering.

We enter his study, which is dark and oppressive, the walls lined with floor-to-ceiling shelves in ebony wood, most of their spaces filled with fossils instead of books. My father is immensely proud of his collection, which includes several dragonflies preserved in limestone, the pelvis of a wooly rhinoceros, and a full archaeopteryx.

I'm not looking at any of that because I see Rocco Prince standing next to my father. Rocco is dressed in a dark suit and tie, with a ruby pin in the lapel that glimmers like a droplet of blood, as if it fell from the corner of his mouth.

"Sit," my father says, indicating the chairs in front of his vast, gleaming desk.

Cat and I sit down, while my father remains seated in his own grand chair and Rocco stands next to him, like a king and his executioner.

"Your fiancé is worried about you," my father says, glaring at me from under his grizzled eyebrows. "He says you were in low spirits last night."

I chance a swift glance at Rocco, trying to guess his purpose.

He's punishing me for slapping him last night. But what does he want, exactly?

I don't know how to reply. Arguing will only get me in more trouble.

"I'm sorry," I say.

"Rocco says you were unhappy all last year at Kingmakers. He said you seemed lonely."

My eyes dart back and forth between my father's scowl and Rocco's smooth, impassive face.

What is this game?

Is he trying to get me to promise to fawn over him at school?

Is he trying to get me to drop out? No. . .Rocco still has two more years at Kingmakers. He wants me there where he can keep an eye on me, I'm sure of it.

"School was new and different at first," I say, cautiously. "But I think I adjusted eventually."

"Your fiancé disagrees."

I clench my hands hard in my lap, my mind racing. I don't know Rocco's angle, so I have no idea how to try to counteract it. My father's clock ticks away on the wall, maddeningly loud.

My father clears his throat, looking between my sister and me. "After some discussion, I've thought of a way to make you more comfortable in your Sophomore year."

I try to swallow but my mouth is too dry. "What?" I say.

"Cat will be attending Kingmakers with you."

Cat gives a terrified squeak in the seat next to mine.

Before I can stop myself, I cry, "What? You can't!"

My father's face darkens and his head lowers like a bull about to charge. "Excuse me?" he says.

I see the flicker of a smile on Rocco's lips. I'm playing right into his hands. By challenging my father, I'm only entrenching his decision.

I try to backtrack. "I only meant . . . what about Pintamonas? Cat's already been accepted—"

"She'll go where I tell her to go," my father growls.

"I'm perfectly happy at Kingmakers! I've adjusted already, Cat doesn't need to—"

"Art school is pointless," my father interrupts. "Rocco has been telling me all he's learning at Kingmakers, the variety of skills taught amongst the various divisions. Cat is timid. Cowardly, even. It would do her good to learn the real work of the mafiosi. If only so she can appreciate what her husband does, when the time comes."

Cat gives me a desperate, pleading look, begging me to think of some way to get her out of this. I've told her how challenging Kingmakers is, how brutal it can be. For me it's a welcome distraction. For Cat it will be hell on earth.

"Please, father," I say, "Cat is delicate. She could get injured—"

"It's time for her to toughen up," my father says ruthlessly. "I've made my decision."

Rocco made the decision, more like. Then he manipulated my father into thinking it was his idea.

I don't want to look at Rocco, but I can't help myself.

I turn my full, furious stare on him.

He smiles back at me, showing his sharp white teeth.

"Don't worry, my love," he says. "I'll take care of your sister..."

2

MILES

For Iggy's album drop, I throw the biggest party of the summer at an old charcoal factory in Bucktown.

I've thrown some ragers, but this one tops them all.

I call in every favor I've got to get The Shakers to do the opening set. That's crucial to bring in top-tier guests and to give the impression that Iggy is even more famous than the most popular band in Chicago.

I set up the stage and sound system on the roof, preemptively bribing the on-call cops to ignore any noise complaints.

Then I pack the guest list with models, influencers, musicians, and photographers, plus all the sexy young socialites from my parents' circle, warning them not to tell anybody about the private event so I can be sure they'll message every last moth-erfucker they know.

I get the swag bags on the cheap, bartering with friends who want to put their luxury goods in the hands of the Chicago elite.

And finally I liberate a freight car of Bollinger from the rail yard, because I want fountains of champagne, and there's no way to get the top-shelf stuff for a reasonable price.

There's no better place for a party than an old factory. The vast open spaces, the hulking furnaces in the corners, the raw concrete walls and the bare beams overhead . . . it gives that sense of gritty authenticity you could never find in an event center. The glitterati want to feel like they're slumming it, and the actual artists need to feel at home.

I've got four of my boys running security.

Much as I want the appearance of an out-of-control bacchana-lia, everything needs to run smooth tonight. Iggy is about to sign a seven-figure deal with a record label in L.A. They want music from the streets, but no actual criminal charges attached to their newest star.

I've known Iggy since we were kids. His dad used to chauffeur my father around when he was mayor of the city. Iggy and I would crowd into the glassed-off front seat, playing music and fucking with the lights, while my parents rode in the back, strategizing for the night ahead.

Iggy is wildly talented. His hooks are catchy, and his rhyme schemes so dense and interconnected that I feel like I have to listen to his songs five times over before I can truly appreciate them.

Iggy's a sweetheart, more poet than gangster. His only personality flaw is his willingness to trust the wrong people.

Which leads us to the biggest tripwire of the night—Iggy's piece-of-shit uncle.

"Declan Poe doesn't get through this door," I say to my boy Anders, nodding my head toward the double steel doors at the entrance. "If you see him, you call me. Don't wait for him to cause trouble."

Anders nods. Beckett and Anders are built like twin refrigerators. They could handle a small army on their own.

I run the party like a maestro in front of an orchestra. I deploy the drinks, the food, the music, the lighting, and the flow of guests with obsessive precision, while creating the illusion of free movement and free choice.

I glide through the crowd, introducing fame-hungry models to sleazy producers, brilliant videographers to marketing reps. Every connection is a new favor in my pocket as I hook people up with exactly what they need.

I hype Iggy up, too. He hates performing, gets nervous every time.

"It's not even a concert," I tell him. "People are just here to hang out. There's no pressure."

There's a metric fuck-ton of pressure. More pressure than the San Andreas fault. But it won't do Iggy any good to hear that.

Everything is flawless. Till I spot another uninvited guest.

She's standing over by the bar, sipping a glass of my extremely expensive stolen champagne, wearing a minidress that uses less fabric than an oversized handkerchief. I can see at least six different men hovering around her, waiting for their chance to swoop in, while she chats up the Cubs' newest pitcher.

The pitcher looks like he took a pop fly to the head. He's staring into Sabrina's eyes with a dazed expression, failing to bring his straw to his lips as he tries to take a sip of his cocktail and pokes himself in the nose instead. Sabrina stifles a giggle, biting the corner of her lip.

I shove my way through the crowd and grab her by the arm.

"Excuse me," I say to the pitcher.

He shakes his head, coming out of his trance.

"Hey!" he says. "We were talking!"

"She's gonna talk you right into Cook County jail," I inform him. "She's sixteen years old."

The pitcher's jaw drops.

Sabrina scowls at me, an expression that only manages to make her look more beautiful. My cousin is fucking dangerous.

"Let go of me," she says coolly.

"Not a fuckin' chance. You're gatecrashing."

"Oh, please," she tosses her long, dark hair back over her shoulder. "You're letting anybody in here. That dude gave up three home runs to the Sox on Thursday."

I keep dragging her toward the exit. "Yup. Everybody's welcome except you."

"Why not?"

" 'Cause I don't want Uncle Nero to cut my fucking head off."

Now Sabrina's really pissed.

"Are you serious?"

"As serious as antibiotic resistance."

"Miles!"

"Sabrina!" I've taken her all the way outside to the ivy-choked alleyway next to the factory. "Look, I get it. You hate being treated like a kid, and you just want to dance and have a couple drinks and make those dudes embarrass themselves for your amusement. On a normal night, I wouldn't have a problem with it. But I've got a lot riding on this and I can't keep an eye on you at the same time."

"I don't need you to babysit me!"

"Yeah, yeah, I know—you can take care of yourself. Go do it at some other party, 'cause your dad's already pissed at me."

I whistle to catch the attention of a cab dropping off another load of partygoers.

Sabrina cocks an eyebrow at me. "You did steal his car."

"I borrowed it for a photoshoot. And I brought it right back again."

"With sand in the engine."

I shove her in the backseat of the cab.

"Goodnight!" I say, slamming the door in her face.

Whatever Sabrina shouts back at me is lost in the pounding bass emanating from the charcoal factory.

With a sigh of relief, I turn back to the party.

I love my cousin, but her dad is a barely-civilized psychopath and my night doesn't need any more complications.

Besides, I've got to focus on Iggy. I can hear The Shakers winding down, which means he's up in just a couple of minutes.

I head back up to the roof, backstage to the little dressing room I set up for him. Iggy's pouring over his lyrics sheet, which looks like the journal of a madman, full of inky scribbles, crossed-out lines, and tiny arrows pointing to revisions.

He looks up when I enter, pushing his shaggy hair back out of his eyes and giving me his slow, sleepy grin.

"The band sounds great," he says.

"You're gonna sound better."

"Not too many people out there?"

"Nah," I lie. "Barely any."

In the bright stage lights, Iggy won't see any different till he's already done.

"That's good," he sighs.

Iggy's normal speaking voice is so soft and slow that the transformation to his rapid-fire rapping jars me every time.

"If your album charts the way I think it's gonna, the contract with Virgin is a sure thing," I tell him.

"We'll find out soon enough," Iggy says.

My phone buzzes in my pocket. I pull it out, seeing a message from Anders:

Poe rolled up with three dudes, but I told him to fuck off. Think he left.

GOOD. I knew he couldn't resist showing his ugly mug, but I'm glad Beckett and Anders were intimidating enough to dissuade him. If he comes back, we're gonna have a much less-friendly conversation.

"Problem?" Iggy asks.

"Nope," I say, tucking my phone back in my pocket. "You ready?"

Iggy folds up his lyrics sheet and stuffs it in his pocket. I know he's already got it all locked up in that insane brain of his—he just likes to look it over to reassure himself.

The crowd whoops and cheers as The Shakers take their bow.

"Sounds like a lot of people," Iggy says mildly.

"You got this," I reassure him.

I walk him to the stairs leading up the backside of the stage. The sound engineer clips on Iggy's mic and gives him the hand-held as well. The opening bars of "Deathless Life" begin to play. Iggy squares his shoulders and I see the transformation wash over him—his eyes narrowing, his lips tightening, his fingers gripping the mic.

Then he bounds up the stairs and starts shouting with the speed of an auctioneer:

THEY SAID I was buried

Desiccated and dead

I'll climb up out the grave

Break the stone on ya head

I'M breathless and reckless

Continually climb

Drink the glass to the bottom

And eat up the lime . . .

BY THE TIME he reaches the chorus, the whole rooftop is shouting the lyrics along with him. Iggy will know that the factory is packed, a mass of people breaking every possible fire code, but it won't matter by now, he's in the swing of it.

I told my boy Kelly to video the whole thing. I'll send that to Victor Kane tonight, and I'll be damned if he doesn't sign the contract on the spot. Iggy's going to L.A., where he'll be free from his bloodsucking relatives.

Right as I'm reveling in triumph, my phone buzzes again.

I pull it out, seeing Sabrina's number.

My cousin wouldn't call just to beg to be let back into the party.

I lift the phone to my ear, already sensing what I'm about to hear.

"Your bouncer needs a lesson in manners," Poe says, in his three-packs-a-day rasp.

"He never passed the etiquette test in the employee training manual," I reply.

"Not you though, huh?" Poe sneers. "You're all jokes."

"I'd call that a quip at best."

"Let's see how funny it is when I strangle your cousin and dump her body in the alley."

I let out a slow breath of air. "Not a good idea. You know who her father is?"

"I don't give a *fuck* who you little shits are related to," Poe hisses. "Get down here and leave your fuckin' bouncers in the warehouse."

"It's a factory," I correct him. "But alright. I'm coming."

I'm annoyed that I have to leave in the middle of Iggy's performance. Even more annoyed that they dragged Sabrina into this. She probably hopped out of that cab the second it went round the corner. She's always been a magnet for trouble.

As I pass Beckett and Anders guarding the door, Anders says, "Something wrong, boss?"

"A small inconvenience," I say.

I could give Anders shit for not calling me when Poe showed up like I told him to do, but this was coming one way or another.

"Wait twelve minutes," I tell Anders. "Then come out to the alley."

He nods slowly, his eyes fixed on mine. I can tell he'd rather follow me right now, but he'll do what I ask.

"Alright, boss," he says.

"Twelve minutes." I tap the Breitling on my wrist. "Use the side door."

Anders takes a quick look at his own watch to confirm the time and jerks his head in the affirmative.

I pass the long line of people still waiting to come inside, all gazing enviously up toward the roof where Iggy's ass-kicking performance is in full swing.

Then I turn the corner to the narrow alleyway where Poe waits with his three goons.

The alley is actually quite pretty, the factory wall carpeted with a thick mat of hanging ivy and the opposite side bordered by an ornate wrought-iron fence. The narrow space funnels the sound so that Iggy's concert sounds much further away than it actually is, and I can hear my footsteps echoing on the concrete.

Poe has one of his idiot friends stationed at the opening of the alley, a rat-faced motherfucker in an oversized leather jacket. He smirks at me as I pass. Poe and his other two goons are holding Sabrina down at the end of the alley in front of a padlocked gate.

The biggest guy has Sabrina's arms pinned behind her back, a position that pulls her tiny dress up even further. His friend—a stocky dude with teardrops tattooed on both cheeks—is standing slightly behind her so he can enjoy the view. If he wasn't so busy staring at her ass, he might notice the glint of metal on her upper thigh.

Sabrina locks eyes with me. There's no hint of fear or remorse in her face. Just pure, burning fury.

It doesn't appear that they roughed her up, so maybe Poe isn't as stupid as he looks.

He does look plenty stupid. He's a walking cartoon character —his blocky, rectangular head sitting on a neck of exactly the same thickness, so it forms one long pillar from skull to shoulders. His face is shaved so high that his pouf of gingery hair perches on top of his head like a toupee. Add to that a drooping mustache and Bugs Bunny teeth.

Still, it would be a mistake to find him comical. Poe is no stranger to violence. The most dangerous man is one who has nothing to lose.

Poe is a six-time convict, petty drug dealer, and fentanyl addict who's about to lose his last meal ticket. He's going to cling to Iggy until his fingernails tear off. Unless I put a stop to this once and for all.

"You're fuckin' disrespectful, boy," Poe hisses. "You throw a party for Iggy's album, and you don't even invite his manager?"

"You're not his manager," I reply. "And you're right, I don't respect you. You're a leech. You've been bleeding Iggy dry since he posted his first song. You don't do fuck-all for him."

"I do everything for him!" Poe rasps, outraged. "Who helped pay his mum's rent after his dad died? Who bought his Christmas presents?"

"You threw them fifty bucks here and there so you could use their house to stash your drugs," I snort. "And the only Christmas I remember seeing you is the one where you had an ankle monitor and you needed a permanent address for your parole officer."

If anybody paid Iggy's rent it was my dad, who helped Iggy's mom land a job as a PA at City Hall after his father dropped dead from a stroke at only forty-eight years old.

"I don't have to explain myself to you!" Poe howls, his face turning the color of a turnip. "You think you can take my nephew away? Well I got yer fuckin' cousin. So you can tear up that bullshit contract with Virgin-fuckin-whoever-the-fuck, or I'll tear her pretty little face off instead!"

I give him a second to recover his breath. Then I reply, calmly, "That's not happening. Iggy's leaving. You're staying here. It's already decided. But I'm willing to discuss terms—we can all walk away happy tonight."

"Fuck yer fuckin' terms!" Poe laughs in my face. "Look around you! There's four of us and one of you."

I pretend to look at his three goons with something approaching respect. Really, I'm just confirming their exact positions. And Poe's, too.

"No need for this to get ugly," I say.

"Oh, we're way past ugly," Poe sneers. "You think you're making a deal here? I'll shoot this bitch in the face just to set the table!"

He yanks a battered .45 out of the waistband of his filthy jeans and points it at Sabrina, cocking the trigger. Sabrina's nostrils flare. I figure I have about two more minutes before she does something crazy. Which aligns nicely with my own timeline.

Poe doesn't want the carrot—it's time to bring out the stick.

"I'm glad you brought up firearms, Poe," I say.

I'm slowly walking forward so that I can position myself between Poe and Sabrina. Poe doesn't care—he's fine with pointing his gun in my face instead. He turns his body, arm outstretched, so that his back is to the ivy-covered wall and Poe's two goons are behind me.

"It's hard to get rid of a gun," I say. "I mean, really get rid of it. You can file the serial numbers off, chuck it in a river. But it's still there, just waiting to be found. And sometimes you don't want to throw it in the river. The damn things are expensive. Sometimes the temptation to keep it is just too strong . . ."

"What the fuck are you blabbering about?" Poe says, mustache twitching.

"Iggy and I have been friends a long time," I say. "Like that Christmas we were just talking about. I spent half the holiday at his house. You probably remember..."

Poe narrows his eyes at me, finger curled around the trigger of his gun. I don't love that he's holding it that way. He's jittery enough to shoot me by accident.

"Iggy and me had just started smoking weed. I think we were fourteen, fifteen maybe. We had to find somewhere to hide his stash so his mom didn't give us shit. We ended up taking down the air vent and putting our baggy in the ducts. Funny, though ... we weren't the first people to hide something in there..."

Poe has a sense of where I'm going, but he doesn't quite believe it.

"You had just gotten out of jail after knocking over the 7-11 on Kedzie with a couple of your buddies. Somebody shot the cashier ... oops. He died two days later. Cops thought it was you, but they couldn't prove it from the security tape, and they didn't have the murder weapon. You hid the gun. But you didn't hide it very well. Uncles and nephews think alike I guess, 'cause Iggy pulled it out of the wall."

"Bullshit," Poe hisses. Though he's shaking his head, he takes a step back so he's almost pressed up against the ivy.

"I'm afraid not," I say quietly, " 'Course I didn't know what that gun was at the time, or where it came from. But when you started demanding that Iggy pay you a forty percent commission . . . I dug up your old case file. I checked what caliber bullet they pulled out of that cashier's neck. And I remembered what we found that Christmas. Only took me an hour to visit Iggy's house and check the vent again."

"I don't know what you're talking about," Poe says. His jaw is stubbornly set and he's sweating.

"It was still there. A .357 Magnum revolver with a scratch across the grip. From how dirty it was . . . I kinda think you didn't even wipe your prints off."

"So the fuck what!" Poe shouts defiantly. "Doesn't mean nothin'."

"It means a lot," I say. "Looks to me like the only evidence the cops need is that gun. They know you were at the gas station that night. They just couldn't prove who pulled the trigger. There's no statute of limitations on murder, unfortunately . . ."

Poe's grip on his gun is none too steady. He's looking back and forth between me and the gangly asshole who's holding onto Sabrina. I'm hoping my leverage is enough that we can end this thing peacefully. But I'm also keeping Poe's goons in my peripheral, counting down the seconds left on that twelve minutes . . .

"You're a fuckin' liar!" Poe shrieks. "You ain't got any—"

He's cut off mid-accusation by the heavy metal door that hits him square in the back. He didn't see it right behind him, covered over by the ivy. Anders comes barreling through the side door at top speed, hitting Poe so hard that he goes flying forward spread-eagle on the pavement, taking several layers of skin off his face.

Since I was waiting for exactly that moment, I have the advantage over the other two idiots. I charge the one with the tattooed face, trusting Sabrina to handle the other guy for just a second.

My dad always told me to attack smart, not hard. When your adrenaline is up, the natural inclination is to come in swinging. You gotta tamp that down if you want to be strategic.

Fists are overrated—too easy to break your hand first punch. Better to use the knees and elbows.

I come at Teardrops with a long knee, using the full momentum of my rush to drive my kneecap directly into his gut. Then, when he doubles over, I bring my elbow down hard on the back of his neck.

Right beside me, Tall n' Ugly has made the mistake of letting go of Sabrina's arms. Maybe he thought she'd stand there helpless while he jumped into the fight. He thought wrong.

In one swift movement, Sabrina unsheathes the little silver knife strapped to her thigh and slashes him across the face, opening his cheek from ear to jaw. He claps his hand to his face, blood pouring through his fingers, and Sabrina uses that opening to stab him under the ribs. He drops like a stone, her knife still buried in his side.

Rat-Face has realized that his guarding of the alley was both unsuccessful and no longer required, so he comes charging at me, trying to pull his gun out of his flapping leather jacket. I throw my cellphone hard at his face, hitting him on the bridge of the nose with a satisfying crunch. I follow that up with a right-cross that takes the rest of the starch out of him.

Meanwhile, Anders is grappling with Poe, who managed to keep hold of his gun despite his brief departure with gravity and the road rash down his cheek. Poe squeezes the trigger wildly, firing two shots up in the air, and a third that narrowly misses my ear.

"Watch it!" I shout.

"Sorry," Anders grunts. He wrenches the gun out of Poe's hand and uses it to crack him across the jaw. A tooth flies out of Poe's mouth, landing next to Sabrina's shoe.

"Ew," she says.

I rip the gun out of Rat-Face's jacket, giving him another kick in the gut to remind him to stay down. Then I examine Tall n' Ugly.

"Sabrina," I say, with an irritated sigh. "Did you have to go for the liver? I wasn't planning on burying a body tonight."

Tall n' Ugly looks up at me, grimacing in pain.

"I'm not dead," he pleads.

"You will be if I pull that knife out of you," I say.

It's buried hilt-deep in his side, and it has Sabrina's prints on it.

Sabrina looks down on him contemptuously.

"You could take him to one of the safe houses," she says. "Or just pull it out and drop him on the side of the highway."

"*I'm* not doing anything," I tell her. "I've gotta wrap this party up. You and Anders take him. Go out that way," I say to Anders, nodding my head toward the padlocked gate. "I don't want any guests seeing him."

"What about the other three?" Anders says, looking down at the semi-conscious groaning assholes.

"They can walk home or pay for their own damn cab."

Tomorrow I'll mail the Magnum to my favorite dirty cop at the Chicago PD. Not because I like snitching—I don't. It's the principle of the thing.

I was willing to give Poe one last payday as long as he left Iggy alone after that. I'd always choose to make an ally over an enemy.

But Poe refused to make a deal. So he's gotta pay the consequences.

Giving Sabrina one last glance to make sure she's okay, I head back inside the factory. I send Beckett out to help Anders with clean up, and then I make it back up to the rooftop just in time to watch Iggy take his bow. As far as I can tell, the music was loud enough to drown out the gunfire. Or else people thought it was part of the backing track—it's all the rage to use "found sounds" these days.

The rest of the night passes in blissful peace. Clips of Iggy's performance go viral on every possible platform. When his album drops at midnight, "Deathless Life" gets a hundred thousand downloads in the first hour.

Victor Kane texts me a photo of Iggy's contract with his signature scrawled in ink across the bottom.

Iggy and I celebrate by taking a bath in the champagne fountain.

"Thank you, man," Iggy says, toasting me with a glass he's too drunk to notice is already empty.

"You're the talent," I tell him. "I just had to shine a spotlight on you."

Iggy sets his glass down, trying to focus his bleary stare on me.

"Why don't you come with me, man? Come to L.A.?"

"I will," I say. "But not yet. I've got two more years of school."

"What do you need a degree for?" Iggy says. "You're already a fuckin' genius."

"It's not the degree," I say. "It's the connections."

As close as Iggy and I have always been, I haven't told him what Kingmakers is really like. I can't tell anyone who isn't a mafioso themselves.

The island is isolated and restrictive. Each student can only bring in a single suitcase. The list of forbidden items includes alcohol, drugs, and most electronics.

At Kingmakers I do exactly what I did in high school, but on a much grander scale: I'm a broker. I provide contraband, smuggled onto the island via a network of fishermen and locals.

I've been hustling since I was twelve years old, saving up every penny in pursuit of my ultimate goal.

I want to be an actual Kingmaker. The appointer of stars. Creator of music, fashion, and cinema.

I don't want to be Justin Bieber—I want to be Scooter Braun.

I have no desire for celebrity. The real power is the man behind the curtain. The producer at the epicenter of global culture.

I want to find a hundred Iggys, and I want to drop a thousand albums. I want to produce the next *Avengers* franchise. And I want to control the billions of dollars of endorsements and ads attached to all of it.

There's one crucial factor of this dream: I have to do it on my own.

I'm building my empire without a penny of my parents' money.

I want to stand on top of the mountain without a single asterisk next to my name.

The American Dream is to be a self-made man.

And that's why I started my bank account at zero, no trust fund, no cheats. Every dollar I earn goes into that account—every hustle, every deal. I'm at $9.8 million now, money earned by my own meticulous, ingenious, and even reckless labor.

The commission I earned off Iggy's Virgin contract will put me almost at $10 million.

I think $12 million is the number I need to launch my empire in Los Angeles. I have it all planned out—the Malibu mansion I'll rent, the office space I'll lease on Wilshire Boulevard. The parties I'll throw and the fish I'll reel in one by one.

I can see it all perfectly in my mind.

Two more years at Kingmakers, and then I'll join Iggy in La La Land.

THE UBER DROPS me off at my parents' house at 5:20 in the morning.

It looks more like an Apple store than a house—a transparent prism of glass propped up on stilts, so that half the floor overhangs the lake. Privacy be damned, no curtains or blinds block any of the windows. You can see right inside the rooms to my father's sleek, modern furniture and my mother's bold paint-spattered art on the walls.

I can see my mom sitting at the kitchen table drinking her morning coffee, wearing her favorite ratty old Cubs T, her hair twisted up in a bun with a pen stuck through to hold it in place.

She glances up as soon as I come in the house, her brilliant smile breaking over her face like she's been awake for hours, and not twenty minutes at most.

"There's fresh coffee in the pot," she says. "Unless you're planning to go to sleep in a minute."

She's poring over a bunch of documents that look like real estate transactions. Probably some new development with Uncle Nero. As soon as one's finished, he's onto the next.

"I'll just have one of those," I say, snitching an apple slice off her plate.

"Congratulations," she says to me.

"For what?"

"Iggy's song. I checked the charts as soon as I woke up."

I can't help smiling. I never told my mom anything about the drop party or the single coming out. She's a sneaky fucker, just like me. Always gathering information.

"He's going to L.A.," I say.

"That's great," my mom replies, with real pleasure. "He's a good kid, he deserves it. You should be proud of yourself, Miles."

Satisfaction is the enemy of success. I'll be proud of myself when I've got the whole damn world at my feet.

"You're a good friend," my mom says.

"I took a nice commission out of the deal," I tell her, grabbing another apple slice.

"I know why you did it," my mom replies. She's looking at me in the way she always does, like I'm the best person in the world. Like she can't help grinning just from the sight of me.

This is not deserved. I can be a selfish asshole. A real piece of shit. My mom doesn't care—she'd always pick a volcano over a pleasant mountain stream. To her, the only sin is to be boring.

"Are you packed for school?" she asks.

"Just about."

Meaning I've packed zero items into my suitcase, but I have considered doing it.

My mom snorts, not fooled for a second. "I bought a couple fresh uniforms for you."

"What size pants?"

"Thirty-four long. You're still growing."

She stands up so she can ruffle my hair. She has to go on tiptoe to do it. I put my arms around her waist and hug her, lifting her off her feet. She laughs and tries to hug me back, but I'm squeezing her too hard.

"It's a dark day when your kids could send you to your room if they really wanted to," she says.

"Don't worry," I tease her. "I'm still scared of Dad."

"Thank god," she says.

I'm not actually scared of my dad. I might be if I only ever saw him on his own, with his electric stare and his way of barking orders that seems to snap men to attention like they've been hit with a whip. But then my mom sidles up to him, taking little jabs at him, making him laugh when you're sure he's never cracked a smile in his life. And you realize he's got a soul after all, however hard he tries to hide it.

He's a good man. My mom's a good woman, the best woman.

I still can't wait to get out of here.

Because I'm a wild thing, just like my mother was once upon a time.

I don't want to be cared for and protected.

I want to hunt.

"Make sure you say goodbye to Caleb and Noelle," my mom says. "Especially Caleb."

"I will," I promise her.

I know how upset Caleb would be if I didn't. He tries to act all tough, but he's a fucking marshmallow on the inside.

Being the oldest is a tricky thing. Your siblings are annoying as fuck for most of your life, but you still love 'em. You can't help it.

And I'll admit, Caleb isn't shaping up too bad. He's a little scrapper at school, he might give our cousin Leo a run for his money on the basketball court one of these days, and he can be pretty funny when he works on his material and keeps his anecdotes tight.

Give the kid a couple more years and a couple more inches, and we might be legitimate friends. For now I can still bend him up like a pretzel if he gets lippy.

Noelle is a different beast. She's smart, and I mean scary smart. She's like an A.I. computer that might discover the cure for Ebola, or else might decide that humanity is the virus and should be wiped off the earth.

Too early to tell with her. For now she looks damn cute in a pair of pigtails and her Sailor Moon shirt.

My dad comes into the kitchen, freshly showered and wearing an impeccably tailored suit.

His hair turned prematurely silver, which creates an alarming contrast with his bright blue eyes. My mom likes to call him a White Walker when she really wants to piss him off.

"He's alive," my dad says when he spots me.

"Where are you going?" I ask.

"Breakfast with Uncle Nero."

"I don't know if that's worth dressing up for," I say. "Since he's probably gonna show up in coveralls."

"I'm not taking tips from somebody wearing moon boots." My dad frowns, shaking his head at my sneakers. "What the hell are those?"

"They're . . . *fashion!*" my mom says, doing jazz hands.

"They're the re-drop of the Nike Air Mag," I inform him. "They only made eighty-nine pairs. I could sell these for thirty-five thousand dollars right now. Used!"

"I will pay you thirty-five thousand dollars if I never have to look at them again," my dad says.

"Tempting," I say. "But if I keep trading up, I might just get my hands on a pair of the solid gold OVOs."

"Please tell me you're keeping at least some of your money in an IRA," my dad says.

"Don't worry, Dad." I grin. "The nice thing about money . . . is you can always make more."

Taking my mom's last apple slice, I head up the floating staircase to the upper level. I was planning to flop down directly on my bed, but I can't because my mom helpfully dumped my empty suitcase there, along with the fresh new uniforms.

Taking the hint, I chuck the rest of my clothes and books into the suitcase, as well as a nice thick wad of cash wrapped up with rubber bands. That's my seed money for the semester ahead. I'll sprinkle that cash amongst the fishermen and the greediest of the school employees, and soon I'll have my own little Silk Road bringing exotic delicacies onto the island that I can sell to my fellow students for exorbitant prices. Tea and porcelain ain't got nothin' on vodka and Molly.

Packing complete, I zip up the suitcase, chuck it on the ground, kick off my sneakers, and roll into bed.

I drift off to sleep counting dollars instead of sheep.

3

CAT

I leave for Kingmakers on the first of September.

I kept praying that something would happen to prevent me from going. My main hope was that I simply wouldn't be accepted, applying so late in the year.

Then a heavy gray envelope arrived in the mail, sealed with wax the color of dried blood, stamped with the crest of the school: a crowned skull. The handwritten address bore my full legal name, Catalina Resmella Romero, in script that looked a hundred years old.

I already knew what it would say before I opened it—or at least, I thought I did.

Catalina Romero,

I am writing to inform you that you have been accepted to King-makers Academy. Having reviewed your application and assessed your qualifications, we have assigned you to the Spy division.

School will commence on the 3rd of September. You will depart from the pier in Dubrovnik at 10:00 in the morning on September 2nd.

Admission to our campus is singular and irrevocable. If you decide to leave for any reason, you will not be permitted to return. Be sure to bring all items you will require for the duration of your program.

Enclosed is a list of our rules and regulations. Sign and return your acknowledgment of the contract, including your willingness to abide by our arbitration and punishment system. Your parents' signature and imprint are likewise required.

We look forward to meeting you. You will be joining an elite institution with a long and storied history. Perhaps someday your name will be inscribed on the wall of Dominus Scelestos.

Your sister distinguished herself in the Quartum Bellum in her Freshman year. I hope to see you do the same when this year's challenge convenes.

Sincerely,

Luther Hugo

Necessitas Non Habet Legem—Necessity Has No Law

I recognized the envelope from Zoe's identical missive the year prior. From its thickness, I assumed that I had been accepted, and that it would include the draconian list of school rules and the irrevocable contract on which my father and I would both have to press our bloody fingerprints, agreeing that Kingmakers has the right to discipline or even execute me if I transgress its laws.

I knew all of that ahead of time.

What I didn't expect was to be put in with the Spies.

Kingmakers has four divisions: the Heirs, who are trained to lead their families as a general leads an army. The Enforcers, who are the soldiers. The Accountants, who handle the finance and investment arms of the business. And then the Spies.

The Spies are the least-numerous and most obscure division. Their job is to surveil and analyze enemy groups—both law enforcement and rival criminals. They predict threats against the family and sometimes liaise with the enemy. And most of all, they ferret out threats from within their own ranks.

I can't imagine a job less suited to me.

Spies have to be bold and cunning. Ruthless and skilled.

I'm terrified of my own shadow. I cry if someone looks at me sideways. I have no skills at all, other than painting and drawing, and I'm pretty good with computers. I've never been in a fight, and I've never fired a gun in my life.

As a Spy, there's no one to protect you. One wrong step, and you'll be tortured and killed.

I feel like a crab ripped out of its shell.

Worst of all, Zoe and I couldn't even travel to Dubrovnik together. The Freshmen start a week later than everybody else, so she's already on campus, while I have to board the imposing ship all on my own, amid the throng of students from all across the globe.

I hear a virtual Babel of languages on the dock, though we all have to speak English once we arrive, as it's the *lingua franca* of Kingmakers.

I try to find the most distant, unobtrusive corner of the ship so I can stay out of the way of the surly-looking sailors, observing my fellow students from a distance.

Everyone looks so much cooler and more confident than me. Plenty of them already seem to know each other, maybe because they're from the same country, or because they've crossed paths with each other before.

I don't recognize a single face. Until a merry girl with blonde curls taps me on the shoulder and says, "Cat? Is that you?"

"Yes?" I say hesitantly.

"I thought so! It's me, Perry!"

"Perry?" I say blankly. And then, "Oh, Perry! Oh my god, you look so . . . so . . . different!"

She laughs. "I got into swimming and lost a lot of weight."

I would never have known her as the same girl I met three summers ago at a resort in Monaco. I was there with my family and Perry with hers. Our fathers seemed friendly. I'm sure they had the same purpose in "vacationing" that week, though I never heard what it was.

It's not only the weight that changed Perry—she looked like a kid when we built sandcastles on the private beach in front of our hotel. Now she's confident and stylish, dressed in a jaunty beret and jacket that perfectly compliment her school uniform.

I feel childish by comparison, with my thick knee socks, flat oxfords, and too-long skirt. I notice that the rest of the girls had their green plaid skirts tailored to hit mid-thigh, which is vastly more flattering. I flush, thinking of all the unspoken rules that other people seem to intuit, which sail right over my head.

"I didn't know you were coming to Kingmakers!" Perry says.

"It was sort of a last-minute decision."

"What division are you?"

"Spy," I say, with a nervous grit of my teeth.

"Ohh," Perry says, eyebrows raised. "Good for you! I'm an Accountant."

"I don't know why they put me there," I admit. "Maybe it was a mistake . . ."

"I don't think they make mistakes," Perry says. "You didn't request it?"

"No." I shake my head. "Definitely not. I expected to be an Accountant, too."

"I wonder what happened?" Perry says curiously.

I hadn't really pondered on it, since it seemed like just one more nasty surprise to pile on the shit heap.

"Well . . ." I say hesitantly. "I do know a bit about programming . . ."

In secondary school, I had a computer sciences teacher who was simply brilliant. She sparked my interest in all things technological. She told me I should go into programming, but I like art so much that I chose graphic design instead. Not that it mattered in the end, since I won't be studying either.

"That could be it." Perry shrugs. "There's a lot of security system analysis in the Spy division. Some hacking, too. Or at least, that's what my cousin told me."

"I wish I was in your division," I say wistfully.

"Me too," Perry says. "We could have roomed together."

My stomach sinks down further than ever. I'm going to be sharing a room with a stranger. Taking classes with strangers. Zoe and I will both be at Kingmakers, but who knows how much we'll see each other. I feel so alone and so intimidated.

I don't know how Zoe navigated all this on her own last year. She's always been braver than me.

At least she told me where to board the ship and what the island is like. She went into all that blind. We don't have any close friends who attended Kingmakers before us—just a few asshole cousins that we avoid at all costs.

I'm theoretically prepared as I cross the wide, empty expanse of ocean leading to distant Visine Dvorca. Zoe even forewarned me that the water will get choppy and rough as we draw close, so I feel the change in the pitching of the ship long before I see the limestone cliffs jutting up out of the waves.

"Wow," Perry whispers next to me. She's staring up at the castle fortress, as is almost everyone else.

I've never seen anything like it.

Kingmakers protrudes directly out of the rock, carved from the same pale limestone as the cliffs. It rises in tiers like a cake, rough and ancient-looking. Dark stains run down from the windows, as if the castle is crying. I'm sure it's only the marks of rainwater, but it gives a strange sense of foreboding that isn't helped by the grotesque and demonic gargoyles menacing each cornice.

Waves beat ferociously against the cliffs. Zoe warned me that the journey into the harbor would be difficult, and sure enough, the ship pitches and rolls so hard that it sometimes looks as if the masts will dip down into the water.

Once we're inside the sheltered bay, however, the sea smooths once more and I'm able to look with interest at the little village encircling the docks.

It's a pretty little town, the weathered wooden buildings stacked right up against the water on stilts, with spaces beneath so that rowboats can take the fisherman all the way to their doors.

The island rises up behind the village—fields and farms, orchards and olive groves, and patches of thick green forest. Then, at the highest and most distant point: the spires of Kingmakers.

The air carries the familiar salt tang of the sea, but also sharper, colder scents—pine and stone. Smoke and iron.

Several open wagons wait to take us to the school. I check to see if my suitcase was safely unloaded from the ship, but there's too many students milling around to get a good look.

"Come on!" Perry says to me. "Let's grab a seat!"

I follow her into the closest wagon, where she squeezes us into a group of kids she apparently already knows. They're pleasant and friendly, but a quick round of introductions reveals that they're all Accountants or Enforcers. I haven't met a single other Spy, which isn't helping my nerves.

Worse still, every time I explain my division I'm greeted with a bemused expression. I really must look as incompetent as I feel.

The Accountants division is the usual catch-all for the studious and introverted children of mafia families. It's the place we can be useful. A job intended to keep us safe.

As a Spy, I'll be nothing but a liability.

I'm scared I won't even survive the classes. Nobody's pulling any punches in Combat. We'll use live ammunition in Marksmanship. Worst of all is Torture Techniques.

"They hook you up to a car battery," a stocky Enforcer says. "You do it in pairs, and you take turns. One of you has to pull the switch, and the other has to take the shock. It's to desensitize you. If you can electrocute your friend, you'll have no problem doing it to an enemy . . ."

Perry's friends are sharing the most outlandish and terrifying stories they've heard about Kingmakers.

"I heard at least five students die every year," a slim Asian girl says.

"Bollocks," a plump blond boy retorts. "It can't be that many, or nobody would send their kids."

"People do die," a red-haired girl with a French accent says. "The year my oldest brother was here, a Senior hung himself in the cathedral."

"Well that's suicide," the blond boy says stubbornly. "That could happen anywhere."

"He only did it because they drove him to it with all the assignments and exams," the redhead says, lifting her chin.

"I hate exams," Perry says, letting out a dismal sigh.

I don't mind tests. In fact, sometimes I take them for fun, if it's something interesting like an IQ test or a personality quiz. But that's a nerdy thing to say, so I keep it to myself.

"Who has siblings here?" Perry asks.

About half the kids raise their hands, including me.

"It's so stupid that they don't let us bring our phones," a short, stocky boy grumbles.

"It wouldn't do you any good anyway," the red-haired girl says. "There's no internet, no cell service."

"No toilets either," a skinny, freckled boy says. "You have to use a chamber pot."

The Asian girl stares at him in horror.

"He's fucking with you," Perry laughs. "They have normal bathrooms."

I force myself to laugh along with the other kids. Honestly, nothing would surprise me when it comes to Kingmakers.

At least the island is beautiful. Visine Dvorca is not unlike Barcelona in that it's sunny and green, with a pleasant sea breeze. I'm guessing it gets colder in the winter, however, judging from the thickness of the pullovers and wool jackets that were included with our uniforms.

Thinking of the winter reminds me that I won't be going home for almost an entire year. For the first time I feel a slight frisson of anticipation—the relief that I won't have Daniela's sharp eyes constantly fixed on me, or my father's hot temper applied to me.

Several of our cousins attend Kingmakers. Zoe cautioned me that two in particular—the hateful Martin Romero and the arrogant Santiago Cruz—have been spying on her and reporting back to our father. That's still less oppressive than living under his roof.

That infinitesimal glimmer of hope is immediately extinguished as we pass through the forbidding stone gates into Kingmakers. I swear the temperature drops twenty degrees within the towering walls, as the sheer size and scope of the castle becomes apparent. I see dozens of grandiose buildings, towers, greenhouses, balustraded terraces, and structures I can't even name. I feel like I've been shrunk down to the size of an ant, dwarfed by the monumental architecture.

The friendly chatter ceases amongst the Freshmen in my wagon as we gaze awestruck all around us.

If I thought my fellow Freshmen were intimidating, it's nothing to how the upperclassmen strike me. They're tall and powerfully built, striding across the grounds with confidence I could never dream of possessing. They don't look like students at all—more like royalty. They're haughty and powerful, with an edge of ferocity that quite frankly terrifies me.

I've been around the children of mafia before. But never like this, never *en masse*. Every single person here is a born killer.

Except for me.

I don't know why I didn't get that particular gene. There's none of my father in me.

I crane my neck, looking for Zoe. She's nowhere to be seen. Her classes started a week ago, so she's probably inside one of

the many buildings, diligently taking notes on some professor's lecture.

The wagons jerk to a stop and the Freshmen unload. There's a
scramble as we try to dig our suitcases out of the wagon full of
luggage. Once we've all secured our bags, we're greeted by a
handful of disdainful-looking Seniors who split us up
according to our divisions.

The Enforcers are the most numerous, and almost entirely
composed of male students. At Kingmakers, boys outnumber
girls four to one. Not all mafia families care to send their
daughters to be trained. My father had no intention of
sending either Zoe or me, before Zoe refused to marry Rocco
Prince unless she could attend college first.

She thought he'd send her to a normal university. Instead he
ordered her to join Rocco at Kingmakers.

Now I've been thrust into that devil's bargain right alongside
her.

The Accountants are the second-largest group, and the only
division with an almost equal split of girls and boys. Most of
the kids in from my wagon happily head off together, taking
Perry along with them. She gives me a little wave as they
depart.

Now only the Heirs and Spies are left.

We're similar in number, but our appearance couldn't be more different. If Kingmakers were a high school cafeteria, the Heirs would be the cool kids: confident, well-dressed, already assembling their circle of admirers.

The Spies are, to put it bluntly, the misfits.

The baker's dozen Freshman Spies show a clear tendency toward heavy piercings, strange tattoos, exotic hair colors, and dour expressions.

Then there's me. I stand there like a lamb among wolves. A schoolgirl in the center of a biker gang.

I can feel the other Spies looking at me, and I don't know how to wipe the stupid doe-eyed expression off my face.

Our guide is a tall, lanky Senior wearing an oversized olive-green sweater vest and a pair of shredded trousers tucked into military boots. His long dark hair hangs over his ears and his hoop earring makes him look a bit like a pirate.

I've already noticed that while Kingmakers students are required to wear uniforms, they seem to have no compunction about styling said uniforms according to their personal preference.

"I'm Saul Turner," our guide says lazily. "I'll show you to the Undercroft."

I have no idea what an Undercroft is, and I don't want to be the one to ask. I fall in line behind Saul, pulling my suitcase along beside me.

Saul leads us to what looks like the very center of the King-makers grounds, to the largest and grandest of the buildings.

"This is the Keep," he announces. "You'll have a lot of your classes in here. Your combat classes will be over there in the Armory," he jerks his head toward a squat building with rounded walls, "and straight past that is the dining hall. Library is waaaay down there." He points to the northwest corner of campus where I can see a tall, spindly tower rising above everything else. "That's basically all you need to know for now."

I wasn't paying attention to much after the mention of "combat classes." When exactly are those going to start? I just know I'm gonna get punched in the face my very first day.

My stomach feels heavy as a stone.

Saul continues walking toward the Armory. We trail after him like a row of obedient ducklings.

"The Undercroft runs all the way under there," he points to the long expanse of open lawn between the Armory and the dining hall.

"Where?" a grouchy-looking girl with a septum piercing demands. She looks around as if expecting a dormitory to materialize from thin air.

"Right under your feet," Saul laughs.

"We're sleeping in a *basement?*" the girl sneers, crossing her arms disdainfully over her chest. Her long nails are filed into points, with silver rings on every finger.

"More of a cellar," Saul says. He seems impervious to rudeness, or to any other emotion we might send in his direction. I get the feeling one of us could be struck with lightning right in front of him and he wouldn't bat an eye. "We go in through here," he says.

We follow him inside a building much too small to house thirteen students. From the rusted empty racks on the walls and the pungent scent of fermented grapes, I think this used to be a wine cellar.

It's not our final destination. Saul leads us toward a wide staircase descending even deeper into the earth, its dark opening gaping like a mouth.

I don't like tight spaces. And I definitely don't like the dark.

My heart is already hammering against my ribs before I even set foot on the stairs.

Even the sulky girl with the nose ring looks slightly unnerved as she falls into step beside me. Our footsteps echo on stone as we descend into the Undercroft.

I'm relieved to see warm light at the foot of the stairs. Even more relieved to see that the Undercroft is, at least, not cramped. The domed stone roof is almost twenty feet high, with thick supporting pillars running down the center of the space, forming a double set of archways.

The first portion of this long tunnel is a kind of common room, with couches, a bookshelf, and a large table with bench seats for studying. Further down, the space is divided into separate dorms.

"Two to a room," Saul says. "Only the ones in the middle are empty, 'cause the upperclassmen claimed everything close to the bathroom and the stairs."

We walk down the hallway, cautious in the dim lamplight.

The double row of doors are identical, but it's easy to tell which have been claimed, as their owners have decorated the scarred wood with stickers and patches. I notice that no one has put up a name tag. You wouldn't be able to find a particular room without already knowing the patch on the door.

The bare doors in the center are the ones up for grabs.

There's a flurry as the Freshmen Spies hustle inside their chosen spaces. It takes me a moment to realize that everyone has already paired off. I stand stupidly in the hallway until only me and the sulky pierced girl are left without roommates.

She stares at me with an expression of disgust even greater than when she learned we'd be rooming underground.

"You've got to be fucking kidding me," she says.

Her disdain hits me like a slap.

I know I shouldn't care what she thinks of me, but I've never been able to ignore other people's opinions.

Humiliating tears prick the corners of my eyes.

Oh my fucking god, I'm not going to cry in front of this girl. Not on the first day of school.

I squeeze my fists so hard that my nails bite into my palms.

"Tough break," I say stiffly. "Looks like you're stuck with me."

The girl rolls her eyes and stomps into the nearest empty room.

Steeling my nerves, I follow her inside.

I expected it to look like a prison cell, but actually our dorm is neat and clean. The beds are low and narrow, rather pretty with headboards and footboards in carved dark wood. We each have our own dresser. The room smells of cedar, soap-stone, and clean earth. No sense of damp or rot.

The only thing lacking is a window.

Two soft, golden lamps provide the only light, because we are indeed deep underground.

My new roommate looks around silently, appraising the space.

"I'm Catalina, by the way," I say. My voice sounds simultaneously timid and over-loud in the small, shared space. "My friends call me Cat."

The other girl glares at me, like she wishes I would spontaneously combust.

"Don't talk to me," she says.

She jerks a book out of her backpack and flops down on her bed.

I start to quietly unpack my own suitcase, neatly re-folding my clothes before slipping them into the dresser drawers.

My wardrobe is easy to organize because all the pieces of the uniform mix and match together: five crisp white dress shirts, six plaid skirts (three green, three gray), a sage-green pullover and another in white. Two gray sweater-vests and one in black. Five pairs of knee socks and five pairs of tights. One academy jacket, also black, with a crest on the breast pocket. Then our gym clothes.

I spend much longer on the task than is strictly necessary, not wanting to sit in frosty silence with my sullen roommate.

I don't even know her name—I was too distracted when Saul read his list aloud. A proper Spy would have paid attention, matching each name with its corresponding student.

That's probably why she scoffed at me when I introduced myself—she already knew my name and everybody else's.

God, I'm fucking this up so bad already.

I sneak one quick peek at the girl, propped up on her pillow with the book in her hands.

Her dark hair is cut short, probably by herself with the wrong sort of scissors, as the pieces are choppy and uneven. She has a narrow face, dark almond-shaped eyes, a long, slim neck.

The pages of her book are thin and colorful. It might be a graphic novel. The cover is bright yellow with a red splotch on it.

That's all I dare to observe, scared that she'll catch me looking at her.

I place my toiletries on top of the dresser, then stack my sketchbooks and pencils on the nightstand. I slide my empty suitcase away under the bed.

Then I sit down on my thin, narrow mattress.

There. I did it. I unpacked.

Now I just have to get through the rest of the year.

4

ZOE

I'm surprised how much I enjoy coming back to Kingmakers.

I never intended to attend a mafia school, but I can't deny that what we learn here is complex and fascinating. Who wouldn't want to know ancient secrets handed down through generations of criminals?

Well, maybe Cat . . .

She looked like she was on death row when I hugged her goodbye at the Barcelona airport. I feel so guilty that she got roped into coming here along with me, all because of that sadist Rocco.

I know he only wants her here so he can use Cat as leverage against me—one more weapon in his arsenal. What fresh torment he's dreaming up, I can only imagine. That's the worst thing about him: the constant unease, like knowing there's a viper in your house without actually being able to see it. Hearing it slither around inside your walls. Never able to rest in case it wriggles out from under your chair and bites you on the ankle.

I hope Cat is settling in as well as can be expected.

It's difficult for me to check in on her, since we're not in the same division or the same year. I'm an Heir, in name at least, even if my father never intends for me to take over his business. That means I room in the Solar with the rest of the female Heirs.

Cat, on the other hand, has apparently been stuffed down in some basement with an Icelandic vampire as a roommate. I've yet to meet this roommate, who Cat thinks is named Rakel, but can't be certain because the girl refuses to speak to her.

I don't have to worry about a roommate. I've got the same little broom cupboard as last year. It's barely big enough to squeeze inside between the bed and the dresser, but I've got a nice big window and I don't have to share it with anybody.

My two best friends are right down the hall. Anna and Chay get on with each other pretty well, except for the times when Chay has an interesting dream and decides to wake Anna up in the middle of the night to tell her all about it.

I'm thinking that's what happened last night, because Chay comes down to breakfast already chattering away a mile a minute, while Anna looks barely conscious and thoroughly grumpy, twisting her silver-blonde hair up in a messy bun on top of her head, and wearing a school pullover that's more holes than sweater.

Chay has on a full face of sparkly makeup, she's prancing around in a brand new pair of knee-high white leather boots, and she streaked her hair bubblegum pink over the summer. She looks like Jem from the Holograms.

"GOOD morning!" she chirps, dropping a tray loaded with an obscene amount of bacon and sausage down onto the table.

"Chay. . ." Anna groans. "Inside voice before nine in the morning, please."

"Is that what you're eating?" I ask Chay, eyeing her pile of protein.

"I'm on keto."

"You're gonna get scurvy," Anna tells her, sleepily stirring several teaspoons of sugar into her coffee.

"And *you're* going to get diabetes," Chay replies sweetly.

I see Cat hovering uncertainly over by the chafing dishes. I wave to her so she can see where we're sitting. She hastily fills a plate with fresh fruit and scrambled eggs and comes to join us.

"This is Anna Wilk and Chay Wagner," I tell Cat, as she sits down beside me.

"Hello," Cat says shyly.

"You're so little!" Chay says cheerfully. "I thought you'd be tall like Zoe."

"No," Cat says, blushing. "I'm not."

I can tell she's embarrassed, because honestly, she looks like a little kid compared to everybody else at Kingmakers. It doesn't help that Cat always leans toward oversized clothes that drown her petite frame. She looks like she's wearing hand-me-downs even in her brand new uniform.

"Doesn't matter!" Chay adds quickly. "I'm pint-sized myself. I still hold my own. Puts you right on level to give somebody a good punch in the balls if you have to."

"Great," Cat says weakly. "I'll try to remember that."

"You'll settle in here soon," Anna says kindly. "Everybody is intimidated their first week."

"Really?" Cat says, eyeing Anna with disbelief.

Anna does not look like she has ever experienced intimidation. Even just rolled out of bed, she has that indefinable air of no-fucks-to-give. Maybe it's her inch-thick eyeliner, or her icy stare, or her low voice that always sounds mildly threatening, even when she's trying to be nice.

"Really." Anna nods. "I wanted to come here all my life, and I was still overwhelmed at first. You'll settle in. Zoe will be here to help you. We'll all keep an eye on you."

She smiles at Cat across the table. I feel a warm flush of gratitude that I have a clique of ready-made friends for Cat. It's the least I can do, after getting her into this mess.

That lasts about five seconds until Rocco sits down next to me, with Dax Volker and Jasper Webb right behind him.

Dax and Jasper are his favorite henchmen. Dax because he's a nasty brawler—thickly muscled, with a square, blocky head and a bulldog jaw, and Jasper because he's almost as cruel as Rocco himself. He's tall with a slim build and long, dark red hair. Beneath the rolled-up sleeves of his dress shirt, I can see tattoos running down both hands, mimicking the bones beneath like a skeleton superimposed on the skin.

Rocco sits right next to me, while Jasper drops down beside Chay and Dax flanks Cat, so all three of them hem us in like a Bermuda Triangle of assholes. There's no need for any of them to share our table—there's plenty of open space in the dining hall. This is obviously Rocco's first foray into expanding our "intimacy" at Kingmakers.

The temperature at the table drops twenty degrees, and the friendly conversation amongst us girls hardens into stony silence.

I hate having Rocco next to me, but I'm even more conscious of Cat's discomfort as she cringes against me, trying to shrink down to nothingness so she doesn't accidentally brush up against Dax's melon-sized shoulder or the tree-trunk thigh straining the bounds of his trousers.

"Thanks for saving me a seat," Rocco says to me. He gives me a thin, chilling smile.

I can't describe the antipathy I feel every time he invades my personal space. Every cell in my body screams at me to get away from him. There's something so off-putting in the way he moves—either holding too still or making swift and unpredictable movements that make me want to jump out of my skin.

However, unlike Cat, I refuse to move away from him. I hold perfectly still, trying not to let him see how much his proximity bothers me.

"I didn't," I reply.

Rocco makes a disappointed *tsking* sound.

"Oh, Zoe," he says quietly. "I thought we discussed this. Is this really the attitude you want to take as we begin another year of school?"

Jasper leans his elbow on Chay's shoulder, his skeleton fingers dangling down just above her breast. Chay has no problem staring him down even with their faces inches apart. She went to boarding school with both Rocco and Jasper, and she is well familiar with their tactics.

"Nice breakfast, biker bitch," Jasper says to her. "I always knew you liked sausage."

Chay picks up one of the brats in her fingers and takes a ferocious bite off the end, chewing loudly in Jasper's face.

"I only like big, thick sausages," she says coolly. "From what I hear, you've barely got an Oscar Meyer weenie."

"Big enough to choke you when I shove it down your throat, you fucking whore," Jasper hisses, his nose almost touching hers.

"Fucking try it and see what happens," Anna says furiously from Chay's other side.

Rocco's hand closes like a pincher on my upper thigh, squeezing so hard that his fingertips dig into my flesh.

On the other side of me, I can feel Cat tense up as if it's her leg in a vice grip. Her eyes are big and round, and I think she's scared to even breathe, caught in the middle of this sudden conflict that blew in like a hurricane.

"Are these really the types of girls you should be associating with at school?" Rocco says to me, looking coldly between Anna and Chay. "An incestuous goth and the school bicycle? What would your father say . . ."

His fingers are tense as steel. They feel hard enough to punch right through my skin. It takes every ounce of strength I possess to sit stiff and upright, while my thigh is shaking with pain.

"He'd say there's nothing in our contract about who I'm allowed to have as a friend," I hiss at Rocco through gritted teeth. "So kindly fuck off and leave us alone."

Rocco's fingers clench all the harder, until I can barely keep from crying out. Then he abruptly releases my leg.

"You disappoint me, Zoe," he says quietly. "We'll talk about this later."

"We have nothing more to discuss," I say.

"Oh, my love," Rocco says, reaching out his slim, pale hand to tuck a strand of hair behind my ear. "That's not up to you."

He stands up from the table, slipping out of his seat with unnerving grace. Dax follows him.

Jasper lingers a moment longer, still engaged in his silent stare-down with Chay. He cracks his knuckles single-handed, using his thumb to pull down each eerily-flexible joint. Chay winces at the off-putting sound. At last Jasper gives a slow, lazy blink, like he never cared at all, and pushes away from the table as well.

Only after they're all gone can I let out a full breath.

"One more second and I was gonna stab my fork into that walking skeleton," Chay says, gripping said fork in her fist.

Anna shakes her head, slow and angry.

"I hate sitting by like that," she says. "But I don't want to make things harder for you, Zoe."

She knows as well as I do that antagonizing Rocco could have long-term consequences for me. It's not like I can irritate him into canceling our engagement. He thrives on my resistance— it only fuels him to worse behavior.

Anna doesn't stop frowning until Leo Gallo drops down next to her, throwing his arm around her shoulders. Anna and Leo are indeed cousins, as Rocco snidely pointed out, but it's only by marriage, not by blood. After a tumultuous first year at school together, the two of them have apparently decided to be lovers as well as best friends, and they're now openly dating. Or at least, as open as you can be at Kingmakers where we're not technically supposed to date.

Watching Anna with Leo is like watching a flower open under the light of the sun. She instantly relaxes against him, the stress leaving her body like a sigh. Her face brightens, and she becomes twice as talkative.

I could be jealous of Leo and Anna. Leo is everything that Rocco isn't—handsome, warm, decent, genuinely affectionate . . . But it's impossible to see the two of them together with anything but a sense of rightness. They so clearly belong with each other, like salt and pepper, or sea and sand. Besides, I never expected to have anything like that myself.

Miles Griffin and Ozzy Duncan deposit their heavily-laden trays next to Leo's. Miles is likewise Anna's cousin, and Ozzy is his best friend. The two of them are the biggest troublemakers at school. Ozzy loves to get in fights, and Miles is the prime procurer of contraband for anyone who needs it.

Miles makes me distinctly uncomfortable, since my goal in life has always been to follow the rules as carefully as possible, while he seems to break every single one for fun.

He has the privilege of that type of behavior since he's the son of an Irish mafia boss turned mayor of Chicago. I expect he's been able to get away with pretty much whatever he likes all his life.

I don't particularly like him. There's something amoral in the way he'll sell anything to anyone—like an arms dealer, with no questions asked.

Not to mention the fact that he applies his particular brand of sarcasm like a switchblade. If he sees the opportunity to make a joke at your expense, he'll cut you without warning.

That being said, there's a marked difference in the mood at the table with these three boys as our dining companions instead of the three that just left. Chay and Ozzy cheerfully trade bacon for a fried egg, and Leo says, "Was that Rocco Prince that just left? He's a creepy fucker, isn't he? No offense, Zoe."

"You could only offend me by complimenting him," I tell him.

"Then consider us on permanent good terms," Leo says, grinning.

"I don't know," Miles says, taking a swig of orange juice. "He's got his charm. If you ever wondered what it was like to meet Ted Bundy."

"I never wondered that," Cat says quietly.

"Holy shit!" Miles says, doing an exaggerated double-take and pretending to peer over the top of the table at her. "There's a kid there! Is it 'bring your daughter to school' day, Zoe?"

"That's my sister, Cat," I say coolly. "She's a Freshman."

"They get tinier every year," Ozzy says, shaking his head in wonder.

Cat's face is flaming. This is a joke that's gonna get real old, real fast for her.

"Alright, knock it off," I say, "she doesn't want to hear it."

"It's okay," Cat mumbles.

She looks so beaten down already, just from one encounter with Rocco and some mild teasing from friends. My stomach sinks lower than ever. I really don't know how Cat's going to survive here. It's her first day of classes, and things are about to get a whole lot worse. She's got Stealth and Infiltration, Counterintelligence, and Combat, and that's all before dinner.

I put my arm around her to give her a sideways hug.

"You're gonna do great today," I tell her. "I better get going—I don't want to be late for Professor Graves, or he'll slam the door in my face."

"Tell him I said hi," Miles says.

"No thanks," I reply. "Out of the whole student body, you're at the top of the list of the ones he hates, and I think I might be in that tiny minority he can actually tolerate."

"That's because you're a good girl, aren't you?" Miles says, with that insulting edge to his voice. "You'd never upset that pompous piece of shit, would you? You just keep smiling and being polite, no matter how big an asshole he is."

I look Miles in the face, really look at him, which is difficult to do, because his steel-gray eyes have a way of fixing on you like he's stripping you bare. It's a nakedness of the soul, not the body. Miles Griffin can look right inside you and see all your insecurities, all your flaws and weaknesses. You can tell he's tallying them up, finding the most vulnerable spot to hit you next.

"Not all of us get to be a rebel without a cause," I say to him.

Miles keeps his eyes locked on mine, his face unsmiling.

"Oh, I've got plenty of causes," he says.

I stand up from the table. As I do, the bruised flesh of my upper thigh gives a painful twitch. My knee buckles under me and my first step is more like a limp.

I recover quickly, straightening up and pretending like nothing happened. But I know Miles saw it. His eyes narrow for just a second before his face smooths out again in placid indifference.

"See you in Psych," I say to Anna and Chay.

I SPEND the morning in Finance, a class mostly full of Accountants. Last year we focused on international banking, this year we're delving into domestic money laundering.

Professor Graves stands at the front of the class in his typical lecturer's stance, hands clasped behind his back, belly thrust toward us, straining the buttons of his tweed vest. He's had his silver beard freshly trimmed for the start of school, and he's looking especially pleased and pompous.

Professor Graves is one of the less-popular teachers at the school, because he lacks the humor of someone like Professor Howell or the fascinating lecture style of Professor Thorn. Graves is strict and fastidious. He hates being interrupted even by valid questions.

On the other hand, no professor at Kingmakers is anything less than an expert, so there's still plenty to be learned in his class. I've managed to stay off his bad side. So all in all, I'm in good spirits as I take notes on the three stages of washing money.

"Placement, Layering, Integration . . ." Professor Graves intones, pacing back and forth in front of our neat rows of desks. "Placement comes first. You take your illegal earnings, and you introduce them to a legitimate financial institution, perhaps through a shell company, smurfing, or trade-based laundering."

"What do you mean by trade-based laundering?" Coraline Paquet inquires from behind me. She's a slim, dark-haired French girl, friends with the Paris Bratva.

Professor Graves gives a long, irritated sigh that simultaneously conveys his hatred of digressions and his disdain that any of us might require clarification.

"*Trade*-based laundering," he says, "as the name would imply, exploits the mechanisms of cross-border trade. Over-invoicing or under-invoicing, misrepresentation of quality, and so forth."

He glares around the room as if daring anybody else to ask a question. When we all keep our mouths shut, he continues:

"Once you've introduced the funds into the legal banking system at a vulnerable point, then you move into layering or structuring. This is when you cut the funds into smaller transactions so they can be transferred into more difficult jurisdictions without triggering reporting requirements."

While Professor Graves explains this process, I feel someone watching me. I turn my head and see Wade Dyer leaning back in his seat with his arms crossed over his broad chest. He's not bothering to take notes. I don't think he's listening at all. He's just looking at me.

Wade is blond and clean-cut, pleasant-looking, but that doesn't fool me for a second. I know damn well that he's from Hamburg just like Rocco Prince. They're friends. Anybody who enjoys Rocco's company has something wrong inside, no matter how benign they look on the outside.

Wade smiles at me, showing dimples on both sides of his mouth.

I don't smile back at him. I face Professor Graves as he talks about Integration, the final stage of money laundering.

"At this point, the funds become eligible for use," Professor Graves says. "They can be used to purchase assets—goods or property—which won't attract attention."

I glance back at Wade.

He's still watching me. Deliberately, he looks me up and down from head to foot. Not that there's anything to see—when Daniela's not picking my outfits, I always cover up. I hate being leered at. Right now I'm wearing a long-sleeved dress shirt buttoned to the neck, a knee-length skirt, and thick black tights. Wade can't see shit unless he's got a knuckle fetish.

I turn my head forward, determined not to look at him anymore for the duration of the class.

The minutes seem to slip by slowly under the awkward sensation of scrutiny. I can hear Wade tapping his pen rhythmically on the top of his desk. I think he's trying to attract my attention.

I'm sure Rocco told him to watch me, and to make it obvious.

He wants me to know that he has friends everywhere on campus, that I'm not safe from him just because we don't have any classes together.

Well, I don't give a shit. Wade has nothing to report except that I filled up four pages with notes. I hope Rocco finds that fascinating.

Still, as soon as class is over I snatch up my notebook and stuff it in my bag.

I hurry down the stairs of the Keep, heading to my next class on the south side of campus. I've got Artillery with Professor Knox, who teaches in the old forge attached to the workshops where the original inhabitants of the castle used to make metal utensils, horseshoes, armor, swords, and pikes.

I can hear heavy footsteps following behind me. A quick glance over my shoulder shows Wade Dyer striding along behind me, hands tucked in the pockets of his trousers.

What the fuck is he playing at?

He's not in my Artillery class.

I debate whether I should turn around and confront him, or just ignore him.

As I'm passing the large octagonal tower the male Heirs use as a dorm, I see something even more unpleasant: Rocco and Jasper coming down the stairs.

Before Rocco can spot me, I take a hard right turn, shooting the tree-choked gap between the tower and an elevated platform that might have been used for weapons training once upon a time.

I spent a lot of time in my Freshman year learning the secret passageways and shortcuts across campus so I could hide from Rocco Prince. I'd never claim to know them all, but I did find a hidden door behind these orange trees that leads up to the ramparts. From there, I can walk across the top of the wall and come down on the opposite side of the forge.

I pull open the rusty, squeaking door, then hurry up the narrow staircase enclosed within the wall. It's always chilly as a tomb inside the stone walls of Kingmakers, even in the warmest parts of the year. When I emerge on the top of ramparts, the sunlight blinds me and the wind buffets me, twice as strong as in the protected cove of the castle.

I head down the long, narrow walkway that runs between the Octagon Tower at my back and the tall, spindly Library Tower straight ahead of me. I like being up here on my own. It's one of the best views in the castle, with nothing but open ocean to the north. I pause for a moment to look over the edge of the ramparts, down the dizzying drop of the limestone cliffs to the dark water below.

The waves hitting the cliffs are probably eight feet tall, though from this height, they barely look like frothy wrinkles on the water.

When I straighten up again, I see two figures blocking my path: one dark-haired, one red.

Rocco and Jasper.

Fuck.

I turn to run back the way I came, but now Wade Dyer is standing there, smiling his charming, dimpled smile.

They close in on me from both sides, swift and silent as wolves.

Wade wasn't following me. He was herding me. Right where Rocco wanted.

I could scream, but it would be pointless. No one would hear me up here. If they heard anything at all, it would sound like a seagull screeching over the water.

Jasper grabs my right arm, Wade my left. They pin me against the ramparts, lifted and tilted backward so I know they could tip me right over if they wanted, sending me plummeting down to the jagged rocks below.

Rocco stands in front of me, hands clasped behind his back just like Professor Graves when he's about to start a lecture. He looks happier than I've ever seen him, his eyes gleaming with malice.

"Oh, no," he says softly. "What a predicament you've gotten yourself into, Zoe. You thought you were a tricky little mouse, didn't you? Always slipping away through stairs and passageways. You forgot that I've been at this school longer than you."

My heart is hammering hard against my chest at such a rapid pace that it's skipping every third or fourth beat, stumbling and then squeezing harder than ever to make up for it.

This is very, very bad.

Rocco leans close to speak directly into my ear. With my arms pinned, I can't shove him away. I can't protect myself. He could take a bite out of my cheek and there's nothing I could do to stop him.

"You only get away when I let you get away," he whispers. "You're a bird with a chain around its ankle. You can fly in circles all you want. But you're bound to me, Zoe. I can take hold of you whenever I want. Soon, very soon, I'm going to close you in a cage. If you want food, you'll eat it out of my hand. If you want water, you'll drink it from my lips. If you want rest, you'll sleep with your head in my lap. And you'll never fly again."

He pulls back just far enough to look me in the eyes.

Looking into those black pupils is like looking down into a well. There's no reason in them. No mercy. Just an empty black hole.

He means every word.

When I marry him, I'll be his slave. He'll never tire of tormenting me. Until I'm broken in my mind, body, and soul.

"Never," I say quietly.

"Never is a long time," Rocco says. "You've taken Torture Techniques, haven't you? With the delightful Professor Penmark? You're a good student, Zoe. I'm sure you were listening when he told you that it's possible to withstand torture for a time. Days, weeks, months . . . But in the end . . . everybody breaks."

Jasper and Wade have an iron grip on my wrists. I look between them, trying to decide if either of them has the tiniest spark of humanity. Jasper's face is cold and expressionless, his green eyes as pale and translucent as sea glass. Wade is much more animated, struggling to hold back his grin.

I turn to Jasper.

"Let go of me," I plead.

Jasper's eyes meet mine and perhaps for a fraction of a second he considers it, but his fingers never loosen on my wrist, and his lips remain tightly closed.

"He's not going to help you." Rocco laughs his strange laugh that's little more than an exhale. "Nobody can help you, Zoe."

He takes a knife from his pocket and flicks open the blade. The steel dazzles in the sunlight—it looks like it's on fire.

"Hold her steady," he says.

The boys hold my wrists and upper arms, shoving me against the stone so I can barely even wriggle. I wouldn't dare thrash around. The knife is too close.

Rocco points the blade directly at my right eye. He brings the knife closer and closer, until its pointed tip presses into the flesh at the corner of my eye.

"I could cut your eyeball right out of its socket," he says. "Then you couldn't give me that insolent look anymore. You could still do everything I require with one eye."

Now I do feel Jasper's fingers twitch around my wrist. He's not completely comfortable with this, probably because he's scared of the Rule of Recompense.

"You can't," I say to Rocco, to remind him.

"Why?" Rocco says, still poking me with the knife. "Why can't I?"

"They'll do the same to you," I tell him.

That's the laws of Kingmakers. If you damage another student —break their arm, cut off their hand, slit their throat . . . the same will be done to you. It's to prevent war from breaking out between families. It's the old law. An eye for an eye.

"That's true," Rocco says softly. "Except . . . you belong to me, Zoe. Your parents already signed the marriage contract. So anything I do to you . . . it's like I did it to myself. There's no recompense."

I don't know if that's true or not.

But I really don't want to find out.

It's clear that Rocco believes it to be true.

"Beg me to stop," he says. He starts to dig the knife into my flesh.

My lips are pressed tight together.

I won't beg. I'll never beg.

The blade bites into me and I feel something warm and wet run down from the corner of my eye, like bloody tears.

The knife feels like a hot brand. I can feel Rocco twisting it, angling the point toward my eyeball . . .

"Stop!" I cry.

"That's not begging," Rocco hisses.

"Please stop!"

Now I am crying actual tears. They run down both sides of my face, stinging and burning when they hit the cut on the right side.

Rocco pulls back his knife. My blood glistens on its tip.

"That's better," he says.

He slashes open the front of my shirt, being none too careful with the knife. It leaves shallow cuts on my chest and the tops of my breasts. He cuts my bra open too, so my tits spill out.

Now both Jasper and Wade are intently interested.

"Holy shit," Wade says. "Who woulda thought she had a porn-star body under those nun clothes."

"I knew," Rocco says, in a tone of deep satisfaction.

Three pairs of eyes crawl over my bare flesh. I've always been ashamed of my breasts. Ashamed of my body. Not because I think it's ugly, but because of the way it betrays me, drawing the attention of the men I least want to notice me.

"Go ahead," Rocco says to Wade. "Touch them."

Wade scans Rocco's face, like he thinks it might be a trick. "You sure?"

"I'm giving you permission," Rocco says in his soft, hissing voice.

Wade doesn't care about my permission. He stares at my tits. All intelligence has left his face. His cheeks are flushed and there's nothing but dull, hungry lust in his eyes.

He cups my breasts in both hands, lifting them and then drop-ping them. My stomach is churning. I've never been more humiliated.

"Fucking hell," he breathes. "You're gonna have so much fun with these, Rocco."

Seeing that Rocco won't stop him, he squeezes my breasts hard in his hands, then pinches the nipples, making me gasp.

He's watching Rocco the whole time. He doesn't give a fuck how I react to this.

"Jasper?" Rocco says, offering his other friend to take his turn.

Jasper considers, his face impassive.

"I'm good," he says at last. He's still holding my right wrist, but not as tightly as before. I don't think he's enjoying this as much as Wade. Not that he's doing fuck-all to stop it.

"What now?" Wade says, his tongue darting out to moisten his lower lip.

"Now Zoe pays her debt," Rocco says, looking at me with his head tilted slightly to the side. In the bright sunshine, his blue eyes with their flecks of black look like panes of shattered glass. "The night of our engagement party, your stepmother promised me something, Zoe. Do you know what that was?"

I try to swallow, but my mouth is too dry. The cut at the corner of my eye still burns, and my breasts ache everywhere Wade touched them. I slowly shake my head.

"She agreed that I was free to consummate the marriage," Rocco says, his eyes boring into mine. "Anytime I wanted."

Through numb lips, I say, "We're not married yet."

"Close enough," Rocco says, and he moves to close the gap between us. To seize me and cut off my skirt, I have no doubt.

As Rocco moves forward, Jasper releases my wrist, stepping back to give him space. Wade isn't holding me at all, having let go so he could grope me with both hands.

I have one brief second of freedom.

Rocco swoops down on me like a vampire, teeth bared in his version of a smile.

I act on instinct, without thought or plan.

All I know is that I have to get away from Rocco. I'll never grovel for him again, I'll never beg. I'll never let him touch me.

He says I'll be a caged bird—well, I'll fly one last time at least.

In that moment of madness, I fling myself over the ramparts.

5

MILES

I'm making the long and tedious walk from the library back to my dorm when someone says, "Stop!"

That's strange, because there's no one around to say "Stop." There's no one around me at all. It's the middle of second period, and all the students are safely ensconced in their classes.

I'm supposed to be annotating a territory contract with Ozzy. We had all our legal textbooks spread out on the table all around us, ready to hunt down every last consideration and clause, until Ozzy realized he forgot the actual fucking document in our dorm.

I volunteered to retrieve it because Ozzy is highly distractible. If I waited for him to do it, I doubt he'd ever return. I'd find him four hours later vaping behind the ice house or lurking around the Solar to chat up some girl.

And now here I am distracted myself by the inexplicable sound of someone saying "Stop."

After glancing in all directions, there's nowhere to look but up.

I see a flutter of movement high on the ramparts—something dark that could be a scrap of fabric or the wing of a bird.

But birds don't say "Stop."

So I find myself pushing through the orange trees, finding the hidden staircase that leads up through the wall.

I'm nosy as fuck, I always have been.

In my line of work, information is currency. I have to know everything that's going on around me at all times. What people need. Why they need it. And how I can get it for them.

I climb to the top of the wall with a sense of curiosity and helpfulness. I'm always helpful, for the right price.

When I peek my head up, I find an unpleasant tableau.

A girl, held in place by three boys.

Not willingly.

It's difficult to see from this angle, but the one closest to me has to be Wade Dyer. Nobody else has that college quarterback build and that Boy Scout haircut. He shifts slightly. Then I see that the dark-haired guy—the one holding the knife—is Rocco Prince.

Which means the girl can only be Zoe Romero.

I'd call Zoe more of an acquaintance than a friend. She's a little too serious for my taste. Not that I can blame her—it's hard to be cheerful when you're engaged to a psychopath.

A psychopath who apparently likes to drag her up on a wall and cut her shirt open.

I watch as Rocco slashes the shirt apart with four quick cuts of his knife. Then he cuts her bra off, too.

My muscles tense and the little hairs stand up on my arms. I really don't like this shit. There's nothing bold about three guys ganging up on a girl to cut her clothes off. It's weak and gutless. It disgusts me.

On the other hand, I'm not the hero type and Zoe isn't my responsibility. Yes, she's friends with Anna. But Anna can't get Zoe out of the bear trap of her engagement, and neither can I. Whether Rocco does this today, tomorrow, or on their wedding night, it's pretty much inevitable.

I consider turning around and descending the stairs again. That would be the smart thing to do. But something holds me in place, transfixed despite the queasy churning in my stomach.

Maybe it's the way Zoe stares them down, standing as tall as she can with her arms pinned at her sides. Ignoring the blood running down the side of her face.

She's tough, I'll give her that.

Apparently with Rocco's permission, Wade starts groping Zoe's tits.

Well, that's surprising. Looks like Rocco is both kinky *and* fucked in the head. If I were getting married, which I'm not, I'd break every bone in Wade's hands before I'd let him touch my fiancée.

The rational part of my brain makes that observation, while the irrational part feels a surging, boiling rage.

Zoe's not my fiancée. She's nobody to me. All I should feel is pity for her.

And yet anger bubbles up inside of me, hot and insistent, telling me I should break Wade's hands regardless, and shatter his arms for good measure.

I watch him touch Zoe and it's like watching a gorilla manhandle the Venus de Milo. It's obscene for a fucking animal like that to touch what is, objectively speaking, a perfectly sculpted body. Have some fucking respect.

Wade lets go of Zoe and I tell myself to calm the fuck down. This has nothing to do with me.

Jasper Webb stands on the other side of Zoe, not touching her but definitely helping to hold her down. I can't see his face as clearly as the other three because his long hair is hanging over his eyes. He doesn't seem to be enjoying this quite as much as that shit-stain Wade.

Wade, Rocco, and Jasper are not people I want as enemies. Each of them is connected, well-liked—in Rocco's case mostly by fellow sadists, but the point still stands—and from a powerful family. I'm not scared of conflict, but in my own family I've seen the disastrous consequences of starting a feud. The endless cycle of reprisals can trickle down for generations.

I should walk away.

I think it's over anyway. Wade stopped groping Zoe. Jasper doesn't seem interested. They'll probably let her go.

That's what I think until Rocco lunges at Zoe, and she turns and leaps over the wall.

I watch it happen in slow motion. She whirls around, lifting her foot and planting it firmly in the indent between the crenellations. She pushes off with all her might, intending to swan dive off the cliff, to plummet some five hundred feet to the rock-strewn water below.

Her dark hair streams behind her like a banner, and there's a look of reckless abandon on her face, a wild determination that is instantly, painfully familiar to me.

It reminds me of my mother.

My mother would jump off a cliff if she had to. And she'd probably drag Rocco over with her.

I'm in motion before I've even registered what's happening. I'm running without thought or decision.

I'm too far away to help Zoe, yet I sprint toward her, desperately reaching out though I know it's too late.

It's Jasper who saves her. He grabs her ankle in both hands. The force of Zoe's fall yanks him forward so he almost tumbles over the wall too, until I grab him around the waist and drag him backward.

Now we're a jumbled mass of hands and arms, Wade Dyer joining in, grabbing Zoe's other leg and helping to haul her back over the ramparts.

Not Rocco, though. He stands watching.

Zoe is limp and pale, whether from shock or because she hit her head against the wall. Blood streams from her nose as well as the right side of her face. She can't stand—her legs collapse beneath her. I try to hold her up, while simultaneously pulling her shirt closed in the front.

Jasper steps back, looking pale and sick himself.

Wade's eyes dart between me and Rocco as he waits for instructions.

Rocco steps forward, lifting his slim, white hands like he intends to take Zoe from me.

I tighten my arms around her shoulders and pull her back out of reach.

"Don't," I growl. "Don't touch her."

"What do you mean?" Rocco says, smiling at me. "That's my fiancée, you know."

While the rest of us are sweating and breathing hard, Rocco looks as fresh as a daisy. You'd never know he'd witnessed a near-suicide, let alone driven a girl to do it.

"Don't fucking touch her," I say again, keeping my eyes fixed on his so he knows I mean it. "I'm taking her to the infirmary."

Rocco's smile is fading, his expression hardening like concrete. His eyes dart between me and the dazed, bloody girl lolling against me.

He looks like a child who's had his lollipop snatched away.

"Be careful, Miles," he says.

He's not talking about Zoe. He's warning me not to fuck with him.

I don't care. Right now all I can think about is Zoe's rope of dark hair laying over my shoulder, and her heart beating so hard against my arm that I'm afraid it might burst.

I start backing away slowly. I'm taking Zoe back down through the door closest to the Library Tower, because it's near to the infirmary and I don't think Jasper will stop me, whereas Wade is blocking the path to the orange grove stairs, arms folded over his chest. Wade looks almost as irritated as Rocco, his handsome face sulky and spoiling for a fight.

The space between us feels like a fragile pane of ice.

The slightest tap will shatter it.

I keep backing up, step by step.

Rocco stays exactly where he is.

He's not trying to stop me. But I can tell from the look on his face that he's very, very angry.

THE INFIRMARY IS A LONG, low building close to the library. Dr. Cross has his apartment at one end, and then there's an open area with several beds, an industrial sink, and glass-fronted cabinets full of medical supplies.

Right now the only other patient is a skinny Sophomore who apparently sprained his wrist in Combat class. Dr. Cross has just finished wrapping up the wrist. When he spots me carrying Zoe through the door, he unceremoniously tells the kid to get back to class.

"Can't I rest a while?" the kid says, looking none too eager to leave the peace and quiet of the spotless infirmary.

"Rest in your dorm," Dr. Cross croaks at him. "This isn't a lounge."

"Can I get some kind of a doctor's note?" the kid says. "How am I supposed to write papers? I'm left-handed."

He holds up his bandaged left arm awkwardly, as if it's been turned to wood.

"It's quite possible to become ambidextrous with practice," Dr. Cross says unsympathetically. "Now get out."

The kid scoots off the bed, scowling.

"What's going on here?" Dr. Cross frowns, peering at Zoe with her bloodied face and torn shirt.

I took off my sweater vest and covered her up as best I could, but it's still obvious that the blouse beneath has been slashed to ribbons.

"She fell on the ramparts," I tell him. "I think she hit her head."

I'm not about to tell Dr. Cross what really happened. It's up to Zoe if she wants to make a formal complaint to the Chancellor.

In response to the rigid rules of Kingmakers, the students keep a code of silence. We don't rat each other out except in the most extreme circumstances.

Dr. Cross glares at me suspiciously. Doubtless he's heard a thousand excuses from injured students. Mine is especially weak.

"Lay her down here," he says, pointing to a fresh bed. "You can leave her with me."

That's what I'd planned to do. I was going to drop her off and get back to the library. But as I carefully set Zoe down on the narrow mattress and lay her head on the pillow, I find myself not wanting to abandon her so quickly.

"I don't think she should be alone," I say.

"She's not alone," Dr. Cross regards me from under shaggy gray brows as thick as caterpillars.

"No offense, Doc," I say, giving him a wink, "But would you want to wake up to yourself? I think she should see a friendly face."

Dr. Cross snorts.

"Keep out of the way, and you can stay," he says, re-washing his gnarled hands at the sink.

With surprising gentleness, he washes the blood off Zoe's face and examines the cut next to her eye.

"Puncture wound," he mutters, as if to himself. "Clean, at least."

Apparently deciding it doesn't require stitches, he disinfects the cut, then covers it with surgical tape.

He carefully feels her skull all over, as if he's a phrenologist. Finding a lump above her right ear, he checks her pupils for signs of concussion.

By this point, Zoe is coming around. She still looks dazed, but she doesn't cry or try to speak. She lays quiet until Dr. Cross is satisfied.

"Here," he says, taking a bottle of apple juice out of the fridge, and handing it to me along with a straw. "Give her this if she wants it." Then to Zoe he says, "Is this delinquent a friend of yours?"

Zoe turns her gaze on me, still hazy and unfocused. After a long moment, she nods.

"You can stay for ten minutes," Dr. Cross says to me. "Then get out of here so she can take a nap."

He shuffles back to his apartment, closing the door behind him.

I sit next to Zoe's bed, feeling awkward and out of place. We've never been alone together under normal circumstances, let alone in a moment like this.

I'm not even sure why I stayed. To check in with her? To comfort her? Both ideas seem ridiculous.

Zoe watches me silently. The sharpness has come back to her stare. She has green eyes, unusual for someone with such black hair. She has a lot of unusual features. Eyebrows and lashes so dark that they looked painted in ink. A straight, imperious nose, like an empress. A wide, full mouth. There's an elegance to her face that makes her look older than her age, but also timeless and eternal.

"You don't have to stay," she says.

Her voice is clear and steady. No quivering, no sobs.

"I don't know about that," I reply.

She frowns slightly, a single vertical line appearing between her dark brows.

"What does that mean?"

"I saw you jump," I tell her. "I guess I'm worried you might do something like that again."

Those green eyes go cloudy once more, this time with anger instead of confusion.

"It's none of your business whether I do or don't," she says coldly.

"Maybe not." I shrug. "Still, I feel invested."

"Ah," she says, mockingly. "I know how much your investments mean to you. But I'm afraid this one won't pay off."

She surprised me with that one. I laugh a little. "What do you know about my investments?"

"That's why you're always passing little packets back and forth all over campus, isn't it," Zoe says, steady and unblinking. "You don't work for the hell of it—I've seen your grades. You must be saving for something."

I don't know if I've ever been speechless before.

"Zoe . . ." I say, a smile tugging at my lips. "Are you stalking me?"

Now she can't help smiling back just a little, though she doesn't want to.

"You're the one that followed me up on the wall," she says. "What were you doing up there?"

"Just passing by," I say.

"I'm not going to thank you," she informs me.

"I wouldn't really deserve it—it was Jasper who caught you."

Her upper lip draws up in a snarl, showing sharp white teeth. She gives an impatient shake of her head.

"I won't be thanking him either," she says.

There's an uncomfortable silence while the unspoken weight of Rocco Prince hangs over us.

"I'm sorry," I say.

It's simultaneously a pathetic, meaningless statement, but also the only thing I can say to her. The only way to express my sympathy for her tragic situation.

"Don't pity me," she says.

Again I see that fire in her eyes. That spark of rebellion that drove her to leap off a cliff rather than let Rocco put his hands on her.

"You know," I say, "I always thought you were a Mozart kinda girl. That was pretty fuckin' metal."

"That impresses you?" Zoe raises a soot-black eyebrow. "Jumping off a cliff?"

"I mean . . . yeah. Assuming you survive." I swallow hard, looking at her closely. "You are gonna survive, aren't you, Zoe?"

She's silent for a moment, then she lets out a sigh.

"Yeah," she says. "For now."

It's the closest thing to a promise I'm going to get out of her.

And besides, who am I to make her swear she won't try to kill herself again?

I might do the same if I had to marry that walking corpse Rocco Prince.

6

CAT

My classes are a nightmare.

Each is worse than the one before.

The professors are harsh and impatient. They expect us to know things that I've never even imagined, let alone studied in detail.

The students who come to Kingmakers are the ones raised to the mafia life. They've been fighting, shooting, and scheming since they graduated from diapers. They learned the history of their ancestors at their grandparents' knees. They always knew what role they'd take in their organization.

I'm the only one plucked out of art school and chucked into the den of lions, ignorant as a newborn babe.

I know this is partly my fault. Zoe paid attention to what our father was doing. I preferred to stay in my room, painting and drawing, or sometimes sneaking down to the kitchen to help our cook make paella and crema catalana.

I loved our house staff. Our cook Celia was gruff but a patient teacher, explaining how to add saffron to the paella to give the rice color and flavor. Our maid Lucia was young and gentle. She used to sneak me magazines so I could look at pictures of party dresses, until Daniela caught our father looking at Lucia one too many times and fired her on the spot.

I'm terrified of every adult at Kingmakers, from the burly grounds crew, to the tattooed kitchen staff, to the professors with their wealth of sinister knowledge.

Worst of all is the Chancellor Luther Hugo. I saw him when he called us all to the Grand Hall to announce the terms of this year's *Quartum Bellum*. He stood before the roaring fireplace, the wild flames behind his dark, imposing figure making him look like the devil himself risen up from the ground.

He reminded us of our duty to our families, the stakes of our future careers in the criminal world, and the dire consequences if we dared to step one toe out of line at Kingmakers.

I could swear his coal-black eyes were boring into me the entire time. His face looked as wrinkled as old leather, but those eyes were agelessly bright.

"Remember," he said, staring into my soul. "Every choice sets the table. Sooner or later, we all sit down to a banquet of consequences."

I think if he ordered me to jump into the fire behind him, I might have done it. That's how much that man terrifies me.

The information that followed was no more cheering.

The Chancellor explained that the *Quartum Bellum*, or "War of Four," is an annual battle between the Freshmen, Sophomores, Juniors, and Seniors. It's an elimination tournament with three separate stages.

Every student participates—mandatory, no excuses.

I was already wondering if I could use the newfound information acquired in my Chemistry class to give myself a convenient case of food poisoning.

I waited until the Chancellor dismissed us before I squeaked to Perry, "How do they expect us to compete against Seniors? Or Juniors or Sophomores, for that matter."

"They don't." Perry shrugged. "You're just supposed to try. Nobody thinks we'll win."

"Don't be so sure," Lyman Landry told her. "The Freshmen did win last year, for the very first time."

"How?" Perry demanded.

"Leo Gallo," Lyman said, his broad, earnest face shining with admiration. "He was the Captain. He's a fucking champion. A god, even. He'll win again this year, you'll see."

"A god," Perry snorted, rolling her eyes.

I could feel myself blushing, because I had met Leo Gallo at breakfast, my very first morning at Kingmakers. He did look like a god. I've never seen someone so handsome—tall, deeply-tanned, with amber-colored eyes and a smile brighter than the sun.

Of course I'd never dare have a crush on him. He's dating Anna Wilk, a moon goddess in her own right, as dark and mysterious as Leo is bright and blinding.

He was kind to me. So was Anna.

I wish I could say the same for my classmates. I haven't made a single friend, other than Perry, who barely shares any classes with me.

Most of my classes are with Spies and Enforcers. I don't know which is worse. The Spies are ruthless, sarcastic, and disdainful. The Enforcers are mostly hot-heads and bullies, the type of jocks who don't just want to win, they want to fucking destroy you.

I hate Combat class most of all. As soon as we face off against our opponents, I can see the change come over my classmates.

Their pupils dilate, they crouch down low, their breathing slows. That's how a predator prepares to attack.

My body chooses flight over fight. My heart rate quadruples in speed and my muscles scream at me to *RUN RUN RUN,* so all I can do is raise my hands in surrender, to duck and cringe.

I've been knocked out twice already.

The first time was by a heavyset Enforcer who looked utterly bewildered when I woke up staring up at him from the mat.

"You didn't even try to block my punch," he said, shaking his head in bemusement.

The second time happened today, courtesy of my very own roommate Rakel. It felt a lot more personal. Anytime she and I get left without partners, I can see her boiling fury that anyone might think she's equally as undesirable as me. She put me in a headlock within five seconds and ignored my hand desperately tapping on her shoulder, begging her to let go.

I woke up face-down on the mats, blood gushing out of my nose.

"A tap-out means you stop," Professor Howell informs her sternly. He's only a few inches taller than me, but he's lean and fit and faster than a jackrabbit. When he's in a good mood, he's one of the more pleasant professors. But when you cross him, he fixes you with a black stare that could curdle milk.

"I didn't feel her tapping," Rakel says, insolent and unrepentant. Even amongst the Spies, Rakel has a perpetual scowl that has made her barely any more popular than me.

"You'll feel the consequences if you try it again," the professor says, scalpel-sharp. "You see that over there?" He jerks his head toward a tall metal cylinder in the corner of the gym. It looks like an Iron Maiden—smooth and featureless on the exterior, with only a glassed-in horizontal slit at eye level.

"Yes," Rakel says slowly.

"That's a deoxygenation chamber. Useful for training for high altitudes or increasing stamina by forcing the body to over-produce red blood cells. I can change the oxygen percentage to any level I like. You ignore a tap-out again, and I'll put you in there for half an hour. You won't suffocate. But you'll feel like you're drowning the entire time. Do you understand me?"

"Yes," Rakel says again.

Professor Howell turns away.

Rakel faces me once more, pure hatred in her eyes. No hint of remorse. She looks so murderous that I almost want to apologize for getting her in trouble. But I squash that thought.

"Face off again," Professor Howell commands.

Fuck me. I was hoping we'd at least swap partners. I need Rakel to cool off a little before we spar again. Like, maybe for the next hundred years.

Professor Howell told us to keep our hands up to protect our faces, and to hold our cores tight. I try to do it, but as soon as someone rushes at me I crumple up in a little ball.

"Ready . . ." the professor says.

No. I'm not ready. I'll never be ready.

"Go!"

Rakel comes at me like a bat out of hell, swooping in, popping me with a jab to the left eye that snaps my head back and makes my already bruised brain rattle around in my skull.

She swings again, and I actually manage to duck that one, just barely. I'm so surprised that I don't see her next blow coming, not even a little bit. She slams me in the right ear, and the whole gym spins around like a merry-go-round. She comes in for a final blow, fist already cocked.

Before I can think, before I can consider what a monumentally bad idea this is, my fist lashes out right at her face.

I hit her in the mouth. Her lips feel horribly squishy and mobile under my knuckles. My fist slides across her teeth, and one of those teeth cuts me. I jump away from her again, saying, "Sorry. Oh my god, you're bleeding!"

Rakel touches her bottom lip, which is already beginning to swell. She looks at the bright red blood on her fingertips as if she's never seen anything like it.

"Time!" Professor Howell calls.

I'm not looking at him. I'm watching Rakel, poised on tiptoe, because if she tries to strangle me, I'm just going to turn and run away.

Strangely, inexplicably, Rakel doesn't look quite as angry anymore. She wipes her fingers off on her gray gym shorts, leaving a dark smear.

When our eyes meet, she isn't smiling, but she isn't scowling either.

"Not bad," she says.

I HEAD to the dining hall for lunch at the usual time, but I don't see Zoe anywhere.

I stand by the chafing dishes, craning my neck to find her, until a Junior slams into me and says, "Get your food or get the fuck out of the way."

Hastily, I fill a plate with pork chops, applesauce, and carrots.

I have no complaint about the food at Kingmakers. Most of it is from the local farms and orchards on the island, so it's all fresh and well-prepared. I just wish I didn't have to eat it all alone. Zoe usually meets me here.

I straighten my shoulders and tell myself to stop being such a fucking pussy. Zoe's eaten every single meal with me so far— it's not fair to expect her to babysit me.

I look around the dining hall, wishing I paid better attention to where everybody sits.

I see a table of Seniors, so muscular and overgrown that they can barely fit next to each other on the narrow bench seats. I'm definitely not going anywhere near them.

Next to the Seniors are a bunch of Heirs. I recognize a couple of them from my year, and a few who are older. One is that friend of Miles Griffin that I met on my first day—the friendly one with the mohawk and the tattoos and piercings all over his body. I think his name's Ozzy. But I only met him the one time, so I don't feel comfortable plopping down next to him.

I spot a group of French students, most of whom are blond. Every one of which looks like they came out of some high-fashion editorial spread. I've never been able to understand how some of the Kingmakers students make their uniforms look so damn stylish.

One of the girls has on a gorgeously tailored white blouse with the collar popped and a stunning gold chain lying across her décolletage. Her wavy sun-streaked hair lays over one shoulder like a mermaid, and her dewy skin looks like it's never been touched by human hands.

The boy on her left resembles her—long surfer hair, high cheekbones, and full lips. He's got a cross earring dangling from one ear, and he's picking at his food with an expression of disgust.

The French students only take up half the table—the other side is empty. I recognize the girl sitting on the end, next to the empty seats. She's the redhead I met on the wagon ride up to the school. Her name is Sadie Grant, I'm pretty sure.

I approach cautiously, ready to be turned away. Sadie gives me a quick smile, saying, "It's Cat, right?"

"Yes," I reply, relieved. I slide onto the empty bench, feeling like I accomplished something momentous by finding somewhere to sit.

"What's your name?" the haughty blond boy scoffs. "*Chatte?*"

"Cat," the glamorous girl corrects him. "It's probably short for something else. Isn't it, Cat?"

She smiles at me, showing lovely pearly white teeth.

"Yes," I say. "Short for Catalina."

"Are you from Spain?" she asks.

"Barcelona," I nod.

"We're from Paris," she tells me. "I'm Claire Turgenev. That's Jules." She nods toward the boy currently regarding me like a raccoon scavenging at his table.

"You're all from Paris?" I ask.

"Mostly. Isn't it funny how we group up at Kingmakers? Sometimes by division, sometimes by year . . . and then some of us came all the way across the world just to sit with the people we knew back home." She laughs at herself in a way that's instantly disarming.

"I'd sit with someone else, if there was anyone worth sitting with," Jules says, his full lip curling up in a sneer.

"You're such a snob," Claire says to him. "I meet people I like every day here. I'm just a creature of habit."

Though Claire's hands are clean, and her fingernails manicured, I can see a hint of dark staining on the cuticles and in the crevices around her knuckles. The same thing happens to my hands when I've been drawing with charcoal or ink. I wonder if she draws. I'm too shy to ask her.

"What's your last name?" Jules demands of me. I can tell by his tone that he's going to judge my answer. I wouldn't be surprised if he told me to take my tray somewhere else if my response doesn't meet his standards.

"Romero," I reply.

He considers this. "You're Zoe's sister?"

I nod.

"She's an Heir," he tells Claire. "Zoe is, I mean."

"Zoe Romero . . ." Claire muses, trying to think if she knows my sister. "Oh, she's the gorgeous tall one with the dark hair and the green eyes. The one who's always carrying around an armful of books."

"Yes," I say, pleased by the connection. I'm always proud when anyone knows Zoe—proud to be associated with her.

"What a waste," Claire sighs.

"What do you mean?" I demand, the hairs prickling on the back of my neck. As much as I like Claire Turgenev already, I won't let anyone criticize my sister.

"No offense to either of you," Claire says, in her clear, enchanting voice. "It's just such a shame that a beautiful girl like that has to marry Rocco Prince. I'm sure you agree that he's repugnant."

She looks across the dining hall to the distant table where Rocco sits with his coterie of thugs, including the two that crashed my breakfast with Zoe.

Rocco radiates a dark energy. It simultaneously separates him from the boys around him yet binds them to his side like magnets. No girls sit at his table. In fact, nobody who isn't part of his gang sits at any of the surrounding tables, creating a vacant halo all around him.

"What do you know about Rocco?" I ask Claire quietly.

Jules gives her a sharp look, like he doesn't think she should answer. Sadie likewise turns her attention on her food, disengaging herself from the conversation.

But Claire answers, without hesitation, "I know what everyone knows. That he's not a criminal . . . he's a killer."

"What do you mean?" I say, trying to swallow.

"Some of us have murdered when we had to," Claire says, in her calm, hypnotic voice. "And most of us will kill in the future. Very few mafiosos make it to the grave with lily-white hands. But only a few of us enjoy it."

I stare across the dining hall at Rocco, at his pale face and his fever-bright eyes. He's not touching his food, either. I don't know if I've ever seen him eat. He seems to prefer to use the time to watch everyone around him.

As if he can feel the scrutiny, he slowly raises his gaze to meet mine.

I drop my eyes at once, face flaming.

"He went to school for a year with my friend Emilia Browning," Claire says, picking up her water glass and taking a sip. "He had a group of friends there similar to the one he has here. *Les tyrans.*" She searches for the word. "Bullies. Assholes.

"They had a boy who followed them around. A sort of hanger-on. They used him as an errand boy—made him buy cigarettes for them, write their papers, that sort of thing. Then one day the groundskeeper found the boy's body dumped in the river behind the school. He had been tortured and beaten for hours, the police said. Cigarettes put out on his body. Eardrum punctured with a pencil. Teeth knocked out."

I feel like I'm going to throw up. With every word Claire speaks, weight settles on my shoulders. Each syllable another brick added to the stack.

"Emilia said that Rocco and his friends bragged of doing it. There was no reason, no provocation. The boy thought they were his friends. There was an investigation, but the boy was no one important, and Rocco and his clique all came from powerful families. Rocco had to switch schools though, because it was so ugly that his parents didn't want it talked about for long."

Jules Turgenev makes a disgusted hissing sound. "Savages," he says, with a flick of his head toward Rocco's table. "No taste. No feeling."

I feel very stupid for not recognizing what was happening right in front of my face.

Since the moment our father signed the marriage contract, Zoe has been sinking deeper and deeper into depression. I knew she didn't like Rocco. But I had no idea what she was actually being forced into.

I got a hint of it that morning at breakfast when I saw him grab her thigh. He'd always been polite, if a little creepy. That was the first time I saw violence between them.

It's not the fact that he grabbed her that disturbs me. It's the way he did it: under the table, secretly, so nobody could see. The way his expression never changed for an instant. There was no hint of rage in his voice. He was calm and collected while he hurt my sister.

All of a sudden, Zoe's absence takes on a new flavor.

I jump up from the table, my tray of food untouched.

"I've got to go," I mumble.

"I'm sorry," Claire says, putting her hand on my arm. "I didn't mean to upset you. I thought you should know. If your parents aren't aware—"

"Thank you," I say numbly. "I appreciate it."

I don't know how to tell her that our father wouldn't care even if I told him that exact story, even if he believed it.

I've been such an idiot.

Zoe has known all along about Rocco Prince. She knew he was a full-blown psychopath. She just didn't tell me. To protect me—because I'm too weak to handle it.

I hurry out of the dining hall, determined to find my sister.

7

ZOE

Dr. Cross tells me that I can stay in the infirmary as long as I like, but I leave that evening, after a long nap that helps ease the throbbing pressure in my skull.

I think I hit my head when Jasper Webb caught hold of my ankle. But that's not the only reason for the pounding headache. It's disappointment, too.

I don't want to be dead. Not really. But god did I want to escape.

Now I'm back in the thick of my own life, and the weight is suffocating.

I'm exhausted from scratching the walls, banging my head against the locked doors. Everywhere I turn, there's no way out.

I've only been back in my dorm a few minutes when I hear a gentle tap on the door.

"Zoe?" Cat calls softly.

I open the door to see my sister anxiously waiting, her dark eyes huge in her delicate face.

"There you are," she says, pushing into my room with a sigh of relief. Then she gets a proper look at me in the lamplight and her face crumples up. "What happened?" she cries.

I touch the tape high up on my cheekbone, which I know fails to cover the beginnings of a nasty black eye.

I open my mouth to give some excuse, to downplay what happened. Instead, I find myself bursting into tears.

I never cry like this. I've never fallen into my sister's arms, sobbing. I'm so much bigger than her that I almost knock her over. I'm instantly ashamed of myself, but I can't seem to stop. My whole body is shaking and I'm making an awful, animalistic sound, a ragged howling.

I never wanted to dump this on Cat. But I can't seem to stop. I'm crying and crying as if my insides are liquefying and pouring out through my tear ducts.

After a long time I realize that Cat has sat down on the bed, and I'm laying with my head in her lap, while she gently strokes my hair.

This is something I did for her many times when she was sick or sad. Especially after our mother died.

I've never been the one in this position before.

The feeling of her gentle little hand on my head is incredibly soothing. It's hard to accept comfort when you feel that you should be the one giving it, never demanding anything in return. It's hard to trust that it might be okay to receive solace, just this one time.

Once my body stops shaking, once I've relaxed, the words come pouring out of me just like the tears—without moderation or control. I tell Cat everything Rocco has done to me, everything he's said, from the moment I met him in the garden of our villa. Up to what happened this morning on the ramparts.

Cat listens silently, absorbing it all. I can feel her legs getting more and more rigid under my cheek, but she doesn't interrupt.

When I sit up to look at her, her lips are so pale that I can barely see them against her skin.

"What can we do?" she asks me.

"Nothing," I tell her. "There's nothing we can do."

"There has to be something!" she cries.

"Cat," I say gently. "Where would I go? Where would I hide? And with what money? Besides . . . I could never leave you with them."

By "them" I don't just mean our father and stepmother. I mean my father's soldiers, and the Princes and their soldiers, and the professors at school, and the other students, and the whole wide underworld that could be used to hunt me down, or to punish my sister for my escape.

"I could go with you," Cat says.

I shake my head. I would never risk what might happen to her if we tried to run away.

Cat was not made for a life of fear and uncertainty.

What I hope is that she'll marry someone reasonable. A strong man who can protect her. Who will appreciate that Cat is beautiful and kind and will be a good wife to him and an excellent mother to his children. Then she'll be safe.

Not all mafia men are bad. She could end up with a Leo instead of a Rocco. There's still hope for her.

As for me . . . well, I can't think about that.

Looking at Cat makes me realize I'm not the only one battered and bruised.

"What happened to your face?" I demand.

"Combat class," Cat says, shaking her head ruefully. "I'm not getting any better."

"You will," I assure her. "I could practice with you in the gym, outside of class hours. I'm not the best at fighting, but I've learned a few things. Chay's better—I bet she'd help."

"Alright," Cat says hesitantly, looking more nervous than pleased at this prospect. Then, returning to the subject topmost on her mind she says, "When you tried to jump off the wall . . . Jasper Webb grabbed you?"

"Yes," I say. "Jasper and Miles Griffin."

"But Miles wasn't part of it. He came along in the middle of it?"

"That's right." I nod.

"Why do you think Jasper helped you?"

"I don't know. Out of instinct. Or to keep me from getting away from Rocco. Or because he was worried he might get in trouble himself. It wasn't out of sympathy for me, I can tell you that. He had no problem holding me down so Rocco could cut my fucking eye out of my head."

Cat gulps, pale and nauseated, and I regret describing what happened in such graphic detail.

"Never mind," I tell her. "I was stupid to run up on that wall to avoid him. I'll be careful not to go to any isolated places."

Cat bites her lip. We both know that avoiding Rocco on campus is only a temporary fix at best. I won't be able to avoid him when we live in a house together as husband and wife.

"What was Miles doing up there?" Cat asks me.

"I don't know," I say.

I can feel my face coloring. I told Cat everything, except my conversation with Miles in the infirmary. I don't quite know how to explain it.

I never expected to experience kindness from Miles Griffin. And I definitely never expected to feel understanding. Miles and I could not be more different. And yet . . . for a brief moment as I lay back against the pillow, and he sat right next to me, not touching me, but only a foot or two of space between us . . . I felt that he could see inside me. He knew what I was feeling, and he understood.

Even more surprising, I felt the same way about him. I looked in his face and for once there was no mask of indifference. His features softened. He looked younger. Miles became a real person to me, with a range of emotions much wider than I thought him capable of feeling.

He uses humor as a shield and a weapon. I've never seen him show anything but ambition, cunning, and the relentless determination to satisfy his own impulses.

As he sat next to me, the walls came down. The real Miles spoke to me. I heard compassion in his voice. Concern. Even respect.

It was bizarre. Unsettling, even. I expected any second that he'd shake his head, crack some joke, and he'd be back to his usual careless self.

Instead, he wanted me to promise that I wouldn't try to hurt myself again.

I could tell that it mattered to him. That he cared.

Why he should care, I have no idea.

I don't think tenderness comes easy to Miles Griffin.

To me either, if I'm being honest. The only person on this planet I truly love is Cat. I never had close friends until I started school at Kingmakers. There's a coldness in me that doesn't melt easily. Maybe because I've had to be so careful, so rigid, all my life. It's hard for me to trust. Hard to open up.

"Miles must be decent," Cat says pensively. "He's cousins with Leo and Anna."

"That doesn't mean anything." I shake my head. "After all, look who we're related to."

THE FOLLOWING weeks at school are uneventful.

I never told Dr. Cross what actually happened, and he didn't press me for answers. He's too used to being lied to by students, and probably doesn't want to hear it.

I don't know whether Rocco is right, whether he's allowed to injure me with impunity. There's no point in reporting what happened either way. Nobody was injured, other than the cuts on my face and body, and the lump on my head. Only serious damage merits an official response.

One thing I did do: I bought trousers from Matteo Ragusa. He's a Sophomore Accountant, and we're about the same size. He was happy to sell me two pairs of pants from his stash of uniforms, though I could tell he was curious.

"What do you want them for?" he said, handing the trousers over freshly laundered and neatly pressed.

"I just ... don't want to wear skirts anymore," I said.

I couldn't explain to him the shame I feel in my body some-times. How much I hate the way it draws the eyes of people like Rocco Prince and Wade Dyer. I'm vulnerable in my school uniform. It was too easy for Rocco to slip his hand up my skirt at the breakfast table. I'm lucky all he did was pinch my thigh.

"You don't need these?" I said to Matteo, holding up the trousers.

"Nah." He shook his head. "I've got plenty. And my mom can send more in my Christmas box."

It wiped out all my pocket money, but it hardly matters. There's nothing to buy at Kingmakers unless I want something illegal from Miles Griffin.

I've been wearing the trousers since. They give me a strange sense of confidence. I feel like Katherine Hepburn or Ingrid Bergman, two women I've always admired. In an environment of skirts, pants are an expression of power.

Nobody has commented on it, other than Professor Graves raising one silver eyebrow the first time I walked into class flouting the usual uniform.

Maybe the pants are working, because Rocco has mostly been leaving me alone. More likely he sensed that he pushed me too far.

I'm not stupid enough to relax. I know he's only regrouping, planning his next attack.

He wasn't pleased with our last skirmish. He doesn't like when things don't go according to plan. Every interaction between him and me is supposed to satisfy some dark impulse. If I don't feed him what he wants, he only gets hungrier.

Rocco isn't the only one watching me. I catch Miles Griffin looking at me more than he used to. We were barely acquaintances before, both of us floating in the orbit of Leo and Anna, but rarely interacting with each other directly.

It may be my imagination, but I feel like Miles is sitting down to eat with us more often, or intercepting us in the commons to walk across the grounds together before parting ways for the next class.

Maybe he just wants to make sure I haven't offed myself yet.

It feels like more than that. It feels like he's listening to my conversations with Anna, taking in every word that comes out of my mouth, even while Leo's chatting away in his other ear.

While he's watching me, I'm watching him.

Miles is much more clever than I realized. I knew his grades were shit and he barely tried in class, basically doing the bare minimum to prevent being expelled. He slacks off in the *Quartum Bellum*. His team was first eliminated last year and he hardly seemed to care. He might even have disappeared for half the match.

But when he's talking about a subject on which he's genuinely passionate, he seems to know everything in the world.

For instance, this morning he's discussing Bitcoin with Ozzy. He's so engrossed in the conversation that his whole face lights up, and he looks much more like Leo, instead of his usual sardonic stare.

"It was the cartels that started Bitcoin in the first place!" he says to Ozzy, gesturing with his long, flexible fingers. "It's the perfect basket for obscuring transactions. I keep expecting the government to regulate it, to refuse transferal to American dollars, but they ignore it."

"They don't understand it," Ozzy says. "Politicians aren't programmers."

We've got a break between classes, and we're sitting on the raised platform amongst the orange trees, enjoying the last truly warm sunshine before the autumn weather begins.

This is the first time I've been over here since my altercation with Rocco up on that wall. The very wall I'm sitting against at this moment, the stone sun-warmed and pleasant against my back.

I can't help glancing upward to the empty ramparts. Miles catches me, and our eyes meet in one swift jolt of understanding, before Ozzy draws his attention again.

We're sprawled out with our bags and books scattered everywhere: Leo and Anna, Chay, Cat and me, Miles and Ozzy, then Ares and Hedeon.

Ares is Leo's roommate. He's a gentle giant—an inch taller even than Leo, with deeply-tanned skin and that particular shade of blue-green eye that you sometimes see in Greeks. He's quiet and studious, so I've always liked him and found him a good study partner.

Hedeon lives on the same floor of the Octagon Tower, with all the male Heirs of our year. I can't say I enjoy his company quite as much as Ares' because Hedeon is touchy and prone to angry outbursts. He'd be good-looking if he weren't so sulky all the time—he's dark-haired, clean-shaven, well-groomed. The only thing marring his handsome face is the slightly crooked bridge of his nose, as if it were broken in the past and never properly healed.

He's improved since our Freshman year. I think Leo and Ares are a good influence on him, because neither of them can hold a bad mood for long.

But right now Hedeon is in as foul a temper as I've ever seen him. He and his brother Silas got into a fistfight at breakfast over the last blueberry muffin in the basket.

I don't know how the fuck Hedeon dares fight with Silas. Silas is a walking leviathan. He looks carved out of stone, and he's about equally as emotive. I've never seen him smile, unless he just finished beating the shit out of someone in Combat class.

Yet they clash with each other constantly, with real fury, over the most petty provocations.

Anna thinks Silas is bitter because their parents appointed Hedeon as Heir. If that's true, I'm not sure what Hedeon is so angry about.

Hedeon gets the worst of it in their fights, but he never backs down. It's like a scab he can't stop picking.

"Gimme some of that water," he demands of Anna. She has a flask full of the lovely, cold, mineral-tinged water that you can pump up from the well next to the dining hall.

"No," Anna says, taking a swig herself. "You already drank half of it, and you should have brought your own."

Hedeon tries to snatch it from her, but Anna pulls it back out of reach. Her dancer's reflexes are as fast as any of the boys. Except maybe Leo.

"Don't know why you're sunbathing," he says to Anna. "I've never seen you catch a tan darker than chalk."

Leo frowns and opens his mouth to tell Hedeon off, but Anna forestalls him.

"Quit barking at all of us because Silas slapped you silly," she says. "It's not our fault your brother's an ass."

Hedeon gives Anna a stare of such furious heat that even Anna looks slightly abashed.

"He's *not* my brother," Hedeon hisses. "There's not a drop of shared blood in our veins."

An awkward silence falls over the group as we all remember that Hedeon was adopted by the Grays, and so was Silas. They were raised together, but it obviously engendered no affection.

Quietly, Chay asks, "Do you know who your biological parents were?"

Hedeon's lips are pressed tight together, his jaw rigid with anger. I don't think he's going to answer her.

Then he says, "No."

It's a twisted, tortured syllable, as if it pains him to let it out.

I've seen Hedeon hit the heavy bag in the gym, over and over and over again, until his knuckles are bloody and his shirt is soaked through with sweat. Those white t-shirts become transparent when wet. Hedeon's back is a topographical map of scars, raised and crisscrossed, newer scars lain over older. They run down the backs of his arms, too, and up the base of his neck.

I think about those scars, and the slightly crooked nose.

I wonder when that happened. Before he was adopted? Or after.

The silence is thick, as most of us want to say something to Hedeon, but don't know what. His expression seems to indicate that he'll bite the head off the first person who tries.

To my shock, it's Cat who pipes up.

"My roommate beat the shit out of me in Combat class again," she says. "But I almost think it's cathartic for us. Really seems to ease the tension in our room afterward."

Chay can't help laughing. "What the hell? Who would want to beat you up?"

"Rakel really seems to enjoy it," Cat says, mystified. "I am learning how to get my hands up. And I knocked her over once today, so that's progress."

Sure enough, Cat's sporting a fresh fat lip to go along with the bruise under her eye from a previous sparring session. It only highlights the innocence of her big, round eyes and her delicate face.

Hedeon looks at her with a bemused expression. He's still radiating anger, but at a less radioactive degree. More asbestos than Chernobyl.

The tension broken, Miles and Ozzy return to their conversation.

"It doesn't do any good to stay right below the ten-thousand-dollar mark for deposits," Ozzy is saying. "They've got algorithms to track that. You put in ninety-four hundred every three days, and they're still gonna pop you. You gotta write your own algorithm to keep it truly random."

"Can you do that?" Cat asks him eagerly.

"Sure," Ozzy says, surprised that she's taking an interest. "Easily."

"Cat's got a knack for computers," I say to Ozzy.

"Ozzy's a fucking genius on a keyboard," Miles says. "Cat couldn't learn from anybody better."

Once again I find our eyes locking, and it feels like so much more intention is flowing between us than the simple words of that sentence.

"Nice outfit, by the way," Miles says, that slow, lazy grin quirking up the right side of his mouth, showing white teeth against his tan skin.

"Thanks," I say, blushing a little. I've got on Matteo's trousers and a pair of suspenders borrowed from Chay, over a white dress shirt, with a pair of flat brown oxfords. I look like a newsie, but Miles seems to genuinely like it. He's a sharp dresser himself, always combining unusual pairings of the uniform pieces with his extensive collection of space-age sneakers.

It's the simplest of compliments. Yet I feel warm all the way down to my toes, and not just from the sunshine.

Ares checks his watch. "I was gonna go finish that paper on Organizational Structure before next period," he says. "You want to come, Zoe?"

He knows I'm always down for a trip to the library. It's probably my favorite place in all of Kingmakers. I like to go there just to breathe the scent of all that ancient paper and ink.

"Sure," I say, scooping up my bookbag.

I raise my hand in a wave, planning to say goodbye to Miles and everybody else. But Miles isn't looking at me anymore— he's staring at Ares with a wholly unexpected expression. Scowling like Hedeon when Silas is mentioned. He looks like Ares just stole his blueberry muffin.

I blink, and the bizarre moment passes. Miles turns his gaze on his expensive sneakers instead.

When I say, "See you later," he responds with a quick jerk of his head.

Ares and I head west along the wall, toward the pointing finger of the Library Tower.

Ares has a calming presence. He's one of those people you can sit with in silence without ever feeling uncomfortable. When I do speak to him, he always answers with a smile. Still, I sometimes get the feeling he's not actually very happy.

"How are you doing?" he asks me gently.

Cat is the only person I spoke to about what happened on the wall. I'm guessing Miles told Leo, and Leo told Ares. That, or Ares is just perceptive. Quiet people see a lot. And it's not that subtle that I'm all kinds of fucked up.

My automatic impulse is to say, "I'm fine," like I always do.

But there's a strange thing about making friends. It doesn't feel good to lie to them.

I've always kept my feelings locked away. Bit by bit, Anna, Chay, Leo, and Miles are bringing me back to honesty. I've even been more open with Cat.

So I don't force a smile for Ares.

I say, "I'm pretty fucking tired. Of school, of family shit, and this fucking unsolvable problem always hanging around my neck."

Ares' jaw tightens. His forearms look strangely rigid where his hands are stuffed in his pockets.

"I understand," he says.

I look at him curiously. "Do you?"

He meets my gaze for just a moment, his dark, untidy shock of hair falling over his eyes. Then he looks away again.

"I think so," he mumbles. "You're smart, Zoe. Disciplined. Loyal. It seems like it has to work out for you in the end."

"Does it always work out for the people who deserve it?" I ask him. "Or is it all just random and fucking awful sometimes?"

He bites his lip, really considering this.

"I don't know," he says at last. "But I'm gonna act like there's some kind of destiny, or karma, or whatever you want to call it. 'Cause otherwise, what's the point of anything? We might as well give up now."

"And you don't want to give up?" I ask him. Sometimes *I* want to give up.

"No." Ares shakes his head vehemently. "I never want that."

We're quiet for a moment, Ares looking uncomfortable, as he always does when he says more than twenty words in a row.

He and I have spent a fair bit of time alone together, but I don't know that much about him. Only that he's from a tiny island in Greece. That the Cirillos were one of the ten founding families of Kingmakers, but they're hardly mafia at all anymore. He grew up on a farm. He's the oldest of four, and his younger siblings miss him desperately—he's always writing letters to them, picking up their responses from the little post office in the village.

I know what everyone else wants to do after we graduate: Anna will take over the Polish *Braterstwo* and Leo will become the Italian Don. Together they'll rule the lion's share of Chicago.

By rights, Miles could take over the Irish territory, but he intends to go to Los Angeles instead, to make his own way in the world.

Chay is the Heir of the Berlin Nightwolves, and she already knows exactly how she'll expand their network of tattoo shops, nightclubs, concert venues, motorcycle shops, and racing teams.

Even Hedeon has been named Heir of the Gray's London-based empire, with his brother Silas ordained to act as his top lieutenant. How they'll manage that when they can't eat breakfast without trying to kill each other is beyond me, but the plan is in place.

Only Ares abstains from talking about the future.

"What will you do?" I ask him. "After we graduate?"

"Take over my father's business," he says at once.

"Really," I say. "That surprises me."

"Why?"

"Well, you're so good at everything here. You've got some of the best marks in the practical classes as well as the academic ones. It's true!" I say, as Ares shakes his head modestly. "Don't think nobody notices just because you're standing next to Leo all the time. Do you really want to be a farmer?"

Ares looks at me, smiling his gentle smile.

"You're kind, Zoe," he says. "Don't worry about me. I like growing things."

"Alright," I say, shrugging. "I'd never tell you there's no joy in a peaceful life. I'd take that deal in a second."

We've reached the Library Tower. I already feel a swoop of happiness as Ares cracks open the heavy, iron-strapped door. The scent of parchment and leather hits us like a cool, dry wind. Mixed with that, a light, exotic note that just might be Miss Robin's perfume. Her apartments are directly above the library, in the attic of its pointed roof.

We climb the spiraling stone steps to the first level. The whole library is one enormous spiral, like the inside of a conch shell. The bookshelves are curved to fit against the wall, and the floor slopes upward like one long, continuous ramp. Wedge-shaped platforms prop up the tables so our pencils don't roll away while we're working. It's a bizarre design that makes the library seem infinite and endless. The thick oriental rugs and book-stuffed walls muffle the sound so you never know who might be on the levels above you.

As we ascend, my shoelace slaps against the stone steps and I stoop to tie my oxfords so I don't trip myself. Ares continues on, not noticing that I've fallen behind.

Shoelace tied, I hurry to catch up with him. I hear Miss Robin's cheerful greeting of, "Aren't you supposed to be in class?" She pauses as I rush up next to Ares, then says, "Zoe too! I should have guessed. I don't think anyone spends more time in here than you two."

"It's Wednesday," Ares reminds her. "Everyone gets a free period in the morning block."

"Wednesday!" she cries, shaking her head. "Next you'll be telling me it's October."

I smile to myself, certain Miss Robin is aware that we're well into October.

When I first met the librarian I thought she was shy and a bit standoffish. She rarely eats in the dining hall, even though plenty of other professors do, and I haven't seen her at any school events.

The more I talk to her, the more I realize she's actually quite warm and charming. She's just wrapped up in her thesis on medieval monasteries. She's never idle when I come in here, always busy scouring old maps and documents.

Even now, I can see traces of ink on her fingertips and a smudge on her cheek. Her dark red hair escapes from her bun in wild, frizzy strands. Her thick grandma glasses have slipped down to the tip of her nose. Because it's perpetually chilly in the library, she's wearing three or four knitted jumpers layered over each other, so she looks plump though I suspect she's actually rather slim under it all.

Miss Robin is pretty, even without makeup, even with her awful orthopedic shoes. She has a low, husky voice. I like to hear her talk—though she never does for long, always heading right back to her own projects.

"I just made tea," she says. "Do you two want some?"

"No," Ares says, being polite.

"Yes please," I say, because I'm not as polite, and if Miss Robin wants to sit with us, I'll take her up on the offer.

She makes the long walk up the spiral to the topmost floor, where I hear a faint creak and thump as she pulls down the ladder that leads to her loft. By the time Ares and I have spread out our books and papers, she's brought down two more delicate china cups and retrieved the steaming pot of tea from her desk.

"I don't have sugar," she says, apologetically. "I drink it plain."

"That's perfect," I say.

She pours the rich, brown, heavily-steeped tea into our cups. It smells of cinnamon and cloves. The spices blend perfectly with the ancient air of the library.

Miss Robin lifts her own cup to her lips and takes a sip.

"How's the thesis going?" I ask her.

"Terrible," she says glumly. "I was so excited when I arrived here—the archives contain documents and schematics you wouldn't find anywhere else in the world. And yet they're uncategorized, unlabeled, unorganized. The sheer volume of materials is precisely what's preventing me from finding the information I actually need. None of it is computerized. And quite frankly, much of it has been damaged by mold and mice."

"The previous librarian was old, wasn't she?" I say apologetically, as if the mess is my fault.

"Ancient—but it's not her fault," Miss Robin says. "The library has never been a high priority for those running Kingmakers. Why would it be? For most of its life, this school has been more of a military barracks than a proper university."

"Is that how the current Chancellor runs it?" I ask curiously.

"I suppose not," Miss Robin says. "After all, he hired me."

"You're his niece though, aren't you?" I ask.

"Twice removed, or something like that," Miss Robin laughs. "But yes, there's nepotism at play. He's very kind to me—other than the vague job description. It was a surprise to show up here and realize that . . . well, that some of my relatives most likely weren't import-exporters after all." She shakes her head ruefully.

That's another reason Miss Robin might not be friendly with the other staff. Most of them have a violent history that would horrify a normal civilian. Professor Bruce was a mercenary, Professor Penmark a debt collector known for his brutality. Professor Lyons was called the Arsenic Witch for her skill at subtle poisoning when she used to take on contract kills for the Saudis. That's just the stories everyone knows—I can hardly imagine what the professors chat about when they sit in their favorite corner of the dining hall.

Still, Miss Robin must be lonely up here.

"Do you spend much time with the Chancellor?" I ask.

"A little," Miss Robin says. "He's not always here, you know—he goes to Dubrovnik sometimes."

"How does he do that?" Ares asks.

"I shouldn't tell you," Miss Robin says, with a mischievous smile. "I think they want everyone to believe that the only way on and off the island is the big barquantine that brought you, or the supply ship that goes back and forth every month."

"What about the fishing boats?" I ask.

"They can't make the crossing." She shakes her head.

"What then?" Ares asks, his expression keen.

"He's got a custom-built cruiser. Beautiful thing—I can't imagine what it cost him. Luther's rich as Solomon, though. The Hugos have always been wealthy. They don't have a golden skull as their crest for nothing."

"Not the Robins, though?" I tease her.

She laughs. "God, no. If we ever had a family crest, which we don't, it would be a robin pecking a breadcrumb."

Ares doesn't seem interested in any of that, returning to the point that piqued his curiosity.

"How do you know the Chancellor has a cruiser? I've never seen one."

"I'm sure you haven't. Because that's how he likes it," Miss Robin says, finishing the last of her tea. "Take your time," she says, nodding toward our cups. "You can bring those to me later."

As Miss Robin heads back to her desk, I say to Ares, "Can you imagine being that rich that you could just buy yachts or jets or anything you like?"

I've never had control over any substantial amount of money, and I know Ares' family is one of the least-wealthy at the whole school.

"Money attracts trouble," Ares says, turning back to his books. Then, after a moment, perhaps thinking that his comment was unnecessarily repressive, he gives me a small smile and admits, "I would like to see that cruiser, though. Bet it's fast as fuck."

I grin back at him. "If I were Hugo's niece, I'd ask to borrow the keys."

8

MILES

I know Rocco Prince won't lay low for long. There's no way he'll just swallow the insult of me interfering with his abuse of his fiancée.

It's impossible for us to avoid each other—we're both Juniors and both Heirs, so at least half of our classes are shared.

We had a cordial relationship up to this point—not friendly, but he used to buy mushrooms off me, and once Ozzy sold him an old iPhone loaded with some pretty fucked up porn.

The iPhones are one of our most popular products. We buy old models super cheap, then pre-download them with music, movies, and pornography, and sell them to students for $500 a pop. We offer an exchange program to swap out your old phone for a fresh slate of content, but most of the time they have to buy a new one 'cause some teacher has confiscated it.

Cellphones are forbidden on the island. Also laptops and iPads. Speakers and iPods are allowed, as long as the only thing they do is play music.

Even just the charging is a hassle. There's barely any outlets in the castle, none at all in the dorms.

No cell phone service, so all calls home to family have to be made from the bank of telephones in the Keep. No internet access. All assignments must be written by hand.

Of course, those rules are for the plebs.

Ozzy and I have GPS phones that work anywhere, and we've figured out how to hack into the school's server. We're about to secure a whole new way of connecting—our very own Starlink satellite. We just have to figure out where to hide it.

That's the project for this afternoon.

This morning I'm dealing with Rocco Prince, Jasper Webb, Dax Volker, and Wade Dyer, who have apparently decided that they're willing to jeopardize their access to the school black market in favor of airing their grievances against me.

We're all in Chemistry class together, in the Keep with Professor Lyons. She looks like your average lab assistant, standing in front of the class in her white coat and her safety glasses, her gray hair cut in a sensible bob. You might even think her grandmotherly, with her sleepy-lidded eyes and her casual lecture style. Yet she has one of the highest kill counts of any former assassin, specializing in undetectable poisons and deaths that could be ruled as heart attack or stroke.

She taught us all about those poisons in our Freshman year. As Sophomores we focused on homemade explosives. Now we're moving on to the manufacture of hard drugs.

"Opium is one of humanity's most ancient drugs," Professor Lyons says, looking a bit like she's taken a hit from the pipe herself as she blinks at us with those heavy-lidded eyes. "The use of opium, both medicinally and recreationally, can be traced back to ancient Mesopotamia. That precious nectar comes from the common poppy—*papaver somniferum,* the very bloom you grow in your garden, from which you can extract seeds for pastries or bagels. The very bloom you see upon your desks right now."

We're sitting at wide tables outfitted with lab equipment. I'm sharing with Ozzy, while Rocco Prince and Wade Dyer sit directly to our right, and Jasper and Dax behind us. If that's supposed to be intimidating, it's not. Dax breathes so loud he'd have no chance of surprising me, and Rocco's dirty looks are B+ at best after you've been on the receiving end of Uncle Nero's death stare.

As Professor Lyons indicated, each table bears a brilliant scarlet poppy with an ink-black center and a fuzzy stem. She instructs us to don our latex gloves so we can slice the poppy's bulb to collect the thick, sludgy opium gum.

Rocco picks up his scalpel but doesn't touch his poppy. He grasps the handle, silver blade pointed in my direction.

"Don't be shy," I say to him. "Or do you need me to hold it down for you?"

I'm provoking him, I know that. The truth is, I'm also holding a grudge from our little confrontation. If I've triggered Rocco's animosity, he's sure as fuck triggered mine.

Deftly, without even looking, Rocco slits the poppy bulb. White sap oozes out.

"I could slit your throat just as easy," he hisses, his eyes fixed on me.

"You could try," I scoff. "You might have an overinflated sense of your own abilities. Not everybody's as slow as your boy Dax. Or as dumb as Wade over there."

Dax shifts his bulk in his chair, and Wade growls, "Fuck you, Griffin. You're not smart enough to mind your own business, are ya?"

Whenever Wade gets mad, he reminds me of a bully in an 80s movie. It's something about his bland good looks, the blond hair and the cleft chin. He looks like Rip from *Less Than Zero*, or Ace Merrill from *Stand By Me*.

Ozzy says, "Wade, you're not the dumbest guy on earth, but you sure better hope he doesn't die."

It takes Wade a couple of seconds to figure that out, and in the interval Ozzy and I burst out laughing at the blank confusion on his face. Professor Lyons gives us an irritated glare.

Under her quelling stare we all go quiet for a minute, but I know it won't last. Dax, Wade, and Rocco are all riled up, like a pack of dogs when somebody drags a stick along the fence. Only Jasper seems indifferent, behind and to the right in my peripheral. He's working on his poppy, his skeletal tattoos still visible through the translucent gloves, seemingly deaf to the storm brewing around him.

"Once you've collected the sap, we'll use solvents to extract the morphine solution," Professor Lyons says, writing the chemical ingredients on the chalkboard.

"I'll get all that shit," Ozzy says, scribbling the list in ink on the back of his hand so he won't have to make multiple trips to the supply cabinet if he forgets anything. "You jerk off the poppy."

Wade follows Ozzy to the cabinet.

I pick up my own scalpel, intensely aware that Rocco and I are now both armed with only two feet of space between us. Holding a knife gives me a strange impulse to slash his fucking face open. Or maybe stab him in the eye, like he tried to do to Zoe. My hand feels twitchy and charged, as if it's taken on a life of its own.

Technically, I'm the one in the wrong. Rocco and Zoe are engaged, and I have no right to interfere in their business.

On the other hand, Rocco fucking sucks and the more I get to know Zoe, the more I think it's tragic for her to be the plaything of this lunatic.

"You don't want to make an enemy of me. It wouldn't be wise," Rocco says. His sibilant voice draws out the "s" in "wise."

Usually I'd say, "*I have no interest in being enemies.*"

I've seen the havoc it wreaks. My family's long and bloody battle with the Bratva in Chicago resulted in my grandfather's death. Uncle Dante was shot, Uncle Nero almost killed. The grudge has lasted twenty years and is still carried on at this fucking school by Dean Yenin, the Bratva heir who tried to drown Leo last year.

The problem is . . . I really don't like Rocco. I don't like anything he stands for. The idea of making peace with him tastes like vomit in my mouth.

So I say, "Zoe's best friends with my cousin. Me, Leo, Anna . . . we're looking out for her. If you don't want to be enemies, then keep your fucking hands off her."

"You have a strange sense of justice," Rocco says, his blue eyes fevered. "Would I tell you not to drive your own car? Or eat the food in your own fridge?"

"You're not married to her yet," I say.

"The contract is signed."

"Yeah? Where's the clause about cutting her eye out? Are you too stupid to take care of your own property?"

"It's none of your business what I do to Zoe. I could set her on fire just to watch her burn."

My stomach churns at the look of amusement on his face. I don't believe in good and bad people. But Rocco radiates a level of evil I've never encountered before.

I'm good at reading people. I look for micro-expressions— hints of fear, anxiety, desire, deception in their face.

Rocco doesn't have micro-expressions. His emotions aren't complex. His intentions are simple: he wants to hurt Zoe for the fun of it. And he wants me to stop inconveniencing him.

"We're not going to stand by for that," I tell him flatly.

"That's your choice," Rocco says. "This was your warning. There won't be another."

Ozzy returns from the supply cupboard, arms laden with baggies and jars. Carefully he sets them down on the table, then slides into his chair once more. He looks over at Rocco, his broad face creased in a scowl, checking to see if we're still barking back and forth at each other. Rocco smiles at him, his thin lips like a gash in the lower half of his face.

Wade finishes gathering his supplies, his arms even more heavily-laden than Ozzy's. He walks slowly and deliberately. As he passes Ozzy, he drops an open beaker of clear fluid all over Ozzy's bare forearm.

Howling, Ozzy leaps up from his seat.

The fluid sizzles on his arm, his flesh instantly lobster red and even bubbling in places. I smell chlorine.

Ozzy tries to run for the door, probably to sprint to the infirmary, but I seize him by the collar of his sweater vest and drag him backward. Yanking the faucet handle, I seize Ozzy's wrist and thrust his arm under the steady flow of cold water to flush the area clean.

"What's going on?" Professor Lyons shouts.

"Wade spilled something on Ozzy's arm," I say. "I think it's hydrochloric acid."

Professor Lyons uses tongs to lift the spilled beaker off the desktop and hold it aloft in front of her safety glasses. She squints at the soaked, blurred label.

"Why was this open?" she demands.

"It was an accident," Wade says, trying to get in front of the story before we can accuse him. "I thought it was benzene."

"Then you're an idiot," she snaps. "Go to the cabinet. Get me calcium gluconate. Try reading the label this time." Then, adjusting the faucet slightly, she says to me, "You keep that water running over his arm for twenty minutes. Not too hard —just like this."

"It wasn't an accident," I tell her.

She surveys the scene with eyes no longer sleepy but sharp as a hawk. "How do you know?" she says. "Wade *is* an idiot."

"He tripped," Dax says from behind me. "Miles stuck his foot out on purpose. I saw the whole thing."

"That's fucking bullshit!" I snarl.

Professor Lyons ignores my profanity. Cursing is common as breathing at Kingmakers.

"Twenty minutes," she reminds me. "Then we'll apply the calcium gluconate."

Ozzy's face is a rictus of pain, his lips drawn back to show his tightly-clenched teeth, his stocky body rigid and trembling as the acid continues to burn the exposed nerves of his arm. I hope the cool water is soothing him a little.

As soon as Professor Lyons moves away to dispose of the empty beaker of acid, I hiss at Wade, "You're fucking dead for this."

He smirks. "They're not even gonna punish me. It's four against two that I'm just clumsy."

"Think twice before you stick your nose in where it doesn't belong," Dax grunts at me, shoving his desk forward so it hits the back of my legs. I'd fucking pop him, but I have to keep holding Ozzy's arm under the water. Ozzy's shaking so hard that I don't think he could do it himself.

I'm ten times angrier that Wade attacked Ozzy than if he'd dropped that shit on me. I'm sure that's why he did it—failing to protect your soldiers is a grave insult in our world. Ozzy isn't really my soldier—he's an Heir himself, the only child of the Duncans, with sole control of criminal activity within Tasmania. But on campus, I make the plans and he helps execute them. As with any set of best friends, one of us has to take the lead.

I feel responsible for this.

The burn is fucking awful, the flesh raw and sure to scar.

"You're gonna be okay," I mutter to Ozzy.

"I know," he grunts, red and sweating with pain. "It's not that. It's my Tails."

"Your Tails?" I ask blankly.

"Yeah," he pauses, grimacing, then continues. "On my arm. He was my favorite. And now look at him."

I look at the spot on his forearm where the doubled-tailed fox used to reside. It's nothing but a red, swollen mess now, with barely a hint of an outline where the tattoo used to be.

"Ozzy . . ." I say. "That was your worst tattoo."

"What are you talking about?"

"It was fuckin' hideous, man. So bad. He looked like a squirrel. Honestly, Wade kinda did you a favor."

I say that low, because fuck Wade if he thinks I'm being serious. He's gonna pay for this, whether the school punishes him or not.

Ozzy laughs, though it comes out more like a groan. "Tails was wonky," he admits. "But that's why I liked him."

When the twenty minutes elapses, Professor Lyons applies the calcium gluconate to Ozzy's arm. She squirts it out of a tube similar to toothpaste. It seems to ease his pain a little. The professor wraps his arm in clean gauze.

"Take him to the infirmary so Dr. Cross can check him out," she says.

"Can I bring a couple of those poppies with me?" Ozzy asks weakly. "Feel like I might need a taste of the dragon, you know what I mean, Professor?"

"You can ask Dr. Cross for painkillers," she says unsympathetically.

"Come on," I say, grabbing Ozzy's bookbag.

I'm sure Dr. Cross will be thrilled to see me again.

OZZY STAYS OVERNIGHT in the infirmary. When he returns to class the next day, his left hand is stiff and swollen and the whole arm is wrapped up, hung in a sling to help protect it from jostling. Ozzy tells me the flesh is still raw. The slightest contact, even over the gauze, is agonizing.

I'm fucking furious that this happened to Ozzy because of me. I hook him up with some of our best edibles to take the edge off, but I need something better than that to cheer him up. So I get up nice and early the following morning and sneak into the Gatehouse.

The Gatehouse is where the Enforcers have their dorms. The rooms are neat and uniform, having been used in the old days as barracks for soldiers. Almost no female students are Enforcers, except for Ilsa Markov, who I'll admit is a pretty fucking badass bitch.

There's a distinct smell of testosterone and unwashed socks in the air. Also the overpowering Aqua Di Gio Wade always wears. I'd be able to find his room even if I didn't already know which one was his.

From what I've observed, he likes to get up nice and early to hit the gym in the Armory before class starts. He's part of the 6:00 a.m. crowd, along with Dax, Dean Yenin, and the rest of the masochists.

I wait outside his door, hearing him rustling around while he pulls on his gym clothes and those spotless white tennis shoes of his. I hear three distinct spritzes as he douses himself in cologne, which assaults my nostrils a few seconds later as the sharp scent seeps through the cracks around the door.

I'm waiting to the right of said door, phone in my left hand, right hand curled around my zippo for a little extra oomph.

The hinges creak and I ready myself.

The moment Wade opens the door, I haul off and punch him in the nose with all my might. It's a sucker punch, totally unexpected, and not something I would usually do. But in this case, it's fully deserved.

Wade clamps his hands over his nose, blood already rocketing out, spurting through his fingers.

"Smile, bitch," I say.

I raise my phone and snap a quick pic of his howling face. Then I hightail it out of there before the rest of the Enforcers wake up and make it something like a fair fight.

I present Ozzy the picture over breakfast. He laughs so hard that tears come to his eyes.

"That was this morning?" he says. "Where is he? I wanna see it in person."

He looks around the dining hall, hoping to see Wade slumped over his pancakes with a couple tampons stuffed up his nose. No luck—he must still be holed up in the bathroom trying to get the bleeding to stop.

"D'you think it's broken?" Ozzy asks hopefully.

"I damn well hope so," I say.

Wade does not appear for our Structural Organization class, though Rocco and Dax must have heard about the retaliation, because they're glaring at us worse than ever.

I'm going against my usual policy of de-escalation, but I don't give a fuck. I was a good boy my first two years at Kingmakers, relatively speaking. It's about time I had a little fun.

"You up for installing that satellite?" I ask Ozzy.

"Yeah," he says. "I only got one arm though, so you're gonna have to do the heavy lifting."

The Starlink satellite dish is small and compact, less than two feet in diameter. It needs a clear line of sight up to the sky, and the higher we mount it, the better. Most of all, it can't be spotted—it was a fuckin' pain in the ass smuggling this thing onto the island. The last thing I need is some school employee ripping it down again right after I put it up.

We need it close, so the obvious choice is one of Kingmaker's six towers. The Octagon Tower in which we have our rooms would be ideal, but it's packed with male Heirs. Even the attic space is occupied. The Library Tower is out because of Miss Robin. Nobody lives in the attic of the Accountant's tower—all their rooms are on the lower levels. But it would look strange for Ozzy and me to be traipsing up there with a suspicious package under my arm.

The Dungeon Tower is empty, but the doors are always locked whether there's a prisoner inside or not—with modern electronic bolts, not the rusty old key-locks I could practically pick with a fingernail. And the Bell Tower was never rebuilt after it was ravaged by fire a hundred years ago. That rickety pile of stones looks ready to tumble down at a moment's notice—we'd be risking our necks just walking through the door.

That leaves the Rookery. It's the smallest tower, nestled up on the north end of the cathedral. It's full of feathers and birdshit, but I think it will suit our purposes.

Ozzy keeps a lookout while I jimmy the lock at the base of the stairs. We slip inside, over steps spattered with dusty white guano. Tiny bits of down float in the still air.

Dozens of homing pigeons used to roost in here. Falcons, too, on the lower levels. The ammonia stench is eye-watering, but it won't matter. We won't be spending much time in here. Once we've got the satellite in place, we can set up our own private network, unsearchable and undetectable unless you already know its name. Ozzy and I will have lightning-speed internet while lounging around in our dorm room.

Assuming he can get back the use of his hand so he can type again. FUCK Wade Dyer, and Rocco Prince, too.

Ozzy must be thinking the same thing. As I organize the tools to cut a hole in the steeply-pitched roof, he says, "Can't wait to get this running."

"Glad I've got you to do it," I say. "I'm not bad with this shit, but you're so much better."

"SO much better," Ozzy agrees, grinning.

"Good thing no girls ever liked you, so you had plenty of time to practice."

He snickers. "They shouldn't like me, but for some reason they do. Girls just don't know what's good for 'em."

"Yeah, neither do guys," I say, thinking about Zoe again.

She pops into my brain multiple times a day. When I'm around Anna and Leo, Chay and Zoe, I can't keep my eyes off her. I don't know what it is. She's not as loud as Chay, not as flashy as the other girls at school. Lately she's been dressing like a boy in her oxfords and trousers. Somehow it only makes her sexier. Maybe 'cause I know what's under those clothes now. I shouldn't be thinking about her figure—I was never supposed to see it in the first place. But fucking hell, I can't forget it. I've never seen a body like that, not anywhere.

And it's not just her looks. It's the way she doesn't talk often, but when she does, anything she says is intelligent and well-reasoned. She has this quiet dignity that reels me in, even when I know she's about the worst possible candidate for a crush.

"Yup, we're just as dumb," Ozzy laughs. "I've got a real bone-head plan for the weekend."

"Oh yeah?" I grin. "What's that?"

"Gonna take another swing at Chay."

I shake my head at him. "What's this, the fifth time?"

"Sixth," Ozzy says.

"Maybe she'll pity-fuck you now that you're a cripple."

"You think?" Ozzy says hopefully.

I'm sure Ozzy's planning to make his move at the Halloween party. If Chay's gonna be there, I wonder if Zoe will be, too? She doesn't always come to parties because her shithead cousins rat her out to her dad. But if I don't let the cousins in . .
.

"Alright," I say to Ozzy, "I'm ready to start cutting. You got the safety glasses?"

"Yup," Ozzy says, passing me a pair. "Pocketed them before Wade flambéed my arm, luckily. 'Cause, being honest, I wasn't gonna remember afterward."

"Yeah . . . well he's not gonna remember what his nose used to look like either," I say.

Laughing, we start sawing through the roof.

Ozzy and I are throwing a Halloween party at the old stables. We're charging a fifty-dollar cover with the promise of unlimited spiked punch. The cover isn't the money-maker. It's the metric fuck-ton of Molly that everybody buys once they're tipsy and dancing.

Throwing a party is all about creating a mood. I hire a couple of Freshman Accountants to make me a thousand black paper bats that hang from the rafters. Then I rig up some spooky red lights, surround the punch bowls with smoking dry ice courtesy of the Chemistry lab, and queue up a killer playlist.

I love music, always have. It does something to my brain. When I've got just the right beat going, and a complicated melody on top, I feel like I can think ten times faster, like my mind is going a million miles a minute.

I invite Leo and Anna, informing Anna that Martin Romero and Santiago Cruz won't make it through the door.

Anna cocks one darkly-penciled eyebrow.

"Is that for Zoe's benefit? You've become so . . . helpful."

"Yeah. I'm a nice guy."

"Since when?" she laughs.

"Just tell her," I say, trying to sound nonchalant. "I never liked those fucksticks anyway. So no loss there."

I don't know if Zoe plans to come, but I'm strangely keyed up as the kids start pouring through the door, some of them dressed in the kind of makeshift costumes you can cobble together from shit you happen to have on hand.

Kasper Markaj dressed as a Spartan, wearing just his underwear and a red velvet curtain draped over his shoulders like a cape. Isabel Dixon teased up her hair and covered herself in charcoal, so she looks electrocuted, while her boyfriend Hiram Stokes hung a paper lightning bolt around his neck.

Everybody's ramped up to celebrate the holiday. The party is bumping ten minutes after I open the doors. Ozzy's collecting the cover charges as fast as he can with just one arm, and I'm pretending to welcome everybody, while actually keeping my eyes peeled for the people I want to see, as well as the ones who can fuck off back to their dorms.

Anna arrives wearing her most tattered clothes, with some pretty impressive zombie makeup all over her face. She's done the same to Leo, but his blinding smile makes him look much too alive to be undead.

"Congrats," I say to him.

Leo was just chosen Sophomore Captain for the *Quartum Bellum*. It was pretty much guaranteed to happen, after the unprecedented victory of the Freshmen last year, but now it's official.

"Thanks," he says. "Can't say I'm quite as excited this time around—knowing what I'm up against."

"Can't be worse than last year," Ozzy says.

"It can always be worse." Leo grimaces.

"Yeah—like having Simon Fowler for your Captain," Ozzy complains.

Simon is a Junior Heir with a high opinion of himself and a generous bankroll from his parents. He openly gave out cash to earn votes for the Captainship. I don't give a shit, because I don't give a shit about the *Quartum Bellum*. But I'm not exactly looking forward to taking orders from someone who would suck his own cock if he were flexible enough.

"Just you two tonight?" I say to Anna.

"Relax." She smiles. "Zoe's coming with Chay."

"I was just asking. For the cover charge," I say quickly.

"You're not gonna charge us!" Anna cries, outraged.

"Absolutely I am. Leo can down an entire punch bowl by himself."

"What's the family discount?" Leo says.

"Two for the price of two."

"I'll pay it," Leo says. "But only 'cause poor Ozzy's having such a shit week. He deserves it."

"Thank you," Ozzy says, taking Leo's crisp hundred-dollar bill and tucking it directly into his pocket. "Couldn't go to a better cause."

When I turn around again, I'm facing an angel.

Zoe's wearing a diaphanous white gown that seems to float around her body. On her shoulders, intricately-cut wings made of paper and wire. Her dark hair is loose and shining. Her skin glows in the moonlight.

"Jesus . . ." I say.

"No." Zoe gives me a small smile. "Just one of his friends."

Chay stands next to her, dressed like the devil in a tight red jumpsuit.

Ozzy gives an appreciative whistle.

"Tell me who I have to kill to go to that version of hell," he says, looking her up and down.

Chay grins. "If you take up the whole sidewalk with your friends and walk real slow so I can't get by . . . eternal torment. If you mix the guacamole too much so it's mushy . . . pitchfork, right up your ass."

"Go on . . ." Ozzy says, looking titillated.

Cat trails behind the older girls, wearing an oversized black pullover and little black cat ears, with whiskers drawn on her face. It's the obvious choice of costume for her, but it's also fucking adorable. She really does look like a fluffy kitten, especially with her black curls wild around her face.

"You look great," I tell Cat. She looks alarmed that I noticed her.

Chay holds out a wad of cash. I wave it away.

"No charge," I say.

"You sure?" Chay asks.

"I never charge friends."

"What the hell!" Leo calls back over his shoulder, still within earshot of this rank hypocrisy.

"Except him," I tell Chay. "He can afford it."

I can feel Zoe watching me. My face feels strangely warm.

"Go on," I say to the girls. "Have a ball."

Chay and Cat head inside, but Zoe pauses as she passes me.

"Where's your costume?" she asks.

I turn so she can see the back of my jersey. "Number 23," I say. "I'm Jordan."

"I thought Leo was the baller," Zoe says.

"Oh yeah, he's way better than me," I admit. "I just wanted to wear the shoes. Air 7s—same ones Jordan wore on the Dream Team at the '92 Olympics."

Zoe admires my sneakers, something that usually would make me supremely happy, but right now I'm not thinking about my shoes at all. I'm looking at her face. I've never seen such smooth, clear skin. It makes me think of the flawless skin all over the rest of her body. I shove that thought away roughly. It's sleazy, something that Rocco himself would dwell on—a view stolen from Zoe without her consent.

"I like vintage," Zoe says.

"Oh yeah?"

"Yes. Especially things from old TV shows and movies. Like if I was ever going to buy a gown for myself, I'd love to get one like Marilyn wore in Gentlemen Prefer Blondes. Do you know the one I mean?"

A crowd of students is trying to get through the door behind us. I'm blocking their way. But I want to talk to Zoe, so I say to Ozzy, "You got this?" and Ozzy says, "Yeah, go on, mate."

"Let me get you a drink," I say to Zoe, as an excuse to keep her right by me.

I lead her over to the punch bowl. "It's good, I promise. Not some mixed-up toilet bowl shit—quality liquor."

"I trust you," she says, smiling up at me.

Those words send a thrill through my whole body.

I pour her a cup of punch, careful not to splash a single drop on her snow-white gown.

"Tell me about the Marilyn dress," I say.

"It was hot pink. Perfectly-fitted. With long, matching gloves. I don't even look good in pink, but the color was so vivid and so powerful . . . you don't think of pink being powerful, but it can be. On the right person."

"I don't believe you," I say.

"What do you mean?"

"I don't believe you don't look good in pink."

Zoe's cheeks flush a shade lighter than her lips, and I say, "See —you're pink right now, and you look better than ever."

Zoe fixes me with those light-green eyes, that always seem to have a storm behind them.

"Are you flirting with me, Miles?" she asks.

I consider denying it. But Zoe is so honest, it demands the same from me.

"Yes," I say simply. "I definitely am."

"Do you think that's a good idea?"

"No. And I don't give a fuck. I'm going to keep doing it, unless you tell me to stop."

I watch her face closely, to see her reaction to this.

She considers.

"I don't want you to stop," she says.

"Good. 'Cause I wasn't going to."

She laughs.

I don't know if I ever heard Zoe laugh before this year. It's a captivating sound, low and intimate, meant only for me.

"I knew you were trouble," she says.

"You have no idea," I tell her.

9

CAT

My first party at Kingmakers is my first party anywhere—not counting the tedious events we had to attend with my father and Daniela from time to time.

I always felt like a show pony, dressed up by Daniela and trotted out for some specific purpose. Usually to dance with some awful business associate of my father's, who would invariably tell me that I reminded him of his daughter before trying to slide his hand down from my waist to my ass.

This was my first time getting dressed with friends, laughing and joking the whole time, after being offered a little pre-party drink from Chay, which I accepted because I was fascinated by the pear bobbing around inside, whole and intact, like a ship in a bottle.

"How on earth did they get it in there?" I asked Chay. "It's a real pear, isn't it?"

"Yes." She nodded. "They attach the empty glass bottle to a branch while the pear is tiny and growing. It grows to maturity inside the bottle, then they cut the fruit stem and fill the bottle with liquor. It's very popular in Germany, very common."

She was doing Zoe's makeup while she explained the drink to me, having already finished her own lacquered red lips and smoky swirls of dark liner all around her eyes.

I was supposed to be finishing my cat costume, but the pear brandy was already having an effect on me, and I wasn't sure I'd be able to draw my whiskers on straight.

"Hold on," Chay said to Zoe. "I'm going to get my other eyeshadow palette."

She hurried over to the wardrobe to rummage around. I took the opportunity to ask Zoe, "Are you sure it's alright for us to go to this? Papa's already furious about my grades . . ."

He wrote me a scathing letter after our cousin Martin ratted me out for my dismal performance in every practical exam I've had so far. If ink were acid, the words would have burned right through the page.

"Fuck him," Zoe said coldly. "And fuck his letters."

Dressed as an angel, her face sparkling with the glitter and her paper wings floating behind her, Zoe's crudity made me laugh.

Zoe laughed, too. She took my hand and squeezed it, saying, "We're going to the party, and we're going to have a perfect night. Who knows how many we'll get, but we're taking this one."

"You look gorgeous," I told her.

I made the wings for her. I'd barely had any time to do anything artistic since coming to Kingmakers, and I missed that worse than I missed anything from home. I cut the feathers using a scalpel stolen from the Chemistry lab.

That was the first time I'd stolen anything, too. Kingmakers is full of firsts for me. My heart was racing so bad I thought I'd puke, but I slipped the scalpel up my sleeve all the same, hands sweating, thinking the professor was going to catch me even as I hurried to my next class.

I stayed up late to work on the wings while Rakel slept in the bed opposite, listening to her godawful metal music on her headphones. I could hear it seeping out, relentless drums and guitars and screaming. I don't know how she sleeps with that racket assaulting her eardrums, when I can hardly stand the little bit I can hear, even with a pillow over my head.

I cut each feather individually. The meticulous process was incredibly soothing, better than yoga or meditation. Each feather became its own universe, perfect and precise, and totally under my control. Unlike everything else that happens at school.

I will say, I've been enjoying my computer classes at least. The only permitted laptops on campus are the ones in the computer lab. Placing my fingers on the keyboard feels almost as much like coming home as working on those paper feathers. Even though I've never done anything like Bitcoin transactions, digital security, or DDOS attacks, I'm picking it up much quicker than anything I've learned in my other classes.

So I've been surviving alright at Kingmakers.

It's Zoe I'm worried about.

She told me what happened the day she was missing from the dining hall. She said Rocco tried to assault her and Miles Griffin helped save her.

Miles is throwing the party tonight, which makes me feel a little better about attending. But also a little worse, because I know that will only make Rocco angrier.

I told Zoe what Claire Turgenev shared with me, what Rocco did at his former school.

Zoe didn't seem surprised.

"I know what he is," she said. "There's nothing I can do about it."

"Why?" I said. "Why can't we at least try?"

"Look around you," she said to me. "Look at this place. It's seven hundred years old. How many students have come through here? Show me the ones who betrayed their families, who walked away and lived a happy life. Show me them. Show me the people who stood up to all of this and won."

Still, even though Zoe told me it was hopeless, I do see a new level of rebelliousness in her. I could tell she was excited as she dressed for the party, and even more excited as we crossed the dark, open grounds toward the distant stables.

The party was already in full swing, students lined up outside the doors to pay their cover charge.

I invited Rakel. Or, I should say, I told her about the party in one of the rare intervals where she wasn't wearing head-phones and she seemed like she might not stab me for daring to speak to her.

"Who's throwing it?" she said.

"Miles Griffin."

There was no need to explain any further. Everyone on campus knows Miles.

"I might go," Rakel said, as if conferring some huge favor on me.

I left it at that, not even brave enough to throw in a, "See you there."

Rakel and I have not become closer friends in the nearly two months we've been sharing a room. The center of our dorm room is an invisible Berlin Wall that I'm not allowed to cross, and we never walk together, even when we're leaving the Undercroft to go to the same class at the same time.

The closest she's ever been to friendly was in our last Security Systems class, when I managed to successfully decode the mystery USB stick handed out by Professor Gillespie. He gave us no instructions whatsoever. I managed to image the USB stick and start forensicating it. It was TAILS, with LUKS encrypted partition. The professor forbade us from using cloud computing or any external system, so I had to brute force the password.

I was first to finish, in what Professor Gillespie informed us was record time.

Rakel leaned back in her chair to get a better look at my computer screen.

"How'd you figure that out?" she demanded.

"I ran hashcat against the LUKS password," I said, showing her all the steps I took.

"How'd you know to do that? The professor never said."

"Just trying different things," I said. "I think . . . sometimes when you know you don't know anything, you can find a solution somebody else might overlook. Trying even the ideas that seem stupid."

On the next challenge, Rakel was quickest to finish.

"Nice!" I said, checking her solution in return. "That was smart."

For a moment, it looked like she was going to smile back at me. She didn't, but she wasn't scowling, either.

I don't see Rakel as Zoe, Chay, and I join the line outside the stables. I do spot a tall boy with white-blond hair walking from the library toward the Armory. He pauses, examining the students bunched together outside the doors in our makeshift costumes. Music thuds out through the open doors, as well as shafts of dim red light and artificial smoke.

The red light strikes the boy's handsome face, illuminating the left side while the right remains shadowed. As he stands watching, his look of irritation turns to an expression of pure fury. He stuffs his hands in his pockets and stalks past, his body so tense that all the muscle on his arms twitches.

"Who was that?" I whisper to Zoe.

"Who?" she says. She's not looking in the same direction as me, all her attention fixed just inside the doors of the old stables.

"That boy over there—the blond one."

I point, but it's too late. He disappeared into the darkness.

"I don't know," Zoe says, sounding distracted.

We're next to go inside. I see Leo and Anna already waiting for us, with Hedeon Gray a few feet beyond them. Miles and Ozzy are manning the door.

Miles greets us warmly, refusing to let us pay our entry fee.

"I told him not to charge you," Ozzy says, winking at Chay. "Don't let him take credit for that. Or for this, either."

He slips Chay a little baggie that she immediately tucks in her pocket.

"Ozzy!" she says. "Are you trying to be charming?"

"Depends." He grins. "Is it working?"

Ozzy isn't good-looking, not compared to Miles, Leo, or Ares, but he does have a brilliant smile with dimples on both sides. It takes over his whole face and makes you think that he might be handsome after all.

Chay seems to think the same as she gives Ozzy a quick kiss on the cheek. Unfortunately, the effect only lasts until she lays eyes on Ares, leaned up against one of the ancient wooden support pillars next to Hedeon.

Ares isn't as flashy as Leo or Miles. He dresses in the plainest, cheapest clothes, and his dark, shaggy hair always looks like it needs cutting. He's reserved and unassuming. But he has a kind of quiet strength that's powerful all the same. I often find myself looking at him, without any particular reason. When he does speak, his voice is deep and resonate. The kind of voice that vibrates in your bones.

Chay is drawn to him like a butterfly to a flower. I can't tell if Ares likes her in return. He strikes me as someone who keeps very tight control over his emotions at all times.

He reminds me of Zoe, actually. Thoughtful. Responsible. Never acting on impulse.

I guess that's why I feel like I understand him, even though we've barely spoken.

You can learn a lot about people just by watching.

I'm not disinterested just because I'm shy. I actually like being surrounded by people, when no one is bothering me. I like seeing the little flashes that pass between people, the hidden indicators of who they are and what they're thinking and how they feel about each other.

I love to see how Leo always checks to see Anna's reaction whenever he's said something funny or outrageous. I like how

Anna touches him continually, her hand alighting briefly on his arm or his thigh, her back leaning up against his chest, as if to reassure herself that he's still there.

I love how Chay is always so conscious that everyone be included in the group. She pulls me into the center of our cluster of friends, dancing with me until she's sure I feel comfortable, then switching over to Hedeon, who at first shakes his head in a sullen sort of way, but then relents and even cracks a smile when Chay tries to twirl him around.

I like how Ares is thoughtful, checking to see if anyone wants a drink before getting one for himself.

I love how beautiful my sister looks, even next to girls as gorgeous as Anna and Chay. My sister's good qualities shine out of her face: her intelligence, her honesty, her determination to do what she feels is right, even when it's difficult, even if it's impossible.

I've never had a circle of friends like this, who make me feel safe and accepted. I know they're Zoe's friends really, but they've welcomed me with open arms, as if I'm just as important and interesting as her, even though I'm not.

Kingmakers still terrifies me. I'm covered in bruises and cuts, from a variety of classes.

Yet . . . I don't hate it here. I could even imagine a time that I might like it. Maybe on my graduation day, if I somehow learn how to fight between now and then, and I stop embarrassing myself every other day. Stranger things have happened.

Speaking of which, I spot Rakel on the opposite side of the stables. She isn't wearing a costume, though she looks like she might be because she's dressed in her normal civilian clothes, which include enough chains and safety pins to set off a whole airport's worth of metal detectors.

I hold up the drink Ares brought me in a kind of cheers.

To my utter shock, Rakel raises her drink in return.

It's not much, but compared to the first day of school, it feels like I've come a long way.

10

ZOE

Hold up," Miles says.

He's looking at the doorway where Dax Volker and Jasper Webb are trying to enter.

"Let me get rid of the party crashers," he tells me. "Go on with Chay and Anna if you like—I'll find you in a bit."

It's difficult to locate my friends in the tightly-packed press of students, with only dim red lights illuminating my way. Miles' parties are always busier and better-organized than the random get-togethers thrown by other students. I'm continually surprised what he manages to pull off under all the restrictions of the island—he's so resourceful.

The professors are well aware that we throw parties in the stables, and they don't seem to care as long as the mayhem doesn't spill out into other areas of campus.

Even in the chilliest parts of winter, it's plenty warm in here, especially once everyone starts dancing. The red lights throw up wild, demonic shadows from the gyrating bodies and the piles of old furniture heaped up on the far end of the space.

I know Anna and Chay will be dancing, because it's their favorite thing to do. I actually love dancing too, though I haven't had as many opportunities to do it other than at stuffy parties with my father and Daniela, or in my own bedroom.

I find the two girls with Cat between them, and Leo, Ares, Hedeon, and Matteo Ragusa completing the circle.

I wish I were as graceful as Anna, or as uninhibited as Chay. I feel a little stiff at first, until Miles' punch takes hold and I start to relax. The music is pounding, the weight of all our bodies shaking the wide wooden floorboards.

Drugs — UPSAHL
Spotify → geni.us/rebel-spotify
Apple Music → geni.us/rebel-apple

After a minute, Ozzy joins us.

"Who's covering the door?" Anna asks, looking sharply toward the entrance.

"Miles is paying Kasper Markaj to do it," Ozzy says. "Don't worry, no assholes tonight. Or at least, none we don't like."

Ozzy is trying to edge his way over to Chay, mindful of his injured arm, but Chay is dancing as close to Ares as possible, so she's not paying any attention to him.

Hedeon seems to have decided that, in the shortage of girls, he might as well dance with Cat. Cat is confused by this at first, and keeps trying to edge away from him, so Hedeon grabs her hands and twirls her around. I have to stifle a laugh at the terrified look on Cat's face. Hedeon may be grumpy, but he's not a bad dancer. He's surprisingly patient as Cat steps on his foot a couple of times before getting into the swing of it.

Anna's definitely the best dancer of any of us. She slips in and out of Leo's arms, sometimes dancing with him, sometimes with Chay and me. Chay had a couple of shots before we came down, so she's plenty loose, grinding up on Matteo until his face is redder than her costume, then turning her attention back to Ares.

Ares lets Chay sidle up against his broad chest, but when she tries to put his hands on her hips, he only holds them there a minute before letting go again. Disappointed, Chay finally gives Ozzy the up-close-and-personal attention he's been craving.

Ares is a mystery to me. He never flirts, which I suppose isn't surprising since he's quiet and reserved. But I've barely seen him look at a girl, even one as beautiful and as obviously interested as Chay.

I don't get the feeling he's gay. Of course, that's just a guess—it's not always easy to tell.

I think the real issue is that he knows no relationship at King-makers would go anywhere, long-term. Especially if Ares plans to go back to Syros. The mafia daughters at our school are expected to make the most advantageous matches possible—which doesn't include the eldest son of a family that lost all its former glory.

It's unfortunate, but true. Ares is a realist, and so am I.

That doesn't stop me feeling a thrill of pleasure when Miles joins us.

"Hey," he growls in my ear, pushing his shock of dark curls back out of his eyes with his palm. "Hope you didn't tire yourself out already."

I can feel his warm breath on my bare shoulder, and the heat radiating out of his body. Pressed together on the dance floor, we're closer than we've been since he carried me to the infirmary.

"No." I shake my head. "I'm not tired at all."

"Good," Miles says, his white teeth flashing in his tanned face. "Let's get to dancing, then."

He pulls a little remote out of his pocket and clicks it to change the song. Instantly the speakers switch to something slower and sexier, with a playful, insistent beat.

Just A Lil Bit — 50 Cent
Spotify → geni.us/rebel-spotify
Apple Music → geni.us/rebel-apple

Miles pulls me into his arms, putting my hands around his neck and his large, warm hands on my hips. He easily pulls me into his rhythm, which is effortless and outrageously smooth.

I've never seen anyone move to music like Miles can. His body flows like he's liquid under his clothes. He's playful and creative, making me laugh as he mixes silly little flourishes into dancing that is, over all, extremely fucking sexy.

Despite Miles booting out anybody connected to Rocco, there's still plenty of students here who could rat me out for dancing with him. Rocco is sure to hear about it, and so is my father.

But right now, in the center of all my friends, I feel a sense of security I've never felt before. I'm free to laugh and dance and enjoy the music, free like I've never been before in my life. Cat is right next to me, giggling as Hedeon spins her around and dips her low, almost knocking over Chay and Ozzy, who are dancing back-to-back so Chay doesn't rub against his injured arm.

Miles flips through song after song, each one better than the one before. Ares gets us all another round of punch. We're hot and sweaty and tipsy, but none of us wants to stop.

"What's your favorite kind of music?" Miles asks me.

"Oh, I don't know," I say. "I like all of this."

"You like Latin dancing?"

"Sure. I mean, I learned it growing up."

He swaps the song to "Señorita," which isn't strictly speaking a Latin song, but as he pulls me into an effortless salsa, I can't help laughing.

"Why are you better at this than I am?" I demand.

"I wouldn't say that," Miles growls, his face very close to mine, my fingers wrapped up in his, our bodies pressed tight together. "I'd say nobody on this dance floor looks better than you."

Señorita — Shawn Mendes
Spotify → geni.us/rebel-spotify
Apple Music → geni.us/rebel-apple

I don't know if I was a good dancer before today, but Miles is bringing out the best in me. It's so easy to match his rhythm, to follow his lead. The sensuality of his body seems to be drawing out the same thing in mine, so our feet move perfectly together, our hips, our thighs, every part of us entwined. I've never felt anything like this. I'm melting into him, dancing without thought or effort, just pure pleasure.

We dance for hours. I never get tired of it. I never want it to stop.

Anna and Leo, Chay and Ozzy, Hedeon and Cat, and poor Matteo all on his own, they come and go around us as they refresh their drinks or take a break to sit and chat on the dusty velvet couch in the corner.

Only Miles and I stay exactly where we are, completely wrapped up in each other, tireless and endlessly driven to keep dancing so this moment won't end.

The couch fills up with half-drunk students. Cat tries to perch on a stack of filing boxes instead. The boxes tip over and she tumbles onto the floor, papers spilling everywhere.

I run over to help her up.

"I'm fine," Cat says, face as scarlet as the punch. "You keep dancing. I'm not hurt, just clumsy."

I help her scoop the papers back into the boxes, though it hardly matters. Everything on that side of the stable is trash, as far as I can see. Stored and forgotten, with no chance of being recovered again.

When we've cleaned up the mess, Cat says, "I'm pretty tired. I think I'm gonna head back to the Undercroft."

"I'll take you," I say.

"I can go alone." Cat shakes her head. Her whiskers have smeared across her face so she looks more like a chimney sweep than a kitten, but still completely adorable.

"No, I'm going with you. It's not safe to be alone in the dark," I say firmly.

I know Cat is making her own way at Kingmakers as best she can, but it's late at night, and Rocco and his friends might be lurking around, pissed about being banned from the party.

"I'll take her," Hedeon says unexpectedly. "I'm gonna head to bed, too."

"Are you sure?" I ask. Hedeon's not one to offer a favor, generally speaking.

"Yes, I'm sure," Hedeon says irritably. "I wouldn't have said it otherwise."

I look to Cat to see if she's comfortable with this.

"Alright, thank you," she says to Hedeon.

Anna and Leo are still dancing, though Anna is tipsy enough that it looks more like swaying, with Leo half holding her up. Ozzy and Chay have disappeared. Matteo passed out on the dusty green sofa.

Now that I've been pulled back to reality, I'm realizing I should probably go to bed myself, before my inhibitions sink any lower.

"I think I'll head out, too," I say to Miles.

"I'll walk you," he replies, not trying to argue with me.

We leave alongside Hedeon and Cat, the four of us sticking together until we reach the junction point where Cat needs to head south toward the Undercroft, and I go north to the Solar.

The night air is crisp and windless. Only a few lights shine out from the windows of Kingmakers, allowing the blanket of stars overhead to glitter dense and brilliant. Hedeon looks up into the sky moodily, ignoring Cat now that they're not dancing anymore.

Cat is so exhausted she can barely walk straight. Her classes are hard on her. She's not used to this level of activity every day. Besides Combat, Stealth, and Environmental Adaptation, which can all be extremely physical, the conditioning classes require us to go for long cross-country runs down in the River Bottoms, as well as grueling workouts in the gym. Even

Marksmanship classes are strenuous—my hands and arms ache after a long session of shooting.

I give Cat a quick hug as we part ways, saying, "Sleep in tomorrow if you can."

She nods sleepily.

I watch her and Hedeon walk away, ensuring that Hedeon stays right by her.

Then it's just me and Miles, alone on the dark, empty campus.

Somehow this feels even more intimate than dancing pressed tight together.

I'm shy, all of a sudden.

Miles breaks the silence between us.

"Did you make those?" He nods toward my paper wings, composed of hundreds of individually-cut feathers, each with its own unique design, like a snowflake.

"Not a chance," I say. "That was all Cat. She's so artistic. She was supposed to go to art school this year, before I fucked it up."

"What do you mean?"

I tell him about the engagement party and Rocco's surprise visit to my house.

We're walking up toward the Solar, slowly because neither of us is in a hurry. The thick sod muffles our footsteps.

"That's not your fault," Miles says, frowning.

"It is, though. When I disobey my father, he always takes it out on Cat. I knew that beforehand. When I rebel, she suffers."

Remembering that immutable fact makes me realize that I'm making the same mistake all over again. I spent the night at the party, dancing and drinking with Miles, heedless of the consequences that might follow.

Reading my thoughts, Miles takes my hand. His hand is large and strong, and immensely warm.

"Your cousins weren't here tonight," he says. "None of Rocco's friends, either."

"They'll still hear. Everybody talks."

Miles doesn't bother to deny that—he knows it's true.

"Tell me about your marriage contract," he says.

"I haven't even read it," I admit. "I wasn't part of the negotiations."

"Do you know what your father's getting out of the deal? What's in it for Rocco's family?"

I explain it to him as best I understand, starting with the wars amongst the Galician clans, and ending with everything I know about my father's business, and the Princes'.

Miles takes it all in, occasionally asking clarifying questions. This is something I've noticed about Miles—he's an information-gatherer. He's good at asking just the right questions to figure out what's really going on.

When I'm done talking, he stays quiet a while, considering.

"There's a personal element on Rocco's side, isn't there?" he asks me.

"Do you mean, is he in love with me?" I say. "I wouldn't call it love."

"He's fixated," Miles says.

"Yes. We've been betrothed since I was twelve. He's been planning what he'll do with me once we're married for eight years now. He's more than fixated—he's obsessed."

Miles' expression is serious as he looks at me. In the infirmary, I realized that Miles has eyes of a color I've never seen before —a pure, clear gray. Under the starlight they shine almost silver, much lighter than his deeply-tanned skin.

"Tell me more about your Marilyn obsession," he says, abruptly changing the subject.

I assume he doesn't want to talk about Rocco anymore, because that topic is depressing. Honestly, I feel the same.

"I love old movies and TV shows," I say. "I always have. I used to watch them at my Abuelita's house—we didn't have television at home. My stepmother is very strict. My Lita was not strict. She'd give us all the treats and snuggles and screen-time we wanted, every time we came to visit. She'd make *leche frita*, and we'd watch *White Christmas, Seven Brides for Seven Brothers, Singin' in the Rain, Some Like It Hot, West Side Story* . . . all the Alfred Hitchcock films, those were her favorite. I think she watched them when she was young to learn English, and never stopped."

"I used to watch *Peaky Blinders* with my Grandma Imogen," Miles says. "She said it wasn't accurate—the Peaky Blinders gang was never that organized. But she liked it all the same, just to hear the Irish accents and see the streets she knew."

"It was opposite for Lita—she wanted to see the places she was never going to visit, like New York or Oklahoma."

"She always stayed in Spain?" Miles asks.

"Yes. We'd go see her every week, Cat and me. Then my Abuelito died, and my father didn't have to send us over there anymore. They were my mother's parents. As long as Tito was alive, he could pressure my father into letting us visit. Once he was gone. . .there was nothing Lita could do." I swallow hard.

"She died last year. I didn't see her for the last four years she was alive."

"I'm sorry," Miles says. I can hear in his voice that he means it.

We've reached the Solar. The wind picks up, rustling the paper feathers of my angel wings.

"I shouldn't have kept you out here so long," Miles says, looking at my bare arms. "You must be cold."

I should be cold, going from the heat of the crowded stables to the crisp, open air. But I'm not. I'm never cold around Miles—my heart is always beating too hard, blood thundering through my veins.

"Your cut is almost healed," Miles says, gently touching the place next to my eye where Rocco dug his knife.

When Miles touches me, it ignites every nerve beneath his fingertips. That one part of my body becomes more sensitive than every other inch of skin combined.

I don't think he means to kiss me.

But one hand on my face becomes two, and then he pulls me toward him, our lips coming together in one smooth movement. Miles' lips are full and warm, firm and yet soft against mine. The kiss is gentle at first, and then it becomes deeper, his tongue sliding between my lips, caressing mine.

The taste of his mouth turns attraction into lust. My heart races so hard that it feels like one, continuous throb. I've thrown myself into his arms. We're clinging to each other, kissing with a kind of desperation that feels wild and reckless and utterly addictive.

Kissing Miles is like dancing with him. We're perfectly in sync. Time melts away. I can't get enough of it, I can't seem to stop. The wind buffets my paper wings, making a sound like a thousand whispers, lifting me slightly like I might fly away.

Slowly, I realize that we're out in the open at the base of the Solar. Even in the darkness, anyone looking out their window might spot me in my white gown.

I break away from Miles.

"I'm sorry," I say. "I shouldn't have done that."

It was Miles who kissed me, but I shouldn't have let him. It's not only dangerous for *me* to break my contract with Rocco. If anything, it's even more dangerous for Miles. The Princes could seek retribution.

"I did it," Miles says, looking at me intently. "And I'm not sorry."

"We can't," I say to him.

We both know we can't, and yet I allowed myself to pretend otherwise. I enjoyed the fantasy that I could talk to a boy I liked, flirt with him, dance with him. I let myself experience the feeling of actually falling for someone, reveling in that sense of mutual attraction. I had never felt it before. It was intoxicating.

But now I've crossed the line. And it felt too good. So good that I'm terrified of what I'll end up doing if I don't stop now.

"I can't see you anymore," I say to Miles.

He's looking at me, face impassive, not answering.

I can't tell what he's thinking. I can't read Miles as well as he reads me.

"You're going to see me tomorrow," he says.

"I'm not."

"You will," he says. His gray eyes are brighter than ever, fixed on mine with an intensity I've never seen in Miles before. He acts like he doesn't care about anything. But I always knew that couldn't be true, because he's the furthest thing from lazy. He's always hustling, always working an angle.

I'm finally seeing what it looks like when Miles is chasing something he wants.

"I can't kiss you anymore," I say. "And I can't be alone with you."

"I'm not going to argue with you, Zoe," Miles says, his eyes burning into mine. "I'm also not going to stop."

Before I can say another word, he turns and strides away from me, across the dark grounds.

I'm staring after him, open-mouthed, my lips still throbbing where he kissed me.

11

MILES

I wake up to Ozzy bursting into our room, his mohawk wildly disheveled and his clothes even worse, the sling missing off his arm and the gauze wrap filthy.

He's grinning like a madman, practically dancing in place as he shucks off his grass-stained shirt, revealing the stocky, muscular frame beneath, and even more of his awful amateur tattoos.

"Where have you been?" I ask, already suspecting the answer.

"With Chay," Ozzy says, beaming with joy.

"How was it?"

"Fucking spectacular. Everything I dreamed of and more."

"Even with your arm all fucked up?"

"Mate, I wasn't in charge of that ride. She's insatiable. All I could do is lay back and try to think about binary code so I didn't nut in two seconds."

"So how long did you last, then?" I tease him. "Four seconds?"

"First time—maybe a minute. Second time round, I was much more successful. By the third time—"

"Alright," I say, "I get the picture. I'm very happy for you."

"Now's the hard part, though," Ozzy says.

"What do you mean?"

"She's gonna try to fuck and chuck me, like she always does. But she's not gonna get rid of me so easy. I may not have stamina in the sack, but when it comes to chasing Chay . . . I'm fuckin' Lance Armstrong."

"Good luck with that," I say, shaking my head at him.

"You think you've got a better chance?"

"With what?"

"The forbidden princess."

I consider lying to Ozzy, telling him I'm not going to pursue Zoe. But it's pointless. He's my best friend. He knew I liked her from the moment she first caught my eye. And right from that moment he started telling me what a terrible idea it was to kick that particular hornet's nest.

"I might," I say.

"You're gonna get yourself killed."

"A lot of people tell me that. It hasn't happened yet."

"Only takes one time." Ozzy grins.

"That arm feeling better?" I ask him, to change the subject.

"Yeah it is," he says. "That's the healing power of Chay."

I roll my eyes. "I bet."

I head to the showers before I have to hear more about Chay's magical pussy powers.

There's a communal bathroom on each floor of the Octagon Tower. Four floors in total, with all the male Junior Heirs residing on my floor, including Rocco Prince.

So it's not totally unsurprising when Rocco interrupts my nice hot shower.

I don't bother to cover up. I've got nothing to be ashamed of.

Rocco stands there in his robe, looking me over. There's something inhuman in the way he cocks his head, his eyes flicking around like some kind of raptor—intelligent, but without the normal range of emotion.

It takes a lot to get under my skin. Still, even I feel a twinge of discomfort, standing vulnerable and naked under the water.

I won't let Rocco see me squirm, though. Not for a second.

"You keep staring and I'm gonna charge you for an Only Fans membership," I say.

"Just assessing the competition," Rocco says. "Wondering what was so alluring to my fiancée last night."

"I don't know what you're talking about," I lie.

I'd like to rub it in Rocco's face that I was dancing with Zoe all night, but my desire to protect her is stronger.

"Don't pretend to be stupid," Rocco says. "And certainly don't pretend that I am."

He strips off his robe, revealing his body—lean, pale, reasonably fit. There's nothing deformed about him. Yet I feel a wave of revulsion, like I turned over a rock and found him underneath.

"Are you thinking you could beat me in a fight?" Rocco says, turning on his showerhead. "Maybe you could. You're taller, heavier. But I think you lack a certain viciousness. The willingness to go past the line. Past what you might consider dishonorable, immoral, even disgusting. I have no line, Miles. None at all. There's nothing I won't do."

He stands under the shower spray, the water flattening his dark hair so it plasters against his skull, his waxy flesh making him look more than ever like some sort of white plastic automaton.

"Do you think you're the first person who's tried to threaten me?" I say.

"No," Rocco replies. "You're a hustler, right Miles? A deal-maker? You think you can manipulate people. Make them do what you want. That's how you feel a sense of power—not by violence, but by bending men to your will."

Despite the hot shower, I feel a chilling cold in my guts.

"You like the idea of taking Zoe from me because you like flouting authority. The school, her parents, my parents, our marriage contract. You like thumbing your nose at all of it. And deep down, you have a little of that hero complex that afflicts your cousin Leo so heavily. You want to save Zoe because you pity her."

"I don't pity her," I growl. "I *respect* her."

"Respect?" Rocco says mockingly.

That's a foreign concept to him. I doubt he respects his own friends or even his family. He admires only himself.

"Yes. I respect her," I say. "You have no idea. You're like a toddler wiping your shit on the Mona Lisa. You couldn't be more ignorant to what she's worth."

"You're wrong there," Rocco says quietly, his gleaming eyes fixed on me. "I see Zoe's qualities. If she was weak, if she was willing, then there wouldn't be any fun in it. It's the challenge of breaking her. The joy of deconstructing her, piece by piece, then rebuilding her the way I want her to be. Reforming her like melted glass. Of course there's always a chance the glass will shatter . . . but if not, I'll make her exactly the way I want her."

My guts are churning. I want to rip his fucking throat out, show him how it feels to be torn to pieces like he imagines doing to Zoe. I've met men who were greedy, violent, callous. But I've never met someone this destructive. Rocco has the soul of an arsonist. If he has any soul at all.

In that moment, I make a decision.

I'm going to save Zoe from Rocco. I don't know how, but I'm going to do it. Not to be a hero. I'm gonna do it because this is fucking wrong, and it can't happen. She can never belong to him.

Rocco sees the spark of decision in my face. He's perceptive, I'll give him that.

It angers him.

"I've never failed to get what I want, Miles," he hisses. "I'm not like the other men you've faced. I don't eat. I don't sleep. I don't give up. I can't be threatened. I can't be bargained with. None of your tricks will work on me."

I turn the water off with a sharp twist, shaking the droplets out of my hair. I pick up my towel and wrap it around my waist, slowly and deliberately, refusing to break Rocco's laser stare.

"You talk a lot," I say to him. "You think you're smart, or convincing. I think you're limited. Stunted. Pathetic, quite honestly. You don't even know what you don't know."

Patches of color come into his face, splotchy and random.

Rocco can read people, but so can I.

I know that what he wants more than anything is to be feared. He wants to seem formidable. He thinks he's smarter and stronger than everybody else, purely because he isn't bound by the usual rules of fairness or compassion.

Well, I don't give a fuck about rules, either.

If Rocco thinks I won't play dirty, he's got another thing coming.

I face him without a trace of fear, cutting off that unholy energy on which he feeds.

"You think you figured me out, because what? I like to make deals to get what I want?" I walk toward him with rapid strides, closing the gap between us in steps. "You think I'm playing around, because that's what I allow you to think. What you need to understand is that if I decide that you're going to lose, you might as well write it on the fuckin' stone tablets. If I turn my wrath toward you, I will not stop raining down hellfire until you and everyone who knows you is done. I will make deals that will ruin your life and any potential life you could have had. Do you think you're the only one here who will do something psychopathic? I'll rip your throat out with my teeth, and I won't lose a single night of sleep over it. You have no idea the lengths to which I'll go."

Rocco takes one startled step back. It's instinctive, compulsive. He means to stand his ground, but he can't.

I laugh right in his face. Because I know that's the thing that will torment him the most.

"You're a fucking ant to me," I say.

I turn around and walk away, leaving him in the echoing silence of his own helpless rage.

BACK IN MY room I pull on my clothes, charged with a kind of energy I've never felt before.

I was ready to strangle Rocco right then and there. God, I wanted to do it. If he'd said one word to me, I might not have been able to hold back.

And now I have this fire in me, this unresolved aggression.

I have to do something with it, before I explode.

There's still an hour before class starts.

I could go to the dining hall. But I have the strangest sense that what I'm looking for isn't there. In fact, I think I know exactly where to find it.

I run down the stairs of the Octagon Tower, taking them two at a time. I'm sprinting across campus, certain that this compulsion is based on something real. I run all the way to the northwest corner of the grounds and rip open the library door.

A bizarre sense of destiny grips me. Nothing and nobody can stand in my way. Glancing toward Miss Robin's desk, I already know it will be empty, that she'll be down in the archives rummaging through maps.

I search for what I'm really here to find. I hunt through the library, pupils dilated in the dim lamplight, blood thundering in my veins, even my sense of smell heightened so that I catch a whiff of that sweet amber perfume before I even see her.

Zoe is halfway up the spiral ramp, her book bag and a hefty stack of textbooks spread out on an open table. She's standing at the shelves, up on tiptoe, trying to reach a leather-bound tome just out of reach.

It must be laundry day, because she's back in a plaid skirt after a week of trousers. As she stretches up as high as she can to hook the book with her index finger, her skirt pulls up, revealing a long expanse of bare thigh.

It's blood in the water.

The effect on me is all out of proportion.

Fueled by pent-up aggression and a newfound insanity, I grab Zoe from behind, one arm around her waist and one hand clamped over her mouth so her shriek doesn't bring Miss Robin running back upstairs.

I seize her and throw her in the crevice between two bookshelves, pinning her in place with my body wedged in the opening. I kiss her with a ferocity I've never known. All the fury I promised Rocco pours out on Zoe instead.

I ravage her mouth, I wrap my hands up in her silky black hair, I inhale that scent off her neck, which reeled me up here like a bright, shining lure. My hands are all over her face, her body, even reaching up under her skirt to grasp the firm globes of her ass.

When I pull back for a second, I see her wide, startled eyes, and her swollen lips open in confusion.

"Miles, what the hell?" she gasps.

I dive in again, kissing her even harder. After the first shock, I feel Zoe give in. Her arms encircle my neck, her body grinds against mine. Now she's on tiptoe for a different reason: to press every inch of her body against me with all her strength. It's like she's drowning and the only air she can breathe is the air in my lungs.

She's just as wild as I am, maybe even more so. She's letting go, fully and completely, maybe for the first time in her life. She bites the side of my neck with her sharp little teeth, digging her fingernails into my back through the thin material of my shirt.

I caress her breasts through her blouse, those full, perfect tits that I haven't been able to get out of my mind since that day on the wall. They're burned into my retinas like the flare of a lightning strike. Her nipples poke stiffly through her bra and I have to free them. I undo one button, then two, then rip the third one open, yanking down the front of her bra to let her tits spill out in my hands.

The moment I touch her breasts, Zoe goes limp against the wall, like I've taken control of her. She lets out a long, tortured groan that I stifle with my left hand, while cupping and squeezing her breast with my right.

Her flesh is soft and firm, the nipple a delicate tan color, flushing darker with every touch of my fingers. I bend my head to take her breast in my mouth, and she bites down on my hand covering her mouth, moaning helplessly.

Once I start going down, I don't want to stop. I drop to my knees and scoop up her thighs, laying them over my shoulders. Hooking my finger under the elastic of her panties, I yank them to the side and bury my face in her pussy.

Zoe is pinned to the wall, lifted up with her legs over my shoulders. My face presses hard against her. I eat her pussy like I'm starving.

I've never tasted anything so sweet. Zoe is already soaking wet. My tongue slides between her lips, then all the way inside her. I find her clit and I gently suck and swirl my tongue around it, until Zoe makes a sound that's almost like sobbing, and I can tell she's covering her own mouth now, trying to stifle her whimpering with both hands.

It's impossible. Her pussy is warm and throbbing, and she's getting wetter and wetter as I slide my fingers inside her and tease her clit with my tongue. She grinds against my face, her thighs squeezing my ears. She won't be able to hold on for long, I'm going to make her explode like nothing she's felt before.

I lick her clit with the flat of my tongue, over and over again, steady and hard. My whole face is smeared with her wetness and I don't give a fuck, no one has ever smelled or tasted better than this girl, I'd take a fucking bath in her pussy if I could.

I find that sensitive place inside of her and I stroke it with my fingers while I lick and swirl her clit with my tongue. When I find that perfect combination where she starts to clench around my fingers, where she's not in control of her hips or her breathing or anything else, then I hit it again and again and again while she cums all over me.

Now there's no keeping quiet. Zoe's whole body shakes like she's possessed. She lets out a strangled scream through her hands that is the sexiest fucking sound I've heard in my life.

I keep licking her, a little more softly now, until I'm sure that every last pleasure shock has surged through her, and her full weight has collapsed on my shoulders.

Then I set her down gently, standing up to smooth her sweaty hair back from her face. Zoe is crying, actually crying, a double track of tears running down the sides of her face. I feel a stab of guilt like I did something wrong. I wipe my mouth off on my sleeve and take her face in my hands to kiss her, saying, "Are you okay, Zoe?"

"I—I—I've never—never felt anything like that," she stammers, her teeth still chattering together, and shivers running through her body in waves.

"It was good, though?" I ask.

"G—g—good doesn't begin to describe it," she says.

I still have her pinned between the bookshelves—not to trap her now, just because it's quiet and hidden, and I want her to feel safe, I want her to feel like we're the only two people in the universe.

Zoe burrows against my chest, her face pressed against my neck. I keep my arms wrapped around her and I stroke her back with the palm of my hand, trying to calm her down, soothing the shakes away.

I didn't intend to have this effect on her.

"I'm sorry," Zoe's muffled voice vibrates against my chest. "I'm embarrassed. I don't cry, usually."

"I know you don't," I say, tilting her chin up to make her look in my eyes. "Don't be embarrassed. You can be however you want in front of me, Zoe. I like you all the ways. And that was sexy as fuck, by the way. I want to do it again right now."

Zoe laughs weakly. "I don't know if I could survive that."

We stay exactly where we are a few minutes longer, whispering and laughing together. Then, when Zoe can stand again, I help her gather up her books to head down to her first class.

"Oh god," she murmurs. "I'm sure Miss Robin heard that."

"She wasn't around when I came in," I say.

"Still," Zoe says, her face pink. "I wish I had a paper bag to put over my head."

"Come on," I say, taking her hand. "I'll distract her while you sneak out."

I walk a little ahead of Zoe, checking if the coast is clear.

Miss Robin is indeed back at her desk, and by the way she peers over the top of her glasses at me, I'm sure she heard something.

"Miss Robin," I say, "Could you check if anybody put an International Taxation textbook in the lost and found? I think I left mine here."

Miss Robin gives me one, slow blink that is much more cheeky than I'd expect from our timid librarian, then says, "Certainly, Miles." She turns to search the lost and found bin behind her desk.

While she's occupied, Zoe hurries by, quiet in her flat shoes on the thick carpet. I get the feeling Miss Robin can hear Zoe anyway, because she spends an abnormally long time hunched over the box, pretending to search the well-organized and easily-perused pile of objects.

Straightening up empty-handed, Miss Robin checks to see that we're truly alone, then says, "I'm not an idiot, Miles."

I give her half a grin, hands stuffed in my pockets. "Sorry, Miss Robin. I'm sure you remember the recklessness of youth. I don't think you're too far out of it yourself."

She smiles slightly in return, but it only lasts a moment before she says, "I hope you know what you're doing, Miles. This isn't a game for her."

"It isn't for me, either. I promise you that."

She examines me with those dark eyes that contrast so sharply with her vivid red hair. The glasses have slipped down her nose again. She doesn't need them to give me an x-ray stare.

"I believe you," she says at last. "Be careful all the same."

"I will." I nod.

I do intend to be careful.

But I can't promise to be safe.

12

CAT

The first challenge of the *Quartum Bellum* takes place at the end of November. It's a slaughter—possibly the most physically wretched day of my life.

We all knew what was coming, because for weeks beforehand we watched the grounds crew building the obstacle course outside the castle: a Rube Goldberg machine of ropes, pulleys, pillars, walls, trenches, nets, and moving parts. We're meant to be the balls rolling though. But this machine is designed to spit us out, not guide us along the path.

The requirements are simple: a race from start to finish. Every single member of each team has to make it through before their time is counted.

Still stung from the upset the year before, it's clear the upperclassmen plan to play dirty. From the moment Professor

Howell fires his pistol in the air and we all bolt off from the starting line, the Juniors and Seniors have no problem knocking the younger students off walls and kicking us into the mud. I hoped their antipathy would be directed at Leo's Sophomore class, but they seem just as determined to make sure that the Freshmen stay where we belong: in last place.

It doesn't help that it rained the whole week before. The churned-up earth is a sea of mud. Within minutes, sludge coats every one of us from head to foot, until I can hardly tell friend from foe.

August Prieto was voted Freshman Captain. He's a Brazilian Heir from a narco family. He's popular in our year because he's handsome and athletic. I think the Freshmen hoped he'd be our version of Leo Gallo. It quickly becomes clear that August does not possess the requisite leadership skills. He takes the fastest and strongest Freshman through the course with impressive speed, but abandons the rest of us to struggle along on our own, an impossible feat when several of the obstacles can't be completed without help.

By contrast, Leo stays at the back of his group ensuring that no stragglers are left behind. When he sees a bottleneck, he coordinates his strongest teammates to help the weaker ones, so that someone like Matteo Ragusa is bodily lifted and flung over the wall by Silas Gray.

I do my best to keep up. As layer after layer of mud coats my body, I can barely lift my arms and legs. I'm falling behind, and I can see that plenty of students have finished the course while I'm only halfway through.

It's humiliating. I don't know what I'll do if I'm the very last one to finish. I could lose the challenge for the entire Freshmen team.

As I try to crawl across a long, flat stretch of mud with barbed wire strung overhead I get a nasty shock—literally. The wire is charged. Every time it touches my bare skin, a jolt of electricity rips through my body, making my teeth slam together.

This is worse for the bulkier students who can't avoid touching the wires. I'm at least small enough to slip under most of them without making contact. One beefy Freshman is practically in tears as he's jolted again and again and again.

I think that's the worst part until I come to the juggernaut, a maze of swinging pendulums and rolling logs and tilting platforms designed to knock us off into the sea of sludge below. Every time we're punted into the mud, we have to start the section over again. I'm knocked in three, four, five times, until I can barely muster the strength to crawl out of the mire.

Only a dozen students remain behind me. Wiping the mud from my eyes, I swear to myself I'll make it through. I try to stop focusing on one bit of the juggernaut at a time, and instead see the overall pattern of movement. There's a rhythm to it, a regular motion.

Hands raw, my entire body throbbing like one giant bruise, I run and duck and jump and slide, until I make it to the other side. I could cry with relief.

The last wall is twenty feet high. No ropes, no footholds. No way to get over without help.

Anna and Zoe help the last of the Sophomores over.

"Cat!" Anna shouts. "This way!"

She's on top of the wall, reaching down one pale, mud-streaked arm to me.

I run and jump as high as I can, but my fingers fall short far below hers.

"Hold on!" she says.

She climbs back over the wall, dropping down on my side.

"I'm sorry," I say, "I'm not even on your team."

"Who gives a shit," she says. "Get up on my shoulders."

She boosts me up and Zoe helps haul me over.

I run with them all the way to the end.

The Freshmen finish last and are eliminated from the competition. At least it's not my fault—eight others lagged behind me.

The Sophomores come in second place after the Seniors. The Juniors finish third, safe from elimination, a result that seems to annoy Miles and Ozzy since it means they'll have to keep competing in the next round. They don't buy into the ferocious hype around the *Quartum Bellum*, especially not when it involves getting this dirty.

"I'm gonna be picking mud out of my teeth for a week," Miles says bitterly, spitting on the grass.

"I can't believe they made me participate when I'm still a cripple!" Ozzy complains, looking at his poor bandaged arm, two inches thick with mud.

"Isn't mud supposed to be good for your skin?" Chay says, pretending to massage the dirt into her cheeks with her fingertips.

"Good point," Ozzy says. "You want that rubbed anywhere else?"

"I wish you could help me," Chay says, pretending to pout. "But as you said, you're barely functional . . ."

"I think you know that isn't true," Ozzy growls, making a grab for her with his good arm.

Chay laughs and slips his grip, dancing away from him, but not too far.

My sister told me that Chay is still refusing to date Ozzy. On the other hand, she's been disappearing for suspicious amounts of time, coming back to the dorms flushed and messy, refusing to say where she's been.

I have no romantic prospects on the horizon, and I'm certainly not looking for any.

However, I'm pleased that my relationship with my roommate Rakel has progressed all the way to entire conversations.

It all started when I asked to borrow her graphic novel.

This was a bold foray on my part, since up to that point, I was pretty sure that Rakel wouldn't lend me her carbon dioxide, let alone her favorite book.

I'd been reading Benjamin Franklin's autobiography as part of my Leaders, Rulers, and Dictators class when I came upon this quote:

> *Having heard that a rival legislator had in his library a certain very scarce and curious book, I wrote a note to him, expressing my desire of perusing that book, and requesting that he would do me the favor of lending it to me for a few days. He sent it immediately, and I returned it in about a week with another note, expressing strongly my sense of the favor. When we next met in*

the House, he spoke to me (which he had never done before), and with great civility; and he ever after manifested a readiness to serve me on all occasions, so that we became great friends, and our friendship continued to his death.

It seemed paradoxical that asking someone for a favor would make them like you more, but Franklin said, "He that has once done you a kindness will be more ready to do you another, than he whom you yourself have obliged."

I thought old Ben probably knew what he was talking about.

So I asked Rakel to borrow the graphic novel, the one I'd seen her reading our very first day of school and plenty of times after.

She stared at me, her dark eyes sharp and suspicious, her pointed nails drumming irritably on the bed.

Then, to my surprise, she dug the book out of her nightstand and thrust it into my hands.

"Don't crease the pages," she said.

I read through the whole thing that night. It sucked me in instantly. It was about a bunch of superheroes called *The Watchmen*. They weren't really heroes. Actually, most of them were complete assholes. And the villain had a plan that was, if not totally reasonable, at least intended for the greater good.

The next morning, Rakel said, "What did you think?"

We talked about it for over an hour, all the way down to the dining hall where we ate breakfast together for the very first time.

The next day she asked if I wanted to borrow her *Walking Dead* comics.

Talking about graphic novels has turned into talking about movies and music.

I ask Rakel about her death metal, confused how that chaotic sound could actually be enjoyable.

"It's not death metal, it's black metal," she says. "There's a difference. And it's not just music, it's a religion to me. It's about mysticism, mortality and immortality . . . The concerts can be hours long, with candles and incense and ceremonial offerings. We call it the *Ulfsmessa,* the Wolf's Mass."

She plays some of the songs for me. I can't say I enjoy them exactly, but I can see that they have more complexity than I realized. They can be haunting and even moving.

"It all comes from living in the land of endless darkness. And worse than that, the midnight sun," Rakel says. "You can't imagine the insomnia in the summertime. That's why I like it down here." She nods her head toward our arched stone roof and our windowless walls. "It's always night when I want to go to sleep."

Most of all we connect over our hacking classes. Rakel tells me that the whole reason she came to Kingmakers was for explicit instruction in dark web techniques. She's wildly frustrated by our restricted access to technology.

"I hate only being able to practice during class time. I want my own laptop and internet access," she seethes.

I hesitate, not sure if I should tell her that might be possible.

"You know Miles Griffin and Ozzy Duncan?" I say.

"Of course." She nods.

"They might be able to help you with that."

As we're leaving our room, we run into Hedeon Gray.

"What are you doing down here?" I say in surprise.

Hedeon scowls at me. "What the fuck business is it of yours?" he says.

"Just asking." I shrug.

"Well just fuck off instead," Hedeon says, pushing past me on his way to the stairs.

"Charming," Rakel says after he's gone.

"He's always like that," I say, though in truth, that was extra rude even for Hedeon.

Behind us, Saul Turner exits his room, likewise heading for the stairs.

"Hey, girls." He gives us a nod as he passes, slouching along with his hands tucked in his pockets.

"You think Hedeon was in Saul's room?" I ask Rakel in an undertone.

She shrugs. "Could be. Don't know why he was being so pissy about it—no rule against visiting other students."

As we ascend the stairs and come out of the old wine cellar at ground level, I can just see Saul's long, lanky frame heading in the direction of the library. Hedeon has disappeared.

"Come on," Rakel said, pulling her sweater tight around her to try to block the wind. "Let's run to class—it's fucking freezing."

13

ZOE

Miles and I have been seeing each other regularly since that day in the library.

It's difficult because we can't be seen alone together. Even when we're in a group with Leo and Anna, Ares, Hedeon, Chay, Ozzy, and Cat, I have to be careful not to sit by Miles too often, not to stare at him too obviously. And especially not to touch him, no matter how badly I might want to do it.

Sometimes one dark curl will fall down over his eye and the temptation to brush it back off his face is almost irresistible. When his hand is only inches from mine at the dining hall table, I want so badly to feel his warm fingers wrapped around mine. It's a physical ache, a craving stronger than any I've experienced for food or sleep.

Then when we're finally alone and I can give into it, his touch on my skin is far beyond pleasure—it's all the way to necessity. I have to have it. The more I get, the more I want.

We haven't had sex. We both know that would be crossing a serious line. My marriage contract states that I will arrive at my wedding night a virgin, and I don't think the Princes will be lenient on that point. So we dance around it, kissing and touching each other, with Miles often repeating what he did to me in the library, sometimes three or four times over until my whole body thrums like a music note, until even the air against my skin feels as orgasmic as his tongue between my legs.

It's not just physical—the more we sneak away together, the more addicted to his company I become.

I don't know what I imagined dating would be like, having never done it before. I suppose I thought it was sex, or formal conversations over dinner. I never imagined it could be fun and playful, like being with Cat or Chay and Anna, but even better, because the laughter and conversation is strung through with this bright thread of attraction, with a rabid interest in each other that's intoxicating, that makes time melt away like sugar in water.

Sometimes we meet up with Leo and Anna to play music and dance around together like we're forming our own tiny nightclub.

Sometimes I show Miles the project I like to work on in my spare time, the thing that I've never shown anybody before, not even Cat.

It's a story. Only it's written like a play, with dialogue. There's long descriptive passages, too. It's about a girl who sees the future, but can't seem to change the outcome of events, no matter how hard she tries.

I was embarrassed to show him. I only did because he asked me straight out, saying, "What's that thing you're always writing?"

"What do you mean?" I said, honestly not thinking about the story. I wouldn't have thought that Miles had noticed me working on it.

"In that green notebook," Miles said. "I know it isn't school-work, because you're never looking at your textbooks and you always hunch over it like it's secret."

My face went hot, realizing what he was talking about. There was no denying it when I was blushing so hard.

I showed him the story, saying, "It's silly, I just work on it to blow off steam. I don't even know what it is."

Miles read through twenty pages, focused and unsmiling, until I couldn't stand the suspense and I snatched it back out of his hands.

"That's enough," I said. "Like I told you, it's silly."

"It's not silly," Miles said, fixing me with his clear gray eyes. "It's fascinating. You're talented, Zoe."

I shook my head, not able to keep looking at him. "It's nothing. Not even a proper story."

"It's not a story," Miles said. "It's a script."

"Like a movie script?" I laughed. "Something has to become a movie before it can be a script."

"That's backwards." Miles smiled at me.

"I mean . . . there has to be some intention for it to be a movie."

"It *should* be a movie," Miles said. "I'd watch it."

"You're just flattering me."

"No I'm not." He was serious again, taking the notebook back from me, wanting to read more. "I know when something's good and when it's not. I wouldn't lie to you."

His compliment meant more to me than any I'd received before. I believed Miles when he said he wouldn't lie. I believed that he was a good judge.

He's smart. So fucking smart. I hadn't realized it before. I'd only ever seen bits and pieces of Miles, never when he was engaged in his actual interests. I'd only seen the Miles who was bored by his classes, or slacking off in the *Quartum Bellum*. When he actually cares about something, he's got incredible focus.

Now he's turning that focus on me, and it's almost frightening. I've discovered this completely different person who intimidates me.

He tells me all about his side businesses.

His distribution network for contraband is shockingly complex. It's not as easy as bribing the fishermen and the shoremen to smuggle things in on the supply ships. He's got an entire interlocking web of barter, including contacts in Dubrovnik, Tirana, and Bari, who source the items and handle payment to the hundred-odd people involved.

"How do you keep track of all this?" I demand.

"Honestly, I don't know," Miles says. "It's the way my brain works. I can see the system as a whole, with all the little junction points. Each of those points is one person, each with a problem and a solution. When you interconnect them all perfectly, the system feeds itself."

What I find fascinating about Miles' methods is how powerful it makes him. Without threats or violence or an army of followers, Miles is one of the most influential people on the island. Everyone knows him. Everyone owes him favors. Nobody wants to fuck with him because they'd risk access to the things that only he can supply.

Everyone except Rocco, of course.

He's the one person uninterested in what Miles has to offer. What Rocco wants, Miles refuses to give him.

The skirmishes of Rocco, Wade Dyer, Jasper Webb, and Dax Volker, versus Miles and Ozzy, are ongoing and escalating. Hardly a day goes by without some kind of altercation. It frightens me because it feels like it's building to something worse. Eventually these fights will burst the bounds of what can be hidden from the teachers, and then there will be consequences of an entirely different sort.

That's not the only conflict we're dealing with.

Leo and his cousin Dean are still on bad terms.

There was a short armistice at the beginning of the school year. I thought maybe Dean realized he had gone too far trying to drown Leo. I even thought he might feel some sense of gratitude that Leo hadn't told the school authorities.

If Dean felt any obligation in that regard, it melted away as soon as he had to watch Anna and Leo openly dating.

He's fallen into a darker mood by the week, and he's been lashing out at everyone around him. His little clique of friends, including Bram Van Der Berg and Valon Hoxha, have become almost as feared as Rocco and his friends. They're vicious without reason. They bully anyone they dislike. Since that mostly includes anybody friendly to Leo, it's brought Dean and Leo into near-constant conflict.

This afternoon we're in Combat class in the Armory. It's mostly Heirs and Enforcers, but Matteo Ragusa is here too.

The trouble starts when Dean deliberately pairs up with Matteo for sparring, ordering Matteo's friend Paulie White to partner with Bram instead.

"Sorry," Paulie mouths to Matteo, too scared to refuse.

Matteo faces off against Dean, his wrapped fists awkward on the end of his skinny arms. He's hunched and already flinching, knowing that Dean has no intention of taking it easy on him.

Dean stalks him with an easy grace that would be beautiful if it weren't so cruel. It has always struck me how alike Dean and Anna look, both pale and fair with the finesse of a dancer. Dean is what Anna would be if she were born male, stripped of all her kindness and humor.

Anna might be thinking the same thing. She watches Dean uneasily, forgetting that she and I are supposed to be sparring.

Dean toys with Matteo, throwing light feints in his direction, making Matteo stumble over his own feet trying to get away from him. Then, without warning, Dean sweeps Matteo's leg out from under him, grabbing Matteo's arm on the way down and wrenching it viciously up behind his back until Matteo shrieks.

Dean lets go of him, but Matteo is cradling his arm, tears standing out in his eyes. His round face is bright pink, and I can tell he's embarrassed as much as hurt, trying not to succumb to the pain.

It doesn't satisfy Dean in the slightest.

"Get up," he barks at Matteo. "Let's go again."

"No!" Leo snaps, striding across the mats. "Leave him alone."

"Here comes the Doberman to protect his little puppy," Dean sneers. "Do you wipe his ass for him too, Leo?"

"He's here to learn how to fight," Leo says. "Not to be your punching bag."

"He isn't, though," Dean hisses. "He hasn't learned a fucking thing. Look at him. He's just as pathetic as he was on the first day of school."

"He's doing fine," Leo says, grabbing Matteo's good arm and helping him back to his feet.

"We're not finished," Dean snaps at Matteo, eyes narrowed. "We've got two more rounds."

"I'll spar you then," Leo says, glaring right back at him.

"Wish I could," Dean sneers. "But we sparred yesterday. Professor Howell says we need to go through all the partners."

"I'll do it, then," Ares says.

Ares was paired up with Leo and had thus far been watching the confrontation silently. His low voice cuts across Dean in a way that makes everyone fall silent.

Dean smirks, unintimidated by Ares' size.

"Even better," he says.

They face off against each other, Dean bouncing lightly on his feet, and Ares standing still with the mats deeply indented under his weight. Dean is a little shorter than Ares, but we all know how fast he is, and how savage. He was a bare-knuckle boxer in Moscow, fighting in the abandoned subway tunnels beneath the city. According to him, he never lost a fight. When he and Leo come to blows, as they have on several occasions, it's inevitably messy and bloody, with no clear victor.

Ares is no pacifist—he got in a brawl with Bram and Valon last year. But he doesn't like to fight, and even in Combat class he's careful and restrained, never losing his temper.

Dean clearly views this as another opportunity to stick it to Leo by beating the shit out of one of his friends. He circles Ares with obvious intent to injure.

He goes in hard, raining down a relentless onslaught of punches almost too fast for my eye to follow. Ares keeps his fists up, but the hail of blows hits him hard in the ribs, the shoulders, and the side of his head. He blocks the worst of it, though I'm sure it still hurts.

Most of the other students have stopped sparring so they can watch. Even Professor Howell shifts position around the edge of the mat, his whistle raised to his lips to stop the fight if necessary, but his dark eyes fixed on the boys with watchful interest.

Unsatisfied by his initial onslaught, Dean attacks even harder, swinging his fist like hammers directly at Ares' head. He lands one hard blow under Ares' eye. Ares responds with a right-cross that knocks Dean backward on his heels. I can see the surprise in Dean's face, and the new level of caution as he circles around, trying to catch Ares off balance.

Dean hits Ares in the body again and again, each thud loud and distinct in the near-silent gym. Ares' jaw is tight, his face stiff. With each blow that strikes him, the patches of color on Ares' cheeks get darker and darker. I get the strangest feeling that he's allowing Dean to hit him. But every time Dean obliges, something builds inside of Ares. Something very like fury.

Dean attacks his head again, buffeting Ares with punches that are both fast and hard, coming at him in a flurry from all directions. It's relentless, furious, far beyond the level of aggression we're supposed to show in sparring.

Professor Howell doesn't stop them. He wants to see how Ares will respond, just as much as the rest of us.

At last it works—Ares snaps. With a howl of anger, he lashes back at Dean with full force. He swings his punches with all his mass behind them, and all the benefit of his long reach. He knocks Dean's fists aside, hitting him in the nose and jaw.

Far from calming Ares, the landed blows only enrage him further. He's totally lost control, roaring like an animal as he hits Dean again and again and again with both fists.

Dean fires back, clipping Ares in the lower lip.

Ares hits him back just as fast, a punch so hard that Dean actually staggers and falls to one knee, something I've never seen before.

Face flushed, eyes wild, Ares cocks his fist again, ready to twist Dean's head around with a finishing blow.

The cold silver whistle slices through the air between them, warning Ares to stop.

Ares drops his fists, chest heaving with heavy breaths. He reminds me of Hercules, driven mad for a moment, shaking his head as he comes back to himself. He looks shocked and a little horrified. Scared, too—scared at how he lost control.

Dean jumps back to his feet, eyeing Ares with a calculating expression. Far from being upset at the surprising turn of the fight, he seems oddly pleased as he spits a mouthful of blood on the ground.

Leo goes over to Ares and claps his hand on his shoulder, making Ares jump.

"Hey. You okay?" Leo asks.

"Yeah. I'm fine," Ares says.

His expression has almost returned to normal. But I can see his hands trembling beneath their wrapping.

"What the fuck was that?" Anna murmurs to me.

"You know Dean," I say to her. "He gets under everybody's skin."

"That he does," Anna agrees. She's still looking at Ares, frowning.

I understand what she's thinking.

I noticed the same thing.

For a minute, Ares didn't look like himself. He was a completely different person.

CHRISTMAS ROLLS AROUND. I always like this time of year at school, because the dining hall is decorated with fresh fir boughs, and the professors take a break from their usual curriculum to teach us lessons that might actually be considered fun.

Professor Lyons shows us how to make LSD candy, which she then invites us to sample. As leery as I am to accept any kind of food from the most famous poisoner of the modern era, I slip two pieces in my pocket thinking that I might work up the courage to try it eventually.

Professor Holland turns out all the lights in his classroom and acts as the Narrator so we can play the party game Mafia, telling us that it's a useful illustration of intention and deception. Since the professor has been sipping out of a pocket flask all afternoon, I'm not sure he actually believes it will teach us anything, but we all enjoy the game regardless.

Not all the students are happy to be trapped at school when they'd rather be at home with their families. This is peak time for homesickness, especially amongst the Freshmen who aren't used to being so isolated.

Luckily for me, the only family I care to see is right here at school with me. Cat and I spend hours together making Christmas cards for our friends.

Cat's cards are, of course, infinitely prettier than mine. She paints landscapes of Kingmakers: the cathedral, the Octagon Tower, the view from the Solar, and so forth.

I choose simple and achievable motifs like a snowflake or a sprig of mistletoe. Since mine are easier, I finish before she does, and spend the rest of the time working on my story, or my "script" as I've begun to think of it, despite how pretentious that sounds.

It's extremely pleasant to scribble away while listening to the swish of Cat's paintbrush and the music playing on Anna's speaker. We snack on paper-wrapped oranges brought up from the dining hall, and hand-made caramels bought in the village.

We're working in Chay and Anna's room because it's larger than mine. Cat and I could barely fit in my bedroom at the same time, and there definitely wouldn't be space for art supplies.

When I hear a knock on the door, I assume it's Chay or Anna coming back from class. Instead, I find Miles standing there, looking spruce in a perfectly-fitted white dress shirt with the sleeves rolled up to show his tanned forearms. Miles always looks tan, even when we haven't had sunshine in weeks. His face is freshly-shaven, revealing the little cleft in his chin and the square lines of his jaw. His dark curls are damp.

"What are you doing here?" I say, trying not to smile too hard.

Miles takes a quick glance into the room to check who's present before replying. He's always careful in that way, which I know is more for my benefit than his.

"I need to see you tonight," he says. "I have a surprise for you."

"I don't like surprises," I tell him.

"You will when it comes from me," he says, showing that crooked smile that has an irresistible effect on me.

A ball of warmth expands inside my chest. It gets bigger and bigger every moment that Miles stands in front of me. Despite what I said about surprises, I'm excited to spend a few hours in his company.

"Nine o'clock," Miles tells me. "I'll meet you behind the Solar."

"I'll be there," I say.

"See you, Cat," Miles calls over my shoulder.

Cat lifts her paint-spattered hand in a wave.

Miles casts a quick glance down the hallway, then kisses me so swiftly that I barely have time to feel his mouth before he's gone. My lips burn all the same, for a long time after.

I wish I had something to give Miles for Christmas. The only person who could sell me a good gift would be Miles himself, and I barely have any money. My father has never given Cat or me a generous allowance.

I did make Miles a leather bracelet. Cat showed me how to do it. It isn't as professional as it would have been if Cat made it, but I was determined to do the work myself, and I think it turned out nicely.

Miles has a distinct sense of style, so I'm hoping he'll like it, or at least not feel obligated to wear it if he doesn't.

I wrap the bracelet in colored paper and write Miles a note in the mistletoe card.

Then I spend a long time getting dressed, wondering what the surprise might be.

What I told Miles was true—I've never liked surprises. But that's because they've usually been unpleasant. I already know him well enough to assume that I might actually enjoy his plans for the evening. In fact, I probably will. I just have to let go of that need to be prepared, that desperate desire for control that I've always felt, despite never actually having any meaningful control in my own life.

When your life is a slow-motion car crash, you try to compensate by controlling stupid, insignificant things. For me it was grades. In Barcelona I wasn't permitted to choose my schedule or my friends, but I could at least get a perfect score on tests. It earned me praise from my teachers, and even occasionally from my father.

I tried to be perfect to please him, and to placate Daniela. It never worked.

I always dressed neatly, shoes polished, hair brushed. I kept my room spotless, clothes organized by color, books lined up flawlessly on the shelf with all the spines at precisely the same depth. I was always on time. I never smoked or swore.

Pointless actions become crucial, even compulsive.

Actually, I see a little of this in Dean Yenin. I see how he lines up his notebooks and pencils on his desk. How his clothes and person are always scrubbed clean. How he washes his hands again and again after Marksmanship or Chemistry classes.

It's plaster over cracks. I see it and recognize it. I don't know what his damage is, but I see how he tries to right his universe, desperately and ineffectually. I'd feel sorry for him if he wasn't such an asshole.

Even my first year at Kingmakers, I tried so hard to follow the rules.

And for what? Did I believe, deep down, that my father would take pity on me and set me free from Rocco?

I know he won't.

Enter Miles Griffin. He's not just a rule-breaker, he's a rule-smasher. He subverts every order, dances around barriers as if they're not even there.

I should be horrified by him.

Instead, I feel like a caveman who just saw a campfire for the very first time.

Miles takes the forbidden and uses it to his advantage—wields it as a tool.

I admire him. And god, how I envy him.

I WAIT behind the Solar for Miles, dressed in a skirt and heels borrowed from Chay, a blouse borrowed from Anna, and my own academy jacket overtop. It's chilly tonight—still and windless, with a hard, frosty bite to the air. The grass is crisp and sparkling under my feet.

I'm not the only one who dressed up and snuck out tonight. I'm pretty sure Chay has been seeing Ozzy on the sly since Halloween. She won't admit to them dating, but on the two occasions I saw her sneaking back to the dorms with obvious JBF hair, she admitted that they'd hooked up again and it was the best sex of her life.

"He's so fucking kinky," she groaned, trying to comb the knots of her hair. "He does things to me I've never even heard of before."

"So you like him?" I said.

"Well . . ." She shrugged. "He's sweet and funny. Smart, too. I just picture myself with more of a Henry Cavill type."

Chay's certainly beautiful enough to snag anyone she wants. But I feel bad for Ozzy all the same, because in other respects —humor, cleverness, persistence—he'd be a great match for Chay.

He's not unattractive—just unique. Call him an Adam Driver or a Benedict Cumberbatch, if not a Cavill.

Attraction is a funny thing. I always thought Miles was good-looking. But with each day that passes, everyone else seems to fade away, and he becomes the standard of perfection. I don't like blue eyes anymore, or brown. I only want eyes that look foggy in the morning and silver in the moonlight. I only want 6'2 with a crooked smile and a wicked laugh.

I hug my arms around my body, bouncing on my toes to keep warm.

I wore the skirt because I wanted to dress up, but if Miles plans to go for a walk outside the grounds, or sit somewhere outdoors, I'm going to freeze.

I don't have long to wait. Miles arrives directly before nine, jogging over the crunching frost. He looks effortlessly stylish in a way that's rare for a man. Men don't often seem to understand the fit and drape of clothing, the best ways to highlight their most attractive features. Miles' pullover and his sage-green trousers cling to his body in all the right places, over his chest and shoulders and the bulge of his thighs.

"Come on," he says to me, making a move to take my hand, and then remembering that he shouldn't do that while we're still outside where someone might see us.

"Where are we going?" I ask.

"This way," he says, his smile gleaming in the starlight.

He takes me west across campus, past the old wine cellar that leads down to the Undercroft, past the infirmary, the library, and the Rookery. I know, from Miles showing me, that he's got a satellite hidden in the roof of the Rookery, giving him full access to the internet whenever he likes. For a moment I think he's going to take me back up the steps of that tower, until he pulls me into the cathedral instead.

I almost expect Anna to be waiting for us inside. She's the one who comes here most often—it's her favorite place to practice ballet.

Instead, the cavernous space is empty and echoing, the faint starlight filtering down in colored patterns from the stained-glass windows, and the tiled floor rippled in places from tree roots pushing up from underneath. A pomegranate tree has sprouted in the chancel, and vines encircle the support pillars.

There's no religion at Kingmakers. The cathedral has been intentionally permitted to fall into ruin. It's the only part of the school where the roof isn't patched or the windows repaired after winter storms. It's a deliberate rejection of one of the many systems of authority to which mafia families will not bow.

Even the other students shun this place. Anna is one of the few who finds the cathedral soothing instead of off-putting.

There's little to entertain anyone inside these walls. The cathedral is cold and dark, unheated and without any electricity.

I'm not sure why Miles brought me here. Until I see that he's dragged in the green velvet couch from the stables, the one that reposed in the Chancellor's office until its ignominious retirement to the pile of discarded furniture, files, and boxes heaped up at the far end of the stables.

The velvet couch isn't the only addition. Miles has brought blankets, drinks, snacks, and a piece of machinery I don't recognize—squat and rectangular, it sits on a pile of crates.

"I had a hell of a time finding one of these that would run on battery power," Miles says.

"What is it?" I ask.

"Take a seat and I'll show you," he says, gesturing toward the green sofa.

I sit down, impressed to see that Miles has even fixed the issue of the missing sofa leg, propping the couch up on a wooden block so it no longer wobbles.

Miles hands me a bowl of popcorn. The popcorn is fresh and crisp, doused in real melted butter and sea salt.

I laugh. "Where do you get these things? How did you pop this?"

"The kitchen staff love me," Miles says. "Nobody enjoys drugs more than line cooks."

Miles fiddles with the little machine, twisting the dials on the side. It whirs into life, shooting a brilliant beam of light across the open space. The opposite wall illuminates, the space where the altar would have been transforming into a wide, bright movie screen.

I gasp as the Paramount Pictures mountain flashes across the screen. The opening credits announce that we are about to behold "VistaVision" for the very first time. Even before Irving Berlin's iconic score begins, I already know the film is *White Christmas*.

"Miles!" I cry. "I can't believe you!"

He drops down on the sofa next to me, draping his arm around my shoulders. He pulls a blanket over our laps, saying, "I've got Milk Duds, too. They were a bitch to find, but I wanted you to have to the full theater experience."

The opening sequence begins with Bing Crosby and Danny Kaye in their war uniforms. The last time I watched this movie was at my Abuelita's house. Instead of popcorn and the dusty smell of the cathedral, the old-timey music recalls the scent of Lita's perfume, the orange blossoms in her garden, and the sugar-crusted *pestiños* she would fry in her ancient cast-iron skillet.

As Rosemary Clooney and Vera Ellen come on screen, singing their famous duet, I remember Lita putting her arms around Cat and me, pulling us close against her sides, saying, "Sisters, see, just like you two. You must always help and protect each other. Sisters first, everything else comes after."

I'm hit with a wave of guilt, knowing that at this moment I'm not putting Cat first, not at all. I'm jeopardizing what fragile protection I've managed to barter for her, all so I can spend time with Miles.

Miles, ever perceptive, takes my chin between his thumb and index finger, tilting up my face so he can examine it.

"What's wrong?" he says. "Were you hoping for *Rear Window* instead?"

I shake my head, my throat too tight to speak.

No one has ever done anything like this for me, not even Cat. It's an impossible gift, something that nobody but Miles could have pulled off. The movie is magical. This moment is perfect. And I can't enjoy it, because I'm afraid what it will cost me later. Or what it will cost Cat.

"You're afraid," Miles says.

I nod my head.

I never would have admitted that before. I hate to show weakness.

I can't lie to Miles, though. It's pointless. He always sees the truth.

Miles kisses me, softly at first, then harder.

He pulls back to look at me, his face illuminated by the projector's light, his eyes silver-bright.

"I'm going to get you free of him, Zoe," he says.

I try to shake my head because that's impossible, but Miles holds my face steady with both hands.

"I will," he growls. "I'll find a way and I'll do it. Do you believe me?"

I look into his eyes.

I've never been so wrong about a person. I thought Miles was indolent and self-centered. I thought he didn't care about anything but his own amusement.

I couldn't have been more wrong. He's the most determined person I've ever met. When he says he'll do this, I believe him. It's absurd and unimaginable, but I trust him all the same.

"I believe you," I say.

Miles kisses me again, without reservation this time. He kisses me like he's already accomplished what he promised. Like he owns me now, fully and completely.

He stops only to pause the movie, switching to music instead.

Often — The Weeknd
Spotify → geni.us/rebel-spotify
Apple Music → geni.us/rebel-apple

The vintage light of the movie screen glows on his skin, glinting in his shining, dark curls. He selects the song he wants without even glancing at the hand-held remote that operates the speaker. Miles does everything he dances: with swift, flawless coordination. I've never seen him stumble or hesitate.

He's always three steps ahead of everyone else, including me. I wonder if he can see the future, like the girl in my script.

Unlike her, Miles seems to have full power to achieve his goals.

The music is sensual and intent.

Miles looks at me with an expression I've come to know well.

The look he gets when he's decided on his plan. When nothing will stray him from his course.

"Take off your clothes," he orders.

I swallow hard.

"I . . . I don't know if we should . . ."

"You trust me?" he says.

"Yes."

"Then do what I say."

"I . . . alright."

"Stand there. In the light."

I stand in the reflected light of the projector, trembling a little, but not from cold. My skin burns in the heat of Miles' stare.

"Take your clothes off," he repeats. "Slowly."

I start to unbutton my blouse. My fingertips are tingling, so stiff that my hands feel like they belong to someone else. Maybe to Miles . . .

I'm mesmerized by his stare. I feel like it *is* his hands doing this, as if I'm not acting on my own volition, but purely according to his will.

I go down the buttons one by one, then I open the blouse and let the silky material slide down my arms and drop to the ground.

The beat of the music vibrates under my skin. I find myself swaying in Chay's high-heeled shoes, my hips moving slightly to the song. I turn around so my back is to Miles, then slowly unzip the skirt, revealing a slice of thong and asscheeks.

I can hear the ancient springs of the sofa creaking as Miles shifts position.

Slowly, I slide the skirt down over my bottom, bending over slightly as it, too, drops down to puddle around my feet. I step clear of the skirt.

"Keep the heels on," Miles barks.

I look back over my shoulder at him. His eyes gleam in the pale light. He leans back against the cushions, his arms resting along the back of the sofa. He looks like a king surveying his concubine. Far from feeling degraded by this, I get a rush of warmth between my legs.

I turn around again, wearing only a lacy black thong and bra now.

Miles' eyes roam over my body. I watch him, feeling equally aroused by his admiration of me. Finally my figure is my friend, because it's securing the attention of someone I actually want. I've never felt as sexy as I do in this moment, seeing myself reflected in his eyes.

I reach around behind my back to unclasp my bra. My breasts fall from their hoisted-up position. Just that movement, that bounce, makes my nipples spring to attention, giving me a deep, desperate ache down low in my belly.

I slip off the bra.

"Touch your breasts," Miles orders.

I slide my palms under my breasts, lifting them and dropping them to experience that exquisite jolt again. I run my fingers over my nipples, pretending it's Miles touching me. Pinching my nipples as hard as I think he would. Each touch sends sparks through my body.

"Now the underwear," Miles says.

Without hesitation, I hook my thumbs in the waistband of my thong and pull it down. I'm soaking. My underwear clings to my pussy lips before pulling away. I keep my pussy trimmed but not shaved clean. For a moment I wonder if Miles likes it that way—I never asked him, the times he went down on me. It gives me a twinge of anxiety. But then I see the naked lust in his eyes and all my fears melt away. He wants me exactly like this. I know he does.

Miles unzips his trousers, letting his cock spring free. I've touched it through his clothes, and once I slipped my hand down his pants and grasped it in my palm. I knew it was thick and heavy. But I've never actually seen it out in the open. I never returned the favor with oral, nervous that I'd do a terrible job.

His cock is bigger than I expected. Quite alarming, actually. It's harder than ever, standing up straight, rigid and aggressive.

I want to close my mouth around it. I'm so aroused that I'm not scared anymore—I want to try.

Before I can act on that impulse, Miles says, "Touch yourself. Rub that pussy for me."

I'm blushing, but the embarrassment is distant. All I can see is Miles in front of me, his burning stare and his dark, scowling brows, and his tightened jaw that looks angry, but I know it isn't anger, it's focus. Every bit of his consciousness is focused on me.

I reach down to touch my pussy, doing it for him, putting on a show for him. My fingers slide easily over the lips, and over the little bit of my clit poking out in between, swollen and throbbing. I touch myself, not the way that I usually would in bed, but the way that Miles touches me—firmly, confidently. Knowing me better than I know myself.

He watches every movement, his hand stroking his cock in tandem. His cock looks enormous even compared to Miles's large hand.

"Taste how sweet you are," he says.

I lift my fingers to my lips.

He's right—the taste is mild and slightly sweet. He wasn't lying when he said how much he loved it.

"Now come here," he says.

I walk over to him, unsteady on my heels because my whole body feels warm and loose, my joints made of rubber.

I drop down on my knees in front of Miles, sliding between his legs. I want to see that cock up close. I want to touch it.

I take it from Miles' hands, running my fingers lightly up the shaft. The skin is smooth and silky, the flesh beneath throbbing hot. When I touch the head, his whole cock twitches like it has a mind of its own.

I run my tongue from base to tip, just like I did with my fingers. It jolts even harder this time. His flesh is like hot tea, the warmest it could be without burning my tongue.

I close my mouth over the head, and his cock fills the space perfectly, like the two were meant for each other. The head lays heavy on my tongue, filling the arch at the roof of my mouth. Saliva floods in, so I can slide my lips a few inches up and down the shaft.

"That's right. Just like that, get it nice and wet," Miles instructs me.

My technique is awkward, the rhythm jerky. Miles takes my head between his hands and directs me, using his hips to thrust into my mouth. He thrusts a little too far and the head of his cock hits the back of my throat. I gag and pull back.

"You okay?" he says.

I nod, swiping the back of my hand across my cheek where tears run down.

Weirdly, I like the feeling of gagging. I like how big his cock is, I like the challenge of trying to fit it in my mouth.

I try again. This time I'm catching the rhythm, figuring out how to dance my tongue across the underside of his cock while I slide my lips up and down the shaft.

Miles groans with pleasure, his head tilted back against the edge of the sofa. The sound is highly gratifying. It makes me want to do this all night long.

Miles has other ideas.

"Climb on," he orders, taking my wrist and pulling me to my feet.

He pushes his trousers the rest of the way down, kicking them off. His cock stands upright again, impossibly erect. I straddle his lap, balanced up on my knees on the sofa, wondering how in the fuck this is going to work.

"Lower yourself down," he says. "Go as slow as you need to."

He positions the head of his cock at my entrance. It's burning hot, wet with my saliva, but so big that I feel like I'm about to impale myself on a baseball bat.

Miles grips my hips between his hands, helping to steady me.

He kisses me. Then he tilts his head to the side and takes my breast in his mouth. He suckles on my breast, rolling the nipple across his tongue.

My wetness melts down on the head of his cock, helping it slide inside of me. Bit by bit, Miles lowers me down.

I keep waiting for a popping or tearing sensation, but it never comes. I slide down and down what feels like a foot of cock, yet somehow I keep stretching to accommodate it. The feeling isn't painful—quite the opposite. It's intensely satisfying. Everything I ever wanted.

At last my ass is all the way down to his thighs, and he's all the way inside me. I feel full in a way that's indescribable. I feel whole and complete.

Miles lets go of my breast to kiss me again, his tongue as deep inside my mouth as his cock is deep in my belly.

His mouth has a new, erotic taste, our arousal as palpable a flavor as vanilla or honey. I want to eat his tongue and his lips. I want to consume him whole.

Miles grips my hips and starts to rock me against him. I hadn't realized we weren't even moving yet. This new friction is so intense that my mouth breaks away from his because I can't concentrate on anything except the feeling of his cock sliding a few inches in and out of me. My clit grinds against his body. The combination of sensations, inside and out, is the best thing since peanut butter and jelly. Something so good and so right that all other metaphors pale by comparison.

The feeling inside me is scary intense. It's so powerful that I know I can't control it. I'm afraid I'm going to wet myself, or cry, or something even more embarrassing.

"Miles!" I gasp. "I can't stop!"

"I don't want you to stop," he growls. "I'm telling you not to."

His powerful hands grip me all the harder, and he rubs me against his body like he's paper and I'm an eraser. Waves of pleasure radiate out of my navel, thick and hot. The climax builds and builds, each stroke more pleasurable than the one before. It's getting too strong, becoming too much. I'm frightened, and yet I couldn't stop if I wanted to. I might be on top, but Miles controls this. And Miles doesn't stop for anything.

"Oh . . . oh . . . OH MY GOD!" I scream, as the orgasm rips through me.

It's an explosion. A detonation. A Krakatoa blast.

It's so intense that I think I might actually have injured myself. There's no way my ovaries survived that.

Miles just chuckles, his laugh as deep and warm as his voice. I collapse against him, feeling the rumble in his chest vibrating against mine.

"You like that, baby girl?" he says.

The climax hasn't dampened my arousal whatsoever. Miles ordering me around, Miles calling me baby, is still an intense turn-on.

"What do you want now?" I whisper in his ear.

"You really want to know?" he says.

"Yes," I say, licking my lips. "Tell me how to please you."

"Stay right where you are," he says. "And ride that cock for me."

Bracing myself with my hands on his shoulders, I roll my hips, sliding up and down on his cock. It's awkward at first, but soon I get the rhythm of it. I'm still sensitive and swollen, almost painfully so. As I keep moving and grinding on him, pleasure overtakes the pain, and it feels better and better by the minute.

"You trust me?" Miles says.

"Yes," I nod.

Miles reaches up with his big hands and closes them around my throat. He does it gently, applying only light, even pressure. Even so, my head begins to swim.

"Keep riding," he orders.

The power Miles has over me is heady and terrifying. He literally holds my life in his hands. I know that if he wanted to cut off my air, there's nothing I could do to stop him.

My blood thunders harder than ever, concentrating in my pussy while my head floats high and light.

The harder I ride him, the more intense the sensation becomes. Miles' eyes are locked on mine, his powerful hands squeezing around my throat, applying just the right amount of pressure to put me entirely under his control. I'm dizzy and hot, and I can't stop, I'm bucking my hips, feeling that intense warmth and pressure in my belly again, that feeling like I'm going to erupt. Nothing on this earth can stop it.

I cum again, even harder than before. My brain soars and I'm delirious, bright flashes of color popping in front of my eyes. Miles lets out a roar that I can barely hear in the midst of my own ecstasy. His cock twitches and pulses, slamming deep inside of me, forcing out one last burst of pleasure for him and for me.

When I come back down to earth, I can't see or speak. I take huge gasps of air, the oxygen tasting like pure, cool mountain air in my lungs.

"What . . . the hell . . ." I moan.

"Did you like that?" Miles asks.

"It was unbelievable."

Miles seizes me and kisses me, biting my lips.

"You're mine," he growls. "All mine."

"I only want to be yours," I sob. "Don't let him take me."

"I promised you," Miles says. "I don't make promises easily. And I never break them after."

He crushes me against his body, holding me so tight that I know for certain he'll never let me go.

I touch my throat with my fingertips. I expect it to feel swollen or sore, bruised even, but it's completely fine. Even in the fever pitch of his arousal, Miles never lost control. He was careful not to hurt me, not even to leave a mark.

I stay on his lap a long time, curled up against him, listening to his heart racing against my ear. Eventually its beating slows, becoming a steady metronome instead.

Hours have passed. It's late at night.

Still, we stay together.

When Miles finally shifts, I feel a stab of disappointment.

It eases when he says, "I don't want to take you back yet. Let's stay a while longer."

"Yes, please," I agree.

Miles picks up the remote again, switching the music to something slower and more romantic. He pulls me up off the sofa and then into his warm embrace. We sway together, naked but not cold, wanting every inch of our skin to touch.

Unchained Melody — The Righteous Brothers
Spotify → geni.us/rebel-spotify
Apple Music → geni.us/rebel-apple

"This is from a movie, too," he says. "Do you know it?"

I shake my head.

"I'll play it for you next time."

I look up into his face.

"How many next times will there be?"

"Infinite," he says.

14

MILES

All through January and February, I strategize how to break Zoe's marriage contract.

The simplest method would be to murder Rocco Prince.

I've considered it. Many times. But it would be risky, for a variety of reasons.

First off, Zoe and I would be the obvious suspects. Despite our best efforts to be subtle, it's widely known that we have feelings for each other. Kingmakers doesn't always enforce its rules when it comes to petty misdemeanors like fistfights and hook-ups, but some rules are sacrosanct. The most iron-clad is the Rule of Recompense. Any serious injury or death is punished in the old way: an eye for an eye. Tooth for a tooth. Life for a life.

Even if we could skirt punishment by the school, the Princes would seek revenge. Rocco, as unlovable as he might be, is their only child and heir.

I don't want to start our life together with a cycle of retribution.

I want to do what I do best: solve the problem, once and for all.

I need to make a deal with the Romeros and the Princes. Something that makes everyone happy.

Zoe has explained to me what her father and the Princes stand to gain from the marriage contract and its accompanying trade deal.

I have to offer them something better.

Something *much* better.

I wish it were as simple as money.

I have 10.4 million now. The full balance of my seed money that I'd planned to take to Los Angeles after I graduate.

If I thought the Princes and the Romeros would take a check, I'd clear my account today. But they stand to make much more than five million each off their deal.

I have to take that ten million and turn it into something more valuable. I have an idea for how I could do that, with Ozzy's help. But I need another player. And probably every penny of cash I can muster.

I work on my plan every spare minute, whenever I'm not in class or sneaking out to see Zoe.

It's starting to shape up, bit by bit.

Only one flaw remains intractable and irascible. Even if I convince the Princes and the Romeros, the one person I'll never convince is Rocco himself. He's the thorn in my side. The one threat I can't remove entirely.

I turn the problem over in my head again and again, but I can never think of anything that will satisfy him. Nothing but Zoe.

I move forward regardless, trusting that even if Rocco is angry, he'll have to abide by what his parents decide.

Rocco knows I'm seeing Zoe, much as we try to hide it. He knows, and his inability to prevent it makes him angrier and angrier.

I've warned Zoe not to go anywhere alone on campus. She's careful to stick close to Anna and Chay.

Rocco retaliates by venting his rage on me instead. I'm an easier target, since we share classes and the same living space in the Octagon Tower.

Rocco and his stooges break into the dorm room I share with Ozzy. They destroy everything inside, slashing up our uniforms, ripping apart our books, and pissing all over our beds.

Ozzy discovers the mess. He's shaking with fury when I join him in the midst of the mayhem.

He holds up the blanket his mother knit for him, one that he's had all his life, torn to pieces and soaked in urine.

"I'll fucking kill them," he hisses.

It takes a lot to make Ozzy mad. But once you do, he's got a hell of a temper buried under the jokes and the smile.

"I can room somewhere else till all this cools off," I say to Ozzy, feeling guilty for bringing this down on his head.

"Fuck that," Ozzy said, dismissing the idea at once. "This isn't just between you and Rocco anymore."

It's true—at this point, Ozzy and Wade Dyer hate each other nearly as much as Rocco and me.

Wade has taken a strange obsession with Ozzy that goes far beyond following his boss' orders. He snipes at Ozzy constantly, shoulder-checking him every time they pass. They've almost come to blows a dozen times, held back only by the presence of teachers or staff.

Wade mocks Ozzy's height, his looks, his accent, his family, and his interests. Ozzy seems unable to shrug it off as he usually would, maybe because Wade is tall and blond and good-looking, the epitome of what Ozzy believes Chay would prefer.

Ozzy and Chay are still hooking up. I don't know if it's good for him. He looks sick every time he sees her chatting with some other guy, laughing and smiling up at them in her usual flirtatious way. His feelings for her deepen by the day, but it doesn't seem to be reciprocated, and it's driving him mad.

The tension eats at me, the secrecy and the strain to find some way out of this. The conflict with Rocco feels like a rubber band stretched to its furthest limit. There's no doubt it will snap. The only question is when.

My only relief is sneaking out to see Zoe.

It's not just for sex. I love that part of it, of course, but more than anything I want the freedom to talk to her, fully and openly, without anyone listening.

I've read through her whole script now, and I think it's brilliant. She has an incredible way with words. She reminds me of Aaron Sorkin or Greta Gerwig, in that her characters are wildly articulate and bold in speaking their minds.

It gives me a look at what Zoe herself would be like, without fear of threats or spies or reprisals.

She's working on the ending. Sometimes she asks me for ideas, and I try to give suggestions, even though I don't know fuck-all about writing. Sometimes we even perform little bits of it, laughing at how awful we both are at acting.

I've never done anything creative before. I think of myself as a facilitator, not an artist. It surprises me how enjoyable it is to map out conflict and resolution within a fictional frame, where the stakes are low and Zoe and I are gods of that world, able to orchestrate events exactly as we want them.

We work well together, Zoe and me.

She's laying in my lap one Sunday afternoon, on the green couch, which I've returned to the stables so Anna can have her ballet space clear again. I'm playing with Zoe's hair, gently combing through the long, black, silky strands with my fingers. She has her notebook propped up on her knees so she can add to it while we talk.

"Should the ending be tragic?" she says. "Or happy?"

"Happy, of course."

"But the whole point all along has been that seeing the future doesn't allow you to alter it. It's a paradox—what you're seeing isn't actually the future, if you can change it."

"I know. But nobody likes tragic endings."

"Romeo and Juliet would beg to differ," Zoe teases me. "Or Titanic."

"The end of Titanic is Jack and Rose reunited."

"In death."

"It's emotional catharsis all the same. You have to give the audience what they want."

"So . . . you think that once our protagonist realizes the nature of her visions, that should give her power over the outcomes. She learns how to manipulate the system. Like in *The Matrix*."

"Maybe," I say. "I guess my point is that I don't believe in no-win scenarios."

"There's always an out?" Zoe says, looking up at me.

"Yes." I nod. "You just have to be clever enough to find it."

Zoe sits up, the dark curtains of her hair falling around her shoulders, soft and shining from my grooming.

She looks at me with those beautiful eyes, pale green with thick black lashes all around. Whenever she looks at me like this, straight on, our faces only inches apart, I'm struck by how lovely she is. Impossibly lovely. A kind of beauty that only increases the closer you examine it.

"What's our out?" she asks me.

"I'm working on it," I say.

"I know you are. I want you to tell me. I want to help you, like you've helped me with the script. I want to work on it together."

I consider this, not unwilling but surprised.

I've never involved another person in my plans. Even with Ozzy, it's only technical details we decide together. The framework is always me alone.

Call me superstitious but I hesitate to say my plan out loud. It's still forming, not fully developed. Exposing it to the air might kill it.

But I trust Zoe, and I value her intelligence. I want to hear what she has to say.

So I tell her. I tell her every idea, every possibility I've considered. I tell her the challenges, the weaknesses, the practical issues I haven't yet overcome. It takes me well over an hour to explain what I have so far. Zoe listens carefully, never interrupting.

When I'm finished, she's quiet a long time, thinking.

Then she says, "You need one more family."

"I know."

"Someone who can take product east, but they have to have an American presence too. Someone with cash to spare, in American dollars."

I nod slowly.

"What about the Malina?"

She's talking about the Odessa Mob. The most ancient and widespread branch of the Ukrainian mafia.

I let out a long exhale. "I considered them. They're perfectly positioned. And I've heard they have cash. A lot of cash. But their reputation . . ."

"I know," Zoe says. "It isn't good."

"They're rapacious. Insular. Treacherous."

"They'd be arms' length away. And if they turn on someone down the line . . . it won't be us."

"We'd have to get the Princes and your father to agree."

Zoe looks at me, smiling slightly. "We need someone highly persuasive . . . do you know anyone like that?"

I grin. "I might."

Zoe's face grows somber again.

"Miles . . ." she says. "This is going to take all your money."

I told her about my seed money. She knows how I intended to use it. And she's right—whether this plan works or not, it will wipe me out. I won't have a bean left over. Not enough to rent an apartment in L.A., let alone build an empire.

"I don't care," I tell her. "I'll make more."

Zoe shakes her head slowly. "I can't let you do that. You worked so hard, all those years. It's your dream . . ."

"No offense, baby girl," I say, "but it's not up to you. I'm doing this, with or without your help. I don't know if it's gonna work, but I'm sure as fuck gonna try. And if this deal's no good, I'll think of another. I told you, this is a jailbreak. Rocco is Warden Norton and you're Andy Dufresne—we're gonna Shawshank this motherfucker!"

Zoe is laughing, she can't resist when I paint a vision of our future together.

I'm likewise riding on cloud nine.

The feeling of working this through with someone else is intoxicating, as if I've expanded my brain to double its size. It's so easy talking to Zoe. She understands everything, and sees things that I don't.

"I love you," I say, without thinking, without planning.

Zoe's eyes go wide. For the first time I see a clear resemblance to her sister Cat. She looks startled and frightened.

"You do?" she says.

I have to laugh. "Why are you surprised? Hasn't it been obvious for a while?"

"When did you start loving me?"

I think back. "In the infirmary. When you told me not to pity you."

She shakes her head at me, a slow smile stealing over her soft, full lips.

"I love you too, Miles," she says.

"Since when?"

Now she's smiling all the way, her eyes gleaming.

"Since I saw you naked," she says.

I laugh, seizing her and kissing her hard.

"Is that the only reason?"

"Yes. I'm horribly shallow."

"You know what, I'm fine with that. I've always wanted to be objectified."

I pull my sweater over my head, baring my chest.

"Feast your eyes."

Zoe does look at me, her amusement turning to lust in an instant. Her eyes rove over my body, and she runs her fingertips down my chest, raising goosebumps on my arms.

She kisses me right over my heart, her soft, warm mouth sending shivers across my skin. Then she runs her tongue softly along the lines of my left pec, and my cock goes rock hard in my pants. I want her tongue in other places. I want my tongue on her even worse.

She's wearing trousers again today, with suspenders over her pullover, and lace-up oxfords on her feet. I love when she looks tomboyish. The juxtaposition between the boyish clothes and the ultra-feminine body underneath is wildly erotic. I pull down her suspenders, then take off her top, and put the suspenders back up on her shoulders again so the wide elastic just barely covers her nipples, pressing down on her breasts, making them look rounder than ever.

"Let me take a picture of you," I say.

"Like this?" Zoe looks down at her near-naked torso, shaking her head and blushing.

"Let me do it," I say. "You're so fucking sexy."

Zoe bites her lip, considering. Then she says, "Alright. Tell me what to do."

If there was any blood left in my head, it all rushes to my groin as soon as she starts taking orders. If there's one thing I can agree upon with that psychopath Rocco, it's that there's no greater rush than having a woman as brilliant and gorgeous as Zoe bent to your will.

The difference is that I want her to do it willingly, gladly. I want her to get off on it just as hard as I do.

"Stand by the window," I tell her.

The golden evening light streams through the dusty glass. The glass is too thick and bubbled and filthy to worry that anyone could see Zoe from the other side—at most she'd be a shadow moving behind the opaque pane.

The light glows on her skin. It highlights the curves of those phenomenal breasts and the indents of her waist. Her figure is an hourglass inside the boxy male clothing. Her thick, dark hair gives her a wild, untamable look. Yet, I'm taming her. She obeys me as I tell her how to stand, which way to turn.

I use my phone to snap the pictures. With each shutter click, my cock gets stiffer and stiffer.

"Lean back against the window. Lift your arms. Lower the suspenders."

Zoe obeys, her eyes fixed on me and her cheeks flushed pink. When she drops the suspenders, her nipples have gone dark and pebbled, jutting out from her chest, tightening her breasts.

Tiny bits of dust float in the sunbeams, dancing around her skin.

"Take off your trousers," I order. "Underwear, too."

Zoe strips, and so do I. I take a few more pictures of her, naked as Venus and twice as beautiful, framed against the window. Then I drop the phone, crossing the room in three long strides. I lift her up, setting her in the window frame, and I shove my cock inside of her without preamble.

Zoe gasps, biting down hard on my shoulder.

Sliding inside of her is like coming home, every time.

I think I remember how good it feels, and then it surprises me, over and over again.

When I'm fucking her like this, I wonder how we ever do anything else. How do I have the patience to eat or sleep or go to class, when I could be doing this instead?

I press my face against her neck and inhale the scent of her skin. I feel her long legs wrapped around me, and her slender arms around my neck. I kiss her, thrusting my cock deeper and deeper inside of her, groaning out, "I love you, Zoe. I fucking love you."

I don't know why I waited this long to tell her. It feels so good to say it. It's what I meant when I told her I'd set her free from Rocco. I meant that I'd do anything for her.

The real, actual words are more powerful.

When she says them back to me, it thrills me to my core. It makes me feel invincible, god-like.

"I love you, Miles," she says, looking up into my eyes. "Always you, only you."

I lift her up from the windowsill, her legs locked behind my thighs, my hands gripping her ass, supporting her. I bounce her on my cock, making her tits bounce on her chest, a sight that is fucking mesmerizing, something I wish I could put on a loop and watch for hours. She's so gorgeous that it's impossible to keep control. From the moment I slide inside of her, it's a battle trying not to nut, making sure that Zoe cums first.

It's a battle I'll lose if I keep looking at those gorgeous breasts. I set her down again, flipping her over and bending her across the cushioned arm of the green sofa, gripping my cock at the base and sliding it into her again from behind.

Zoe likes it this way. She likes how hard I can fuck her from behind, especially if I reach around and rub her clit at the same time. I slide my fingers up and down her slit, finding that sensitive little clit and giving it just the right pressure in time with my thrusts. My hips make a smacking sound against her ass. I fuck her harder and harder, knowing she can take it, knowing she fucking loves it.

"Beg me to cum in you," I growl.

"Cum in me, please!" she gasps.

"Tell me you want it."

"I need it!"

It sounds like this is for me, but it's not. It's for Zoe. I'm giving her permission to ask for what she wants, to beg for it even. And sure enough, as I knew it would, it tips her over the edge. She likes begging and she likes obeying me.

Her pussy locks around my cock as she starts to orgasm, the waves hitting her in time with my thrusts.

I was barely clinging on to my control. As soon as her pussy starts clenching, the dam breaks and I shoot inside of her, hard and hot and fast. The cum pours out of me, an eruption I could no longer hold back even to save my own life.

Nothing in the world has ever felt this good. No deal, no win, no triumph. Zoe is the ultimate prize.

The only thing I want in this moment is to secure her. To make her mine forever.

THAT SUNDAY, I call my mom.

I've wanted to tell her about Zoe for a while. I was going to wait until I figured out the solution to my problem. But now, as I move into the endgame, I feel something rare and unusual: I want my mom's advice.

As soon as she picks up, I say, "Mom. I met someone."

"What kind of someone?" she says. I know she's trying to keep the excitement out of her voice. She doesn't want to scare me away.

She doesn't have to worry. I'm way past a fear of commitment.

"I met the one," I say without hesitation.

I can almost feel my mom gripping the receiver tight. Yet there's a long silence on the other end of the line.

"Why do I get the feeling there's trouble involved," my mother says.

"Why would you think that?"

"Because you never do anything the easy way, Miles. You never want the simple thing. You love the challenge."

I can hear my mother's exasperation mixed with something else. Something like understanding. And maybe even pride.

"Yeah? Where do you think I get that from?"

"You'd do better to take after your father instead of me."

"That isn't true, Mom," I say quietly. "I admire you. You know that, don't you? No one has a fire like you. No one loves harder. No one will go further to get what they want."

She swallows, her throat making a clicking sound.

"Thank you, baby," she says. "That means a lot to me. You're my firstborn, and I'm so fucking proud of you. I sometimes worried that you wouldn't ever experience what your father and I have. Not everyone does. Not everyone wants to."

"Where's the 'but?' " I say.

"No 'but.' Just be careful, baby. You're coming into the real world now. Real stakes. Real consequences. Love makes you desperate. It makes you risk . . . everything."

"It's worth it, though. You can't tell me it isn't."

"It's worth any price. But it's not always you that pays the price, Miles. Remember that. Remember what happened to your Grandpa Enzo."

I know the story as well as the people present at that fateful wedding. Leo's father Sebastian married Yelena Yenina, daughter of a Bratva boss, despite the fact that their families were mortal enemies, engaged in a bloody battle over territory.

As soon as the vows were said, Alexei Yenin tried to slaughter my family. He shot Uncle Nero and Uncle Dante. And he gunned down my grandfather, riddling him with so many bullets that he had to be identified by his watch.

I should have been at that wedding myself, a baby in my mother's arms. She and my father were only excluded because the Bratva feared retribution from the Irish mafia. I could have been a casualty of someone else's love.

I hear my mother, and I understand her.

But nothing can stray me from my course.

I won't give up Zoe.

I can't.

I want her, or nothing at all.

15

CAT

The second challenge in the *Quartum Bellum* will be much more pleasant than the first, because I get to be a spectator instead of a participant.

It's the perfect event to watch: an MMA tournament, with three champions chosen from the Sophomores and Seniors, and only two from the Juniors as punishment for finishing third in the obstacle course. The spectators get to sit on outdoor bleachers erected around a large canvas-floored ring.

I watch Leo agonize over which three fighters to put forward for the Sophomores. The obvious choice is Dean Yenin. To Leo's credit, he admits that at once, making the request of Dean during lunch hour in the dining hall.

Leo intercepts Dean as he carries his tray to his usual table stuffed with Bratva and Dutch Penose. I'm sitting close enough to hear them talk, and close enough to see how Dean bristles up the moment Leo approaches, expecting conflict instead of conversation.

"I'm picking the fighters for the *Quartum Bellum*," Leo says without preamble. "I thought you should represent us."

Dean narrows his eyes at Leo, looking more offended than flattered. "Obviously," he says.

I've never heard Dean speak before. I'm surprised how low his voice is, since his face is almost pretty. That's a strange thing to say about someone who looks mean enough to drop-kick a puppy, but it's true—Dean Yenin may have bruised, bloody knuckles and a perpetual scowl, but those features are paired with long lashes, violet-colored eyes, and full lips.

Dean is the boy I saw outside the stables the night of the Halloween dance. I pointed him out to Zoe a week later, and she shook her head, saying, "That's Dean Yenin. Stay away from him."

"Why?" I said, out of curiosity, not because I had any intention of speaking to him. With the exception of Zoe's friends, I never approach upperclassmen.

"He's Leo's cousin," Zoe said. "But they hate each other. Their families are enemies. They came to school already wanting to kill each other. Then they both fell for Anna."

That was so intriguing that I had to know more. Having something of a girl-crush on Anna myself, I could perfectly imagine the kind of obsessive rivalry she might inspire.

"Did Anna like Dean?"

"At first," Zoe says. "Until she got to know him. He's dangerous. He tried to kill Leo—he'll fuck with you just for being Leo's friend."

"I don't think he knows I exist. Don't worry, I'll keep it that way," I promised Zoe.

So I watch Dean and Leo from a table away, careful not to stare too obviously.

"Yeah," Leo says, trying to keep his temper. "You're one of the best fighters. So I—"

"*One of* the best?" Dean scoffs. "I am the best. And it's not close."

Leo grits his teeth, torn between his desire to argue and his need to secure Dean's cooperation.

"You'll do it, then?" he says.

Dean doesn't answer immediately, savoring his power over Leo, the delicious dynamic of Leo forced to come begging for a favor.

"Who else are you picking?" he demands.

I don't know whether that will influence his choice, or if he's just curious.

"I'm not sure," Leo says. "Maybe Silas Gray . . ."

Dean gives a curt nod, as if he was expecting that. "He fought well in the final challenge last year. But he's not strategic. All size and rage."

"Who would you suggest?" Leo says, half irritated and half actually wanting the advice.

Dean is silent a moment, thinking.

"Ares surprised me," he says, at last.

Leo casts a swift glance back at my table, looking at Ares calmly eating a chicken salad three seats down from me. I fix my gaze on my own half-eaten food, not wanting to be caught eavesdropping.

Over the din of the dining hall, I can just barely hear Leo's lowered voice saying, "I don't know if he'd want to."

"Why not?"

"I don't think he'd like it. With everybody watching."

"He's shy?" Dean sneers.

"I dunno. I haven't asked him. Who else would you suggest? We need three."

"Aren't you picking yourself?" Dean queries.

"Not necessarily," Leo says. "I can fight, but I've never done it in a ring."

"Hm." Dean sounds surprised that Leo wouldn't jump on the chance to put himself in the spotlight. He's mildly less irritable as he says, "What about Kenzo Tanaka? Or Corbin Castro?"

I sneak another glance at Dean. This is the first time I've seen him and Leo in close proximity without open aggression. Their expressions are curiously alike as they consider the problem.

"Kenzo could be good," Leo agrees. "He's smart and fast, and I've seen him take some hard hits without going down."

Dean nods. Then he seems to remember who he's talking to, and his face stiffens once more, the chill returning to his voice. "It won't matter who else you pick. I'm gonna win the whole thing."

"I hope you do," Leo says evenly. "It would send us to the final round."

He and Dean part ways without further conversation.

I can hear Anna's relieved exhale as Leo rejoins her.

"He'll do it?"

"Sounds like it," Leo says.

Ares has a textbook propped up against his milk glass and he's reading as he eats, oblivious to the drama going on around him.

"He had some other suggestions for who he thinks should fight," Leo says.

"Oh yeah, who?" Anna says.

"Ares," Leo replies, looking over at his friend.

Ares glances up, eyebrows raised. "Does he know we won't be fighting each other? 'Cause it sounds like he wants a re-match."

"You rung his bell." Leo grins. "Knocked a little sense into him."

"Maybe if I punch him fifty more times he might turn halfway decent," Ares says, returning to his textbook.

"You want to do it?" Leo asks.

"Punch Dean? Of course."

"No. Do you want to compete?"

Ares pauses, eyes still fixed on the page. Without looking up he says, "I don't think so."

"Why not?"

A muscle jumps at the corner of his jaw. "You know I don't like that shit. I wanna help the team, but there's better fighters than me."

Leo doesn't argue. Everyone knows Ares hates attention. Even I know it, and I'm barely an acquaintance.

"What about you, Hedeon?" Leo calls down the table.

Hedeon is a pretty good fighter—the fact that he can hold his own with Silas is proof of that, even if he only wins one out of four fights.

"Fuck that," Hedeon snarls, shoving away his tray. "Not interested."

He might be offended that Leo didn't ask him earlier. It came off like he was the fourth choice, after Dean and Ares and maybe Kenzo Tanaka.

Or he's just having one of his days. I don't know what his problem is, but Hedeon seems to suffer from a particular brand of bipolar that vacillates between mildly grouchy and full-out homicidal.

We accept Hedeon's outbursts like we accept Ares' modesty. It's a part of them and not likely to change.

THE MORNING of the second challenge dawns bright and clear with a light breeze. Perfect weather for sitting outdoors.

As I leave the Undercroft, Rakel says to me, "Don't forget to index the source materials for our History paper."

I agreed to do the indexing if Rakel proofread my paper.

"I tried yesterday," I tell her. "But I can't find any book that has replicas of Shimizu Jirocho's letters."

"They're not in a book," Rakel says, that old note of why-are-you-so-fucking-dumb creeping back into her voice. "They're down in the archives. Ask Miss Robin to get them for you. Or Saul—he's a library aide. He's allowed down there."

"I will," I promise.

"But meet me at the computer lab first, 'cause that project's due tomorrow."

"Right." I nod. "Lab first, library after."

I've been doing a lot of my schoolwork with Rakel, and my grades have improved somewhat. She's bossy, but she has a better background on subjects like the history of the mafia clans. I'm picking up some of the chemistry and programming faster than her, so we're useful to each other.

I hurry to breakfast, and then I follow Zoe through the stone gates to the outdoor bleachers assembled around the boxing ring. I'm glad I get to sit with Zoe and her usual group of friends.

For once Leo gets to sit back and watch a challenge, instead of having to orchestrate the victory. I'm not sure he prefers it this way—he looks tense and nervy, even with Anna cuddled up next to him.

Chay and Ozzy sit on their other side. You might think they were a couple, if Chay didn't keep protesting otherwise. She looks plenty comfortable leaning against Ozzy's shoulder while she chats with Anna. Ozzy finally got his bandage off, but his arm looks awful—the skin a mat of puckered scar tissue, mottled red and purple, only half-healed. The scars darker in the patches that used to be tattoos.

Hedeon and Ares sit in the row in front of ours. I don't see Miles anywhere—I ask Zoe what he's doing. She shrugs, unconcerned. "I'm sure he'll be along soon enough."

The Sophomores, Juniors, and Seniors mostly cluster in their respective groups so they can cheer for their fighters. The Freshmen have already been eliminated, so it doesn't matter where we sit or who we support.

I'm cheering for the Sophomores, though the only fighter I know is Dean, who terrifies me.

Leo ended up selecting Dean Yenin, Silas Gray, and Kenzo Tanaka. The Juniors picked Kasper Markaj, an Albanian

Enforcer who Zoe tells me was a team Captain in last year's *Quartum Bellum*.

"He's decent and hardworking," she says. "It was a shame his team was eliminated so early. I know he felt bad about it."

Their other fighter is Jasper Webb, the boy with the skeletal tattoos who harassed Chay during my first breakfast at King-makers. The one who helped hold my sister down while Rocco cut her clothes off. Needless to say, I fucking hate him and hope he gets his face pounded in the first round.

The Seniors selected Calvin Caccia, an Italian Heir who Zoe says was also a Captain last year.

"I don't like him as much," Zoe tells me. "He's arrogant and rude, and he's got a grudge against Leo."

"So do a lot of people," Leo says, from the other side of Anna. "Don't hold that against him. If you hate everybody who hates me, you won't have many friends left."

Zoe laughs. Leo may have enemies, but he's still one of the most popular students at our school.

"Who are the other two?" I nod down toward the last two fighters warming up at the edge of the ring. One is a tall black guy with a ripped physique and a shaved head. The other is beastly in size, but he looks more fat than muscular.

"That's Zeke Golden and Lee Sparks," Anna says. "Zeke is skilled. And don't be fooled by the extra fluff—Lee's no slouch, either."

The fighters reach their hands into a sack to pull out an opponent's name. Leo gives an irritated grunt when Silas draws Lee Sparks, and another when Dean is paired up with Zeke Golden. It's bad luck that two of the Sophomore fighters will have to face experienced Seniors. Kenzo Tanaka draws Jasper Webb. The two previous Captains—Kasper Markaj and Calvin Caccia—are the first to enter the ring.

The fight is swift and decisive, Kasper easily outclassing Calvin Caccia, ending with a TKO after only one round.

"Ha!" Zoe cries, not having dropped her dislike of Calvin. "Good for Kasper. Bet that makes him feel better about last year."

Silas and Lee Sparks face off next. It's a battle of titans, the two heaviest fighters charging each other like bulls, clinching and thrashing around as if their horns are locked. Each time one throws the other to the ground, the crash echoes around the bleachers.

Hedeon is sitting right in front of me, close enough that he could rest his spine against my shins if he leaned back. He watches Silas swing his heavy ham-like fists into his opponent's face. With every blow his brother lands, Hedeon flinches. His skin has turned almost as gray as his name.

Silas wins, but only at a heavy cost. He's battered and bleeding, not that it seems to bother him any. Lee looks even worse and has to be helped out of the ring and taken directly to the infirmary.

Hedeon rests his face in his hands, looking ill.

I want to ask if he's okay, but I don't dare do it.

"You want a drink?" Ares says, passing over a bottle of water.

Hedeon raises his face, wild-eyed and angry, like he's going to snarl at Ares. He stops himself, just barely.

"Thanks," he mutters, taking the water and drinking it down.

Dean is up next, against Zeke Golden.

Tension sweeps the crowd. The Seniors have already lost two of their fighters—if Zeke doesn't win, they'll lose the challenge and be eliminated from the *Quartum Bellum*.

The pressure is visible on Zeke's rigid frame, and on Dean as well. Both fighters look strained as they climb into the ring. Unlike the first two pairings, both Dean and Zeke are experienced boxers, hands wrapped with professional care, both falling naturally into their stance before Professor Howell has even tapped the starting bell.

"Fucking hell," Anna breathes as the fight begins.

Dean and Zeke are so fast that I can hardly keep track as they attack each other with rapid, intricate combinations. This is the difference between trained and highly-trained, boxers vs. brawlers. The crowd collectively holds their breath, the punches landing too fast even for cheers.

The fight goes the full three rounds. I can't tell who won, though I suspect it might have been Dean. His face is almost unmarked, other than a small bruise under one eye.

The judges—Professor Howell, Professor Bruce, and the Chancellor himself—bend their heads over their scorecards. The crowd silently waits. The Chancellor gives Dean an approving nod as he announces the unanimous decision.

The Seniors howl with rage. They're out of the *Quartum Bellum* without even the dignity of advancing to the final round.

Dean looks angry instead of pleased. He probably wanted to win that fight outright, not by decision.

"I can't believe it!" Anna cries. "We're safe!"

"Yup," Leo says with a strained smile.

"That was intense," Anna sighs.

"Dean's a good fighter; that's why I picked him," Leo says, trying to keep the jealousy out of his voice.

Anna catches it anyway. She grabs his face and kisses him.

"You'd knock the shit out of any of them if you were down there," she says.

Leo smiles, mollified. "I don't know about that. I'd definitely beat that fucker Calvin Caccia though, wouldn't I, Zoe?"

"That's right." Zoe grins.

With only Sophomore and Junior fighters remaining, the matches continue for bragging rights, and possibly an advantage in the final challenge.

The last pairing is Kenzo Tanaka against Jasper Webb.

I know who I want to win, and not just because I'm supporting the Sophomores. Any friend of Rocco deserves an ass-kicking.

Jasper Webb climbs up in the ring. He looks calm and unphased, even as the surrounding students scream down at him. He shucks off his shirt, revealing a chest and back tattooed in the same manner as his hands, with a perfect anatomical representation of the bones beneath the skin.

"Why do you think he did that?" Zoe says quietly, beside me.

"I don't know," I say. "To remind himself of our inevitable end, I suppose. Or he just thinks it looks scary."

I say it mockingly, but in truth Jasper does cut an imposing figure as he tosses his long, dark red hair back out of his face. His body is lean, hard, and pale, with ripples of muscle beneath the tattooed bones. Even from up here, I can see that his green eyes are vivid as my sister's, though infinitely colder.

He faces off against Kenzo Tanaka, who has his dark hair brushed into a retro-style pompadour, and his shirt likewise stripped off to show the dragon tattoo running from thumb to shoulder.

"It's the battle of the ink," Leo says. He's trying to sound casual, but his eyes are fixed on the ring. He wants Kenzo to win. He wants the Sophomores to triumph.

We're all destined for disappointment. Kenzo starts out strong, hitting Jasper with some vicious kicks and punches to the head. Jasper barely seems to feel it. He takes blow after blow, never staggering.

The second round begins, and Jasper walks to the center-ring as fresh as if the fight is just beginning. Kenzo fires a few more combinations at him. Jasper slips them easily. Waiting patiently for an opening, he shoots the gap and hits Kenzo with a single hard right-cross straight to the jaw. Kenzo goes down limp and boneless.

The crowd roars. Jasper isn't popular, but no one can deny the perfect precision of that punch. Professor Howell hoists Jasper's arm in the air. The cheers are deafening.

Howell calls a short break before the second round of fights. Only a couple of students leave the bleachers. Though the final round of the *Quartum Bellum* is already assured, the Sophomores and Juniors are still intently interested to see whose fighter will triumph. The Freshmen and Seniors likewise seemed glued to the ring, eager to see who will have to fight Silas next and whether Jasper will be able to employ that sledgehammer punch against a different opponent.

Miles scales the side of the bleachers, squeezing into the gap between Anna and Zoe.

"Where have you been?" Zoe says, her cheeks flushing pink just from the sight of Miles.

"Thought you might be getting hungry," he says, passing around a paper bag of fresh-baked chocolate chip cookies. They're warm and soft, the chocolate chips still melty from the oven. I scarf my cookie down in two bites.

"A present from your friends in the kitchen?" Zoe laughs.

"I told you, they'll trade their souls for the right baggie." Miles grins.

"No milk?" Leo complains.

"Only for Zoe," Miles fires back, pulling a chilled glass bottle out from under his shirt and ripping off the paper top.

"Zoe. I will pay you five hundred dollars for that milk," Leo says, eyes fixed on the bottle. "I'll do all your homework for a year. Please. I need it."

"There's plenty," Zoe says, taking a sip and passing it along. "I'm happy to share."

"And she doesn't want your homework help," Anna laughs. "It wouldn't improve her grades."

"I've been studying this year," Leo says, pretending to be hurt.

"Not as much as Zoe."

"Well if that's the standard, then none of us study."

"Except Ares," Zoe amends.

I'm only half-listening to the conversation because I'm looking across the ring at the double rows of seats reserved for the teachers. Miss Robin sits at the edge of the second row, her red hair flaming in the sunshine and her lumpy, oversized cardigan ill-suited to the warm spring weather.

"Look at that," I say to Zoe. "Miss Robin came."

"It's funny seeing her in sunlight," Zoe says.

"Well, now you know for sure she's not a vampire."

"I bet she's finally getting comfortable at the school," Zoe says. "I'm glad—I'm sure it takes a while to get used to this place. And the other professors."

"I like Miss Robin," Miles says, taking the milk back from Leo and washing down his cookie. "She did me a solid the other day."

"What did she do?" Anna asks.

I see a quick, amused glance pass between Miles and Zoe.

"She found my textbook in the lost and found," Miles says.

Professor Howell climbs up into the ring, easily vaulting over the top rope though it's chest-high on him.

"Ready for the second round?" he shouts up to the crowd.

The students roar their approval, not nearly satiated yet.

The fighters draw lots again, and this time there's an audible gasp as Silas is paired up with Jasper Webb. Jasper barely had time to recover from his last fight, but he takes his position, looking cool and uncaring even in the face of Silas's granite bulk. Jasper cracks his knuckles, the sharp popping audible all the way up in the stands.

The fighters raise their fists. Professor Howell rings the bell.

This time Jasper is careful to avoid Silas's blows. He dances and dodges with a speed almost approaching Dean's. Silas is ferociously strong. When he clips Jasper with even a glancing blow, the impact is brutal. Jasper begins to bleed from nose, lip, and eyebrow.

Still, he's giving almost as good as he gets. Sniper-like, he fires off sharp, snapping punches that hit Silas precisely where Jasper intends. He opens a cut over Silas's left eye, then hits him again in the same spot, sending a torrent of blood into

Silas's eye, half-blinding him. Staggering around off balance, Silas is struck again and again.

By the third round, Silas tires. Jasper redoubles his speed. He's just as fast as he was to start with, maybe even faster. But Silas is so massive that Jasper's blows don't have the same effect as they did on Kenzo Tanaka. Silas stumbles and reels without going down.

When the bell sounds, it's clear that Jasper has won on points. Both he and Silas are a mess, blood raining down on the canvas.

By contrast, Dean makes short work of Kasper Markaj. Zoe wants to cheer for Kasper, even though he's a Junior, but it's clear from the start that he can't keep up with Dean.

Dean moves through his footwork with balletic grace. Each blow is swift, calculated, and horribly strong. His fists are scythes, slicing through the air.

Miss Robin leans forward in her seat, her dark eyes locked on the fighters. Her cheeks are flushed, and she looked trans-fixed, barely breathing.

It strikes me that she might have come to this particular event because she likes boxing. It's a curious preference for someone so gentle, but people don't always resemble their interests. There are plenty of grannies that love wrestling, or bikers who like to bake.

Dean knocks Kasper to the canvas three times in the first round. On that third fall, Kasper doesn't get up. He concedes the victory, stumbling out of the ring supported by Professor Howell.

Dean raises his own gloved fist in victory, stern and unsmiling. He doesn't seem to get any joy from his wins. Yet I can tell how badly he wants them.

Professor Howell announces one more break before the final round.

Not a single person leaves their seat.

Everyone is wildly curious whether Dean will continue to prevail, or if Jasper will prove some kind of dark-horse phenom.

"I didn't even know he was that good a fighter," Leo says.

"I did," Miles replies, unsmiling. "I've seen him in Combat class."

"Still . . . taking down Silas . . ."

"Silas was pretty beat up from his first fight," Ares says.

Hedeon isn't joining in the conversation. The milk and cookies seemed to revive him slightly, but he's still broody and pale.

Dean and Jasper take their places in the ring. Jasper is heavily marked from his battle with Silas, while Dean's face is almost pristine. Neither boy shows a trace of nervousness—just cold intention. Dean has removed his shirt as well, his body is a testament to endless hours in the gym: focused, repeated training sculpting each muscle to superhuman perfection.

"God almighty," Chay says quietly.

Anna shoots her a quelling look, probably for Leo's benefit.

"I'm sorry!" Chay cries. "I know we hate him, but he's a fucking specimen. Don't worry, Leo, you are too—I saw you naked in the dining hall, so I know what you're packing. I'm just saying . . ."

Leo doesn't seem bothered, but Ozzy has fallen quiet on the opposite side of Chay.

The bell rings and Dean and Jasper close the space swiftly and silently. Like hawks they swoop and twist and dive at each other, clinging and breaking apart only to attack again, even faster than Dean's fight with Zeke Golden. I have my hands pressed against my mouth, biting hard on my knuckle without even realizing it.

The blows hit in near-constant tempo, both Dean and Jasper wincing and spitting blood, but neither slowing for an instant.

Jasper pins Dean against the ropes and hits him with a punishing combination that seems like it might just win the fight. Dean fires back with a volley of punches that are the first Jasper truly seems to feel. He drops to his knee and Dean hits him again, knocking him flat on the canvas.

The fight is over. Dean won.

"Maybe Jasper could have made it if he didn't fight Silas first," Chay says.

"I doubt it," Leo says, shaking his head. "Dean's so fucking good."

I know the animosity between Leo and Dean is still raw, but Leo's pragmatism won't let him deny Dean's skill. He's realistic, whether he likes the truth or not.

"You're the one who picked him!" Anna reminds Leo. "We won the second challenge!"

"Dean won it," Leo laughs.

"Under your excellent leadership," she gives him a light kiss on the mouth.

I see Miles and Zoe exchange another glance. Probably wishing they could be affectionate whenever and wherever they like. Wishing that, like Anna and Leo, their marriage contract was a license to date and not a prison sentence.

"Well," I sigh. "I'd better get going. I'm supposed to work on a coding project with Rakel this afternoon."

"She talking to you now?" Chay laughs.

"Sometimes!" I say. "A lot, actually."

"I bet poor Anna wishes I'd give her the silent treatment once in a while," Chay says, grinning at Anna.

"Only after midnight," Anna grumbles.

I climb down from the bleachers, planning to head to the computer lab in the Keep.

Heavy footsteps follow after me. I turn, expecting to see Leo or Miles, or maybe even Ares. Instead, I find Hedeon only an arm's reach away.

"Oh, hello," I say. "You have a class in the Keep, too?"

"No," Hedeon says shortly.

He still looks pale and out of sorts. I don't think he enjoyed the fights at all.

I don't expect him to walk with me or talk to me either. We may have danced together at Halloween, but Hedeon and I are not friends. I'm sure the dancing was purely out of necessity—there's a dearth of girls at Kingmakers, and Chay, Anna, and Zoe were already occupied.

So I'm surprised when Hedeon keeps pace with me, silent and scowling, like a grouchy, elongated shadow.

"You're good at those hacking classes, huh?" he says abruptly.

"Uh, sure . . . good enough," I reply. "I'm learning."

"You have access to the school computers?"

"Yes . . ." I say hesitantly. "Limited access."

"Could you get more?"

He's watching me with sharp blue eyes under the straight, dark slashes of his brows. His voice is calm, but I hear the hidden edge underneath, like a razor blade buried in a cupcake.

I stop walking. "What are you asking me, exactly?"

Hedeon grabs my arm and pulls me into the shadow of the Armory, out of the flow of students heading toward the Keep.

"I want to know if you could hack into the school server."

"I have no idea," I say, staring up into his face. "I wouldn't try."

"I could pay you," Hedeon says. I hear the urgency now, how badly he wants this.

I should just tell him no. I shouldn't even be discussing this. But I'm prickling with curiosity.

I used to mind my own business. I used to be timid and safe.

Ever since I came to Kingmakers, I've become much more inquisitive. There's a world of secrets and lies all around me. I'd like to know the answers to a few things . . .

Maybe the Spies are rubbing off on me after all.

"I have to know what you're looking for," I say. "Or else I won't know if I can do it."

Hedeon narrows his eyes at me, suspicious.

I try to maintain my innocent, wide-eyed expression. Like I only want to help him.

"I need access to student records," he says. "Old records."

"You think they're on a server?" I say. "I thought everything at Kingmakers was written by hand."

I'm thinking of our acceptance letters, our contracts, our assignments, our grades. My impression was that it was all kept on paper so it could be burned or disposed of with no permanent record.

"There's nothing in the archives," Hedeon says, frustrated. "The records must be somewhere else."

I hold my breath, realizing that Hedeon already asked Saul this question. That's why he was in Saul's room the day I bumped into him down in the Undercroft—he wanted Saul to check the archives, which Saul has access to as a library aide.

Saul must have told him there were no records down there.

Which means they must be online.

Or stored somewhere else.

"I don't know if I can even look," I tell Hedeon. "All our keystrokes are tracked in the computer lab. I'm sure they have some pretty hefty protection against us accessing the school server."

Hedeon is already turning away, disappointment clear on his handsome face.

It's that look of anguish that pricks me, turning curiosity into guilt. I do want to help him.

"Wait!" I say, calling him back.

"What?" Hedeon rounds on me, angry as well as discouraged.

"What about the stables?"

He frowns, not understanding me.

"The night of the Halloween party, I was sitting on a stack of boxes and I knocked them over. There were a bunch of papers inside. Old documents. That couch is from the Chancellor's office, everybody says. Maybe the papers are too?"

Hedeon considers this, lips pressed tight together.

"I'll look," he says. And then, as an afterthought, "Thank you."

"No problem. I hope it helps."

His face darkens once more and he growls, "Don't tell anyone about this, Cat. Nobody. Not even Zoe."

"I won't," I say. "I mean, I don't even know anything."

Hedeon looks at me closely, then stalks off.

It's true, I don't know anything.

But if Hedeon wants old school records . . . then I'm beginning to guess.

16

ZOE

The weather warms rapidly as we move into spring. Students start throwing more parties out of doors, down at the Moon Beach and in the River Bottoms.

I've received three extremely nasty letters from my father after my cousins reported me attending those parties. I crumpled the letters up and threw them away half-read. It might be madness, but I'm starting to think that the plan Miles and I formulated might actually work, which makes me uncharacteristically reckless.

Either way, my father can't touch me here. He could punish me over the summer. But if Miles' visit is successful after the school year ends . . . everything will change.

I'm trying not to hope. Trying not even to think about it.

Which isn't that difficult, because my mind is filled with Miles himself. I've never had such a difficult time paying attention in class. Every minute that we're apart I'm fantasizing about sneaking away with him again. I'm picturing his crooked smile, his low, mocking laugh, his clear gray eyes that remind me of steel, of smoke, of early morning light . . .

I'm picturing his body with his rich, nut-brown skin and his dense muscle, his warm flesh and his even warmer hands that grip and manipulate me like a doll in his arms, while I'm carried away on waves of pleasure that are steep and endless . . .

I had never been happy before, not really. I never knew what it felt like.

Happiness is exhilarating, intoxicating. I'm drunk on it. It makes me believe I can do anything. It makes me believe that everything will be okay.

It's changing me. And it's changing Miles, too.

"I've never seen him like this," Anna tells me. "I'm not saying he was a dick before—I mean, he was always nice to me. When he felt like it. But he was obsessed with doing everything his own way, without help. Everybody's his friend and everybody owes him favors, but ultimately it was about Miles and what he wanted. You're bringing out the best in him, Zoe. Giving him something to care about outside of himself."

"I don't know about that," I say, blushing. "I'm not trying to change him. I like him exactly as he is."

Anna laughs. "Oh you do, do you? Have you forgotten the Miles of last year? You really must be falling hard."

I stare at her open-mouthed. I *had* actually forgotten that I disliked Miles in my Freshman year. It seems impossible now, like I was a completely different person. Somebody uptight and miserable, which of course is true.

"I hope you keep liking him." Anna smiles at me. "We could be family."

The idea hits me like a bolt of pure joy. Anna and Leo as actual family, not just friends . . . Miles as my family . . .

I want it. I want it so badly that it feels like it will tear me apart.

"Are you coming out with us tonight?" I ask Anna.

"I wish I could," she sighs. "I have three different papers due. Leo's gonna keep me company in the library, though I shouldn't let him. He's more distracting than helpful."

"Come join us later if you can—"

Chay interrupts us, barging into the room with arms laden with books. She dumps them down on her bed, crying, "Fuck class! Fuck homework! When's our picnic?"

"In an hour," I laugh. "Lend me something cute to wear."

Chay, Ozzy, Miles, and I planned to have a picnic down outside the school grounds. I was hoping Anna and Leo could join us too, but it sounds like they'll be occupied in the same manner as Cat, drowning in midterm papers.

Anna helps us get ready anyway, picking out a pair of jeans and boots for me to wear. Chay lends me an oversized Queen shirt. I can't borrow pants from Chay because she's so much shorter that they'd fit more like capris.

"Let me do your makeup," Chay demands.

"Not too much," I warn her.

"I never do too much! On you . . ." Chay amends, laughing.

Chay gives me a nice subtle smoky eye and a little lip gloss. I pull my hair up in a messy ponytail. With the band shirt and Anna's boots, I feel a tiny bit rockstar. I like it. I never felt "cool" in my life before I met these girls.

Chay spends forty minutes more redoing her own elaborate makeup, until I'm fidgeting with impatience and almost pulling her out the door.

"Alright, alright!" she says, "I'm coming!"

Chay looks surprisingly sweet and feminine in a white summer dress, cardigan, and espadrilles. The pink streaks have faded from her hair, so now it's just a soft fluffy mane of her usual strawberry blonde, which contrasts nicely against her golden tan.

When we meet up with Ozzy and Miles outside the stone walls of Kingmakers, Ozzy stares at Chay with a stunned expression.

"You're just . . . perfection," he says.

Instead of laughing and agreeing like she usually would, Chay says, "That's really sweet of you to say, Ozzy."

"He stole the words right out of my mouth," Miles growls, slipping his arm around my waist. "What can I tell you now— what's better than perfection?"

"This," I say. "This moment right now."

The evening is warm and still, the fresh scent of new grass sweet in the air. Tiny paper-white butterflies flit over the wildflowers in the field. The light is golden and soft.

I shouldn't let Miles touch me while we're still within sight of the school. But there's no one around. I feel safe and flushed with happiness.

"Where should we go?" Chay asks.

Ozzy hoists his backpack on his shoulder. "I was thinking we could go to the cliffs above the Moon Beach," he says. "Watch the sun go down."

We tramp across the field, through a strip of woods, and then westward through the vineyards. The vines are just beginning to flower, the leaves green and lush but the grapes still tiny and hard.

"The deck behind my parents' house is covered in fox grapes," Miles tells me.

"Oh really?"

"They're old vines, brought all the way from Italy two hundred years ago."

"Your family brought them over?"

Miles nods. "We had this old Georgian house in Chicago. It was in the family for generations. My grandfather Enzo lived there, my mom was born there, lived there all her life. The fox grapes grew up the side of the house and over the pergola on the roof. But the house burned down."

I groan with sympathy.

"Actually," Miles gives a short, mirthless laugh. "Dean's grandpa set it on fire. Alexei Yenin—just picture Dean, with KGB training and an even worse attitude. Leo's father married Alexei's daughter, you know that?"

I nod. Anna told me when she explained the tortured history between the cousins.

"Anyway, Leo's dad Sebastian, he was in the house at the time, with Dean's father Adrian Yenin. Alexei didn't care. He fire-bombed the house with his own son inside. Sebastian left Adrian to die, and he almost did. He was burned over half his body."

Ozzy and Chay are listening as intently as I am, though I'm sure Ozzy at least has heard this story before.

"Uncle Seb fought Alexei Yenin. He killed him. It was revenge, because Alexei had already killed Grandpa Enzo. Tried to kill the rest of my uncles, too. Seb and Uncle Miko—Anna's dad, you know him."

Chay nods.

"They beat the Bratva. Took back their half of Chicago. But the house was totally destroyed—the books, the photographs, my grandmother's piano, even Uncle Nero's cars in the under-ground garage. My family was devastated. They didn't try to rebuild.

"The next spring, my mother came back to the lot before it was going to be cleaned up and sold. She found one sprig of the fox grapes still growing. Green where the rest of the vines were nothing but ash. She dug it up and replanted it out at the lake where she and my dad were just starting to build their own house. It grew perfectly. The grapes are thicker than ever. The bees and the wasps get drunk every fall."

I've never heard Miles talk like this before. He loves to discuss his plans for the future. I've never heard him sentimental.

"The lake house is gorgeous," Ozzy tells me. "I visited—you can see trees and water from every room."

Miles told me about the house, about his little brother and sister, and about his parents—the stern Irish mafia prince and the wild Italian princess who were married against their will to avoid all out war between their families.

Obviously, I hate the idea of any kind of forced marriage, but Miles assured me they didn't stay enemies for long.

"Once they were done trying to kill each other, they got along great," he laughed.

That's an outcome that could never occur for Rocco and me.

One I wouldn't even want, now that I've fallen head over heels for Miles. There's no other happy ending for me. I want Miles, and no one else.

"I want you to see it," Miles tells me now, "I want you to see the grapes and the lake house. I want you to meet my family."

"I'd love that," I say, swallowing hard. In truth, I'm intimidated by the description of Miles' parents. They're brilliant and ruthless—they run half of Chicago. Having never known affectionate parents myself, I have a hard time picturing powerful people who might also be loving and supportive to their children.

"I told my mother about you," Miles says.

"You did?"

I'm stunned. For all the promises Miles made to me, this is something different, something concrete and real. He wouldn't have done that if he wasn't serious about moving forward with our relationship.

"Have you told your mother about me?" Chay says to Ozzy, in her teasing way. She's only joking—she wouldn't expect Ozzy to tell his parents about their hook-ups.

But Ozzy looks her in the eye, his face serious.

"Yes," he says. "I did."

Chay is taken aback. She's quiet for a moment, then she says, "What did you tell her?"

"I told her I met a girl who's bold and funny and creative, and absolutely fucking gorgeous, and that I'm crazy about her."

Chay's blue eyes are wide and startled. For once, she's not laughing.

She opens her mouth to reply but doesn't seem to know what to say.

It doesn't matter—we've arrived at the cliffs, so she's saved from responding.

Ozzy unzips his backpack, taking out a blanket, a bottle of wine, several packs of sandwiches, and a half-dozen apples.

"No glasses," Ozzy says. "Seemed like they'd only end up smashed."

"You remembered the bottle opener," Miles says, popping the cork. "That's all that matters."

The wine is from the very vineyards we just traversed. The bottle is stamped with the plain, dark label showing an outline of the island, no text. It's a rich, dark pinot noir that you have to drink carefully, because the effects creep up on you quickly.

Chay is uncharacteristically quiet as we eat and drink, looking out over the sparkling water at the setting sun.

We've come just in time to watch the heavy orange sphere sinking down into the waves. Enough clouds blanket the sky that we can look directly west, watching the colors change from pink to orange to a deep, bloody red.

"Tell me about your family," Chay asks Ozzy, once we've drunk more than half the wine.

"I'm an only child," Ozzy says, taking an aggressive bite out of an apple. "I've got a million cousins, though. We grew up wild and feral in Tasmania. We'd go surfing in the Bay of Fires—there's orange lichen all over the rocks, so it really does look fiery, especially when you've got a sunset like this one going. We'd run through the lavender fields in February when they bloom. There's tulip fields too, and raspberry farms—it's fucking gorgeous, really. Nobody knows how pretty 'cause nobody comes to see it."

Ozzy's face is half-lit by the setting sun. The shadows bring out the rugged lines of his broad nose and jaw and the deep dimples as he smiles. Ozzy may not be conventionally handsome, but his warmth and charm are undeniable, especially when he's speaking in his bright, lilting accent.

"I'd like to see it," Chay says softly. She's looking at her hands when she says it, and then she chances one quick glance up at Ozzy.

"Don't tease me, girl," he growls. "I'll buy you a ticket right now."

I'm leaning back against Miles' chest, feeling warm as toast with his arms around me. As the sky darkens, the rhythm of his breath rocks me, and I become sleepy and peaceful.

"What are you thinking?" Miles murmurs in my ear.

"I'm thinking this is the best day of my life," I say. "All the best days have been with you. They just keep getting better."

"My mother told me that once," Miles says quietly. "When you find your soulmate . . . every day is the best day."

He tilts my head back so he can kiss me.

"I didn't understand it then," he says. "I'm starting to now."

I reach my hand up to tangle my fingers in his thick, dark curls. The kiss deepens, and Chay says, "Ozzy, take me for a walk so I can sober up a bit before we head back."

"Sure," Ozzy says affably.

I know they're leaving to give Miles and me a little privacy, and I appreciate it.

As soon as they're out of sight, walking south along the cliffs, Miles starts to undress me. Now that the sun is almost down, a breeze blows in off the water. It feels cool and delicious, liquid against my bare skin. Miles strips me completely naked, then trails his fingers lightly over my flesh, tracing the profile of my nose, lips, and chin, then drawing the curves of my breasts, slowly circling inward until his fingertips stroke my nipples into hard, aching points.

He runs his hand lightly down my navel. His fingers caress me like the breeze, like I'm a maiden that fell asleep in a field and he's the god of wind, come to ravage me.

"You're the most beautiful sight I've ever seen, Zoe," he growls, his voice low and thick. "No sunset, no painting, no creation of god or man is more stunning than you." He laughs. "Not even in Tasmania."

I should be afraid—I'm naked as a jaybird, out in the open on the cliff-top, where anyone could see me. Students roam all over the island.

But I feel nothing but pure bliss. Miles is a drug—its effects are reckless abandon.

"Take me," I beg him. "Right here, right now."

I don't have to ask twice. Miles puts his face between my thighs, pushing my knees apart with his hands to spread my pussy open the way he likes. He licks me everywhere, making sure I'm wet and throbbing and ready for him. He never tires of eating my pussy. He enjoys it even more than I do, if that's possible—he wants it every single time.

I've never thought of this as a dominating act, but Miles never has more control over me than when he's between my legs, orchestrating a symphony of sensation that blasts through every cell of my body, taking me over from head to toe. He owns me like this. I'll give him anything in the world, as long as he doesn't stop.

He makes me beg and cry. He makes me feel like I'm dying. And when I'm limp and shaking with pleasure, that's when he mounts me and thrusts his cock inside of me. All I can do is cling to him with my arms around his neck as the sensation begins to build all over again.

I never knew sex could have so many personalities. Sometimes Miles orders me around, and the power play of his dominance and my submission is achingly erotic. Sometimes we fuck like animals, driven to claw and bite as we mate. And sometimes sex is like this: slow and sensual, sweeter than honey and warmer than a bath.

Our bodies melt together, our mouths locked, our tongues entwined. I can hardly tell where Miles ends and I begin. The waves washing against Moon Beach below are distant and soothing. The sky is fully dark now. The cocoon of that darkness makes me feel that Miles and I are alone in the world, two people that are really one person, one being.

"I love you," I whisper. I don't know if I said it out loud or only in my head.

"I love you," Miles says, at the same time.

I've never felt connection like this, or pleasure like this.

I can't give it up. Not for anything.

Miles fucks me deep and slow and hard. The head of his cock hits the furthest point inside of me, which should be uncomfortable, painful even. I'm so aroused that it isn't painful, it's deeply satisfying instead. In fact, I'm beginning to feel an intense pleasure at that hidden spot, nerves that have never been touched before stroked into firing. They blaze into life, a totally new sensation, and I start to orgasm in a way I haven't before, in a spot I didn't even know I could feel.

The orgasm pulses out in waves, clenching and squeezing around Miles' cock. He starts to cum too. He can never hold back if I cum while he's inside me.

Miles crushes me in his arms, he drives deep inside of me and holds his cock there while it twitches and pulses in response to my climax. I'm still cumming, one long, continuous orgasm that perpetuates just as long as his, maybe even longer.

We're both panting and sweating in the cool breeze. I hate that I have to pull my clothes back on, because I'd much rather lay in his arms all night long.

I barely dress myself in time, before I hear Ozzy calling out, "Break it up, lovebirds, we gotta head back."

I can hear Ozzy and Chay tramping through the high grass before I see them. Ozzy's bright grin gleams on his face, and Chay's hair looks tousled enough that I'm guessing their walk turned into something similar to what Miles and I were doing.

Ozzy starts packing up the picnic supplies while Miles shakes off the blanket.

"We should have brought a flashlight," Chay says.

"The moon will be up in a minute," Miles says. "We'll make it back alright."

Sure enough, the moon rises bright and full, a flat silver disk that drowns out the stars.

It's bright enough that we don't stumble as we head back through the vineyards.

I don't think I'd stumble anyway—I feel like I'm floating, with my hand wrapped up in Miles' and my feet barely touching the ground.

Nothing could ruin this moment.

Until we come out of the trees that border the vineyard and a horribly familiar voice says, "There you are. We thought we missed you."

Four figures stand in the field south of Kingmakers: Wade Dyer, Dax Volker, Jasper Webb, and Rocco Prince. They form a barrier between us and the castle.

Miles' fingers lock tight around mine as his body goes tense as stone. He casts a quick glance behind us. I know he's contemplating telling me to run. But the only thing behind us is the cliffs, and the path down to Moon Beach, which is another dead end.

We got sloppy. Rocco hasn't spoken to me in weeks. He lulled us into a false sense of security, which I'm sure was exactly his intention. He let Miles and I get wrapped up in each other, forgetting that Rocco even existed. While he never forgot about us at all.

"What do you want?" Miles says.

I know he's afraid, because he can see the ugliness of our situation just as well as I can. But there's no hint of fear in his voice. He sounds as strong and clear as ever.

"I want what I always wanted," Rocco says softly. His pale face looks flat and waxy in the moonlight. "I want Zoe."

Before I can open my mouth to reply, Miles steps in front of me.

"No," he says.

Rocco laughs. His laugh is more breath than sound, eerily repetitive.

"We're going to beat you until you barely blink, Miles. Then I'm going to take what was promised me. I'm going to fuck Zoe right in front of you. Maybe I'll let Wade and Dax and Jasper take a turn. You'll lay there watching, choking on your own blood. When I'm finished, you'll both finally understand the truth. She belongs to me. She always has, and she always will."

He jerks his head toward Chay and Ozzy. "You two can go."

Chay scoffs right in his face. "Who the fuck do you think you're talking to? You're not touching our friends."

I've never loved Chay more than in this moment. But unlike Miles, her voice isn't calm and confident. It's tight with fear, coming out an octave higher than normal.

Ozzy backs her up, addressing Wade, Dax, and Jasper, because he knows there's no point reasoning with Rocco. "Don't be stupid," he says. "This won't end well for any of you."

Wade smirks, his handsome face not looking handsome at all when it's twisted up in disdain.

"Please tell me this wasn't a double-date, Chay," he scoffs. "Fucking this grubby little degenerate is one thing, but actually going out with him . . . say it isn't so."

Chay meets Wade's scorn with a cold stare.

"He's ten times the man you'll ever be," she says.

Wade stops smiling. "He'll be ten times the man when I rip him into pieces," he seethes. He strides forward.

I scream, "No!" trying to step out from behind Miles, but he won't let me, he blocks me with his arm.

"Leave them alone!" I shout over Miles' shoulder.

"Come with me now and I will," Rocco hisses, his eyes dark and gleaming in his white face.

"No *fucking* way," Miles barks, before I can answer.

"So be it," Rocco says, flicking out the blade of his knife.

Wade, Dax, Jasper, and Rocco all charge us at once.

Wade and Dax run at Ozzy, Jasper at me, and Rocco at Miles.

It's a blur of motion and confusion in the weak light.

Half of what I perceive is through grunts and yells, rather than what I can actually see.

Rocco slashes his knife wildly at Miles, the blade winking in and out of sight as it reflects the moonlight. Miles twists and dodges, the tip catching him at least twice, slicing through his shirt and slashing his arm.

Jasper comes at me just like he attacked Dean in the ring—with breathless speed and absolute silence. I try to slip his grasp, but he's much faster than me. His arms lock around me, harder than iron.

Trying to remember everything I ever learned in Combat Class, I stomp down hard on his right foot, and whip my head backward, hitting him in the mouth with the back of my skull. I hear Jasper's grunt of pain. Warm blood spatters my arm.

Jasper's python arms barely relax for a moment. When I try to twist away from him, he locks his forearm around my throat instead, pinning me against his chest.

Head swimming, I see Wade and Dax pummeling Ozzy, a maelstrom of punching fists where Ozzy gives as good as he gets because he's stocky and powerful. His tight punches rocket out from his body, slamming into the other two boys with echoing thuds. Still, Wade and Dax are bigger and just as used to fighting. They'd overwhelm Ozzy in minutes, if they hadn't forgotten Chay.

She jumps on Dax's back, locking both arms around his throat and choking him hard. Dax stumbles backward, trying to shake her off. Meanwhile, Ozzy tackles Wade. They roll around in the trampled grass, hitting and throttling each other.

I'm still squirming and flailing my elbows, trying to hit Jasper in the body. The more I struggle, the more he tightens his arm on my throat. I'm so dizzy I can barely stand.

Rocco takes another slash at Miles' face. This time, Miles manages to catch Rocco's wrist and hold it. Rocco punches Miles with his free hand, three times over in the side of the face, but Miles maintains his death grip on Rocco's knife with both hands, twisting Rocco's wrist until the knife flies through the air and lands in the grass next to Ozzy's boot.

Now Rocco and Miles are brawling in earnest, and I realize that I've underestimated Miles yet again. I've never seen him fight before. In this moment, Miles is no dancer or deal-maker. He's a fucking killer. He looks crazed as he hits Rocco over and over, savage blows with no caution behind them, no hint of restraint.

Rocco is a snake, but Miles is a lion. No matter how Rocco gouges and bites and claws at him, Miles responds with twice the fury.

I take heart from Miles, redoubling my efforts to get free of Jasper. I twist and flail until I manage to reach back and smash him in the balls with the side of my fist. That's what finally forces him to let go. I break free right as Wade Dyer hits Ozzy with a punishing blow that knocks him back to the ground.

Dax is staggering as Chay cuts off his air. Wade charges at Chay and punches her in the side of the face, hard enough that she loses her grip and tumbles to the ground.

Both Miles and Ozzy roar with outrage. Miles flings Rocco off while Ozzy stumbles up and charges at Wade. Miles hits Dax twice in the face, which is enough to finish him, still dizzy and gasping from Chay's headlock. Meanwhile, Ozzy pummels Wade with hitherto unseen fury. Wade elbows Ozzy in the face, with a crack of bone-on-bone that breaks his nose.

Miles is so enraged that he leaps on Wade, hitting him again and again.

Wade's face is a mask of blood, and still Miles hits him.

Miles looks insane, completely out of his mind.

"STOP!" I scream, grabbing him by the shoulder and dragging him back.

Miles tries to break free, his bloody fists still raised, but I seize his shirt and pull so hard that he falls over backward on top of me.

Wade looks demonic, his eyes bright chips in his blood-soaked face.

Howling like an animal, he charges at Ozzy, who gropes in the grass beside him and snatches up Rocco's knife.

Wade jumps on Ozzy and Ozzy swings the knife.

"NO!" I scream.

The knife disappears into the side of Wade's neck.

My shout still echoes while absolute silence falls over the group.

Rocco stands up, his eyes fixed on Wade and his face utterly expressionless.

Jasper has taken several steps back. He stands alone, one skeletal hand pressed to his bleeding lip.

Dax is half-conscious, unaware of what's going on.

Chay is wide-eyed, both hands clapped over her mouth.

Ozzy freezes in place, horror-stricken at what he's done.

And Miles looks like he's about to throw up.

"Don't move," Miles says to Wade. "Don't touch it . . ."

Wade frowns, confused, as his hand fumbles against the side of his neck, his fingers brushing the handle of the knife.

He takes one staggering step forward. He opens his mouth to say something. All that comes out is a strangled, gurgling sound, and a large quantity of blood.

Then he sinks to his knees and topples forward, face-down in the grass.

"We have to get help," Ozzy cries.

We all know it's too late.

17

MILES

I'm in the Prison Tower, in the cell next to Ozzy.

Rocco Prince is on my other side. Dax and Jasper in the cell next to him.

The girls aren't being disciplined. All accounts agreed that they were not voluntary participants in the fight.

For Rocco, Dax, Jasper, and me, the punishment is seven days without food, and only 500 mL of water.

The torment is extreme. The starvation I could deal with, but the thirst is constant torture. My lips are cracked and parched. My throat and tongue so swollen I can barely speak. My skin gritty with salt.

I'm filthy. We have no extra water to bathe. I can't sleep because I dream of cool, flowing faucets, and I wake up gasping.

Yet none of this compares to the anguish of knowing that my best friend is about to be executed.

Many rules at Kingmakers can be bent. Some can even be broken. The one irreversible decree is the Rule of Recompense.

An eye for an eye. Tooth for a tooth. Death for a death.

Ozzy has already been sentenced.

Tomorrow he dies.

"Take a look at that sunset," Rocco hisses from his cell. "It's your last one."

Ozzy doesn't reply. He stopped talking two days ago.

It's me who responds.

"I will fucking kill you for this, Rocco. I will strip your flesh off, and stab your eyes out . . ."

I can't finish my threat because my throat is too dry to speak. It ends in an impotent rasp.

Wade's parents arrived this morning. I saw their ship come in, through the tiny window in my cell.

They haven't taken his body home. They're staying to witness the execution.

I would do anything, anything to save Ozzy.

I've tried to think of a way out of this. Day and night I racked my brains until I was delirious.

There's nothing I can do.

As our cells grow dark once more, I whisper, "I'm sorry, Ozzy."

I don't expect him to answer.

But after a long pause, he says, "It's not your fault, Miles. You stopped . . . I didn't."

18

CAT

They force the whole school to attend the execution.

I don't want to go.

I try to hide in the bathrooms of the Undercroft, but Saul Turner finds me and says, "You better get up there. The Chancellor's not exactly in a good mood."

I'm already crying as I take my seat in the Grand Hall. My guts are churning, and I think I might vomit. I don't want to watch Ozzy die.

Rocco, Dax, Jasper, and Miles are forced to sit in the front row, bound to their chairs. They look ragged and filthy, skinny from their week of starvation and wild-eyed from lack of water. Rocco is the least affected, though his face is now lean to the point of emaciation. Miles looks like a completely different person—no hint of his former swagger. He's beaten and broken.

Zoe is pale as a ghost. I don't think she ate this week either. She stumbles and almost falls as we take our seats. Leo has to help support her. Anna already has her arm around Chay. Silent tears run down Chay's face, as they have in a continual flow every time I've seen her. Her arms are raw where she's dug her fingernails into the skin.

A rigid tension runs through Leo, Ares, and even Hedeon, as if they want to mount an attack—break Ozzy and Miles free, help them escape.

We all know how impossible that would be. Even if we could overwhelm the professors and the staff, the grounds crew who double as security, and the Chancellor himself, it would all be pointless. Every family who sends a student to this school signs a contract in blood. Ozzy's sentence has been passed. A hundred mafia families would ensure that it was carried out—on him, and anyone who tried to help him.

The silence in the Grand Hall is an oppressive weight. No whispers, no fidgeting, no creak of chairs. Once the students are seated, you could hear an eyelash fall.

Even the cavernous hearth is silent, no fire burning in the grate.

The banners of the founding houses hang limp without a breeze to stir them. I look up at those banners, hating every single one. Hating the cruel and merciless power they represent. Hating this way of life where we're driven to extremes, then punished when we overstep the bounds.

Luther Hugo sits in a high-backed chair, facing the students.

He wears a black double-breasted suit, his long, dark hair combed straight back from his forehead, his pointed brows like inverted Vs over those glittering beetle-black eyes. He stares at the accused and then at the rest of us, his eyes piercing each student in turn. There's no enjoyment in his expression and no pity, either.

I wonder how many times he's done this.

Mr. and Mrs. Dyer sit to the left of the Chancellor. Wade's parents are as blond and beautiful as their son. I hate them, too, and feel no pity for their loss. They raised a garbage son. Even in death, he hasn't stopped hurting people. It's his fault we're all sitting here today. His fault, and Rocco's most of all. But only Ozzy will pay the ultimate price. He'll die to satisfy the Dyer's bloodlust.

To the right of the Chancellor sits a plain, dark-haired woman wearing a blue dress. Her face is pale and sober. I wonder if she might be the Chancellor's wife—I never heard if he was married. She's younger than him by twenty years at least.

That's common amongst the mafiosi. My stepmother is twenty-two years younger than my father.

The professors stand sentinel around the perimeter of the Hall, along with a dozen other Kingmakers staff. I realize how stupid I was to think that these burly stone-faced men were here simply for menial tasks like building the obstacle course and tending the grounds. I see them for what they are, now —soldiers.

Even the professors in their dark suits remind me of their former professions as mercenaries, assassins, torturers, and criminals. I see no tears in Professor Lyon's eyes, or even Professor Howell's. I fell into the pleasant fiction that these were my teachers, this was my school. I forgot why I was so terrified to come here in the first place.

At least Miss Robin stayed away. I couldn't bear to see her standing by, emotionless, like the rest of them.

The Chancellor stands in one, quick, sweeping motion. With all the impressive feats I've witnessed from Leo and Ares and Miles, it's easy to forget the difference between a man of twenty and one fully grown. The power that only comes from long experience—the difference between a sapling and hardened oak.

The Chancellor is massive, rough-hewn, lines etched in his face as deep as hatchet strokes. His visage is that of an ancient god, his voice thunder as he says, "A student was killed on our grounds. Wade Dyer died at the hand of Ozzy Duncan. Our laws are simple —a life for a life. The debt was incurred. Now it must be paid."

His voice echoes around the Hall long after he stops speaking.

The faces of my fellow students are sickened, stricken, but no one so much as dares to cry audibly. Not even me.

The Chancellor nods toward the double doors at the end of the hall. Professor Holland and Professor Knox shift from their military positions to pull them open.

Ozzy is led into the Hall by Professor Penmark, so weighed down with chains that he can barely walk. His hair is lank and unwashed, his face as hollow as Miles'. His hands are bound behind his back, and his chains make a horrible clanking sound with every step. His walk seems endless—perhaps he's moving slowly because he knows these moments are his last.

He's still wearing his school uniform, filthy and tattered as it has become. Somehow that seems the most awful thing of all to me—a symbol of his trust in the institution that now turns on him with such callousness.

I don't want to look at him, but it seems cowardly to turn away. His mouth is set, his gaze steadily fixed on the floor just in front of him. He doesn't look at any of us. I think he's trying to die with dignity, if nothing else.

Professor Penmark forces Ozzy to kneel in front of us, directly before the cold, empty hearth. Professor Lyons hands the Chancellor a long, steel knife, with a carved handle and a razor's edge.

My stomach lurches.

It's barbaric. Insane. I can't believe they're going to exsanguinate him like a pig.

I expect them to let Ozzy say a few final words, but his mouth remains firmly closed. I don't know if that's his choice, or if mafiosi are required to go silent to the grave.

Dax and Jasper's heads are bowed, staring down at their knees. Miles faces Ozzy, straining against his ties, weak and exhausted though he might be. I can't see Rocco's face, but I know, I fucking know he's smiling.

The Chancellor grips the steel knife in his right fist, testing the blade with his thumb.

The woman in the blue dress stands. She walks forward, placing herself in the gap between the Chancellor and Ozzy's kneeling figure. She sinks to the ground, taking Ozzy's head in her hands and whispering something in his ear. Ozzy's head jerks up. He turns to look at her face, startled and horrified.

Ozzy hadn't seen the woman, fixated as he was on walking in a straight line. The look of anguish on his face tells me who she is. Not the Chancellor's wife—this must be Ozzy's mother.

"NO! NOOOOOOO!" Ozzy screams, as Professor Penmark seizes him by the shoulders and drags him back.

Now Mrs. Duncan is kneeling in his place, straight-backed and resolute.

Calmly, she smooths her dark hair back from her face and places her palms flat on her thighs.

"NOOOOOOO!" Ozzy bellows, his voice tearing.

Before I fully understand what's happening, the Chancellor seizes a handful of Mrs. Duncan's hair and tilts her head back. He places the steel blade against her pale throat and draws it across in one quick slash. A gash opens up like a grinning mouth. Blood pours down the front of her dress, dark as wine. Ozzy's mother doesn't make a sound. She dies silent, slumping to the ground.

Several students scream and others shout in outrage.

Chay faints, falling forward so fast that Anna barely has time to catch her before her head hits the chair in front of her.

My stomach contracts. I have to clap both hands over my mouth, whipping my head to the side to avoid the sight of that still figure on the ground.

I see Dean Yenin sitting behind me. His face is pale as death, his eyes wide open. He looks electrocuted.

Ozzy is still shouting. He hasn't stopped, though his voice has broken to a barking rasp.

Professor Penmark lifts Mrs. Duncan's limp hand, testing her wrist for a pulse. He gives his nod to the Chancellor to confirm what we can all see with gruesome clarity.

The Chancellor faces the Dyers. With cold formality he announces, "The debt is paid."

The Dyers stand. Mrs. Dyer looks down at the fallen body of Mrs. Duncan, at the sheet of blood still spreading across the polished floor. Her upper lip twitches and she turns away, without even a glance to spare for the sobbing Ozzy.

The Chancellor raises his hand to dismiss us.

I barely hear the rumble of the students standing. I'm deafened by my own heartbeat pounding in my ears. I feel trapped, hemmed in by the mass of bodies slowly filing out. I shove my way through, dashing out of Grand Hall, across the short stretch of lawn, running for the bathrooms in the Keep. I stumble into the closest stall and collapse to my knees, vomiting in the toilet. I hear at least two other students doing the same.

I want to hide in here forever.

Take On Me (MTV Unplugged) — a-ha
Spotify → geni.us/rebel-spotify

Apple Music → geni.us/rebel-apple

I can't go back out. I can't go to dinner this evening in the dining hall, or sleep in my bed tonight. I can't return to class tomorrow, to study and practice as usual.

I don't understand how humans can participate in this madness, then go on like normal, like nothing happened.

Yet, after several minutes of kneeling on the cold tiles, I find myself standing and walking to the sink to splash water on my face.

And then I leave the bathroom, still able to stand, still able to move. Floating in this strange, numb state.

I don't want to be here anymore. I want to leave this place.

But where would I go? I hate home, too.

I wander down the hallway in a daze.

As I pass the door to the boy's bathroom, I hear a sound that breaks through the fog.

Sobbing. Desperate, anguished sobbing.

A boy is crying, harder than I've ever heard before.

Crying so hard it seems like it will kill him.

I listen and I think, *Thank god, someone understands. Someone felt how horrible that was, how intolerable.*

His grief is my grief. In fact, his grief is even worse.

I can hear the depth of his pain, dwarfing my own. It's a private, lonely sound, and yet I feel a compulsion to comfort him.

I push the door open and slip inside.

I weave my way through the labyrinth of sinks and stalls, cupboards and closets. The boy is way back in the furthest corner of the space, his echoing sobs making it difficult to find him.

My head throbs and I can hardly see straight.

Still, I'm driven on, pulled helplessly toward the boy.

Maybe I'm not here to comfort him. Maybe I want solace myself.

I find him at last, a lone, tall figure, hunched over the very last sink, his face in his arms, his shoulders shaking as he cries like his heart is breaking. I barely register the lean body, the white-blond hair. I walk up unheard behind him and place my hand on his shoulder.

He whirls around, grief turning to fury in an instant.

I've made a terrible mistake.

This is no boy—this is Dean Yenin.

And he looks ready to rip out my jugular with his teeth.

His face is wet with tears. He knows that I see it. He knows I heard him crying.

He seizes me by the throat and slams me up against the wall, my head jolting against the tiles.

His fist draws back. I catch one glimpse of bruised and swollen knuckles, before he propels it directly toward my face.

I shriek, squeezing my eyes tight shut.

I hear the shattering of tile as his fist hits the wall next to my ear.

I open my eyes and immediately regret it, because Dean's face is right against mine, his eyes purple fire and his nose pressed against my cheek. He hisses, "If you tell anyone . . . *anyone* . . . I'll fucking kill you."

Dean lets go of my neck so abruptly that I fall to my knees on the cold floor. A piece of shattered tile cut my cheek—a droplet of blood falls from my face to the floor, blooming red against the white marble.

By the time I look up, Dean has disappeared.

I kneel there for a long time, shaking helplessly.

19

ZOE

I tried to see Ozzy and Miles while they were locked in the Prison Tower, but no one was allowed inside, no messages permitted.

The Chancellor interrogated Chay and me. We told him everything that Rocco had done since the very first week of school. It didn't matter. All they cared about was Wade's death.

The guilt is choking, crushing, suffocating me.

I can't even apologize to Ozzy because he took his mother's body back to Tasmania, and he won't be returning to Kingmakers.

I write him letters, letters to his father, too.

He hasn't responded. I don't expect him to.

He already said what he wanted to say, in a note left on Miles' bed, addressed to both of us:

It's not your fault. Be safe and be well.

Neither Miles nor I believe it.

It is our fault.

We wanted what we were forbidden to have.

The mood at Kingmakers is somber and dark in the weeks following Mrs. Duncan's death. None of the students had witnessed an execution before. We all knew the rules, but the reality was distant. Now it's right in front of our faces. Fun and games are at an end.

People whisper as I pass. They stare at me.

I feel like I'm cursed.

Anyone who tries to help me is cursed, too.

I'm scared to be around anyone, even Anna and Chay and Cat. Especially Cat.

Now that Rocco has wounded Miles so successfully, shaming him and cutting away his best friend, I can't help but fear that he'll attack Cat next. He wants to isolate me from everyone I love. He won't allow me any help or support.

He's started following me again. He watches me everywhere I go. Always staring. Always smiling.

Chay is devastated by what happened to Ozzy, and even more unhappy that he's gone. She begged him to stay at school, or at least come back in the fall, but he refused.

Since he left she's fallen into a deep depression, stumbling to class barefaced and red-eyed, her hair in a tangled bun, a state in which I had never seen her even once before.

She's developed a hatred for Rocco that almost surpasses my own. She always disliked him from their days in secondary school. Now she harbors a burning rage that frightens me, because I worry that she might act impulsively, given the chance.

Rocco is a plague unleashed by me.

There's only one way to stop it.

Two weeks after Ozzy leaves, I visit Miles in his half-empty dorm room. As soon as he sees my face, he knows why I've come.

"Don't," he begs me. "Don't say it."

"I have to."

I swore I wouldn't cry, but something hot and wet is already running down both sides of my face.

"I can't see you anymore," I tell him.

Miles looks at me. He's still thin from his week in the tower. I doubt he's been eating since. Shadows mark his under-eyes and the hollows of his cheeks. His gray eyes look large and dark. Veins stand out on his arms and the backs of his hands.

Yet he's beautiful. So fucking beautiful.

He's beautiful when he's sad and when he's scared. When he's happy or when he's angry. He's a diamond with a hundred facets. Each one is pure and perfect to me.

But he doesn't belong to me and he never did.

I was never meant to have such a treasure.

"I'm going to marry Rocco at the end of the school year," I say. "There's no point putting it off any longer. He'll only make life miserable for the rest of you."

"I can't let you do that," Miles says quietly.

"It's not your choice," I tell him. "It was never a choice, for any of us."

Miles looks at me the way he always does, fully and completely, taking in every part of me.

"I made you a promise," he says.

"It was an impossible promise. I know you would have kept it if you could."

He looks at me. Then he stands up from his bed in one quick motion, and closes the space between us. I think he's going to kiss me, and I don't know how I'll find the strength to push him away.

Instead, he takes my hand and lifts it to his lips.

He looks into my eyes, his mouth pressed to my knuckles, his touch telling me more clearly than any words could do that he loves me, that he'll always love me.

And I love him. I love him and Cat and Chay and Anna, Ozzy and Leo and Hedeon too.

Which is why I can't be selfish any longer.

I leave Miles' room planning never to return.

20

MILES

I had a long time to think in the Prison Tower.

Even longer in the weeks that followed, when Ozzy was gone and I was alone in the dorm room.

What I realized is this:

If not for Zoe, it would have been *my* mother who was executed.

I was in a rage that night.

I wanted to kill Wade, Jasper, Dax, and most of all Rocco.

They pushed us and pushed us, crossing every fucking line. In that fight—with Zoe in danger, and Chay and Ozzy hurt—I lost control. I could have killed any one of them.

It was Zoe who screamed for me to stop.

She was the one who dragged me back. The only person who could have brought me to my senses in that moment.

Ozzy struck the killing blow.

But it could just as easily have been me.

Then it would have been *my* mother who traded her life, who took the punishment, who paid the debt. I know she would have done it, unhesitatingly. Just like Ozzy's mom.

It would have killed me. It would have poisoned my soul.

For all the guilt and horror I feel at what happened to Mrs. Duncan, still one thing is certain: I need Zoe. I fucking need her. I'm no good without her.

Zoe brings out the best in me. She makes me smarter, stronger, more determined. And most of all, she holds back that dark and reckless part of me.

She's my rudder, my guide.

I can't fly without her, or I'll crash and burn, I know it.

And I fucking love her. That's the most important part of all. I like her, I love her, I admire her, I adore her. I'm not abandoning her to Rocco's torment. She doesn't deserve that. I don't care what it costs to save her, or what I have to risk.

It wasn't a mistake to oppose Rocco. My mistake was letting this go on too long.

I need to end it. Now.

So when Zoe leaves my room, I wait less than a minute before getting to work.

No more planning. It's time to act.

The first thing I do is call Ozzy.

I don't expect him to pick up first try, but to my surprise, he answers almost immediately.

"If it's another apology, I don't want to hear it," he says. "I'm fucking drowning in guilt, I can't handle you wallowing in it, too."

"How are you?" I ask him. "How's your dad?"

"He's a fuckin' mess. Wants to kill the Chancellor. My uncles had to tie him down. Literally."

"He didn't know . . ."

"No. My mom got the letter from the school. Hid it from him. He didn't even know she had left Tasmania until . . . well. We don't need to talk about that. Suffice it to say we're in a fuckin' state. But surviving."

"I am so, so sorry, Ozzy."

He takes a long breath with a catch in the middle.

"I know, mate. I know you are. I'm sorry, you're sorry. We got ourselves in a mess together, but it was me that grabbed the knife. So just fuckin' save it. I can't think about should'ves and would'ves or I'm gonna drive myself insane. She didn't want that."

His voice is fully cracking now.

I never met Mrs. Duncan. Ozzy came to visit me in Chicago, and we'd planned that I'd come out to Tasmania this summer or next. But that won't happen now.

I never even spoke to her. Yet I feel I knew her all the same, because Ozzy talked about his parents all the time.

I knew that Mr. Duncan ran an illegal mining operation, as well as trafficking black market metals and stones. He was from criminal stock tracing back to the days when Tasmania was Van Diemen's Land, and before that, to the professional cracksmen of London.

Mrs. Duncan was the governor's daughter. She sang in the church choir. She wasn't supposed to walk down the same hallway as Mr. Duncan, when they were teenagers attending the same secondary school.

They fell in love anyway.

Ozzy was the result.

They married young and stayed together, happily by all Ozzy's accounts.

He said his mom was funny and playful. That she dragged Ozzy and his dad along to church, but she also loved dice games and shooting. She was shit with technology but she bought Ozzy his first gaming rig.

I know all these things, so I know this was a good woman who died. I know what Ozzy and his father have lost.

I watched how she took Ozzy's face in her hands with tenderness, without a second's hesitation as she offered her life in place of his.

"What did she say to you?" I ask.

I have no right to ask, but I want to know all the same.

"She said, 'I love you, bub. No more violence from this. Go on happy and strong.'" Ozzy pauses to swallow. "She didn't want me to try to get revenge. But I don't know if I can do that. In five years, ten . . . when it seems unrelated, when nobody remembers but me . . . I want to kill them. Rocco, Jasper, Dax."

"If you want that, I'll help you," I promise him. "Whatever you feel is just . . . I'm there."

"I hoped you'd say that," Ozzy says, quietly.

"I'd like a measure of revenge right now," I say. "On Rocco. Though I'll admit, this is self-serving . . ."

"You want to take Zoe from him. You want to go through with the plan."

Ozzy already knows. He's been expecting this.

"Yes. I want to do it immediately. Is the server ready?"

"I finished it yesterday."

"You haven't been working on it still . . ."

"I knew you'd call. Sooner rather than later. And I needed the distraction."

"You're okay with me going forward?"

" 'Course I am. If you don't, he gets what he wants."

Now it's my turn to feel my throat swollen too tight to speak. I can barely manage, "Thank you, man. Seriously. I can't tell you—"

"Nah, you can't, so don't even try. It's beautiful work. Best yet from yours truly."

I end the call, then unearth my list of highly hard-to-come-by contacts. Men whose personal cellphone numbers are only known by five or six people in the world—sometimes not even their wives.

When you call a number like that, you always get an answer.

I call two such men. And I set up two meetings, for the same time tomorrow night.

Both parties don't want to attend. I have to use all my powers of persuasion. I have to make aggressive promises, with catastrophic consequences if I fail to deliver.

Finally, they agree.

Now, I have two more problems to solve, and I think that one single person might just be able to help me.

I've gotta find my new best friend, Ares Cirillo.

No surprise, I track him down on the second level of the Library Tower. Even better luck, Zoe isn't with him. He's all alone at a large table that looks small with his rangy frame wrapped around it. He hasn't cut his hair all year—it hangs shaggy around his face as he hunches over his paper. Writing everything by hand is a fucking nightmare at Kingmakers, especially when you've got a hand the size of an oven mitt like Ares. I can barely see the pencil eraser poking out the top.

"I knew I'd find you here," I say, sliding into the seat directly beside him.

Ares looks up, startled and wary.

Ares has always seemed a little jumpy around me. I don't think he's ever entirely trusted me. Which shows that he really is intelligent.

"Hello, Miles," he says, in his deep voice. "I'm really sorry about your friend. I liked Ozzy."

"Me too. He's not the one who's dead though, he just went home, so you can use current tense."

"Sorry," Ares says again, wincing. "I just meant . . . well, you know."

Now he's even more off balance, which I think is good for me. I want him feeling guilty.

"Ozzy and I were working on a project. Something we want to sell to the Princes and the Romeros. Something to help Zoe. You want that, don't you Ares? You want to help Zoe? You're good friends, aren't you?"

Ares shifts in his seat, glancing at me in a guilty way.

"We're *just* friends," he says. "I hope that's clear. We never—"

"Of course not," I say, clapping him on the shoulder a little too hard. "You're just buddies."

"Right."

"*Definitely.* Anyway, you agree that Zoe is a fucking treasure, one that Rocco Prince does not deserve. So I'm sure you'll do anything you can to help her."

Ares narrows those baby blues at me. He's kind of a Boy Scout, so I don't think he's gonna like this next part,

"What exactly do you want me to do?" He says.

"Nothing too onerous. First, I need you to get me the contact information for the Malina."

Ares' head gives a convulsive jerk. That's about the reaction I expected when I mentioned the Ukrainian Mafia.

"Why would you think that I'd have—"

"I know your family has Bratva connections in St. Petersburg."

"What are you—"

"Ares. You know I know everything. So cut the shit. Your dad's inactive but not unconnected. I know he can get me that number, I've got a phone right here so you can call him. You don't even have to wait for Sunday."

Ares stares at me, his lips tightly pressed together.

After a moment, he says, "I could ask him. But I think you're making a mistake."

"Why is that?"

"You don't want to do business with the Malina."

"I know what they are."

"You don't know. Whatever you think, they're ten times worse. They have no honor, none at all. The schemes they'll use are several sewer-levels below what you could possibly imagine."

"They're only gonna form a limited part in the plan. I've considered the risks. Thank you for your concern," I tell Ares, firmly.

I have to use the Malina, there's no other choice. So there's no point arguing about it. They're the only ones perfectly situated for everything I need.

"What's the second thing?" Ares asks. His arms are folded across his broad chest now, and I can tell he's even less excited for the second request.

"This one's even easier," I say. "I just need you to drive a boat."

"What boat?" Ares says, frowning.

"One to get off this island."

Now his expression is past a frown—it's all the way to absolute negation.

"No," Ares says. "I can't do that."

"Why not? I know you know how."

"I'm not leaving. We could get expelled."

"What do you care? You're not even going into criminal enterprise."

"I don't care. I want to graduate. It matters to my family."

"You won't get expelled. Because we aren't getting caught. We'll be out and back one night, no one will miss us."

"You can't possibly guarantee that. And besides, what boat are you going to use that . . ." he breaks off, realizing. "No," he shakes his head even harder, "Absolutely not. How do you even know about that?"

"How do YOU know?" I demand, even more curious. Ares does not seem the type to have discovered the Chancellor's secret ultra-fast, ultra-fuckin-fancy speedboat.

"One of the teachers told me," Ares mutters.

"Well, the Chancellor won't like that. But he'll like a big old scratch down the side of his boat even less, so you better drive me. I already know where he keeps the keys. I just need my chauffeur . . ."

I know Ares doesn't want to do it. Not at all.

In fact, he's terrified. Because Ares is a good boy who follows the rules. Like Zoe used to be.

Unfortunately for Ares, I'm a very corrupting influence.

I rest my hand on his shoulder again, squeezing tight. I lean forward to look Ares dead in the eye.

"I'm on a very tight schedule, and I don't have time to barter. So here is an unprecedented opportunity for generosity. A level of largess I may never match again in my life. Tell me what it is, Ares. Name your price."

Ares looks at me steadily, making some silent calculation I can only begin to guess.

I wait and wait, knowing better than to stomp on a blossoming answer.

Finally he replies.

"A favor," he says.

"What favor?"

"That's the rub. A favor of my choosing, to be determined at a time of my choosing. In the future. But the promise comes now."

"Is there any limit on this favor? You're not gonna ask for my firstborn with Zoe?"

Ares allows a very small smile.

"No," he says. "Nothing that would upset Zoe."

"Then I agree. Any fucking favor at any time, I promise you."

"Alright then," he holds out his hands to shake, to seal the deal now and forever. "I'll do it."

It's so hard not to release the sigh of relief locked up in my chest.

"Great," I say. "Perfect. Let's make that call to your dad."

ARES and I will have to steal the Chancellor's boat.

He keeps it locked up in a private berth in the caves directly below Kingmakers. You can't access it from the land side—you have to go down under the school itself.

Kingmakers extends for several levels underground.

Everybody knows about the Undercroft and the swimming pool beneath the Armory. They know about the archives below the library, though only Miss Robin and her aides are allowed access.

But that's less than half the space under the school.

I discovered the tunnels in my Freshman year. It took months for me to get access to one of the skeleton keys, and months more to make a copy. Apart from the Chancellor, only two professors and one of the grounds crew have access. Now me as well.

I break into the Chancellor's office to get the keys to his boat. Picking the lock on his door is easy—it's having the balls to enter his personal space that's difficult. The second I set foot over the threshold, I'm hit with the scent of his cigar smoke and expensive aftershave, the smell of metal and leather, and I'll admit, I want to turn and run.

For all the rule breaking I do at school, Luther Hugo is not somebody I want to fuck with. I've always steered clear of him, intentionally. Wade Dyer's death was the first occasion that forced us to speak face to face.

On that particular day, I had already been dragged up the steps of the prison tower and chucked in a cell, so I've never actually visited this office before.

I'm on the top floor of the Keep. Rich, dark wood with inlaid panels cover the walls and ceiling. A bank of windows on the far wall overlooks the castle grounds. I'm discomfited to see how wide the view is, how much the Chancellor can observe from up here. The opposite windows look directly over the cliffs to the sea below.

Waves smash against the rocks. You would think there would be no exit on that side—after all, the barquentine has to come around to the lee side of the island to enter the sheltered harbor. But the Chancellor's vessel is no sailing ship—it's a sport yacht, shaped like a bullet, that can cut through almost any swell.

I'm quite sure he keeps his keys in here because the one time I observed him leaving the island late at night, he made a quick stop at his office first.

I should have been in the Spy division, like Cat. I've watched the Chancellor from afar plenty of times. He's a curious figure to me. Fabulously wealthy, as all the Hugos are. And yet he chooses to stay at the school the majority of the time, never marrying, never fathering children, running his business interests from afar.

Maybe he likes the power of controlling the school, shaping the minds of the next generation of mafia. Still, it's an unusual vocation for a man once known as the Widowmaker.

He might fear retribution from all those widows. The island is a good place for semi-retirement—quiet, and difficult to attack.

He still has all his luxuries around him. The office is stuffed with books, newspapers, cigars, cognac, a bearskin throw, and a box of unopened truffles. The Chancellor's acquaintances likewise keep him company in the form of framed photographs on every wall.

I look them over in a glance, curious but knowing I don't have time to snoop around as I'd like to. I recognize politicians and celebrities, as well as famous mafiosi. In the civilian world, the Hugos are known for their philanthropy and patronage of the arts. Most of these photographs were taken at charity events.

Other locales I recognize from the island. The photograph hanging to the left of the Chancellor's desk shows Luther himself standing next to four students—three boys and one girl. Luther shakes the hand of the girl, who looks flushed and pleased, while the three boys, all significantly taller than her, range in expression from disappointed to bitter.

I'm guessing these are the Captains of some round of the *Quartum Bellum.* In which case the girl likely captained the winning team. She's pretty, dark-haired, blue-eyed. Too young to be a Senior. I could probably find her name on the wall of winners down in the Armory.

Luther himself looks much younger—his hair is fully black, thick and wild-looking. His face is still lined, but only around his eyes and forehead. His cheeks are smooth and beardless. Usually that makes a man look shorn or weakened, but in his case, it shows that he was handsome once, in an aggressive, wicked sort of way.

I wonder if the girl became famous later, and that's why he kept this picture. Everyone else on his walls is someone important.

I'm more interested in the set of keys hanging on a small hook directly next to the photograph. I snatch them up, stilling their jingling with my fingers.

I slip back out of the office, making sure to re-lock the door behind me. I even check that I haven't left footprints on the plush rug.

From there, it's an easy jog down the staircase to meet Ares on the ground floor. He's holding my laptop under one arm, shifting uneasily from foot to foot.

"What took you so long?" He hisses.

"That was less than five minutes." I hold out my hand for the laptop. I want to keep it with me, as it's a fairly crucial part of the plan.

"Let's just go," Ares says. "The sooner we leave . . ."

"I know, I know. The sooner you can get back in your cozy bed and pretend that none of this ever happened. Come on, follow me."

"I thought we were going out?" Ares says, looking confusedly toward the front doors of the Keep, as I lead him further inside instead.

"Not out . . . down," I reply.

I take him to a recessed door next to a musty old tapestry. The door is narrow and might well be a closet. If you didn't know what you were looking for.

The lock turns with a screech. Ares winces, but I ignore it. There's no one around to hear.

This staircase is darker and damper than the ones above ground, the stone smooth and slick in places. I use my phone to light the way. The roof hangs so low in places that Ares has to stoop to avoid banging his head. I try to give him a warning every time I duck under some new outcropping of raw rock.

The path winds and spirals. Sometimes we traverse an almost flat tunnel, and other times we descend stairs so steep that my quads burn.

"How far down does this go?" Ares says, sounding somewhat nauseated. I understand: picturing the hundreds of tons of rock and castle on top of us is not particularly pleasant. Especially when you remember that limestone is porous, and can degrade as water seeps through. Still, I like to think that any castle that stood for seven hundred years is unlikely to fall on my head tonight.

"Almost there," I tell him, with slight exaggeration.

Ten minutes later, we do indeed arrive at the Chancellor's own private sea cave. The boat bobs on the water, its pointed nose rising up and down like a horse tossing its head, anxious to be free to run. It's at least sixty feet long, sleek and shining, painted graphite black with darkly tinted windows.

"You could be ten feet away from this thing and not see it on a night like this," I say to Ares.

Ares stares, shaking his head slowly.

"I've never piloted anything like this," he says.

"I'm sure you'll get the hang of it."

I toss him the keys. Ares catches them easily, left-handed.

"See. Those are the kind of reflexes I'm counting on to get us through the currents."

Taking a deep breath, Ares starts to cast off. I can tell he knows what he's doing, just by the way he handles the ropes. I've already jumped on deck, impatient to be on our way.

Ares joins me a moment later, throwing one last nervous glance back toward the doorway.

"Relax," I tell him. "You've never noticed the Chancellor leaving any other night. Why should anybody see us?"

"I wasn't paying attention," Ares grumbles. "I was sleeping in my bed, like I should be right now."

"Come on," I grin. "Do it for Zoe. And for the fantastic leverage you'll have over me. I can't wait to see what you'll make me do. Streak the Super Bowl? Assassinate the president?"

Ares ignores me, refusing to have fun while we're risking our necks.

He starts the engine and carefully steers us out.

I thought this would be the tricky part, navigating the narrow stone passageway.

But once we're in open water, it's much worse. The waves batter us from all sides, without rhythm or reason, as if intent upon lifting us up and smashing us against the rocks like the boat is a piñata and the ocean a gang of rowdy partygoers.

Ares has to gun the engine hard, then pull back, steering us in and out, timing the gaps to shoot us forward again, always maneuvering the boat so we aren't hit broadside and flipped.

It doesn't help that it's a black, moonless night. Several times rocks seem to rear up out of the water like sea monsters. Ares misses them by mere feet.

My heart is in my throat. All I can do is call out warnings, while Ares strains against the wheel, every muscle standing out on his forearms.

At last we've made it through the worst of it, and we're out in open ocean, heading in a swift and regular course toward the unseen shore. Ares stands pale and silent, not wanting to celebrate with me.

"That was fucking insane!" I shout, clapping him on the back.

"We have to do the same thing on the way back," Ares reminds me, "with the waves pushing us forward instead of holding us back, which might be even worse."

"Don't worry," I tell him. "If the Malina kill us, we won't have to come back at all."

Ares turns to glare at me. "Don't joke. Don't even think about trying to be fucking funny with these people. The only thing that would make them laugh is cutting your throat."

"Hey," I tell Ares, serious now. "You don't have to worry about that. I'm not going to let Zoe down."

Ares looks at me, reading the truth in my face.

"I know," he says. "That's why I agreed to this."

The Chancellor's boat is infinitely faster than the barquentine, but it's still going to take us an hour or two to get to shore. I can only spend so much time looking out over endless black waves before Ares seems relatively intriguing by comparison.

"I know I was giving you shit about Zoe," I say, "But how come you never dated her, or Chay, or any of the other many, many girls who like the strong, silent type?"

Ares shrugs. "I'm not interested in dating."

"Girls, specifically, or . . ."

"I like girls," he says, flatly.

"Just not the ones at our school."

He takes his eyes off the water for a moment to scowl at me. "Why are you so curious?"

"It's my nature. I like to figure people out. I have a hard time with you—you don't make sense to me."

"Sorry to disappoint."

"You like cultivating that air of mystique?"

Realizing that I'm not going to drop it, Ares lets out an irritated sigh and turns to face me.

"There's no point, is there? Any girl like Chay who thinks she might like to date me for a minute . . . she'd change her mind quick enough if she ever came to Syros. I may be at Kingmakers, but I'm not like the rest of you."

"Why come here, then?" I demand. "Why not go to a normal school?"

"I wish I had, sometimes," Ares says, and now his face is dark, full of some anger he's barely holding back. "You do whatever you want, Miles. You don't understand what it's like to owe something to your family. They demand it from you, and you try to give it, even when it's impossible."

I suppose the Cirillos want him to carry on their name and legacy at the school, even if they're barely mafia at all in real life. They were a founding family, after all. One of only seven still surviving. They must look at the wealth and status of the Hugos and think that's where they could have been . . . perhaps where they should be . . .

"I understand family demands," I tell him. "I'm an Heir, remember? I'm supposed to take over for my father in Chicago. But I'm not doing it. Let my brother take his place, or my sister. I'm making my own way. You can do that, you know. You don't have to do what they ask."

"Maybe not in your case," Ares replies. "My family isn't yours."

I try to draw him out again as the boat speeds on, but apparently Ares has decided that's enough conversation.

WE PULL up to the marina in Dubrovnik. Ares throws the ropes down, planning to disembark with me, but I tell him, "Stay here with the boat."

"Don't you want me to come in with you?" he asks, glancing in the direction of the Oasis hotel.

"Nah," I shake my head. "They'll either take the deal or they won't."

"You should have someone there backing you up," Ares says, gripping the rope tightly in his hands.

"I appreciate it man, but I'm outnumbered either way. Stay here, and if I'm not back in three hours, go back to King-makers on your own. Can't have you getting expelled on my account."

Ares frowns, but stays onboard.

I walk up the dimly-lit streets of Old Town on my own, laptop tucked under my arm. Golden lamps burn all along the sea wall. The red-roofed buildings glow as if each one is a burning furnace.

I booked the presidential suite in the Oasis, which encompasses the entire top floor and includes its own private concierge. That alone cost me $20,000 of my bankroll, but it's a drop in the ocean compared to what I've spent. I've cleaned out the whole fund, and I don't regret a penny of it, not for a minute. I only hope it works.

The concierge greets me, looking surprised when I give him my name. It's the school uniform—I'm sure he expected someone older.

"Right this way, Sir," he says. "I have your suit ready."

He takes me up to the top floor, to the four-room suite. I survey the private boardroom, the full bar, and wide-open glass doors leading out to the rooftop deck. The sea breeze blows in. I could probably see Ares from here, if the boat wasn't stealth-painted.

My clothes are indeed laid out on the bed as the concierge promised.

I ordered a midnight blue Brioni, along with calfskin loafers, a crisp white dress shirt, and opal cufflinks. The concierge also provided an array of toiletries on the marble countertop of the sumptuous bathroom.

I rinse the sea salt from my skin, shave, dress, and then style my hair, tucking a silk pocket square into my jacket.

The man looking back at me in the mirror seems ten years older, infinitely confident, anticipating the night to come. The small part of me still squirming inside tries to voice an objection, and I crush it down ruthlessly. There's no room for fear or nervousness. One thing I know for certain: no man on this planet ever accomplished a goddamn thing without believing he could.

I check my watch. 12:50. Ten minutes to go.

I seat myself at the opulent boardroom table, the laptop closed and quiet, the only item on the table. I take the head seat, which may offend some of my visitors, but will set the appropriate tone for the evening.

Three minutes later, the concierge buzzes:

"Your first guest is here."

"Send him up," I say.

The door to the suite is unlocked so Alvaro Romero can walk right in. He strides in, shoulders stiff, jaw already tight, eyes bright with fury. He chooses the seat at the other end of the table, directly opposite me, and I suppress a smile because that's exactly where I want him. He's refusing to cede the position of power—I prefer to have him at the end where his objections will be distant.

"You have a lot of nerve summoning me here, boy," he snarls, by way of a greeting.

And yet, I notice that he dressed just as carefully as I did. Which means he's not uninterested in what I have to say. He just wants to vent a little spleen first.

His thick gray hair is freshly combed, and he's as neatly attired as Zoe herself. Other than that, I don't see much of his daughter in him. He's coarse-featured and weak-chinned, whereas Zoe radiates beauty and confidence.

"Thank you for making the journey," I say. "As you know, I'm a little restricted in how far I can travel at the moment."

"Yes . . . I wonder how your Chancellor would like to hear that you've taken a field trip to Dubrovnik. I could solve my problem with one phone call."

"I'm sure I'd be expelled," I say, calmly. "I don't think that would solve your problem, however."

Romero leans across the broad expanse of shining table, his dark eyes blazing. "I don't know where you get the gall to speak two words to me, when you've been defiling my daughter in defiance of your own school contract and her marriage agreement. I ought to have you castrated, boy."

That's the second time he's called me "boy." I'd like to shove the pejorative back down his throat, but I tuck it away in a mental file of grievances, so I can stick it to him later if I want to. For now, I need to focus.

"Mr. Romero," I say, politely, "Though we haven't met in person, I feel that I have some sense of you all the same. Your daughter Zoe is brilliant, disciplined, deeply loyal. I know those characteristics must have come from her parents."

He narrows his eyes at me, not liking my familiarity with his daughter, but influenced by the compliment all the same.

"I think you're a man of honor. A man who wants to uphold his agreements. Also a man intelligent enough to recognize an opportunity when it presents itself."

"I have an opportunity in place," he says, coldly.

"Yes, but it comes at a cost. The cost is your daughter. I don't expect you to bend to sentiment . . . but you cannot be unaware of Rocco Prince's nature."

Romero's heavy brows sink so low that his eyes become mere slits underneath.

"This younger generation," he hisses. "You're soft. *Romantic.*" He utters it like a curse. "Daughters are not sons. Your parents may allow you to play these games. My daughters will OBEY."

I hear the venom in his voice. This is a touchy point for him. His pride is hung here, and his anger at Zoe for the sin of being born a girl.

Dieter and Gisela Prince walk into the room.

Romero startles, because I didn't inform him that his intended in-laws would be attending this meeting.

I'm likewise surprised. I was only expecting Mr. Prince, not his wife.

They seat themselves on my left side, a little closer to me than to Romero, which I think is a good sign.

Dieter Prince is in a little better mood than Romero. He examines me with cold blue eyes not unlike Rocco's. His black mustache conceals the expression of his lips.

"My helicopter is waiting," he says, briskly. "I only intend to stay an hour. So please explain to me why I shouldn't gut you here and now for trying to steal my son's bride."

"Because you don't care about the bride," I reply. "Neither do the Romeros. This is a business deal—Zoe is simply the wax seal. Can we all dispense with the fiction that the marriage is an integral part of the arrangement?"

"You show your inexperience," Prince says, sternly. "Contracts fall apart. Agreements change. Marriages last. Only a marriage ensures that the future of both families is entwined. It's the only way to assure that our interests align over time."

"What is that worth to you?" I say. "Ten million? A hundred?"

"You don't have that kind of money," Romero snaps from the bottom of the table.

"No," I say. "But you could."

Prince and Romero exchange glances. Romero snorts, stubbornly dismissive. I see a spark of interest in Dieter Prince's eye. The money matters to him. The number matters, I can see it.

"What are you talking about?" Prince demands.

"You're building a distribution route," I say. "From Barcelona to Hamburg. It's a good route, undoubtedly. Alvaro Romero's product and your men. But what if it was five times larger? What if it spanned out to Kyiv, and down to Turkey? What if you could take orders from every city in Northern Europe, all at the same time? Untraceable and undetectable."

Prince's dark mustache twitches.

"Explain," he says.

"The choke point in contraband sales is the ordering system. You need a network of low-level dealers to sell the product in person. Have you ever heard of Amazon?"

"Of course," Romero says, still irritated.

"You'd be the Amazon of drugs."

"How do you figure that?" Prince inquires.

"Online ordering via the dark web, funneled through a private server. You send the product along your distribution channel. You don't have to accept the money in person and deal with all the pesky inconveniences of exchange rates and transport and laundering. You take payment in Bitcoin, utterly untraceable. Then we exchange it for American dollars."

"How?" Prince says. "Who exchanges it?"

I check my watch. "That's the last piece of the puzzle," I say. "They should be arriving as we speak."

"This is fantasy," Romero spits. "All talk. You can't do any of this."

"I already have," I say. "It's already done."

I flip open the lid of the laptop and turn the screen to show him. He leans forward, squinting to see. A stream of numbers pours down the screen like running water, right before his eyes.

"Those are orders," I say. "In real time. People ordering your product as we sit here."

Prince and Romero stare, the numbers reflected in their irises. Numbers representing a river of cash running directly into their pockets.

In that poignant silence, the Malina walk through the door.

Marko Moroz is a beast of a man—near seven feet tall, broad, with a mane of reddish-brown hair the color of fox fur. His eyes have a yellowish cast, and his lips are thick and fleshy. His hands are so large and scarred that the fingers permanently curl. He wears a military-style jacket and boots, his four soldiers likewise attired in combat gear.

These soldiers have been chosen for size and brutality. I told Moroz we would be meeting without arms, without body-guards. Yet he brought his four largest, as a show of strength.

They're marked with the tattoos of their accomplishments. Ukrainian tattoos are similar to Russian—a burning woman chained to a stake, showing vengeance wreaked on one who has betrayed. A hand holding a tulip, to indicate that the bearer turned 16 years of age inside a prison camp. A snake-wrapped dagger proclaiming the wearer a master-thief.

These men make Dieter Prince and Alvaro Romero look like bankers by comparison. They don't try to blend in. They wear the evidence of their violence proudly.

Discomfort grips the room. Dieter and Gisela Prince sit poker straight in their chairs, and Romero is wide-eyed as a schoolboy. He licks his lips, his eyes darting toward the open door as if he's considering fleeing right now.

"I hope we're not late," Moroz says, in his deeply-accented voice.

"Right on time," I say. "Please, make yourself comfortable."

I gesture to the open side of the table. Moroz sits while his men remain standing, fanning out in the room.

I have to move fast, because the Princes and Alvaro Romero will want to get out of here as quickly as possible. They won't want to do business with the Malina, nobody does. Not unless their greed is powerful enough to overcome their reservations.

"Marko Moroz has American dollars," I say. "A large quantity from his operations out of Brighton Beach. He's looking for an investment opportunity. The Malina can expand our distribution network from Germany all the way through Poland, Lithuania, Latvia, and Estonia, down through Belarus to the Ukraine, then across the Black Sea to Turkey. They can take the Bitcoin and use it to purchase property in Dubai. They'll provide you with clean American dollars in return. For that service, they ask only a thirty percent cut of the profits, and an additional five percent for the exchange."

"Ten," Moroz cuts across at once. He smiles, showing several gold teeth. "Ten percent for the currency exchange, and *forty* percent of the profit. It seems fair, for all I'll be providing."

This is not what we discussed, though I anticipated Moroz trying to strong-arm me at the first opportunity.

I smother my irritation, and the rising sense of panic that Prince and Romero won't accept that deal. It has to be sweet, or they won't work with Moroz.

"A ten percent exchange fee is reasonable," I agree. "The profit should be split evenly three ways—33.3% each. Let's keep it simple for the accountants, shall we?"

Dieter Prince watches closely to see if Moroz can be reasoned with.

Moroz takes a long time considering, then he gives a slow nod.

"Yes," he chuckles. "Let's not confuse the accountants."

"It's agreed, then," I say, glancing around at the Princes and Romero to confirm. "Equal profit share. Ten percent to the Malina for the exchange to American dollars. And an additional one percent fee to the bitcoin wallet. A bargain for clean washed money."

It's a beautiful bargain, and everyone at this table knows it.

Prince and Romero exchange glances. I kept the laptop screen turned toward them both, so they could watch the orders piling up even as we spoke. Several million dollars have already accrued in the short time the program has been running.

They don't want to work with the Malina. They know the money is sitting in an open bear trap that could snap on their hands at any moment. But they also don't want to refuse Marko Moroz while he sits directly across from them. I was counting on his intimidation factor to work both ways.

"What do you get out of this?" Mrs. Prince says, suddenly, surprising us all. She hadn't spoken all throughout the meeting, sitting like a pale, silent shadow at her husband's elbow.

"I get Zoe Romero," I say, simply. "No money, no drugs, no cut. I only want her. In return, I hand over the platform, the server, the bitcoin wallet—all of it."

"You can't be serious," Dieter Prince snorts.

"That must be gold-plated pussy," Moroz laughs, slapping his ham-sized hands on his thighs.

Romero scowls at the slight to his daughter, then immediately wipes his face smooth when Moroz glances in his direction.

"That's what I want," I say, quietly. And then, realizing that Zoe will require one other thing to be happy, I say, "Catalina, as well. No marriage contract for her. She marries whoever she likes, after she graduates."

Romero is freshly outraged, sputtering down at the end of the table. He's required to sacrifice the most of anyone present— the girls are his only two children. His only pawns. But after all, pawns aren't worth much in the eyes of chess masters.

With all the trouble Zoe has given him, he may be sick of marriage contracts.

The silence stretches out. No one wants to speak first.

Moroz has the least patience.

"What, then?" He demands, banging his massive fist on the table, making all of us jump. "I have a pile of cash and no time to waste. Do we all agree?"

"Yes!" Romero yelps, more out of nerves than anything else.

Dieter Prince looks at his wife. He seems to be searching for a way to extricate himself from this deal without getting in trouble.

Mrs. Prince has a different perspective.

"This way is better," she says, softly. "More money. More allies. No marriage contract."

Her blue eyes meet mine for one swift second.

She doesn't say anything else, but I'm certain that deep inside of her, there's some measure of sympathy for Zoe. And very little love for her son.

"So be it," Mr. Prince says. "Rocco is young. Plenty of time for him to find someone else."

He sniffs, dismissing Zoe in a breath as he stares at that laptop screen again.

I'd like to smash it over his fucking head. But I'm too elated by what I just managed to pull off. The biggest fucking deal of my life. For the greatest prize imaginable.

"Let's toast," I say, "While I draw up the contract."

By the time we've all signed and shared three rounds of drinks, I know I'm barely going to make it back to the dock in time. Moroz has been pouring shots that fill his tumbler, and he's starting to get a crazed gleam in his eye. I want to get the fuck out of here before he gives me a backslap that knocks my fucking head off my shoulders.

We bid our farewells and part ways in the lobby, all of us waiting for the Malina to leave first before we feel comfortable heading out in the dark on our own.

I sprint down to the docks, still wearing my suit, having forgotten my uniform back at the hotel.

I'm ten minutes past the three hours Ares and I agreed upon.

Yet the sleek black boat waits at the end of its berth.

"You were supposed to leave without me," I tell Ares.

"I know," he sighs. "I kinda need you to get back through those rocks."

"And you were mildly concerned that I might be dead."

"Concerned, or hopeful?"

"Definitely concerned."

"Only 'cause I thought I might miss out on my cut of this super important deal."

I laugh. "There is no cut. I'm broke as fuck now. Spent it all."

Ares shakes his head at me. "That doesn't sound like a very good deal."

I picture Zoe's face when I tell her what I've done. The way her disbelief will melt into a smile brighter than the dawn.

"It's a fucking fantastic deal," I tell him. "The best I'll ever get."

21

CAT

When I don't see Zoe at breakfast, I worry that something awful happened to her again.

Instead, she comes bursting into my room down in the Undercroft while I'm stuffing my backpack with books.

She rarely comes to visit my dorm—nobody who isn't a Spy likes to come to the Undercroft. They find it creepy, and to be fair, the Spies are less than welcoming.

We're the only division where the male and female students share the same floor. While I've gotten to know some of the older students like Shannon Kelly and Isabel Dixon, I hate visiting the bathrooms at the far end of the tunnel, because it means I also have to pass the doors of some of the absolutely terrifying residents like Jasper Webb and my own asshole cousin Martin Romero.

Their rooms are caves, and I have a sneaking fear that if I don't run past their door fast enough, they might reach out a tentacle-like arm and drag me inside.

For all these reasons, it's usually me that visits Zoe in the bright, clean Solar.

Today I'm simply relieved to see her at all, especially since I can tell at a glance that her face is beaming with excitement.

"He did it!" She cries, her voice choked with emotion. "Miles did it!"

"Did what?" I say, blankly.

"He convinced the Princes to dissolve the marriage contract."

I stare at her, open-mouthed, not able to process what I'm hearing.

"How . . . are you sure?"

I want to celebrate with my sister, but I'm afraid this can't possibly be true. I don't want her hopes dashed as quickly as they rose.

Zoe lowers her voice, though we're alone in my room. Rakel already left for class.

"He snuck out last night with Ares. They went to Dubrovnik and Miles made a new deal with the Princes and our father."

Zoe sounds feverish. I haven't seen her this happy in . . . maybe forever.

"Does Rocco know?" I whisper.

"Not yet. But he will."

Zoe is triumphant. She can't wait for Rocco to hear that his schemes have been ripped out from under him.

I, on the other hand, feel a new level of dread.

Rocco isn't going to take this well. Not at all.

I don't want to say that to Zoe, however. I don't want to eat away at her joy in this moment.

So I just throw my arms around her and hug her hard.

"I'm so, so happy for you Zo," I say. "You deserve this."

She hugs me back even harder, her slim frame shaking with excitement. "The deal is for you too, Cat. Our father won't make a contract for you. He's not allowed to. You won't have to marry anyone you don't like."

I let out a long sigh. That was a future horror I had never even considered, because it scared me too much.

"Miles did that? For me?" I say.

"Yes," Zoe pulls back to look at me, smoothing a few wild curls back from my face. They immediately spring forward again, disobedient as ever. "He knows how much I love you."

I've never imagined a free future for myself. It's overwhelming. I don't know where to begin making plans. I feel like I'm standing in front of a buffet with a thousand dishes.

What would I do, if I could truly do anything in the world?

Would I go to Pintamonas?

That's what I planned, before I came here.

But I don't know if I want that anymore. My progress at King-makers has been hard-won. I started at the bottom of my class, the weakest, the least competent. Slowly over the school year, I've grown. I've learned things. Discovered reserves of strength and ingenuity I never knew I possessed. Bit by bit my grades have improved, so I'm no longer failing. I might even find myself at the middle of the pack.

Who knows where I could be in another year? Or two or three?

I once pictured myself on graduation day, as strong and confident as a Senior like Saul Turner.

That no longer seems like an impossible fantasy.

"I'll have to thank Miles," I say to Zoe. "Though I don't know how you can ever thank someone for something like that."

"I know," Zoe says. "I just can't believe it."

But she can. She absolutely believes it.

It takes me calling home to my father to be fully convinced. I phone him on Sunday, which is the day we're permitted to use the old-fashioned bank of telephones in the ground floor of the Keep.

I never call my father, usually. He communicates via letters that I detest opening.

However, today he seems to be expecting my call.

"Hello, Catalina."

He never calls me Cat. He never has.

"Hello, father."

"I assume your sister told you the news."

"She said you made a new deal with the Princes. A more advantageous arrangement."

I'm trying to flatter him. I know my father's pride. If he senses any hint of triumph in Zoe or me, he'll be furious.

"I don't expect you girls to understand the complexity of my business. But yes, you could say it is infinitely more advantageous," he says, with pompous magnanimity.

"I—I'm very happy for you, father."

"It's an embarrassment for your sister to be cast off by her fiancé. She better hope the American is serious about pursuing her. I doubt anyone else will be interested after the way she's behaved."

"I think he's very serious about her," I say, quietly.

My father responds with a disgusted sniff.

"I hope you'll never behave in such a whorish way, Catalina. I raised you to understand what a wife owes to her husband. A woman's value is easily diluted. Like a bottle of wine, once the cork is popped—"

"I understand, father," I say, quickly.

I'm seething with anger, my hand shaking around the receiver. How *dare* he talk about Zoe that way, when he's never felt love or devotion in his life. He's a hypocrite, a reptile, a slimy fucking—

"See that you do understand," he says, shortly, hanging up the phone.

I slam the receiver down in return, wishing I'd had the courage to do it before him.

I hate him. I hate him so much.

I loathe the idea of going home this summer. I wish the school year would never end, a sentiment I never thought I'd feel, but now I embrace it wholeheartedly.

I prefer Kingmakers. I can say that now. For all its faults, for all the ways it terrifies me, at least this place is honest in its intentions. No one pretends to love me here, pretends to have my best interests at heart, while poisoning me from the inside out.

My father doesn't know anything about who I am, not really.

I am a fucking Spy.

Luther Hugo made no mistake when he chose my division. He looked at my school transcripts. He noticed what my father never bothered to see. Nascent skills. Embryonic expertise.

I've been building those skills all year.

Now it's time to put them into practice.

I'm tired of terror, tired of waiting for men to attack so I can fumble in reaction.

It's time to face my last fear at this place.

Time to go hunting for Rocco Prince.

ONE OF THE few classes I enjoyed at Kingmakers, right from the beginning, is Stealth and Infiltration. In that class it's an advantage to be small and insignificant, easy to overlook. Even Professor Burrows is a short and trim man, with a quiet, carefully cultivated British accent, and a plain, unremarkable face. The only thing memorable about him is his strangely tiny, baby-like teeth, that only reveal themselves on the rare occasion when he smirks at his own joke.

Professor Burrows has been teaching us how to stalk our quarry without being noticed.

"The first step is research," he tells us. "You should have a good idea of where your subject is going before they ever leave the house. If your intent is to follow them to an unknown locale, keep your distance, monitor their position via indirect sources such as window reflections, and be prepared to alter your appearance *en route*. Caps, sunglasses, and reversible jackets can be of use."

When I start following Rocco Prince on campus, I try to make use of all Professor Burrow's tips. I borrow one of Rakel's beanies to cover my hair, and I slip in and out of my academy jacket. I hide behind stacks of textbooks in the library and beefy Enforcers in the dining hall. I remember the Professor's directive not to follow behind the subject at all times, but rather to walk on parallel or diagonal pathways, to sometimes overtake and sometimes pause out of sight.

Rocco is a predator with finely-honed instincts. If I even look at him too long, his head jerks up and his cold blue eyes sweep around, searching for the source of that prickling along the back of his neck, that sixth-sense that he's being observed.

But he doesn't see me. Because I've learned how to hide behind pillars and in the shadow of stairwells, how to sit perfectly still without flinching, my face turned down to a book, even while his gaze passes over me.

Everyone knows when Rocco learns of the dissolution of his engagement, because he destroys the dorm room he shares with Dax Volker. He smashes up the furniture, rips the mattresses apart, even throws a chair through his own window. For that little tantrum, his family is fined and he's forced to suffer the humiliation of working on the grounds crew for two weeks.

I expect him to retaliate against Miles and Zoe immediately, but he doesn't. He doesn't so much as speak to Zoe, which she sees as a good sign.

"I know he's pissed, but he has to abide by his parents' decision," Zoe says to me.

Zoe looks lovelier than I've ever seen: her skin glowing, her hair dark and lustrous, her eyes bright as spring clover. She's still wearing her favorite trousers, but her blouse is partly unbuttoned and the sleeves rolled up. A belt cinches her slim waist, showing her figure in a way she never would have done before.

She's secure for the first time in her life, safe as if Miles' arms are wrapped around her, even when he's not actually in the room.

I don't want to puncture that safety, not for a second. But I'm frightened for her, and I can't seem to shake it.

"I just . . . don't believe he'll let you go so easy," I say to Zoe.

"Fuck him," Zoe says, tossing her head imperiously. "There's no contract anymore. If he tries to hurt me at school, he'll be punished. Outside of school, I'm staying with Miles. You can come with us too, Cat. Come to Chicago this summer. Father won't care—he'll be drowning in cash from this deal. Miles says it's already running, it's already working."

She's high on triumph, blissful and full of plans.

I'm afraid that Miles is the same.

They can't see what I see.

They're not watching Rocco as he gets paler and more venomous by the day. He's a snake that's starving, and that only makes him more dangerous.

"I think he's losing his friends, too," Zoe says. "Jasper was pissed about that week in a prison cell, and from what I hear Dax is none too happy that Rocco fucked up their room."

I have noticed that Rocco's friends don't seem particularly happy in his company. Jasper barely speaks, and Dax is sulky and easily irritated. Some of the hangers-on disappeared entirely after what happened to Wade Dyer. Rocco snaps at anyone who remains, until his group of a dozen minions dwindles to three or four.

Still, I follow him as the school year draws to a close, until there's only a few weeks left. Because I don't trust that he'll let us board that ship without one final confrontation.

A WEEK before the final challenge of the *Quartum Bellum,* I study in the library. Much as I usually enjoy this place, I'm longing to be outdoors where the orange blossoms are in full bloom, the sun shining, the grass fragrant. The weather is fully warm now. Nobody wears sweaters or jackets anymore, or even stockings. The girls lay out on the lawn with their skirts pulled up to get some color on their legs. The boys hang around tossing footballs and baseballs, pretending not to watch.

I'd like to be down there, but I'm close to achieving actual decent grades, as long as I can stick the landing on my final exams. So I'm one of the only people inside the tower, resisting the siren call of early summer.

Or at least, that's the case until I hear several sets of footsteps coming up the ramp.

Instinctively, I slip out of my seat and hide between the book-shelves.

The footsteps are heavy and male. The lowered voices have an edge of malice all too familiar to me.

"Did you see her laying out on the grass with her head in his lap? Fucking flaunting herself."

Rocco's hissing fury makes my flesh go cold and clammy. I stay exactly where I am, wedged in the tiny space only feet away from the boys.

"Well, he paid enough for her. Let him have her. I would have kept the cash, personally."

I hear Dax Volker's ugly laugh.

I expect them to keep walking up the ramp, but they appear to have stopped. There's a scuffing of chairs and a thud of books being thrown down as they toss their belongings onto a table close to the one I was using.

"She thinks she won. She thinks she can prance around with him, laughing in my face."

"She did win. It's done. Give it up."

I'm not as familiar with that voice since I've barely heard him speak, but I'm quite sure the low, disdainful comment came from Jasper Webb. I'm certain of it when it's immediately accompanied by the sharp pops of Jasper cracking his knuckles in rapid sequence.

"That's what you'd do, isn't it?" Rocco hisses. "You'd give up. Like when Dean Yenin beat your fucking ass to the canvas."

"He didn't have to fight that mobile mountain first," Jasper bites back. "What the fuck do you know about it, anyway—you weren't down in that ring. You don't even box."

"I'll put my knife up against your bony fists any time," Rocco snarls.

"Knock it off," Dax says, simultaneously bored and irritated. "I'm sick of you two sniping at each other. I'm sick of this school and this whole fucking year. Can't wait to spend my summer in Ibiza, fucking coked-out bikini bitches."

Rocco is silent for a minute, but his mind obviously keeps returning to Zoe, like a hamster in a wheel.

"It isn't over," he says.

I hear the exasperated sighs of the other two, clearly at their breaking point with this topic.

"Yeah, what the fuck are you gonna do about it?" Dax says, openly hostile now.

"Whatever it is, you can leave me out of it," Jasper adds. "I don't fancy another run-in with the Chancellor. Unlike you two, I don't have some sweet mommy who wants to get her throat cut on my behalf."

"I doubt mine would offer," Rocco says, quietly.

It's the first time I've heard him admit something that could be construed as vulnerable. But he doesn't say it with any sadness. He's only stating a fact. He's calculated to what uses he could put his mother, and self-sacrifice simply isn't on that list. He doesn't care whether she loves him or not.

"What, then?" Dax says, with an air of wanting to get this over with. "What's your plan?"

"My plan is to wait," Rocco says, in his gentlest voice. "I'll wait two years, three years, four . . . I'll wait until after we graduate, and after they're married. Maybe I'll wait until she's pregnant." He laughs softly, enjoying that idea. "Eight months pregnant, about to welcome their first child. Then I'll find her. I'll knock on her door. And the moment she opens it, unsuspecting, unaware, I'll take another beaker of that acid and I'll throw it right in her face. Burn her, blind her, fuck her up. Let's see how much he wants her then, when she's a fucking monster."

Dax and Jasper are silent, not even able to muster a chuckle as the depravity of this plan lays over their table like an icy mist.

"You think you'll still care in four years?" Jasper says, trying to hide his disgust.

"I'd wait fifty years to do it," Rocco replies. "But I won't have to. Happiness is an anesthetic. They'll get comfortable much sooner than that. They'll believe I've given up because that's what they want to believe. I'll never forget. I'll never forgive. Not until I get what I want."

My stomach heaves, abruptly and without warning. I have to clap my hand over my mouth, like I did in the Grand Hall the day Ozzy's mother was killed.

However much I've changed this year, that vomit reflex is the one thing I can't control.

Perhaps Rocco hears the slap of my hand. He seems to tense up, demanding sharply, "Whose bag is that?"

I can just see my backpack hanging over the corner of my abandoned chair. I forgot to grab it when I hid between the bookshelves.

My instinct is to flee, but Rocco can't see me. He can't know that I heard.

"I dunno," Dax says. "It's been there the whole time. Probably someone forgot it."

"Pick it up," Rocco barks. "Look through it. See who it belongs to."

Dax's chair scrapes across the carpet as he stands, planning to do as Rocco ordered.

Now I'm in a panic, knowing that my name is written inside several of my textbooks. If Dax looks through them, he'll tell Rocco, and Rocco will fucking know I'm somewhere close by.

He'll know it isn't a coincidence.

I'm about to burst out of my hiding place like a grouse flushed from ground, when I hear a light voice saying, "Did someone forget that? I'll take it."

Ms. Robin's oversized cardigan and mane of frizzy red hair sweeps into view as she snatches up the bag, right before Dax's big hand can close around it.

"Thank you, boys," she says, already striding away.

"Did she hear any of that?" Rocco says in a low tone, after she's gone.

"No," Dax says. "And who cares—she's a fuckin' space cadet. You ever seen her drooling all over those crumbly rat-shit scrolls? Thinks she's a fuckin' medieval monk, or a nun or some shit." He gives another of those awful laughs. "Dresses like a nun, too. I'd still bend her over the desk. I like a redhead. So does our boy Jasper, don't ya Jasper?"

"No," Jasper says, coolly. "I'm not interested in fucking the librarian."

All this seems to have distracted Rocco enough that he forgets about the mystery backpack.

"Let's go," Dax says. "I don't feel like studying."

"When do you ever," Rocco says, waspishly.

"It's almost dinner, and unlike you two I actually like to eat."

"If you call the pig-slop they serve at this place eating."

Not waiting for Rocco to agree with anything like grace, Dax gathers up his books. Rocco and Jasper follow.

I stay exactly where I am, legs too weak to support me even if I was brave enough to move.

I heard every word that Rocco said. And just like Dax and Jasper, I know he wasn't joking.

Rocco will get his revenge on my sister. He'll wait as long as he has to. Neither time nor distance will erase his hatred. He's a danger to her for as long as he lives.

This problem has only one solution.

I don't want to admit it. I don't want to allow the thought in my mind. But I know it, as surely as I can see the sun rising in the morning and the moon in the sky at night.

The only way for Zoe to be safe . . . is for Rocco to die.

22

ZOE

The last few weeks of school are the most blissful of my life.

Rocco is so bitter that he won't even look at me, which is exactly what I like.

Miles and I are free to spend every possible moment together. We walk to class hand in hand, we sit together for every meal, we stay up late at night laughing and talking, watching old movies, or fucking like rabbits every chance we get.

The joy of being flirty and romantic out in the open is ten times greater than I imagined. I've never felt so light and so free.

Often Anna and Leo join us for movies or exploring the island. Chay comes along sometimes, but I know she feels a bit like a fifth wheel. She's been in an awful state over what happened to Ozzy's mom. She only cheered up once Ozzy started accepting her calls on Sundays. Miles gave her a cellphone, and now she's holed up in her room for hours at a time, talking to Ozzy.

"I'm going to visit him in Tasmania," she tells me. "As soon as school lets out."

"As friends, or . . .?"

"It's not a pity thing," Chay tells me, fiercely. "I've missed him since he's been gone. Missed him a lot, actually."

"That's great, Chay," I say, honestly. "I always thought Ozzy was good for you."

I've got my own visit planned for the summer holidays—I'm going to Chicago to meet Miles' family. I asked Cat if she wanted to come with me. Neither of us has been to the States before, and I really don't think our father will object. Miles showed me the ongoing transactions on the offshore server, which are already surpassing the generous projections he made that night in Dubrovnik. Our father will be too busy counting his money to do anything else.

Cat didn't seem as excited as I expected. She's been strangely quiet lately, almost avoiding me. She says she's busy studying, but I wonder if it makes her feel isolated to see me so wrapped up in Miles. Like she thinks I'll forget all about her.

I try to tell her that will never happen.

"You know you'll always be my best friend, and I'll always take care of you, Cat. No matter what happens with me and Miles, that will never change."

"I know," Cat says, looking at me with her huge dark eyes that seem to take up half her face.

"What's wrong, then? Are you still worried about Rocco? He hasn't said a word to me. I really think he's going to drop it. The Princes won't want to jeopardize all the money they're making. Miles could still shut down the server if Rocco tries to fuck with us."

Cat just looks at me, solemn and pale.

"Is it final exams?" I prod her. "Your grades are much better now, I'm sure you—"

"It's nothing," she says, shaking her head. "I'm just tired. It's been a long year."

THE LAST EVENT of the *Quartum Bellum* takes place on a sweltering Friday in May.

The sun beats down on our heads like we're in the tropics, every member of our team sweating before the challenge has even begun.

The Sophomores face off against the Juniors. Bleachers have been re-erected around the open field so that the rest of the school can watch.

Leo is, of course, hoping to lead us to victory for the second year in a row. If we're champions four years running, he'll beat the record previously set by Adrik Petrov, the St. Petersburg Enforcer whose name has gone down in legend as the only Captain to win three years in a row.

Adrik graduated right before I came to Kingmakers, so I never laid eyes on him, but Miles assures me that his exploits are not exaggerated.

"He was the fuckin' man alright," Miles says. "I never saw somebody so good at absolutely everything. Some people thought he was an asshole, but I liked him."

"You like assholes," Leo says.

"That's why we've always been good friends," Miles grins.

"I'm gonna beat his record," Leo says, full of competitive fire. "In the *Quartum Bellum,* and everything else."

"Good luck with that," Miles says. "You're off to the right start today—I don't think it's gonna be that hard to beat the Juniors."

"That's your team," I remind him.

Miles and I are standing across from each other on the field, him in a black shirt, me in white. Technically we're adversaries and I'm supposed to do my best to defeat him. In practice, I can't stop staring at his handsome face, and I think I'd hand him a trophy right now if he asked for it nicely.

Miles looks around at the rest of the Juniors, which include the Captain Simon Fowler, Kasper Markaj, Jasper Webb, and Dax Volker, as well as the Bratva Heir Claire Turgenev and her cousin Neve Markov, and my own cousin Martin. That would be their "all-star lineup," if you wanted to pick out the best. The rest range from mediocre to poor in strength and skill-set.

"My team's shit," Miles says, bluntly. "It's just the way it goes. Some years are stronger than others. I don't care. I'd rather you beat us quick so I can get out of this heat."

"Where's Rocco?" I say suddenly, looking around.

Rocco is a Junior. He's supposed to be here on the field. Attendance to the *Quartum Bellum* is mandatory.

"Who cares?" Miles says. "It's his problem if he gets caught skipping out. Kinda wish I had the same idea. Too late now, though—Professor Howell already saw me."

Professor Howell strides to the center of the pitch, his favorite silver whistle bouncing against his chest. Sweat already gleams on his lean, tanned face and in his tightly-cropped black hair.

"Ready everyone?" he bellows.

There's a weak, heat-blasted cheer from the crowd, and an even weaker shout of acknowledgment from the competitors.

Professor Howell raises his starter pistol to the cloudless sky and fires.

23

MILES

The final challenge is essentially one vast game of tug-o-war, with a net instead of a single rope. The net is strung with a line of flags down the center. The first team to pull those flags into their own end zone wins.

Because there are so many students on each team—nearly seventy in total—the tactics involve shifting manpower to different areas of the net. The teams alternate between abrupt bursts of aggressive power, and long, gritty struggles where the students sweat and strain, the net barely moving at all.

I fucking hate it.

I find the *Quartum Bellum* tedious and pointless, and I tend to exert the minimum effort required so my teammates don't notice that I'm barely working at all. That's hard to do when everybody is dripping in sweat in five minutes flat.

The rough rope burns our hands, scraping the skin off our palms. The sod beneath our feet is soon torn up by dug-in heels, and players are frequently jerked off their feet, dragged along with the net until they're skinned up and covered in grass stains.

I hoped it would all be over soon, but it quickly becomes apparent that we're in for the long haul. While the Sophomores and Juniors have bursts of triumph where they manage to drag the net several feet toward their end zone, this progress is immediately undermined by the opposing team hauling it back again.

Leo has the better strategy, as per usual. He uses unexpected shifts in force and direction to literally jerk us off our feet. He moves his players around, relieving those at the highest tension points as soon as they start to flag. Bit by bit, he's pulling the net closer to his side.

Still, it will be an hour or two until my team realizes they're beat.

I occupy myself by staring at Zoe.

She's toiling away like a good little worker bee. Her black hair has come loose from its ponytail, sticking to her face. Her cheeks flushed pink in the sun. In fact, she looks quite similar to when she's on top of me, riding my cock, which makes said cock wake up inside of my shorts. That thought is the only thing that could make me enjoy this fucking competition. I don't mind if it drags on, as long as I get to watch Zoe laughing and shouting, using that goddess-like body to its best advantage.

She catches my eye and grins at me, showing a flash of white teeth.

"You could try pushing instead of pulling," she cries. "We'll put you out of your misery."

"You'll never respect me if I let you win," I shout back, giving a sharp jerk to the net that yanks her forward.

Zoe just laughs and plants her filthy sneakers in the churned-up dirt, pulling as hard as she can to go absolutely nowhere.

Dean Yenin stands a little to Zoe's left. He gives an irritated toss of his head, annoyed at our exchange. He, of course, is treating the challenge like the fate of the world depends upon it. He snarls with annoyance whenever Leo shouts an order, but follows the strategy when the benefit is obvious.

Silas Gray isn't listening as carefully. As Leo yells for them to pull left, he yanks the net in the opposite direction, putting unexpected force on the section held by Dean.

With a sickening jolt, Dean's arm is ripped sideways. He gives a strangled yell, letting go of the net. His arm hangs at an upsetting angle, the shoulder dislocated from the joint.

"You fucking idiot!" Dean snarls, his face scarlet.

Silas stares at him, impassive and unrepentant.

Leo lets go of the net to come look. He grimaces at the dangling arm.

"You'd better go to the infirmary," he says.

"You think?" Dean bellows, teeth gritted in pain.

"I can send someone with you—" Leo starts.

"Don't fucking bother, he yanked my arm out, not my legs," Dean spits, stalking off across the field with his good arm pinning the loose, swinging limb in place against his body.

"What a shame," I say to Kasper Markaj. "Couldn't have happened to a nicer guy."

Kasper snorts and takes a fresh grip on the net.

"Come on, you lazy shits!" Simon Fowler bellows to our team. "We've got 'em right where we want 'em, they're dropping like flies!"

I sigh.

"He's no William Wallace, but he's trying his best."

24

CAT

Rocco has to die, and I'm the only one who can do it.

It can't be Zoe or Miles. They're the obvious suspects.

If they kill Rocco, the Chancellor will find out, or the Princes. Their new life together will be destroyed before it even starts.

In fact, I have to make sure that when Rocco dies, it's glaringly obvious that Zoe and Miles had nothing to do with it.

Which is why it has to take place during the final challenge of the *Quartum Bellum*.

Zoe and Miles will be competing in full view of the entire school. No one can accuse them of attacking Rocco.

I, on the other hand, will need a different alibi.

But I'm getting ahead of myself.

The first step is to bait the trap.

I start by leaving notes in Rocco's pockets. This is risky, because it involves sneaking into the Octagon Tower and picking the lock to his room.

Lock-picking is one of the very first things you learn at King-makers, at least in the Spy division. We covered it our first week. I've gotten quite good at it, as delicate, tricky handwork is something I've practiced while making jewelry and paper art.

The more difficult part is dodging all the male Heirs that might wonder why I've snuck into their tower. Also, overcoming my creeping disgust at touching anything that belongs to Rocco. His clothes have a sickly-sweet smell that reminds me of rotting fruit.

The notes I leave for Rocco are deliberately vague and tantalizing.

Things like:

I know what you did.

I have evidence.

I'll expose you.

You'll have to pay to keep me quiet.

I don't actually expect Rocco to feel threatened by these notes. Quite the contrary: I think they'll irritate and enrage him, because he won't understand them. It will drive him mad not knowing who's doing it, or why.

He may think I'm referring to the story Claire Turgenev told me: the boy he tortured and murdered at his old boarding school. Or perhaps he'll connect it to one of the hundred other cruel and disgusting acts that must lurk in his mind like un-exhumed bodies.

It doesn't matter what he thinks—it only matters that I spark his curiosity.

I leave a dozen notes over three days, hidden in the pockets of his trousers, backpack, and between the pages of his textbooks. Then I stop.

The hiatus is important to throw him off balance. To make him even more paranoid. To ensure that he responds when I leave my final note.

Three days before the *Quartum Bellum,* I sneak out of the Undercroft late at night. I steal stones from the crumbling Bell Tower on the northwest corner of campus, and I carry them up onto the ramparts. Heavy stones, each one five to ten pounds in weight. I hide them under my shirt and take them up one by one until my legs are shaking from dozens of trips up and down the stairs.

Then I search the stables. I look through the piles of broken furniture, moldy books, worn-out chalk-brushes, and old filing boxes.

I haven't been in here since I told Hedeon Gray he should check these boxes for old student records. I pause in my search to examine the boxes myself, wondering if he found what he was looking for.

The files have clearly been rifled through, but I don't see any student records. I never looked at the papers that closely on Halloween—it might have been a stupid suggestion. Either that, or Hedeon found what he was looking for and took it away.

Resuming my own quest, I find a large canvas sack full of old scuba equipment. I dump out the scuba gear and take the sack.

All I need now is rope.

THE DAY before the *Quartum Bellum,* I leave my final note. I place it right on Rocco's pillow where he can't possibly miss it. I tell him the time and place to meet me, and I instruct that he brings $5000 to ensure my silence.

Of course, I don't expect him to bring any money.

The money is a distraction.

I can't tell if my plan is reasonably clever or extraordinarily foolish. I've been moving through the motions in a kind of daze, doing what I feel must be done, while not actually believing I can go through with it.

I'm not a killer. I never was.

And yet, I have to kill him.

I haven't told Zoe what I plan. She can't know, and neither can Miles. It's the only way to keep them safe. If something goes wrong . . . well, I can't think about that. My sister was willing to sacrifice her life for mine. She was going to marry Rocco to keep me safe. I have to risk the same for her.

As I hurry down the stairs of the Octagon Tower, I forget to listen for footsteps coming up. It's a small mistake, but one that proves disastrous when I run directly into Dean Yenin.

He seizes me by the throat, slamming me up against the curved stone wall.

Instantly, I'm back in the bathroom of the Keep, where Dean confronted me with a rageful, tear-streaked face.

He must remember the same thing, because his hand tightens around my throat until I let out a strangled scream and claw at his fingers.

"What are you doing in here?" He snarls, his breath hot on my face.

"Nothing!" I squeak, trying to pull his hand off my neck. I might as well try to bend steel. His fingers only dig in further, until my head is swimming and my legs disappear beneath me.

"Why are you here? Are you looking for me?"

I have done nothing but the exact opposite since that day in the bathroom. I've avoided Dean Yenin like he's Medusa and his very gaze upon me would turn me to stone.

"No!" I gasp, my head starting to loll as the world goes black around me.

Dean loosens his grip enough that I can breathe, but he still keeps me pinned against the wall with his cable-like arms on either side of me.

"Why are you here, then? Don't fucking lie to me."

"I was just looking for Miles!" I lie at once, with all the appearance of being too terrified to do so. "I had a message from Zoe."

"A message?" Dean sneers. "Are you their errand-mouse?"

He lets go of my neck. I massage my throat, trying to swallow.

"She's my sister," I say. "They're dating, you know."

"Of course *I know*," Dean says, rolling his eyes at my idiocy. "The whole school knows about your slut sister."

"Don't call her that!" I snap. My indignation is undermined by the fact that my voice comes out a raspy little squeak. Still, Dean rounds on me with fresh fury, startling me so badly that I stumble backward and fall on my ass on the steps.

"What the fuck are you gonna do about it?" He hisses, fists clenched at his sides.

Down at ground level, I see my opening—I dart under his arm and sprint off down the stairs. Dean doesn't bother to try to catch me.

My heart really is racing like a little mouse as I keep running all the way from the Octagon Tower to the Undercroft. It was a narrow escape—and I'm damn lucky that was Dean instead of Rocco.

THE MORNING of the *Quartum Bellum,* I'm too nervous to eat. I have to go to breakfast, however, as it forms a crucial part of the plan.

I sit at Zoe's table, along with Miles, Leo and Anna, Ares, Chay, and Hedeon. Chay is looking more cheerful than I've seen her in weeks, and she's started wearing makeup again. Hedeon, by contrast, is as glum as ever. He picks morosely at his food, only looking up to glare across the dining hall at his brother, who's shoveling down a half-dozen eggs and twice as much bacon.

"Eat up," Leo urges the Sophomores. "I need you all in top shape for the challenge."

"You're gonna captain our breakfast now?" Anna teases him.

"Absolutely I am. I will fork-feed you if it helps you perform better."

"No thank you," says Ares.

"You sure?" Leo says, picking up a big bite of pancake and pretending to airplane it over to Ares' mouth.

"Don't even—" Ares tries to say, and Leo stuffs the pancake in his mouth.

This results in a two-minute scuffle, during which Ares shouts something about non-consensual pancakes and Leo yells at Ares to quit wasting his strength while they both try to wrestle each other out of their seats.

The fight is the perfect distraction. I pick up my knife, which, like all the knives at Kingmakers, is heavy and serrated, with a carved bone handle and a tempered steel blade. It looks a hundred years old. God, I hope it's not infected with tetanus.

Pathetically, this is the part of the plan I dread the most.

Under the cover of Leo and Ares' roughhousing, I slash the knife down my own arm in one, quick swipe. The serrated teeth rip my flesh open, and blood pours down on my plaid skirt before I can jerk my arm away.

"Ouch!" I shout.

"Cat!" Zoe cries. "What happened?"

"My knife slipped," I say, pouting out my lower lip. Said lip trembles. It's not acting—my arm really does hurt, and I'm nauseated at what I've done to myself. I meant to make a nasty cut, but it's bleeding more than I anticipated, and I'm starting to feel dizzy.

Hedeon is closest. He grabs a linen napkin and clamps it down over my arm.

"You'd better go see Dr. Cross," he says. "That will need stitches."

"Good idea," I say.

I get to my feet, wobbling slightly.

"I'll take you!" Zoe offers.

"I can do it," Hedeon says.

"Do you want me to come?" Zoe asks me, eyebrows drawn together in worry.

"No," I say, quickly. "You guys go ahead, I'll be fine. The challenge is about to start."

"Hurry back," Leo says to Hedeon.

Anna slaps him on the arm for being inconsiderate.

"We need him!" Leo says. "But also, get better Cat. Sorry about your arm."

"I'll send him right back," I promise.

I need Hedeon to leave, and quickly, so I'm only too happy to go along with Leo's request.

Still, I'm grateful that I can lean on his arm on the way to the infirmary. I really was a little overzealous with that knife. I had to make sure I cut deep enough for stitches, but I overdid it.

"Went a little hard on those pancakes," Hedeon says, throwing a sideways glance at me.

"I know, I'm clumsy," I say, in my best sad baby voice.

Hedeon bites the edge of his lower lip, not quite believing me.

I've got a few things I'd like to ask him in return, but now's not the time for sleuthing, or for antagonizing him. I really do need him to carry me along. Hedeon is nowhere near as big as his adopted brother, but he's still 6'1 and strong. I kinda want to ask him to throw me over his shoulder because, like Leo said, I want to conserve my strength. For different reasons than the *Quartum Bellum.*

"Guess you'll miss watching the challenge," Hedeon says.

"I'll support you in spirit from here," I say, nodding toward the long, low building of the infirmary.

"You want me to come in?" Hedeon asks.

"No," I say. "Thank you, though. For the napkin and the arm."

I let go of his warm, substantial bicep.

Hedeon squints down at me like he wants to say something else. Instead, he jerks his head in a surly *you're welcome,* and heads back toward the dining hall.

Dr. Cross opens the door after one knock.

"The challenge hasn't even started yet!" He squawks in outrage. "How are you injured already?"

"I cut myself at breakfast," I say, pulling back the blood-soaked napkin to show him the damage.

"Cut yourself with what? A saber?" He howls.

"The knives are sharp."

"And the students are idiots, apparently."

"That can't be a surprise to you," I say, giving him a disarming smile. "How long have you worked here?"

"Since before you were born, and probably your parents, too," Dr. Cross says, rolling his eyes behind his thick glasses. "Well, it's not so bad. I can stitch you up. You might have a scar, but better on your arm than on your face."

He washes his hands at the steel sink, then begins to bustle around, gathering up his supplies.

"Sit on the bed before you fall over," he barks.

"I am a little dizzy," I admit. "I didn't get a chance to eat my breakfast. You don't think I could have some tea, maybe?"

"This isn't the Four Seasons!" Dr. Cross barks. But a moment later he softens, saying, "I'll start the tea and you can drink it once I've stitched you up. Keep pressure on the wound while I'm gone."

He heads back to his apartment to fetch the kettle and cups. I hear him banging around in his little kitchen, and I take the opportunity to retrieve a pair of capsules from my pocket. I made them myself, with a carefully measured dose. One should do it, but I plan to use both just to be sure.

Dr. Cross returns several minutes later bearing a teapot and two mugs. The mugs are chipped and unmatching, but the tea already smells lovely.

"I don't have cream," he says, gruffly.

"I like it plain," I say.

"Let it steep a minute," he barks, though I hadn't tried to touch it.

Dr. Cross fills a syringe with lidocaine and injects my arm in several places. The whole arm is so hot and throbbing that I barely feel the needle poking at the edges of the wounded flesh.

"We'll give that a minute to settle in," he says. "You can pour the tea now."

I lift the pot with my uninjured arm, and pour two careful mug-fulls.

"Forgot the sugar," Dr. Cross grouses, heading back to his kitchen.

I drop both capsules into his mug. The clear coating instantly dissolves in the hot tea, leaving only a fine white powder at the bottom of the mug that he shouldn't notice unless he looks carefully. I desperately hope I've dosed it right—I really don't want to hurt the doctor.

I lift the other mug, sipping the tea even though it's scalding.

"It's so good!" I say to Dr. Cross as he returns.

"You don't want sugar? Oh that's right, you said plain. Healthier for you, but I never quite got rid of my sweet tooth."

He dumps three lumps into his tea and stirs without noticing anything amiss.

"Ah!" He says, after a satisfied slurp. "Let's get to it, then."

He sets down his mug so he can pick up his needle and thread. I resolutely turn my face toward the window. I don't want to watch. Dr. Cross works swiftly, in spite of his arthritis-ridden hands. When he's done, the line of stitches down my arm is neater than the jagged wound deserved.

"There!" He says, with satisfaction. "I'll put a bandage on it, too. Keep the wound clean. Come back for fresh wrapping when you need it. The stitches will dissolve on their own in a few weeks. Don't pick at it, whatever you do."

"Can I rest a little longer?" I ask him. "I'm still dizzy."

He glances at the clock. "If you like. You'll miss the challenge, but that may be for the best. It's damn hot today. No good sitting out in the sun."

He tidies up swiftly and efficiently, then washes his hands once more. As he turns to leave, I say, "Dr. Cross! You forgot your tea!"

"So I did," he says, lifting the mug and taking another swig. "Still warm."

Thank god for that.

He sits down on the bed next to mine to continue drinking. He slurps with every sip, but it's not an uncouth sound. In fact, it's strangely comforting.

"What's your family name?" he demands, squinting at me through the inch-thick lenses of his glasses.

"Romero," I tell him.

He makes a dismissive sound. "Never heard of it. I barely know any of the families anymore."

"Is your family mafia?" I ask him.

"My mother was an Umbra," he says, proudly. When he perceives that I don't know what that means, he adds, impatiently, "They were a founding family, girl, good god, what are they teaching you out there?"

I'm relieved to see that he finished his tea. Even more relieved to see that his blinks are becoming longer and slower.

"I'm getting too old for this," he says morosely, gazing at the washed and sterilized instruments he has yet to put away.

"Why don't you rest and I'll put those in the cabinet?" I offer.

"Well . . . go on, then," he says, leaning back against the pillow with his fingers interlaced over his chest. "I may as well rest a moment. There's sure to be another injury or two before the day is done."

He closes his eyes, his breath already slowing.

Quietly, I unlatch the glass-fronted cabinet and put the instruments back in their carefully-labeled places.

I'm trying to move silently, trying not even to breathe.

Soon Dr. Cross's mouth hangs open and long snores come rasping out.

I wait for five, then ten agonizing minutes. I have to be sure he's deeply asleep before I leave.

The dose I gave him should knock him out for hours.

Some parts of this plan are well-organized, but others rely on chance. It was dumb luck that I was the only person to require Dr. Cross' services this morning, and I'd like to keep it that way. The *Quartum Bellum* is the complicating factor. It's a rare challenge that doesn't result in at least a few injuries.

I need to leave and return as quickly as possible.

I also have to beat Rocco to our meeting place.

Creeping around on tiptoe, I lock the door to the infirmary, then crack the back window just wide enough for me to shimmy out. The heavy wooden sash creaks. I cast an anxious glance back at the slumbering Dr. Cross, relieved to see that he hasn't shifted position whatsoever. His continued snores soothe my fears of an overdose.

I slip out the narrow space, then hurry across the deserted grounds, as outside the castle gates I hear the distant shouts and groans of the *Quartum Bellum*.

I check my watch. I have to be up on the wall early, in case Rocco tries to get the jump on me.

I scale the staircase inside the wall, coming up on the ramparts where Rocco Prince trapped my sister so many months before. He may know already, simply from our meeting place, that the notes relate to Zoe. I hope that will be all the more incentive for him to come.

The biggest risk at this point is Rocco bringing a friend. He has to come alone. If he doesn't, all I can do is abandon the plan and run.

I'm early. Rocco is late. The appointed time ticks past, then ten minutes and twenty minutes longer. The sun beats down on my head. I can still hear the ongoing cheers of the challenge, though they seem weaker than before, the audience exhausted by the heat.

If Rocco doesn't get here soon, I'll have to leave. I can't risk anyone coming to the infirmary and finding the door locked. That may have happened already. God, this plan is full of holes. I was desperate, trying to find a time when my sister would be safe from suspicion. All my schemes seem childish and destined to fail as I examine them in the harsh light of reality.

I touch the loose loop of rope resting on the ramparts behind me, then I tap the wooden pin jammed into the wall directly behind my heel. The pin is taught and straining. It could pull free any moment.

I'm no engineer. I barely had the strength to set this up. I don't know if this will work. I don't think Rocco will come. God, I'm an idiot. What was I thinking?

I'm about to abandon it all. About to turn and run. Then I hear a distant creak that sounds very like a door.

I pause, frozen in place like a deer, my ears straining for further sound.

I hear a scrape that might be footsteps on the stairs.

Then a long pause.

Then finally, a slim, dark figure ascends to the wall.

With all the time I've spent around giants like Miles and Leo and Ares, I sometimes forget that Rocco, while modestly proportioned, is still much taller than me. Faster, too, and infinitely stronger. He strides toward me with eerie speed, jaw lowered and eyes burning right through me.

He doesn't stop until we're face to face, mere inches apart.

"What a disappointment," he says, in a disgusted tone.

"Did you bring my money?" I say. I hoped to muster a semblance of confidence, but my voice always betrays me. It comes out high and weak, with a crack in the middle of the sentence.

"*Money?*" Rocco scoffs, and for one of the only times in my remembrance, he laughs. "You thought I'd bring money?"

"If you didn't—" I begin.

"If I didn't, then *what?*" He hisses, taking a hideously quick step toward me, so I have to back against the wall. I fumble behind me, feeling for the loop of rope that seems to have disappeared.

"I'll expose you!" I squeak.

"What in the fuck are you talking about?" Rocco cries, confusion the only thing preventing him from throttling me. "I only came up here to see what sneaky suicidal shit was leaving notes in my pockets! I was going to carve my name across their chest. But now that I know that's it's *you* . . ." he pulls his knife from his pocket quicker than a blink and flips open the blade. "Now I think I'll have to come up with something more creative for Zoe's little sister . . ."

"Wait!" I cry, desperately grasping for time while my fingers miss the rope, "We can make a deal!"

"As fun as that would be," Rocco hisses, reaching for me with his slim, pale hand, "*I fucking hate deals . . .*"

My fingers close around the loop and I grab hold, throwing the lasso around Rocco's wrist. He stares at it, mouth open in amused derision.

"What in the fuck—"

I kick the pin as hard as I can, knocking it free from the wall.

I only had one chance to do it. Rocco watches the rope hiss over the ramparts, comprehension dawning on his face, right as the loop yanks tight around his wrist, jerking him forward.

He swings at me with his knife, trying to plunge it into my chest. I'm already dropping down to my knees, flinging my arms protectively over my head.

Rocco drops the knife, grasping at me desperately with his free hand as he's yanked forward. If I were any bigger, this wouldn't work. He'd grab hold of me and pull me over along with him. But after all, I'm very small. I curl up like a little mouse while Rocco is dragged right over my head, the toes of his shoes skimming my head as he flips over the wall, tumbling down with a blood-curdling scream.

The canvas bag of rocks drags him down. It weighs over two hundred pounds, much more than Rocco himself. Without the pin holding it in place, it plunges straight down and Rocco is dragged along after it, screaming all the while. I don't hear the impact, but I hear when the scream stops, the silence sudden and abrupt.

I don't want to look over the edge.

Yet I have to.

I have to be absolutely sure.

With both hands clamped over my mouth, and my legs shaking beneath me, I force myself to stand. I peek over the ramparts.

I see a dark shape broken on the rocks below. The canvas bag has split, spilling its stones all around.

I want to sink back down and hide here, shivering, for as long as it takes.

But I have to get back to the infirmary.

No part of this plan is harder than the journey back. I have to stop three or four times, my stomach heaving. Luckily there's nothing in there but tea, so I keep the sick down. I can't leave vomit as evidence.

I'm not worried about prints on the rope. The rough jute shouldn't hold fingerprints, and the tide is coming in. The waves will beat against the remains of Rocco Prince, washing away fibers and hairs. Maybe even washing away the body.

No, it's my alibi I'm struggling to protect. I have to get back inside that infirmary before anyone notices I'm gone.

I race across campus, unseen as far as I can tell. I slip around the back of the building, pausing outside the window.

For a moment I think I hear a sound, something almost inaudible, a footstep on sod. I whip my head around wildly, seeing nothing at all. I can certainly hear Dr. Cross snoring.

I shove myself back through the gap in the window, lowering the sash as quietly as I can. Then I slip back under the blankets of my unmade bed.

I don't think Dr. Cross has moved an inch.

I watch him for several minutes, my heart still jittering in my chest. My brain runs even faster.

You're a murderer. A murderer. A murderer.

I stuff that thought back down.

I'm so fucking lucky that it worked. I think it worked, I hope it worked . . .

I could still be caught. There's so many things I might have missed. I'm no criminal. I'm not even a Spy, not really. I don't know what delusion gripped me, thinking I could pull this off. It was pure luck if I did.

I check the clock.

Then I clear my throat, loudly. When that doesn't work, I get out of the bed and shake Dr. Cross.

"What is it?" he grumbles, coming to abruptly.

"I'm sorry, Dr. Cross. I just thought you wouldn't want to sleep too long. It's been fifteen minutes."

A lie. Over an hour passed. I can only hope he wasn't watching the time.

He glances at the clock, blearily.

"Yes, right," he says, shaking his head. "Don't want to sleep too long. Is the challenge still going?"

"I have no idea," I say

"How's the arm feeling?"

"Good as new, almost," I say, showing him the unmarked bandages.

"Good. Help me change these sheets, then," he says, indicating the two despoiled beds.

"I'd be glad to."

We strip the sheets, and Dr. Cross carries them to his laundry. While he's gone, I hear an aggressive banging on the door. My heart leaps into my mouth. I run to the door, realizing I forgot to unlock it. I quickly turn the bolt, opening the door to see Dean Yenin's angry, sweat-soaked face. He's holding his left arm pinned against his body, the shoulder at an awful angle.

"Get the doctor!" he barks.

I run to oblige.

Dr. Cross hurries back into the room, assessing Dean at a glance.

"We'll have to pop that back in," he says. "Girl—what was your name?"

"Cat," I stammer.

"Hold him steady."

I do not want to touch Dean Yenin. But I jump to action, by long habits of obedience. Gingerly, I take hold of Dean's good arm, the muscle iron-hard beneath the skin. He turns to look at me, eyes narrowed, a strange expression on his face.

"Bite on this," the doctor says, stuffing a strip of leather in Dean's mouth.

Dean bites down hard as Dr. Cross swings his injured arm upward. Dean lets out a strangled scream, his good hand clutching convulsively at my skirt. He grabs my thigh, and I don't even feel the pressure of his hand, because I'm distracted by how vulnerable Dean looks when he's in pain.

He lets go of me abruptly. I do the same.

Dr. Cross manipulates Dean's arm gingerly, ensuring that his shoulder joint is back in the socket.

"Better?" he says.

"Yes," Dean replies, his face still pale and sweating.

"I'd better go," I say. "I'd like to catch the end of the *Quartum Bellum*. Is it still going on?"

"It is," Dean says, his eyes fixed on mine.

"Well . . . thank you Dr. Cross," I say, edging to the door.

"I'll follow you out," Dean says.

I don't like that one bit, but I can't exactly stop him.

As soon as we're outside the infirmary, I say, "I'm going to run to catch the end!" and I sprint away from him, with the paranoid sense that I'll hear his footsteps chasing after me.

He lets me go.

Still, I'm too unnerved to even look over my shoulder as I run through the gates to the makeshift bleachers, hiding myself in the crowd.

25

ZOE

After several grueling hours, when our palms are hamburger and it feels like all of us are about to have our arms pulled out of our sockets like Dean, the Sophomores finally manage to drag the line of flags into our end zone.

We're too exhausted to even cheer.

The crowd of watching students and teachers is equally tired of sitting in the blazing sun, and can barely muster a response as Professor Howell hoists Leo's arm in the air, declaring his team the winners of the *Quartum Bellum* for the second year in a row.

Leo, at least, retains a little enthusiasm. Sweat-soaked and reeling, he still flashes a bright grin, handing out fist bumps and backslaps to as many teammates as he can reach, while pulling Anna tight against his side with his free arm.

Miles passes me a bottle of miraculously cold water, retrieved from god knows where.

"Can we be friends again, now that we're no longer mortal enemies?" he grins.

I gulp the water down and pour it over my face in blessed relief.

"I'll be your best friend forever just for that water," I promise him.

"I'm gonna hold you to that," Miles says, sweeping me up in his arms and kissing me, not giving a shit how filthy and sweaty we've both become.

I can't get over the fact that he can kiss me on the field now, not caring who might see us.

His lips burn hot from the sun and exertion. I feel limp and weak in his arms, and not just because I'm exhausted.

"What do I have to do to get you away from all these people?" Miles growls, setting me down gently on the churned-up grass, but not letting go of me.

"I would love to sneak off together," I tell him. "I should check on Cat, though. That was a nasty cut this morning, I don't know why the knives are so goddamn sharp at this place—"

"I think she's right over there," Miles says, nodding his head toward the stands, where the students lethargically descend, joining the crowd heading back toward the castle.

I spot Cat walking with her roommate Rakel. Cat obviously visited Dr. Cross because her left forearm is wrapped in a fresh white bandage, but she still looks pale and shaky.

I jog over to join her, Miles following after me.

"Hey! How are you doing?"

"I'm fine," Cat says, her voice wobbly. "How are you guys? Congratulations, by the way."

"Are you sure you're alright?" I ask, brushing the hair back from Cat's cheek to see her face more clearly. "You look a little—"

"I told you, I'm fine!" Cat cries, shaking me off.

It's unlike her to snap at me, but after all, Cat's grown up a lot this year. I shouldn't baby her, especially not in front of her roommate. I know Cat wants Rakel to respect her.

And indeed, the two girls look quite friendly as we pass through the stone gates into the school grounds, Rakel saying, "I hope they have lunch ready. You gonna come eat with me, Cat, or will you wait for this lot to take a shower?"

"I need a shower," Miles agrees, "and I better get in there before all the hot water runs out."

"No! You should eat first," Cat says, abruptly. "We should all stay together."

"Sure, if you like," Miles shrugs. "I'm fucking starving."

"Did you see Dean at the infirmary?" I ask Cat. "Silas Gray almost pulled his arm off."

"He came in right as I was leaving," Cat nods. "He—"

"What's the hold-up?" Miles says, annoyed with the crowd of students clogging the bottleneck between the Armory and the dining hall.

The students ahead appear to be looking up at something. Sure enough, as we push our way forward, I see a flock of noisy sea birds circling in the air above the north wall. The white birds wheel and caw, diving down to squabble on the rocks below.

"What are they doing?" Miles says.

"Why's there so many of them?" Rakel asks.

Cat stares up at the birds, silent.

I have the oddest sense of foreboding. Maybe it's because I watched The Birds with my Abuelita. That strange, sharp call of gulls has had a sinister sound to me ever since.

"Who knows why birds do what they do," I say.

"There must be something down there," Miles says.

"Who cares, let's go eat," I say, dismissively.

I don't want to think about that particular cliff, having had too close a view of it myself.

Understanding me at once, Miles takes my hand and turns toward the dining hall, saying, "Hope they have fresh bread."

"I'm not feeling well," Cat says, in a small voice.

"All the more reason to eat," Miles says, taking Cat's arm as well.

Rakel is still gazing up at the wall.

"Somebody climbed up," she says.

Irresistibly, I turn back. Someone has indeed scaled the stairs, and now they're bending over the parapet, peering down. Silhouetted by the sun, I can't be sure who it is, but by the lanky frame and the uncut hair, I think it might be that Senior Spy—Saul-something.

He shouts down to the students at the base of the wall.

"What's he saying?" I ask Miles, unable to hear.

"I think . . . I think he said there's someone down there," Miles says.

Cat turns and vomits on the grass.

26

MILES

The body at the base of the wall is Rocco Prince.

The rumor flies around the school long before the professors confirm it.

And though this information is not publicly shared, one of the grounds crew tells me that Rocco was found with a noose around his wrist. On the other end of the rope, a canvas bag of stones.

"A noose around his *wrist?*" I ask, confused.

"That's right," the crewman says, shaking his head grimly. "This shit is gonna kick off a whole other round of fuckin' headaches."

The students are confined to the dorms while the death is investigated. The staff bark orders at us with a new level of tension. This is the first time in Kingmakers' history that two students have been killed in a matter of months.

Nothing can stop the speculation.

"I think he killed himself," Simon Fowler says to me. "He was always off his rocker."

I don't believe for two seconds that Rocco would voluntarily jump off that wall.

Still, I feel an immense relief knowing that he's dead. The only problem is the suspicion bound to fall on my head.

For the first time in my life, I'm actually innocent. But nobody's going to believe that.

Even Simon seems wary.

"If I hadn't been standing right next to you all day, maybe I'd think you pushed him . . ." he laughs, giving me a sideways glance.

"I wish I could shake the hand of the guy that did," I reply.

I suppose it's possible Rocco tied himself to a bag of rocks and pushed them off the ramparts because he lacked the courage to jump. But I just don't fucking believe it.

Which means there's a killer on campus. Someone who hated Rocco as much as I did.

"Maybe it was Dax," Simon says. "He was pretty fucking pissed about that week in the cell. Not to mention Rocco smashing up their room."

"Keep going, Horatio," I laugh. "You've got a whole lot of theories."

Simon smirks, unbothered by the sarcasm. "It's not hard to come up with a list of people who hated Rocco Prince."

That's true. But I do find the timing suspicious.

Inconveniently suspicious.

I'm hauled into the Chancellor's office immediately.

He sits behind his scarred, ancient desk, his hands folded in front of him. I pretend to look around his office for the first time, like I wasn't just in here a couple of weeks prior. His silver keys are right back on the hook where I returned them.

"Nice setup," I say to Luther Hugo, nodding toward his array of photographs. "Is that the British Prime Minister shaking your hand?"

Hugo ignores me. He watches me with those graphite eyes, under black brows speckled with silver. Professor Penmark stands on his left and Professor Graves on his right. Not my two biggest fans, unfortunately.

"Were you involved in the death of Rocco Prince?" Hugo asks, bluntly.

"I think it was mostly the rocks that did it," I say. "And a little bit the fall."

"Now would be a good time to lose the insolence," Hugo says, in the kind of voice that feels like a set of incisors closing around the base of your neck. "Unless you want to spend another week in a cell, you'll answer my questions fully and honestly."

"I get why you'd think it was me," I tell him, looking him in the eye. "But if you haven't heard, I already worked out a deal with Zoe's father, and the Princes as well. Rocco wasn't a problem for me anymore. Not to mention, I was competing in the *Quartum Bellum* while Rocco took his swan dive."

"You expect us to believe that?" Professor Penmark snaps, his bony white hands twitching. He seems irritated by this relatively civil line of questioning. I bet he wishes he had me strapped down to a table with the full array of his nasty implements laid out so he could "persuade" me to cooperate.

"I don't think you operate off 'belief' here," I say. "Let's look at the facts: there's no evidence I killed Rocco. Because I didn't."

"Then who did?" Professor Graves demands, in his usual pompous way. "Enlighten us."

"Half the school hated him," I say, shrugging. "Or maybe he did it himself. He was kind of a pouty little bitch, after all."

Luther Hugo hasn't taken his eyes off my face, not for a second.

His black, glinting eyes are like uncut gems, pressed deep into the sockets.

"Truth is your only chance for mercy," he says, quietly.

An absolute lie. There is no chance for mercy.

"The truth shall set you free," I tell him, not allowing a hint of nervousness to show. "I never touched him, and I don't know who did."

That statement is ninety-nine percent accurate.

The one percent is the caveat I'd never share with the Chancellor, or the professors.

I don't know who killed Rocco. . .but I have one wild, improbable suspicion.

TEDIOUSLY, I have to repeat my conversation with the Chancellor that evening when Dieter Prince phones me.

He doesn't sound like a man who just lost his son.

He sounds like a man who suffered a minor irritation on par with an unexpected tax bill, or the loss of his favorite golf clubs.

"Were you involved in Rocco's death?" He demands, the moment I pick up the phone.

"No," I say. "I was very happy with our arrangement. Rocco hadn't said a word to Zoe or me. I trusted that he intended to abide by the agreement."

Not entirely true . . . I wouldn't trust Rocco to lick a stamp for me, but I don't need to get into that with Dieter Prince.

"I assume the Chancellor told you I was in full view of the entire school at the time of the incident."

"That was his impression," Prince admits, stiffly.

"That's a fact," I repeat. "I've got hundreds of witnesses."

"You could have hired someone to do it."

"Who?" I'm almost laughing. "The whole school was there."

Dieter is silent for a minute, considering.

I notice that he hasn't rushed to Kingmakers to retrieve his son's body.

And the money's still piling up in the joint account. He's just about to receive his first infusion of American dollars from the Malina. He wants it. I know he does.

"So our arrangement continues as agreed?" He says, after a long pause.

"I certainly hope so."

"So be it," he says briskly, ending the call.

Zoe's in a daze the week after Rocco's death.

I know she's deeply relieved. But at the same time, she seems unable to celebrate.

"I just can't believe it," she says, shaking her head. "I almost wish I'd seen the body. It seems impossible . . ."

"He's definitely dead," I assure her. "The Chancellor wouldn't be giving me so much shit otherwise."

"Fuck Rocco, I'm thrilled," Chay says ferociously, spearing a fried potato with her fork as we sit eating breakfast in the dining hall. "Wish we had time to throw a party to celebrate before school lets out."

Cat is quiet, picking at her food.

"You gonna come to Chicago with us?" I ask her.

She hesitates. "Oh . . . I don't know. I'm sure you two would rather be alone . . ."

"No we wouldn't," I say. "Zoe needs company so she's not too scared to meet my family. They're pretty intense, I'm not gonna lie—but they're going to love you girls. I'll warn you, Caleb will hit on you, he won't be able to help himself."

Cat blushes, squirming in her seat.

Zoe smiles at me encouragingly. I know she really wants Cat to come.

"We can go see a Cubs game . . . and there's this bakery with a purple coconut cake . . ."

"I like coconut," Cat says, perking up a little.

Cat has seemed even more shaken by Rocco's death than Zoe herself.

I understand that for these girls Rocco was a boogeyman, a terror almost as powerful in his absence as in his presence. He was a huge fucking source of stress in my life, too.

But I can't help thinking . . .

Only a very few people were out of my sight when Rocco was killed.

One of those people was Cat.

She had all the reason in the world to want Rocco dead. Like me, she must have harbored a suspicion that Rocco was still dangerous to Zoe. That he wouldn't give up so easily.

I'd broken Zoe's marriage contract, but I never thought for a second that Rocco had ceased to be a threat. He was an unsolved problem that continued to hang over my head. I knew I'd have to deal with him eventually.

Now he's gone. Wiped off the face of the earth.

And I'm glad, so fucking glad.

But I can't help wondering who I have to thank for that.

Cat was in the infirmary with Dr. Cross. Hedeon walked her over there, and Dean Yenin followed her back. So technically, she was never alone. Her alibi is almost as solid as mine.

Still, I wonder . . .

I look at her sitting there, small and shy and about as physically imposing as a newborn lamb.

Even though Cat has come a long way this year, the idea that she could murder Rocco Prince is laughable. I feel ridiculous even considering it.

At the end of the day, it doesn't matter who did it.

He's fuckin' dead. And he's not coming back.

27

CAT

The week after Rocco's death is a fog of constant paranoia, where I'm certain that any moment I'll feel hands closing around my arms and I'll be jerked out of my seat, dragged off to the Prison Tower by the Chancellor's minions.

Even when I'm lying sleepless in my narrow bed down in the sunless cave of the Undercroft, I expect to hear the door broken down at any moment.

But it never happens.

No one comes to arrest me.

No one even speaks to me.

Miles is interrogated by the Chancellor. That, too, sets my guts churning all over again, terrified that they'll chain him up and

I'll have to admit that it was me, not him, who murdered Rocco Prince.

But after a week of incessant gossip and rumor, where students and teachers alike seem to talk of nothing else, the storm fades away as quickly as it blew in. The Princes send a lieutenant to retrieve the body. And everyone else seems to forget that Rocco ever existed.

Dax and Jasper attend class as usual, faces impassive, as if they didn't just lose two of their supposed best friends.

There's no consequence or punishment for anyone.

"They don't want to admit that they can't find the murderer," Chay says, over lunch. "They just want the whole thing to disappear."

"Maybe Rocco really did kill himself," Ares says.

"I doubt it," Zoe shakes her head.

"It's only blowing over because the Princes don't care," Miles says. "He's their Heir—but they didn't love him. How could they?"

"Still . . ." Zoe says. "Their only child . . ."

"They might have made a bigger fuss a year ago," Miles says. "Dieter Prince is distracted."

"He's a sociopath like Rocco," Zoe says, coldly. "He doesn't feel anything."

"That's a good thing," Miles tells her, gently. "Otherwise this might have been a bigger problem. As it stands . . . we're lucky."

He casts a quick glance in my direction.

Twice now I've seen Miles looking at me as if he might suspect my secret.

In the past, I would have given the truth away immediately.

But now I have the ultimate poker face.

I'm numb inside, hollow and emotionless.

I killed someone.

I'm a murderer.

I know Rocco was awful. I know he wanted to hurt my sister. I know he had to die.

And yet . . . I feel so fucking guilty.

I can't crush it down.

I can't make it stop.

For all the things that terrified me about my plan—the possibility that Rocco would torture or kill me, the chance that I'd be caught and executed, or just the fact that it might not work at all, that I'd fail and Rocco would still be walking around free to seek revenge upon my sister . . .

The one thing I never considered is how awful I might feel afterward.

I've done something irrevocable.

Whatever happens for the rest of my life . . . I'm different now. I'm no longer innocent. No longer good.

I can never take this back.

And I *wouldn't* take it back—that's the maddest part of all. I don't regret it. My sister is safe and happy. It's what I wanted.

But even that fact only serves to prove that I truly am an evil person.

I know myself in a way I never did before.

I killed without hesitation. And I'd do it again.

Thank god the school year is over. I muddled through my final exams, distracted and foggy-headed. Yet I passed them all, retaining enough of the hard-won information I learned this year.

Now I've allowed Miles and Zoe to convince me to accompany them to Chicago, at least for a couple of weeks. I'm going to see America for the very first time.

I can't feel any emotion as pleasant as excitement. But I will be relieved to be away from this campus, where I won't have to pass that stretch of wall where I committed the ultimate crime.

I hope a long summer will dull the pain, and I'll be able to return here in the fall, pretending that nothing happened.

It helps that no one wants to talk about Rocco Prince. By September, they may truly have forgotten him entirely.

THE WAGONS HAVE COME to take away our bags, and to ferry us down to the harbor. All the students take the same ship back to Dubrovnik, so I'll be with Zoe this time. We're going to fly directly to Chicago.

I'm nervous to meet the Griffin family, but I know Miles will make us comfortable, and that Zoe can't fail to charm them with her intelligence and beauty. I'll be her quiet shadow as always, safe at her side.

The Undercroft is nearly deserted, most everyone having carried up their luggage early this morning, then spent the rest of the remaining time laughing, talking, and wrestling in the summer sunshine.

I'm lingering down here because I want to be alone. I want to sit in the cool, dry darkness a little longer.

I have my sketchbook out, unpacked, and I'm trying to draw a picture of a girl sitting on the rim of the well in the commons —the well next to the dining hall that provides the coldest and most delicious water on the island.

I love that moss-stained well. Yet in my drawing, it looks sinister and dark, like a blank eye leading down into the center of the earth.

I hear a scrape of metal in the lock. I think it's Rakel turning her key. She must have forgotten something in her dresser.

Instead, the door sweeps open and Dean Yenin steps inside.

His broad shoulders fill the doorframe, his head only an inch below the lintel. His fair skin and hair look white as ash in the dim light. As always, his person is flawlessly neat—trousers pressed, shirt crisp and snowy white, hands clean as marble. The only color on him is those violet-blue eyes, beautiful in a way that only deadly things can be.

I haven't taken a breath since he stepped into my room.

I'm frozen in place on the bed, my pencil tumbling numbly from my fingers. It rolls away from me across the floor. Neither of us looks to see where it lands.

Reaching behind him, Dean closes the door with a soft *snick*.

That motion, more than anything, tells me his intentions aren't good.

He walks toward me, slow and deliberate.

I stand to meet him. Even at my fullest height, the top of my head lands far below his chin. I'm looking at his chest, where the hard slabs of muscle strain the buttons of his shirt. I have to tilt my head all the way back to look him in the face.

Dean has a terrible beauty up close. He's the sort of monster where it could kill you to look at him.

Gracefully, he stoops to pick up my sketch pad. He examines the drawing, dark lashes swooping down as he looks at every part of it.

"This reminds me of Timoclea," he says. "Do you know it?"

His words are a cold frost that sweeps through my body, freezing the blood in my veins, stopping my heart.

The Baroque artist Elisabetta Sirani painted a scene recounted by Plutarch in his biography of Alexander the Great.

When Alexander's forces seized the city of Thebes, a Thracian captain raped Timoclea. After the assault, he demanded if she knew of any hidden money. Telling him she did, Timoclea led him into her garden, where she promised gold could be found inside her well. As he bent over to look, she pushed him in, and threw stones down upon his head until he was dead.

I look in Dean's eyes, and I see that he holds my life in his hands.

With awful tenderness, he strokes his finger down my cheek.

"I know what you did," he says.

I can't speak. I can't even blink. All I can do is tremble.

"I saw the strangest thing as I walked to the infirmary. You. Climbing in a window."

I shake my head, silent, horrified.

"Yes," Dean assures me, his eyes fixed on mine. "I saw you. You lured him up on that wall. And you pushed him over."

He knows. He knows. He knows.

"Alexander pardoned Timoclea," Dean says. "But no one will pardon you."

My tongue is ice in my mouth, but I have to speak.

"Please . . ." I whisper.

"You want me to keep your secret?" Dean asks me, his voice as soft as a caress.

I nod. I would fall on my knees before him to beg, if I were capable of moving.

"I won't tell," Dean promises. "But understand this . . . I own you now. When we come back to school, you're mine. My servant. My slave. For as long as I want you."

Dean cups my chin in his hand, pressing his thumb against my lips. Sealing me to silence.

Then he leaves me there, plunged into dread deeper than any I've ever known.

EPILOGUE
ZOE

Chicago

I t's Sabrina Gallo's birthday.

We celebrate at the Shedd Aquarium, where the dinner tables are arranged around floor-to-ceiling glass windows looking in upon the sharks, rays, and turtles floating around in their underwater world. The pale blue rippling light makes it feel as if we're all underwater, too, particularly the couples circling dreamily on the dance floor.

I'm glad I've met most of Miles' family separately by this point, because they're quite the intimidating crowd. The Gallos are all beautiful, with the nut-brown skin, thick dark curls, and surreal gray eyes that I've come to know and love on Miles. That, at least, makes me feel a sense of familiarity, though each of them differs enough in their sharp and provoking personalities to keep me on my toes.

No one is more beautiful than Sabrina Gallo herself. I've never seen a girl so exotic and breathtaking. She's entirely in her element receiving her pile of presents from family members, and the kisses and well-wishes of friends.

A continual rotation of boys orbit her, battling for her attention.

"How old is she turning?" I ask Miles.

"Seventeen. One more year until she comes to Kingmakers."

"I can already see she'll be popular."

"She'll be trouble, more like," Miles shakes his head. "Sabrina causes more problems than the rest of my cousins put together."

Even Miles' uncle Dante has flown in from Paris with his three children and his supermodel wife who I remember from the magazines and billboards of my youth. Dante is so big that he makes Silas Gray seem petite by comparison, and his eldest son Henry is his mirror image, only a little darker-complected, with a slightly gentler face. While Dante is terrifying, Henry has a softness to his deep brown eyes and full lips that has almost as many female eyes turned in his direction as the flock of males circling Sabrina.

The Griffins have come to the party as well, including the elegant Riona Griffin with her handsome rancher husband and their four redheaded sons. The sons cluster around a table in the corner, playing some sort of card game that evokes plenty of laughter, but also moments of tension where it seems like all four burly country boys might break out into a fistfight that would smash the table and chairs like kindling under their combined mass.

Anna and Leo dance together, Anna looking particularly ethereal as she twirls on the axis of Leo's hand, a massive manta ray floating directly behind her as if they're engaged in some kind of cross-species *pas de deux*.

Leo's parents sit at the table closest to the dance floor, feeding bits of cake to Leo's little sister Natasha who will be celebrating her own first birthday soon. The surprise baby seems to have revitalized his parents. As they laugh and tickle the giggling, frosting-smeared infant, Sebastian and Yelena look barely any older than Leo and Anna.

Miles' parents are deep in conversation at their own table, their knees close together and their heads almost touching as Aida tells her husband some animated anecdote with much gesturing of hands. Callum Griffin listens to her intently, occasionally chuckling, and always keeping his steel-blue eyes fixed on her face.

I was terrified to meet them. I could hardly breathe when the taxi pulled up to their house. Then Aida came running out onto the lawn, barefoot and wearing a pair of cut off denim shorts, immediately pulled me into the longest, warmest hug of my life. She started peppering me with questions, teasing Miles, and fussing over Cat and me, until I was too distracted to be nervous.

Miles' father Callum is polite and genteel, but terrifying in his intensity. He has that analytical stare that seems to break you down into pieces, tallying up every bit of you. I only managed to keep my composure because I'd encountered it before in Miles himself.

Also like his son, Callum is incredibly devoted to the people he loves, beginning with his wife, and trickling down through Miles, Caleb, and Noelle. He takes an acute interest in each of his children, even little Noelle, who every night has been adding to her scale model of the Helix Bridge with her father's help.

Their house is always full of ongoing projects, talk, laughter, and delicious food. Aida brings home delicacies from all over Chicago for us to sample, in case we missed any while sightseeing.

It's strange how their modern glass prism can feel so cozy and welcoming, while my father's villa has always seemed more like a rented hotel.

Daniela runs the villa like an austere foreman, while Aida is so warm and irreverent that it's impossible not to feel at home around her. Like Miles, she has a wicked sense of humor with a kind heart underneath.

In the few weeks we've been in Chicago, she's set up a dozen different activities for Miles and me, often sending Caleb along with Cat to keep her company. Caleb is a little younger than Cat and he can be intense and aggressive, but he's taken his role as tour guide very seriously, trying to show Cat every inch of the city that he thinks might be of interest to her.

Cat is easy to please. She's immersed herself in every museum, monument, and historical site. She even agreed to join us on a helicopter tour over the city, though I know she doesn't love flying on any type of aircraft, least of all one that can fly in between skyscrapers.

Right now she's dancing with Dario Gallo, Dante's youngest, who has a slimmer build than his father and brother, and no insignificant skill at spinning Cat around. Cat looks pink-cheeked and breathless, and very pretty in the blue sparkly dress we bought this afternoon on the Magnificent Mile.

I bought a new gown too, jade green and backless, something I never would have dared to wear before. It hugs me like a second skin, and keeps Miles' eyes pinned to me constantly, which is all I could want out of a dress.

"Do you want to see the rest of the aquarium?" Miles asks me.

Nero and Camille Gallo rented out the whole place for their daughter's party. The long glass galleys are almost entirely empty, as most of the guests seem to prefer eating, drinking, and dancing to viewing the fish.

"I'd love to walk with you," I say.

Miles takes my arm. We stroll through the long underwater tunnel that allows eels and sharks to swim directly over our heads.

The light turns our skin faintly blue, and brings out hints of topaz in Miles' eyes. He looks extraordinarily handsome in his stylish tuxedo, with the crisp white collar and black bow-tie highlighting the masculine lines of his jaw.

He pulls me tight against him under the watery, shifting light, kissing me until my head spins. His mouth is warm and soft, and tastes pleasantly of champagne.

"I want to talk to you about something," he says.

"What is it?"

"I want to preface this by saying that you don't have to agree. I won't be angry if you don't like this idea."

"You're not going to try to convince me?" I laugh. "I'll believe that when I see it."

"Well, I didn't say that," Miles grins. He takes a breath, one dark eyebrow cocked. "I sent your script to a friend of a friend in Los Angeles. He was interested."

"What?" I gasp.

"He's an agent of sorts—and he works as a script doctor himself. He liked your story. He thinks you should try writing a version that could be shot as a TV pilot."

"Miles, you didn't tell me you were going to do that!"

"I was just putting out feelers."

I look at him closely, at his set shoulders and his focused expression. I know Miles well enough that I can guess where this is headed.

"I know what you're up to."

Miles tries to hide his smile. "Oh yeah? What?"

"You want me to come to L.A. with you."

Miles laughs. "You *are* figuring me out, you tricky minx."

He takes both my hands and brings them to his lips, keeping those keen gray eyes fixed on me.

"I don't care about graduating," he says. "I already got what I wanted out of Kingmakers. And I don't think you're that attached to the place, now that you're not buying time on your engagement. I could stay another year, but after I graduated, you'd still have a whole year left. I don't want to be apart from you."

I consider what he's saying, my brain spinning.

It's true—I don't want to be separated from Miles when he finishes school before me. That's another year out, but I understand the point he's making: if we already know we want to start building a life together, then what are we waiting for?

Still, I hesitate.

Miles already knows the reason, I don't have to explain it.

"You don't want to abandon Cat," he says.

I nod. My sister's safety and comfort mean the world to me. I hate the idea of leaving her anywhere alone. Especially somewhere as dangerous and unpredictable as Kingmakers.

"Rocco's not there anymore," Miles says. "She'll still have Anna, Leo, and Chay to keep an eye on her. And I don't know if you've noticed . . . but Cat has changed a lot. She's not a kid anymore—she can take care of herself."

It pains me to hear that, even though I know it's true and I want my sister to be confident and independent. Miles is right

—Cat has grown by leaps and bounds. I don't think she even dislikes Kingmakers anymore, or at least, it's become a challenge instead of torture.

"I'd have to talk to her . . ." I say, hesitantly.

"Of course," Miles replies, with the gleam of incipient triumph in his eye. He knows he's working on me. He knows that the idea of the two of us in warm California sunshine, in the sea breeze under the palm trees, is incredibly enticing to me. I've always wanted to see L.A. Always wanted to be in the place where all my favorite movies were made.

"There's another issue," I say, wincing. "I don't have any money, Miles. I spent two month's allowance on this dress. I have no savings. And unfortunately, you had to clear out all of yours to help me."

I bite my lip, feeling sick inside. I'm incredibly grateful for what Miles did for me, but I've never been able to shake the guilt of costing him all that money, all those years of work. I don't see how he can pursue his dream of becoming a broker and producer if our combined net worth is one green dress.

Miles just laughs, as unconcerned as ever.

"Let me show you something," he says, pulling out his phone. He opens a strange little app with a plain green block as its icon.

Inside I see a digital counter, increasing by a fractional amount every second.

"What is that?" I ask, frowning.

"When I made the deal with your father, the Princes, and the Malina, we all agreed that the three parties would split the profit evenly three ways. On top of that, the Malina would take ten percent for the service of exchanging Bitcoin for washed American dollars."

I nod, following so far. Miles explained that to me before.

"In addition, the Bitcoin wallet charges a fee of one percent."

I nod again, still not understanding.

"I'm the Bitcoin wallet," Miles says.

I stare at him, at his laughing, mischievous face.

"You're taking one percent?"

"I have been the whole time. I didn't mention it at the meeting, because I wanted to make sure I got what I really wanted, which was you and Cat free of your father's bullshit plans. Nobody asked about the Bitcoin wallet—it's a reasonable fee. Generous, even."

I look at the number again, finally understanding. There's already $187,962 in the account. And, as I watch, an additional $1.53 added in the space of a minute. The money rolls in, bit by bit, skimmed off the vast sum flowing to the Malina, my father, and the Princes.

"It's enough to get us started," Miles says.

I shake my head at him in wonder.

"Always working an angle."

He shrugs. "I can't help it. I'm just so damn good at making money."

He hasn't given up on his central point.

"Will you come with me, Zoe? From here straight to L.A.?"

I look in that handsome, determined face. A face I fucking love. I face I could never say no to.

"Yes," I whisper. "I would love to come."

Miles sweeps me up in his arms, kissing me over and over again.

Kissing turns to running his hands down my body in the thin, clinging gown.

"Come here," he growls, pulling me into the next room.

We're in a quiet, dark space where the far wall is one vast plate of glass, looking into a tank full of jellyfish. Their floating bells and trailing tentacles drift peacefully through the water, the transparent bodies tinted with shades of pink, yellow, and blue.

Miles pulls me down on the closest bench, making me straddle his lap so the gown pulls up high on my thighs. He grips my waist, grinding me against him so I can feel how hard his cock is, like an iron bar laying down the leg of his trousers.

He kisses me deeply, exploring my mouth with his tongue.

Then he slowly massages my thighs, using his big, warm hands to wake up the muscles, to send blood surging through my body. He knows exactly what he's doing. As the neurons in my legs come alive, my pussy begins to throb, as if it too has come out of slumber. It aches to be touched. I want his fingers stroking me there and everywhere. I'm hungry and greedy for this man.

Now I'm grinding against Miles of my own accord, pressing my whole body against him, sucking and biting on his lips.

Miles unzips his pants and releases his cock. He pulls my underwear to the side and pushes his cock inside of me. There's something so hot about him fucking me without undressing me, too eager to even take my panties off.

My skirt somewhat hides what we're doing, but there's no way anyone could be confused about the way I'm bouncing up and down on his lap, my legs wrapped around his waist, my hands tangled in his hair. Someone could walk through here any minute and I don't give a fuck, I have to have him right now, I can't stop riding him.

Miles puts his hands under my ass and stands, lifting me in the air. He carries me over to the aquarium window, pressing my back against the cool glass. Now he has leverage to fuck me as hard as he wants, using his powerful legs to drive into me. I'm sandwiched between the cold glass and his burning body.

I press my face against his neck, smelling his cologne and whatever he uses to tame those curls, the scent of his skin and his sweat. An intoxicating cocktail. My head reels. I lick the sweat off the side of his neck, and then lick his ear as well, sucking the lobe and biting it hard between my teeth.

"You naughty fucking girl," Miles growls, driving into me harder and harder.

His fingers dig into my ass. The friction of my pulled-aside panties rubbing on my clit is driving me wild. It's rough and almost too much. But nothing is ever too much with Miles. I can never get enough.

"Fuck me harder," I beg him. "I want your cum dripping out of me the rest of the night."

"You're crazy," he groans, and I know that he loves it, I know that he saw that spark of madness in me that very first day up on the wall. He knew that I wasn't as quiet and controlled as I seemed, and he loved me for it, he wanted to unleash that in me all the more.

I want that, too. I want to be as bold as Miles, as brave as him. I want to go after everything I want in life without fear or hesitation.

"Make me cum and I'll go anywhere in the world with you," I promise him.

Miles pins me against the glass, fucking me senseless. I cum hard and fast, deep inside me in the place that only Miles can find, the only place that satisfies. As soon as he hears me moaning out, "That's it, oh my god that's it," Miles cums too. That's how I want it, that's how I always want it — together, perfectly in sync.

We collapse against the glass, Miles still inside of me. He kisses the side of my neck, sending shivers down my body as if we didn't just fuck. I want him again already, before he's even pulled out.

"You make me so happy," he says, pressing his forehead against mine.

"You've changed my whole life," I tell him in return.

WHEN WE'VE TIDIED ourselves up enough to avoid rousing suspicion, Miles and I return to the party. Cat flops down at our table, exhausted from dancing with Dario Gallo, Caleb Griffin, and Teddy Boone in quick succession.

Miles goes to get drinks.

I take the opportunity to speak with Cat while we're alone.

I tell her that Miles wants me to move to Los Angeles with him. I tell her that I'm thinking of going.

Cat listens, her big dark eyes already tugging at my heart.

"I want to go," I say. "But I don't want to leave you. I'm worried about you going back to school on your own."

Cat sighs and gives me a small smile. "I'm going to miss you, Zo," she says. "But you have to go."

"I don't *have* to . . ."

"Yes you do. You never know how much time you have to do things. None of us know. You can't waste another two years babysitting me."

"But what if—"

"Go, sis," she interrupts. "Go, and don't worry about me. I'm nineteen. Next year I'll be twenty. I'm not a kid anymore. I'm not even the same person I was last year. I've learned things.

Done things." She swallows. "Just go. I'll be mad at you if you don't."

I take her hand and squeeze it hard.

"You're sure? You won't miss me too much?"

"I'll be fine," she says.

Cat always tells me the truth. But there's something in her face I don't like. Something unspoken. Something weighing on her.

I hold her hand in both of mine, looking at her closely.

"You know you can tell me anything," I say.

Cat's eyes meet mine for just a moment and then drop to our linked fingers as she shrugs and says, "Sure. Of course."

"And you can call me every day . . . I'm sure Miles can get you a phone."

"Sundays will be fine," Cat says, squeezing my hand in return. Then, deciding that's not enough, she leans forward and hugs me. "I love you, Zo. You deserve happiness. You always did."

"We both do," I tell her.

Cat nods without answering.

Miles sets fresh drinks in front of each of our seats.

"What did I miss?" He asks.

"Dance with me and I'll tell you," I say.

"I love that offer," he says, already pulling me to my feet.

He takes me in his arms, swaying me in that smooth, fluid way that seems to bend the music around us, as if the rhythm follows us instead of the other way around.

I look up into his eyes.

"I'm coming with you," I say. "Whenever you want."

"Good," Miles grins. " 'Cause I already bought your ticket."

Want to follow Miles & Zoe to L.A.? →

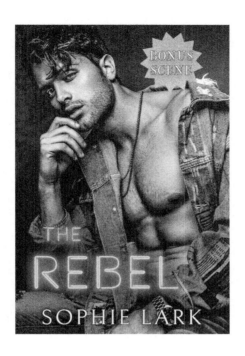

Bonus Scene

Miles and Zoe are throwing their first Hollywood party and it gets a little wild... 🔥🔥🔥

Click to Download

geni.us/rebel-bonus

HAVE YOU MET MILES PARENTS CALLUM & AIDA?

CALLUM & AIDA – BRUTAL PRINCE

MIKO & NESSA – STOLEN HEIR

NERO & CAMILLE – SAVAGE LOVER

DANTE & SIMONE – BLOODY HEART

RAYLAN & RIONA – BROKEN VOW

SEBASTIAN & YELENA – HEAVY CROWN

SERIES PAGE – BRUTAL BIRTHRIGHT

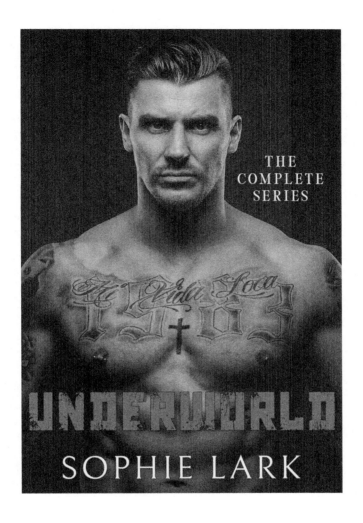

THE
COMPLETE
SERIES

UNDERWORLD

SOPHIE LARK

You'll want to read Snow before The Bully...

★★★★★ *"The heroes are Alpha males, the women are strong and fierce. Each story is set in a different location, with a unique plot and obstacles to overcome... Scorching hot! So intense and entertaining you won't be able to put them down."*

"Underworld" is an action-packed, supremely sexy romance series, full of thieves, detectives, mafia princesses, and Bratva bad boys. Each book is a stand-alone and can be read independently. However, if you read in order, you'll find hidden connections to make the story even more fun. There's no cheating or cliff hangers, but there are plenty of spicy scenes, including rough sex and spanking.

BOOKS 1–8 BOXSET – FREE KINDLE UNLIMITED

Printed in Great Britain
by Amazon

83762857R00302